THE
LOMBARD
HEIRESS

THE LOMBARD HEIRESS

by

VIRGINIA COFFMAN

SEVERN HOUSE PUBLISHERS

This title first published in Great Britain 1986 by
Severn House Publishers Ltd of
4 Brook Street, London W1Y 1AA
First published in the USA by Arbor House
Publishing Company

British Library Cataloguing in Publication Data
Coffman, Virginia
The Lombard heiress.
I. Title
813'.54[F]   PS3553.0415
ISBN 0-7278-1296-3

Printed in Great Britain
at the University Printing House, Oxford

For JEAN WILSON of the
Book Shop
Boise, Idaho

and

for GARY JOHNSON of the
Chapter House Bookshop
Boise, Idaho

Booksellers that every writer dreams of meeting
and so few writers ever encounter.
My gratitude to both of them is boundless.

CHAPTER
ONE

THE FACES of the diners appeared to glow in an elegant hell-fire, thanks to the little red lamps on the Ruby Room tables. Despite their elegant surroundings, these gourmets seldom let themselves be distracted from the dining room's excellent cuisine. Tonight, however, the two young women who entered from the hotel lobby proved the exception.

Several of the red-hued faces looked up from their plates, having recognized one of them. Together the girls presented a nice contrast—the one a tall, leggy blonde, the other petite and dark, with enticing curves and an enchanting smile.

Luckily, Ramon, the maître d', recognized the dark-haired Lombard girl from the picture which had appeared that morning in the San Francisco *Chronicle*. She had been part of the entourage at San Francisco International Airport seeing off her grandparents Steve and Randi Lombard as they left for Tokyo.

"Some class!" Ramon had observed that morning to his wife, who was clearly impressed at the thought of the glamorous trip. "The richer they are the more freebies they get. I'd have to pay through the nose to get us across the Pacific, but these Lombards go for nothing."

Sure enough, a caption beneath the photo stated that the Lombards were to be the guests of the Japanese government, which was honoring Steve for his efforts in behalf of Japanese-American trade. As a kind of afterthought, the *Chronicle* had added another line under the photo:

"Seeing them off was their only grandchild, Andrea Lombard, a class of '62 graduate of the University of California at Berkeley last May."

So, Ramon thought, tonight the poor little rich girl is out on the town. Ramon gave the Lombard girl another look. As the only Lombard grandchild, he figured that she must be in line, after her father, to inherit one of the largest fortunes in America. This knowledge inspired Ramon to use his special talent, the ability to bend graciously before an "unknown" whose family could, if it chose, buy and sell San Francisco's stately old St. Francis Hotel.

"A table...?" He made a suitable hesitation. "But, of course, *mesdames*. Let me see..." He applied deep concentration to the half-filled Ruby Room with its scarlet-and-black brocade walls and its comfortable banquettes.

He included in his bow the heiress's tall, blonde friend, quite attractive in her own right, but for his purposes mostly unimportant. The gray suit came from Macy's. Maybe the Emporium. The black pumps? Anybody's guess. Good legs, though.

Surprisingly enough, the heiress, with her full head of curly black hair was also good-looking, even without the Lombard money. Her khaki shantung suit was a Marc Bohan original, if Ramon knew his designers, and he did. Even more, the Lombard girl had a contagious smile and a good deal of unexpected charm.

"I'm so sorry. You are—"

"Ramon, madame."

"Yes. Well, Ramon, I'm afraid we've no reservations. We decided to stop in, just like that." The snap of her fingers briefly revealed the flash of an oval diamond in a dinner ring. Nice little bauble but surprisingly modest for anyone in her family's tax bracket. Hardly over a carat. Ramon always noticed things like that.

He managed to locate an empty banquette and led the girls across the room. As he had expected, some of the diners recognized Andrea Lombard and the buzzing began. Good for the image of the ultra-expensive Ruby Room, Ramon reasoned. One thing about the heiress, she was friendly and polite, not like some of the snobbish rich kids that had come in. The attention didn't seem to bother her and she smiled at anyone who caught her eye.

The blonde was another matter. Aloof and tight-mouthed,

her contempt for the onlookers was clear. Ramon wondered how she felt about her friend. You couldn't tell by their attitude toward each other. The Lombard girl seemed almost anxious to please her blonde friend.

Must be real tough to be rich, Ramon thought sarcastically...you spend all your time wondering if you're loved for yourself or for those millions you're likely to inherit some day...

So this was Andrea Lombard. Certainly not what he would have thought her to be...He figured a lot of people would like to get their hands on that girl.

Faith Cortlandt snapped her thin, gold-plated cigarette case shut. Before taking a puff of the Pall Mall between her fingers she nodded at the retreating headwaiter with the lighter.

"Took his time lighting my cigarette, you notice. There was a time the Cortlandts could have bought and sold that pipsqueak. I hate to think how quickly he'd have jumped to light you up."

Andrea, who heard variations on this theme from her friend every day, tried to turn her attention to the huge parchment menu.

"I don't think he saw you at first. He was seating that old lady with the blue hair." Luckily, she found the right line on the menu. "Look, they've got *noisettes* of lamb. Your favorite."

Faith puffed a couple of times, trying to prolong her pique, but finally broke down and grinned.

"Damn you! Okay. I'll *be* a lamb. I hate it when you wheedle me out of my well-deserved sulks. But we'll have to make this fast. Frank's seminar is over at eight. He'll be crossing the Bay and parking that jalopy of his out there in Union Square any minute now. No limos waiting for Frank. Not on an assistant professor's salary."

After ordering vodka on the rocks for Faith and a gin martini for herself—also, not coincidentally, her Grandpa Steve's favorite drink—Andrea took a pill out of a polished silver box and quickly swallowed it with little sips of water, clearly trying not to call attention to the act. Most of her college friends jeered at the idea of a sheltered heiress with ulcers. But the duodenal

9

ulcer came and went with her tensions, and the pills had become a habit, representing to her a kind of protection against any potential anxiety attacks.

She caught Faith's glance at the pillbox and slipped it back into her handbag. Then she concentrated on the menu, wondering why *she* should suddenly feel guilty because Faith's boyfriend Frank Kelly got much less than he deserved.

"You're sure close with your grandfather." Faith stared at her cigarette. "Isn't there anything he can do?"

Andrea's grandfather, that eternally busy, eternally young Steve Lombard, owner of nearly half the real estate on the West Coast, was among other honorary positions a regent of the University of California. Though he confided in Andrea as in no one else, she could hardly ask him to raise Frank Kelly's salary, no matter how much she might wish to help Faith.

"Maybe they'll give him an associate professorship," Andrea said brightly. "He certainly deserves it. Without him, I'd never have graduated."

"Come on, Andrea, if you don't talk with Steve Lombard about what he can do for you, then what the devil *do* you talk about?"

Andrea became evasive. Everyone, especially Faith, would laugh at the truth. No one except her grandmother Randi was aware that Grandpa Steve had been coaching her along, giving her what amounted to a crash course in banking, investments and the handling of people across a conference table.

Her grandfather had let her know that she was being groomed to help her father on that painful and distant day when he took over the reins from Steve. They both knew it would have to be handled with great subtlety. Tony Lombard was the last man in the world to accept advice from anyone, least of all from his daughter. But she would be older then. Andrea knew she would have to approach the matter with enormous care if she was to at least save Tony from some costly mistakes. *Somebody* had to keep Tony from making the disastrous decisions with the Lombard estate that he had already made as production chief of Prysing Productions.

Steve had begun Andrea's real education a little more than a year ago, when she came up from her father's hillside mansion

10

in Hollywood to enter Cal-Berkeley for her senior year and major in business management. She still had a lot to learn...

It would all be so much easier, she knew, if her father would listen just once to Grandpa Steve, but that was clearly impossible given their long-standing rivalry. Even Andrea recognized that her passionate, emotional father, with his stubborn streak and lack of business sense, could quite easily run Steve Lombard's vast fortune and holdings into the ground....

Faith needled her.

"I suppose you and Steve Lombard talk about money. What else?"

Andrea shrugged. "Oh, sure. What are you ordering?"

"Like you said, *noisettes* of lamb. And the caesar salad. Well, I've been meaning to ask you now that you're an unattached twenty-one-year-old college graduate—what worlds do you intend to conquer?"

She closed her menu, and confessed.

"What I'd really like to do first is to meet a lot of devastating men. Nothing heavy. Just fun. I want to see the world on my own...I barely got a sample of it on those trips with dad and my stepmother, Jany. But this has been better, dad letting me take my final year up here at Berkeley instead of close to home and his precious studio in Hollywood. They wouldn't have let me live here if I hadn't promised to stay with Aunt Brooke and my grandparents in that mausoleum on Nob Hill."

"Lucky for me you did."

Andrea smiled, glad to hear at last that Faith liked the arrangement. Andrea had wheedled her college friend into the old Lombard mansion as Great-Aunt Brooke's social secretary and thus provided herself with a companion her own age. Besides, it pleased her Lombard relatives who had known the East Bay Cortlandt family in their more prosperous days before the Depression, bad war investments and attrition stripped them of their fortune. Faith Cortlandt's presence also suited Great-Aunt Brooke, a vivacious widow who liked to be surrounded by youth. Andrea was happy to discover now that the arrangement satisfied Faith as well. Sometimes with Faith, it was hard to tell. She could be a lively, bright companion, but she was sensitive about her family's lost glory, and very prickly.

11

She prickled now, just a little.

"Well, if *you* can't land those devastating guys, with all your many assets, I don't know who can."

Ramon approached their table with stately grace, following in the wake of waiters and a trolley with the makings of their caesar salad. He then took over the show, obviously taking for granted that the two young women would be studying his swarthy, handsome features with more than a little interest. After much fuss the salad was divided onto two plates, and Ramon departed, followed by busboys pushing his wheeled accoutrements.

During the silence that followed, Andrea eyed her friend surreptitiously over the salad. No doubt about it—Faith was looking happily expectant for a change. Most of the time she was so cynical about everything, but now she seemed excited. Andrea envied her, imagining that it would be the greatest thrill in the world to find herself in love and to know that a man as attractive and intelligent as Frank Kelly actually cared for *her*—and not for some distant fortune piled up in the wings.

Faith was puzzled by Andrea's pensiveness.

"What the devil are you thinking about?"

Andrea turned her attention to her plate.

"Sorry. Just jealous."

"Ha! That's likely." Faith frowned, then went on. "Look, Andrea, I don't even know what Frank feels about me. We have good times together. He's fun in a quiet way. Not pushy. Clean-cut. But for all I know, it might be nothing but good old friendship."

Andrea's response delighted Faith.

"You forget. I saw the way he used to look at you during lectures. I won't say moon-eyed, but—"

Faith quickly changed the subject, glancing around the room. She noticed that Andrea's eyes kept avoiding the other diners.

Faith exhaled impatiently. "What's the matter with you?"

"I don't know. I hate being stared at like this."

Faith laughed. "I know what's bothering you. If there is a hell it must look like this place. Gleaming eyes, all aimed at you. Full of malice."

"Malice!"

12

"Well, envy. Jealousy. They all wish they were you. So do I."

To get her friend's mind off this subject, Faith looked around, tilting her head and patting the bun of blonde hair low on the nape of her neck.

"Speaking of those men you wanted to meet, get a look at what just walked in."

Andrea shifted against the plush crimson seat, trying not to be too obvious about it. She had recovered her spirits, and her wide green eyes sparkled.

The newcomer *was* worth a second glance. Taller than the average man. Dark-haired. Trim. Suntanned...elegantly dressed.

Faith read Andrea's thoughts. "Looks like money. Sure sign he's broke. Did you hear his accent? He's British." She shrugged. "Not that it matters. He's really something!" She tilted her head again and leaned forward across the table to whisper to Andrea. "How do you like that? He's got a clear view of you. And he's making the most of it. Lucky you."

Startled, Andrea looked over at the stranger again. He caught her stare and returned it with what appeared to be amused curiosity. He obviously didn't recognize her. It was hard to guess from that one look whether he was a charmer or just plain calculating. One thing she could tell. He carried himself like a man of the world, used to the very best.

His eyes were a deep brown—intense, unreadable. But that was as much as she could learn about him. He seemed puzzled by her interest, and rather cool, so she tried not to glance across the room again.

Andrea was relieved when Faith got edgy over her upcoming date.

"How about if we skip the dessert? These places always take so long, and I don't like to keep Frank waiting. He has an eight o'clock lecture tomorrow morning and the poor guy lives out in East Oakland. Has to get up at the crack of dawn."

Andrea knew she had been dawdling, but she didn't want to see her own evening end. She had to do something about her social life. It was getting duller by the day. There had to be a few friends who enjoyed her company for herself, not merely because she was a Lombard—no matter what Faith hinted.

"I could call Herb," she murmured, then could have bitten her tongue. Faith leaped onto the name.

"My God! You *are* hard up. Not Herbie Liversedge. What a creep!"

"He means well, and he does have one great asset."

Faith knew what that was. Herb's uncle, Sam Liversedge, had been the Lombards' banker and investment counselor since before the Fire. Sam owned the major interest in the Consolidated-Mercantile Bank, "Con-Mer" to San Franciscans, and Herbert was his only living relative. Nobody could suspect poor, fat Herbert of shopping for an heiress. Faith rolled her eyes.

"Don't let him get going on his wine-tasting scheme. Sure cure for insomniacs."

Andrea shrugged off Herbert's lack of glamor and excitement. She signed the bill which would go on her St. Francis charge account. It was monitored and paid every month, like all the others, by Sam Liversedge's office, which then sent a copy to her father in Hollywood.

As they left the two girls passed close to the interesting Englishman but he didn't raise his head from the huge menu.

The headwaiter rushed over to escort the young women out to the elegant hotel foyer. Just then the man with the British accent looked up at Andrea, one dark eyebrow raised, still without any further sign of communication. Still in all, he was the first man ever to stir her in this way. He excited her, and she hadn't met any men who excited her quite that much.

She was relieved when Ramon began to fuss.

"And we do hope we will have the pleasure of seeing you again soon."

Andrea smiled, and assured him that everything had been perfect.

Faith had more important things on her mind. Across the big, high-ceilinged lobby with its old-fashioned marble pillars she caught a glimpse of Assistant Professor Frank Robert Kelly. He had a newspaper in his hand, folded in quarters to one column.

14

Nothing equivocal about his face, Andrea thought again, comparing him to the tall man in the Ruby Room. His tousled hair was tawny in color and his eyes were green like her own. He had an athletic build that he kept in great shape. Frank Kelly had been a poor boy, according to Faith, born in a tough neighborhood. He had scratched his way up, working at everything he could find that would get him through college. And he had made it.

Faith hurried along, rapidly outdistancing Andrea. Frank Kelly saw the two girls then and got up to greet them. He took both of Faith's extended hands and kissed her cheek. While Faith held one of his hands he offered the other to Andrea with a smile.

"Haven't seen you lately, Andrea. You're looking wonderful. Not that I'm surprised. I'll bet you dumped your schoolbooks weeks ago."

She grinned mischievously.

"Day after commencement."

Faith gave her a funny look, and Andrea said quickly, "I'll be running along. Have a swell time, now."

"No. Wait." Frank caught her arm. "I just want to get a bite to eat. I was tutoring someone during dinner. Come along with us to the Wharf. We could all share some cracked crab at one of those steam pots."

"After our enormous dinner? Frank, we've just finished what you might call a lavish spread." Faith looked to Andrea.

"Too true." Andrea patted her own stomach, made still smaller by her little waist-cincher. "You run along. Have a good time."

She turned away but was stopped by Faith's sudden insistence, sounding a little abrasive but firm.

"Don't be a fool. We're not going to do anything exciting. And Frank wants you to join us. Don't you, Frank?"

"I do. Honestly."

Andrea weakened. She knew it was a mistake, yet she couldn't deny what she saw as Frank's sincerity. Maybe he just felt sorry for her.

"No. I don't think..."

Faith didn't let up. "Now, tell the truth. You'd have a better time with us than with Herbie Liversedge, and you know it. Come on, let's get going."

Uneasy but giving in, Andrea let Frank take her arm again. She was aware that several people had begun to watch them. Probably by this time everyone leaving the Ruby Room knew who they were, she thought, and saw that she was the spare tire. The third wheel. Whatever you called a useless part.

At least, she was satisfying the eagle-eyed vigilance of her family. She certainly felt safe enough in the company of friends like Faith Cortlandt and Frank Kelly.

CHAPTER
TWO

AS THEY waited for Andrea to get her coat, Frank whispered to Faith, "She's been sheltered all her life. She shouldn't be running around alone. You don't mind if she tags along, do you?"

What could she say? "Why should I mind? She's a friend of mine."

And Andrea really was her friend, one of the few people whom Faith ever permitted close to her. In college Faith had had followers who imitated her makeup, the way she wore her clothes, the height of her heels. Men and women both were attracted to her understated allure. But a part of her still wondered why people all seemed to forget that the Cortlandts were among the foremost families in the Bay Area—long before Andrea's grandmother, Randi Gallegher, the daughter of a poor Irish dock worker and a mother no better than she should be, married into the Lombard family. Depression in the thirties had started the long Cortlandt slide. The use of plane service and the collapse of postwar passenger ships in the Pacific among other bad investments had plunged the Cortlandts so low that Faith had grown up in a stucco duplex in East Oakland. . . .

Faith preferred not to dwell on those days before she was twelve, when she had still been the golden girl in the Cortlandts' elegant Piedmont home set against the Oakland hills. True elegance.

It was in this home that Grandmother Alma Cortlandt Gault had tipsily confided her sad love story to the eleven-year-old Faith. Once upon a time Grandmother Alma had loved Steve Lombard, but he married Randi Gallegher instead of her.

"She pretended to be different, virtuous. You know the sort of creature."

Faith had nodded, wide-eyed, thrilled to be in on these adult secrets.

"Good," said grandmother, her lips thinning as they closed, then added after a sigh or two, "We wouldn't be in our present straits, I can tell you, if it weren't for the Lombards. If I had married Steve instead of Ed Gault—" She cuffed Faith's cheek gently. "Well, it's all in the past. But just remember, the Lombards owe us plenty. That whole family! Keep it in mind."

There were other times, other conversations, when Faith was older and grandmother lived in the next-door half of the duplex in East Oakland after her second divorce. How she hated it! Poor grandmother died in that house, still hating it. And all that time the Lombards were across the Bay, in that Victorian mansion high upon Nob Hill.

Somehow, that made it worse. Then, when the family scraped together every cent to get Faith into the university, the Lombard girl popped up in the same courses. And of all things, she went out of her way to hang around Faith. What was Faith supposed to do? Spurning her shy friendliness was absurd. Faith wasn't capable of that.

When Faith was talked into the part-time job as social secretary to Brooke—which included living in the Lombard house on Nob Hill—her biggest shock was Randi Gallegher Lombard herself, a quiet, busy, elegant woman who accepted Faith without fuss and without condescension. Still, she was a Lombard by marriage, and they possessed all that the Cortlandts had lost. . . .

Meanwhile, as Faith walked out of the hotel beside Frank Kelly that summer night, she felt his nearness tingle her skin. She longed to be alone, to have him hold her in his muscular arms and quiet her fears. She wanted someone to take care of her for a change.

As the two women crossed the street, Andrea caught her heel in the cable slot. Frank grabbed her arm tightly, restoring her balance. Faith reflected with regret that it was a shame she herself didn't stumble, though Andrea did it all with such an innocent air. Faith knew that Andrea's friendship and admiration for her was genuine. Perhaps her generosity was patronizing, but Faith gave her credit for being well-intentioned.

If she would just stop being so damned lucky, a person might really return all that good will! Any more of the Lombard luck and it would be impossible to think of Andrea with anything but bitterness, if not downright hatred.

Andrea would normally have loved a night on the town with friends her own age. But tonight everything around her was misted and blurred, seen through the heavy white fog of a typical San Francisco summer. "Shivering weather," as her stepmother Jany had called it in her accent that still retained its French flavor after seventeen years in the United States.

Although Andrea and her stepmother were fond of each other, they had little in common except a devotion to Andrea's father, the attractive Tony Lombard. Andrea seldom saw her real mother, two-time Oscar winner Eden Ware. The movie star's busy schedule took her from Hong Kong to Marrakesh to Dubrovnik in one year, but Andrea had a great deal of fun with Eden on those rare occasions when they got together. Eden knew everybody and did everything daring and dramatic.

Andrea's father, the chief executive of Prysing Productions, was in desperate trouble now, after his studio's last two disastrous years. Another season like that and the stockholders might vote him out. Even Andrea felt that he ought to stop pouring money into overblown extravaganzas reminiscent of the thirties and get into the more practical TV market.

Andrea's close relationships were with her family rather than with friends her own age. Sooner or later, every man she met found himself compared in her eyes to the darkly handsome movie tycoon Tony Lombard, or to Andrea's grandfather, the dynamic and youthful Steve Lombard who, with beautiful "Gran" Randi was at this moment receiving the plaudits of Japanese industry for his commercial efforts on their behalf after World War II.

Andrea was very much in awe of Grandmother Randi, possibly San Francisco's most admired woman in public life. In her quiet way Randi got things done, so consistently and successfully that everyone "left it to Randi" when the big jobs came along. Andrea didn't envy her. She loved her, but couldn't understand how Tony could adore his mother and feel so equivocal about his father.

There seemed to be a lifelong business and professional rivalry between father and son, Steve and Tony. She knew her grandfather had little faith in Tony's ability, in Hollywood or elsewhere. The worst of it was that Tony's creative efforts tended to justify Grandpa Steve's judgment.

It was hard for Andrea to discount her grandfather's opinion on anything. In her eyes he was the smartest man she had ever known. She was aware that her father and grandfather spoiled her outrageously, making the outside world harder to cope with by comparison. If only one of them could be here tonight, to go wandering through the murky fog with her, perhaps ending up in North Beach and eating Hangtown Fry, that Gold Rush delight, at three in the morning!

The street outside the hotel was still busy and the first two cable cars that rattled past were filled with people as they started up the Powell Street hill. The street would level off temporarily on Nob Hill a block from the Mark Hopkins and Fairmont hotels. This was two blocks below the Lombard mansion where Great-Aunt Brooke lived like royalty between her trips to Europe.

Frank Kelly grabbed Andrea on his right, Faith on his left, and swept them over the throbbing cables where they managed to squeeze onto the third cable car that showed up in minutes.

Trying to do her part for Faith, Andrea let other passengers get between her and Frank as the car pulled up the hill. She pretended to be fascinated by the busy cableman in his box above the street where the complicated crossing of the cables took place between the Powell and California Street cars. But this didn't free her—Frank, too, was interested in this operation. Over the noise around them he tried to explain how the cables worked. The California Street cable car had clanked past the big stone Lombard house on Nob Hill every day, but she still knew little about them. Aunt Brooke had her limousine call for her and never used the cars, but the rest of the family, including Gran Randi, often hopped on and off when they wanted to get down to the financial or the shopping districts.

When the car plunged down the hill to cross over the North Beach district, Andrea lost her balance. Frank pulled her inside against him. She found herself uncomfortably attracted to him and wondered how she could be attracted to two men at the same time...

During her years at Cal-Berkeley and at the restrictive girls' college in Southern California, Andrea hadn't gotten very far along on such subjects as sex. Technically, she was no longer a virgin, but the two experiences with fumbling, anxious Colley Sessions had been huge disappointments.

They must have been just as disappointing to Colley. He had avoided her ever since, even among the eight hundred students in some of her class lectures. She had wondered uneasily if she could be frigid, though she wasn't sure of the complete meaning of the word...

Tonight her interest in the tall, sophisticated man in the Ruby Room had proved she could be aroused, and here was Frank Kelly, exciting her by his touch and his warm, friendly eyes.

"You remind me of Sleeping Beauty," he teased her, paying no attention to several snickers around them. Faith was on the other side of the car from where they stood.

"Me?"

"Sure. This is all new to you, isn't it?"

She thought of the times she had gone exploring like this, usually with her grandfather, but she agreed with Frank.

"Sort of."

The car rumbled onto Columbus Avenue.

"I used to live there." He nodded his head. "On the second floor of that three-story Victorian with the bay windows. They sell Italian newspapers downstairs. I got quite an education. In the language and the politics."

"Italian?"

"American. Wildly antifascist. I was born early in the Depression, and I remember my friends during the war. Stuck their switchblades into Mussolini posters."

Several of the crowd on the car looked at him. Frank grinned back. After all, the war had been over for seventeen years.

"That's how I got to be one hell of an expert with the switchblade, let me tell you."

21

Irish Kelly in Italian North Beach. She was amused by the idea until she caught Faith Cortlandt's eye. Faith revealed nothing except rigidity. She was separated from Frank Kelly by several other riders, all swaying with the car as it rattled toward track's end and a view of the big Alcatraz fog light on the horizon. Andrea had an uneasy sense that she was still being watched by Faith. And maybe others.

She had known this sensation before. Her father, and even Great-Aunt Brooke, accused her of being paranoid. It was a standing joke. Even she laughed about it. Nevertheless, she had always been aware that strangers pointed her out and watched her. Andrea seldom flattered herself that there was any other reason for their interest than her inheritance.

Andrea bit her lip and looked away, pretending not to hear Frank's next remarks. When he persisted, she waved one hand and shrugged, as if she didn't understand. It was important for her not to offend Faith. Faith was one of the few people she knew outside the family who she felt wasn't interested in the Lombard money. Faith spoke up whenever she liked, didn't bother to agree politely when Andrea expressed a different opinion and was fussy about paying her own way in any reasonable enterprise. If Andrea chose expensive restaurants, as she often did, Faith shrugged but saw to it that Andrea ate her next meal paid for by Faith at a hamburger stand on Market Street.

Besides, in her brusque way Faith had been Andrea's first real friend at college. Andrea couldn't bring herself to hurt Faith.

They jumped off the cable car at the end of the Mason Street line and strolled along Fisherman's Wharf. Andrea hurried a few steps ahead. When she looked over her shoulder at Frank and Faith they were huddled together, wrapped in the clinging mists off the Bay.

The three of them reached the sidewalk stalls of steaming crab and other shellfish. Frank ordered a paper cone of crab with a tiny cup of seafood sauce, and tried to feed the girls. Andrea refused, pleading that she couldn't hold a bite, but Faith's appetite had renewed itself, and she and Frank shared the modest meal.

Andrea wondered if they were lovers. There were areas about Faith's life and feelings that remained securely locked against outsiders. She envied Faith. She shifted her position, backing further away to give the couple more privacy. A dozen passersby, mostly tourists, bumped into her. Tonight wasn't the easiest in the world.

Andrea turned abruptly and walked into a bedraggled young girl standing on the corner selling newspapers. The girl wore a badly knitted poncho over a man's faded jeans. Andrea took a dollar bill from the outside pocket of her handbag and offered it to the girl in exchange for one of the papers whose print came off at once on her glove. The girl had a big smile.

"Thank you, sister."

Andrea wasn't sure whose sister the girl thought she might be. She turned away just as a flashbulb went off, jumped, then recognized the limping man in the street as the freelance photographer who had recently made a spread of pictures on her Grandpa Steve and Grandmother Randi when they took off for Japan.

The photographer waved to her.

"Hi, there, Andrea. Out slumming? Hold it! 'Richest Girl Donates to Hippie Commune.'"

Andrea forced a laugh. "No, no. Please." She waved a hand in front of her face to avoid another picture. She had heard from Grandmother Randi how persistent this photographer had always been.

"You Andrea Lombard?" The girl selling newspapers opened her eyes wide, then signaled to a man leaning against the wall of Tarantino's Italian Restaurant. "Hey, Eddie, it's the heiress, the one we just read about!"

Andrea saw the man called Eddie straighten up and start toward her. He had a stringy red beard, worn jeans and an army fatigue jacket. But even the blur of fog didn't wipe out the awful grin spread on his face. Andrea stepped back into the street, just missed a bus and found another bulb flash in her face.

It was the photographer again. She pushed past him, ducked into a nearby souvenir shop, lost herself among the roving tourists along the center aisle and was relieved to find that no one paid any attention to her. She breathed deeply and looked back, trying to make out Faith and Frank across the street. Throngs of tourists along the sidewalk blurred her view. She decided to wait in the store until the photographer had gone, or at least until she caught sight of her friends again.

She looked up suddenly and found herself staring across a counter at a tall man who smiled back at her and began to walk over to where she stood. Just then two middle-aged women, bundled in blue fox and with teased hairdos, walked up to the counter. The man disappeared into the crowds out on the street. Was this the man from the Ruby Room? Andrea could have sworn he was. But now she had no way of knowing for certain.

Feeling let down, she went to the doors and looked out at the passersby. The photographer was gone. Across the street she spotted Faith and Frank Kelly heading west on the sidewalk toward remnants of the fishing fleet all neatly anchored side by side, behind the big restaurant. Frank seemed to be studying every dark hold and corner and Faith was peering into the street ahead.

Andrea went out to the curb and called them. They looked so distraught she felt like a guilty child for causing them worry. They cut across the street against the traffic to meet her, both talking at once.

"You really had us going," Faith angrily informed her.

Frank was nicer. "Girls like you have to be guarded, you know."

"From what, for heaven's sake?"

"From yourself," he joked.

"You look like you've just seen a ghost. What happened?" Faith looked concerned.

"Not a thing." After a beat Andrea added, "Not a damn thing!"

"Well, don't look so sorry about it, for God's sake."

That was Faith. Sharp-eyed as always.

They dropped a tired Andrea off at the Lombard mansion and then headed out toward the Bay Bridge to Oakland. Frank was hesitant to bring Faith to his apartment but she seemed anxious to break away from the Lombard house.

They had made love only once, a spur-of-the-moment thing that only served to increase her attraction to him. Faith didn't know why he obsessed her so. Maybe because he was so hard to land. All his female students had crushes on him. They were forever visiting his office with pleas for help in his literature courses.

"I can't get you back across the Bay in the morning, Faith. These summer sessions begin early. I have to be in Berkeley by seven forty-five."

She grinned. "No problem. There's always the bus and the Bay Bridge."

He reached across and took her hand. "If you say so. Here goes."

He headed the Dodge down Taylor Street and wove his way toward the complexities of the bridge ramp.

In the golden glow of the tunnel lights as they crossed Yerba Buena Island, Frank drew her closer. She settled against him while he pulled off toward Oakland's gleaming lights on the horizon dominated by the Tribune Tower.

"How I hate Oakland," Faith said quietly.

"It's a great city. Hell of a lot bigger future than Frisco on that crowded little peninsula."

"Oh, Frank. It's—it's Oakland. You know. Bourgeois. Middle-class."

He looked at her in a funny way, as if seeing her for the first time.

"Nothing wrong with being middle-class. You can climb up. Or down. Someday...give me a little time—" He broke off, went on firmly. "With tenure, someday I'll earn a full professorship."

Faith didn't argue with him, though she knew that his idea of wealth and hers obviously were vastly different. They drove the rest of the way in silence.

When they got to his apartment Faith walked slowly up the stairs of the two-story stucco building. The apartment itself was worse than she expected, faded and shabby, but in an odd way this made Frank more dear to her. She felt for him a tenderness she had never experienced before, and the warmth that feeling aroused in her was contagious. Frank caught her in his arms

25

and for a little while Faith forgot her distaste for the small apartment, the kitchenette, the view of the dingy, dark, silent street so like those others she had known most of her life.

"Love me," she whispered. "Show me."

He did. He was ready, unexpectedly virile. They came together hard and fast.

Afterwards, Faith vowed to herself that one day they would make love in a decent place, and that she and Frank would have more of the life which she felt they both deserved.

THREE

ANDREA TOLD herself that she certainly wasn't going to wander all over San Francisco in the hope of running into the tall Englishman again. So it was purely "coincidence" that her trips around the city during the following days took her to places where tourists were often found.

Fortunately, Aunt Brooke, who was wise to this sort of thing, was busy being wined and dined by Sam Liversedge, her brother Steve's banker-friend and her own lifelong suitor. But it finally penetrated even Brooke's notoriously self-centered mind that every time she came home late in the evening her carefully reared grand-niece was also just getting in. Alone.

It was all very mysterious, not at all like the virtuous Andrea she was used to. What was she up to? Brooke wondered. One night she greeted Andrea by presenting her cheek as usual, patting Andrea's shoulder and then complaining to Sam Liversedge.

"You can't very well demand accountability of a twenty-one-year-old woman."

"Oh, I don't know. She's certainly safe with my nephew. They were out last night, weren't they?" Sam's face crinkled into a grin, though his eyes studied Andrea until she turned away self-consciously. "Andrea's as nice a child as any I've known. She's not like those wild and woolly rebels over in Berkeley. Our little girl knows enough to listen to her elders. Isn't that so, honey?"

Andrea rewarded him with a smile—anything to save the peace.

"Anyway, Aunt Brooke, I wasn't anywhere, really. Goodnight, all."

She was halfway up the heavy Jacobean staircase when she overheard Aunt Brooke's voice and then Faith's.

"You really shouldn't let her run around alone, Faith dear. I like to think I can trust you to look out for her. You're such a capable girl."

There was an eternally youthful quality about Brooke Lombard Huntington Ware Friedrich. (She had taken back her maiden name since the war.) Like her vigorous brother Steve, she would never grow old. Her only son, Alec Huntington, a dour, middle-aged television executive in New York, was often taken to be Brooke's own age.

Brooke's curly hair was as red as ever, thanks to expert color jobs. Her pretty, mischievous face looked almost girlish in a flattering light. Her figure could still attract most males over forty if she set her mind to it, and a few under forty. She liked almost everyone and was liked in return. But her emotions were shallow and no one ever took her too seriously. She was everything Faith Cortlandt was not, and vice versa.

Brooke wasn't the only one curious about Andrea's comings and goings. Faith was apparently having trouble with her own love life. She seemed to have a suspicion that her dear friend Andrea—"So innocent, so in need of protection, and *so very rich*," as Sam Liversedge remarked one day—was responsible. It was all due to that unfortunate night when Andrea had gone with them to the Wharf.

When Andrea asked one day how the romance was going, Faith snapped, "Who knows? He certainly flutters around *you* like a mother hen."

"Not me! I haven't seen him since the night we went to the Wharf."

Faith didn't say another word.

Maybe she was just coming under the influence of that "old barn," the Lombard mansion itself. Andrea wondered that it had been in the family so long. It was very dark and Victorian, with heavy rooms, archways, beams and two added-on wings, one for a large ballroom which was seldom used. The other wing included the swanky dining room which even Andrea admitted was a splendid affair with crystal chandeliers and sconces, all glittering when there was a formal dinner for the

28

mayor or the governor, or a visiting head of state with whom Steve had dealings.

Andrea caught herself thinking far too much about the tall Englishman. He looked like a man who was used to elegance. She wished he could see this house.

Her thoughts were interrupted, though, by the sudden arrival of Andrea's mother, on her way to British Columbia for a sweeping film epic about the Klondike.

Eden Ware's visits were always fun, especially with her stories of her current films. Her age had had no effect on her popularity. She had moved onward into exciting, mature roles and kept her fans and box-office records despite two recent bad films made under her ex-husband's supervision.

Arriving unexpectedly on a windy summer day, she managed to appear on the entertainment page of the *Examiner* with the barest mention of her Lombard ex-in-laws. A superb achievement in itself.

Her news photo showed the well-known face with its thin, fly-away hair, the famous high cheekbones and wide mouth, the lean, almost boyish figure. Not the qualities one looked for in a glamorous movie star. Nor did she dress like one, except when doing public relations work at her ex-husband's premieres. But Eden Ware's physical attributes were not the kind to fade with age. Many critics claimed she looked better now in a simple silk jacket and slacks than she had at twenty in tulle and rhinestones.

But it was accepted by the family, including her daughter, that the payment for all this luck, talent and longevity was a lifetime of devotion to one thing—her career.

As a girl she had traveled around Europe with Brooke Lombard and they still got on well. Brooke welcomed her now with an affectionate embrace.

"Eden, you must go off to New York with me after you finish this tiresome movie. A couple of shows, some good restaurants and a few divine men."

"You and your divine men!"

Eden rolled her eyes roguishly at her daughter, giving Andrea the pleasureable sense of being in on a private joke. She then hugged her tightly.

"Brooke, I wish I could, but this damned clinker I'm about to wade into is going to keep me up north. I'm off tonight, as a matter of fact."

It was Andrea who felt the keen disappointment.

"Oh, mom, no! Can't we at least have an evening together? I so badly wanted to talk to you about everything that's been going on here."

Eden hugged her again.

"Important stuff, huh? Sweetheart, next time for sure. But today is all jammed up...How's your ulcer? Any better?"

"No problem. Jany gets my prescription filled for me and sends it up." Getting off the subjects of both her ulcer and her stepmother, Andrea went on as before. "If we could just spend a few hours talking. Gossiping. I've missed you."

But Eden was under her usual pressure. "It's absolutely imperative that I have a little talk with your Aunt Brooke's boyfriend. About business."

Brooke opened her eyes at that.

"Don't tell me you're borrowing money. I read in Sheilah Graham the other day that you're making two hundred thousand dollars a picture. To be honest, dear, I didn't know my nephew had that kind of money to pay you...Or is it belated alimony?"

"Don't be catty, darling. Poor Tony is contractually obligated to pay my salary, but with the movie industry in the doldrums I've been turning most of it back into the coffers of Prysing Productions."

Eden let Andrea go and pointed a finger at Brooke, only half joking.

"If you tell that around, Brooke, I'll chew you up and spit out the pieces. Worse. I'll give your correct age to the press."

Brooke made a face. "You stinker! I wouldn't put it past you...Now don't worry. I *certainly* don't want my friends to know my nephew is on the rocks. They'll expect *me* to come to his rescue. Maybe Steve will help out when he gets back from the Orient. He owns some Prysing stock."

While Andrea listened uneasily, Eden shook her head.

"You know how Tony is about proving something to his

father. He's counting on Sam Liversedge to bankroll a percentage of next year's schedule."

"Why doesn't Tony go to the Los Angeles companies? Didn't Bank of America bankroll his 1960-61 program?"

Eden said nothing, but it was clear to Andrea that her father had been turned down this year by Hollywood's principal financial backer. Much as she hated to see her father in such trouble, it annoyed her that he wouldn't listen to advice from anyone. He refused to get into television, and he was fighting a losing battle. Everyone Andrea was acquainted with had a TV set. True, a black-and-white image on a small screen couldn't compare with Cinemascope and color in a huge theater. But didn't he realize that if things went on at their present rate he would be showing his epics to empty movie palaces? He was doing that already.

But Tony Lombard was stubborn. "Bullheaded," Grandpa Steve called him. Tony had set his mind against TV, partly because his father was investing heavily in every aspect of television, including color and the new gadgetry. Tony was hurting himself.

Eden called Sam Liversedge's office. Sam's female assistant was delighted to talk to Eden Ware and put her on hold, twittering that Mr. Liversedge would just adore seeing her.

It was a long hold.

When her voice came back, the mood had gone from euphoria to embarrassment and confusion.

"That man! He sneaked out the other door while I've been typing up some trust department reports."

Eden repeated this to Andrea and Brooke without inflection. Then she put on her charming movie-star act.

"That's my Sam. Tell him that just for that, he can take me to dinner."

"He...a...left a note here. It says he's on his way to Pebble Beach to play golf. I'm terribly sorry, Miss Ware."

Eden Ware cleared her throat, managed a laugh that was commendably light.

"Naughty man! Well, I'll have to stop in and say hello on my way back from the Klondike."

31

She hung up. Andrea took her hand and squeezed it hard. Her father wasn't getting any help from Sam Liversedge.

"Mother, that was an Oscar-winning performance. You were wonderful."

Eden grimaced. "Wasn't I, though? Well, what the heck, Tony's a big boy, and little Jany will comfort him."

Brooke laughed. "That little Frenchwoman absolutely smothers him. She'd do anything for Tony. I swear she'd kill for him, if she thought it would make him happy."

Andrea looked at her mother and was prouder than ever. Eden merely shrugged at this disparagement of Andrea's stepmother, but took no part in it.

"Tony needs attention and adulation. I never gave it to him." She took a big breath, turned to Andrea. "All right, sweetheart, since Sam refuses to give me a few minutes of his time, you've got my undivided attention for—" She squinted at her watch. "About ten hours. Then I'm off to the frozen north."

It turned out to be a day of mixed blessings. Andrea always felt self-conscious when people pointed her out, so it was twice as bad when she went shopping with her mother. Eden spent half their lunchtime signing autographs at the Bourgogne Restaurant and was even accosted on the street by teenagers who boasted audibly that three Eden Wares would get them a genuine Tony Curtis.

Eden laughed at Andrea's indignation.

"Shows you I'm worth something. One-third of a Tony Curtis."

All the same, Andrea sensed that Eden flew north from San Francisco still worried about her failure to promote the backing for Tony Lombard's new production schedule. Almost nothing in all the world, as Andrea knew and Eden would have confessed, was as high on her list of priorities as her career— nothing except Andrea herself. But an Eden Ware without her present fame was unthinkable.

Andrea had also kept an eye out for the tall Englishman, but no luck there either. The presence of her famous mother could have scared him off, she mused.

She had almost come to give up hope of ever running into

him when one noontime she met Frank Kelly at the Top of the Mark quite accidentally.

Andrea was being shown to a table she had specially picked out, visible to everyone who stepped out of the elevator and into the skytop room. This was a kind of last hope, just in case that man dropped in for a drink. She didn't see Frank until it was too late. She did not want to rekindle Faith's jealousy, and quickly looked away, but he waved to her and got up at once, introducing his two friends to her. She recognized their names as All-Coast football stars of former years.

Andrea congratulated herself on recognizing the names of Cal's football rivals. She hadn't entirely wasted her senior year at Cal studying business management.

"I can't stay," she protested when they invited her to join them. "I'm sorry."

"Well, you aren't going to drink alone. Are you?" Frank demanded.

"N-no. Only—"

He seemed to assume, in a very protective way, she thought, that she shouldn't be here without a man.

"So you just sit here. Take my chair. Waiter? Another chair. Right here. Thanks. Now. What on earth are you doing up here alone? I know. Waiting for a girl friend."

She nodded. She was still too inexperienced to argue with such a good-looking man.

"I don't see her anywhere. Guess she couldn't make it. But that's okay. You sit right here and we'll order. Waiter, a Bloody Mary for the young lady. That all right?"

"Fine. I can't stay long." She looked around once more, failed to make out anyone she might know and sat on the edge of her chair pretending an interest in the men's sport talk.

Frank Kelly had been rambling along about Cal's chances for the Rose Bowl this season when he noticed the boredom in her eyes. Good-naturedly he clapped one hand over hers on the table.

"Sorry. This can't be much fun for you."

He raised his head, laughed and motioned to someone be-hind her.

"Well, I'll be! Why didn't you tell me who you were waiting for?" He raised his voice. "Over here!"

She swung around. *"He's here?"*

Fortunately, no one heard her over the din of voices in the room. Then Andrea saw whom he was referring to. Faith Cortlandt was standing there, looking ominously cool but very chic in a soft tweed suit the color of her hair, topped off by an Hermès scarf that had been Aunt Brooke's Christmas present to her last year. She wore an elegant hat that fitted around her loose French twist. The only kind of hat Andrea could wear, with her thick mop of black hair, was a pillbox in imitation of First Lady Jacqueline Kennedy.

Andrea snatched her hand out from under Frank's, but the gesture itself attracted Faith's attention. Her lips tightened. Andrea pushed her chair back.

"Just in time, Faith. I've got a date and here's a vacancy. Take my chair."

After a moment's hesitation Faith relaxed. "Thanks, Andrea." She slipped in, presenting her pale cheek for Frank's kiss.

Andrea gave them all a casual wave and headed for the elevator. She knew she had surprised Frank and his friends by her abrupt departure, as well as Faith, who watched her leave with a puzzled look.

It was a relief for Andrea to get into the elevator and ride down with strangers. Her friends provided too much tension lately.

Out on the street she saw the big gray stone Lombard house only a block away. Aunt Brooke was entertaining the Palace of Fine Arts committee today, and Andrea was on the committee. She sometimes felt more comfortable at museums, zoos and aquariums than she did with friends her own age. But the men and women who made up committees to support such echoes of the past were, for the most part, Aunt Brooke's age and their favorite topic of conversation was the past.

She decided not to return to the Lombard house. It was an early September day, and she stood a moment enjoying the sunny blue sky, thinking of the handsome man she would never meet.

Her future suddenly loomed terrifyingly before her—a vast, empty space. She felt she had none of the Lombards' ambitious drive, nor did she have the social ease and confidence of Aunt Brooke. Andrea didn't know what was going to become of her life.

If only someone could point her in the right direction.

CHAPTER
FOUR

HAVING DECIDED to play hookey from the committee meeting, Andrea salved her conscience by going shopping for a few small presents. She wanted to buy Faith a leather notebook to carry in her handbag, and decided she would go to the Wharf.

The devil with that mystery man! Andrea walked through the Mark Hopkins lobby with her hands thrust into the pockets of her jacket, deep in thought.

She tried to ease her mind by telling herself that her parents and grandparents were all vigorous, healthy, active people. She wouldn't have to worry about all that heiress business for many, many years. In the meantime she must do something with her life. All the other Lombards were busy building up or tearing down things—movies, television, shopping centers, old buildings, industries, airplane parts.

None of those appealed to Andrea. Nor did the charity and volunteer work that Grandmother Randi took part in. But there were other challenges. Once, Grandpa Steve had given her a block of Pacific Telephone and Telegraph common stock and she had "played" with it, selling it for AT&T and IBM, buying more during the split, working it up. She now had an eight-thousand-dollar profit and was prouder of that than of all the Lombard properties. She wondered if perhaps she should become a stock manipulator....

Meanwhile, the Mark Hopkins doorman waved a taxi out of the little forecourt and over to the steps. She got in and let him take her on the roller-coaster ride down to the Wharf. She wandered past souvenir stores and restaurants, wondered where to have lunch and what presents to buy everyone. She was only a block from the big shop where she thought she had seen the man from the restaurant.

She glanced toward the Bay. The choppy blue waters were dotted with sailboats, fluttering like moths around a big, sleek, white passenger vessel in from Australia, New Zealand and Tahiti by way of Hawaii. Andrea pictured herself returning to Hawaii, her birthplace as well as her mother's.

"I've got to do something with my life," she reminded herself firmly, and walked on. She was passing the little basin where the fishing fleet had returned with their day's catch when a man's voice broke through the noise around her.

"I say! It's you again."

Andrea took her time before she looked up and saw her mysterious stranger gazing down at her with a crooked grin.

"I see we frequent many of the same places." So that *was* he in the souvenir shop that night!

Before she could say anything he said, "You must be a tourist in town, too. I'm not even sure of my direction here. Care to join me for a cup of coffee?"

"Look here. I don't even know your name." She thought his nerve was colossal, though it seemed safe that he didn't know who she was. She found herself drawn to his easy, almost impudent manner. He was certainly a charmer...

"I'll get to that. But do come and join me for a bite to eat at—what is it? Ferrante's. Is the food good?"

"Of course it is," she said, accepting his invitation.

She was dying to say yes anyway. He swept her around the corner into Ferrante's and upstairs.

He certainly had a way with him. It was the first time in ages that she didn't have to wait for a table in the popular seafood restaurant, especially on the deck usually reserved for cocktails.

They were ushered to a table next to the rail with the fishing fleet below them and the Golden Gate with its bridge and fluttering sailboats outside the piers. On the horizon to the west the Maritime Museum was a proud little monument to the passionate attention of Steve Lombard, who had used a lot of pressure and spent a lot of money to glorify the memory of the old ferry boats and the deep-water sailors who made San Francisco "The City" for men who sailed before the mast.

Andrea's intense pride in anything Steve Lombard accomplished spilled out of her.

"My grandfather worked hard to get that building. He loves the romantic days of sail—that's what he calls them. When grandpa was a boy there were still a few sailing vessels out there."

"This grandfather of yours. He's still living?"

"Very much so." What a question, she thought, her suspicion aroused. But she recovered rapidly, pleased that her identity remained secure.

"Now that I've told you all about me the least you can do—"

"*All* about you? For a start, what am I to call you?"

She offered him part of the name with which she was christened, Eve-Andrea. "My name is Eve. What's yours?"

He gave it some thought while he sipped his scotch. "I'm . . . Lee. For Leland."

They shook hands. Across the room two women who appeared to be mother and daughter put their heads together and whispered while they stared at Andrea and her companion. They seemed to have recognized her, but she lost interest in them.

During lunch Leland made a good deal of small talk, asking Andrea questions that led her to reveal more about herself than she intended. She, on the other hand, learned remarkably little about Leland except that he had spent some time in the States and was reasonably harmless.

"I suppose you have *some* faults. Or do you keep them secret?" Andrea asked, surprising herself with her coyness.

"Not at all. I have expensive tastes." He pointed to her plate. She had ordered a Hangtown Fry and was enjoying the fried oysters. "How do you eat all that revolting mess?"

"I love them. Father says I have plebeian tastes. He even named the seafood plate in the commissary after me."

The way his eyes looked up slowly from the plate to her face gave her an odd feeling that she was talking too much, revealing more than she should. It was as if that blank gaze of his might be a facade hiding a very keen interest.

"Your father is a restaurateur?"

She backtracked, talking too fast, a bit rattled.

"Sort of. I mean, it's pretty small, like a diner. In fact, it is a diner."

Leland glanced over the water toward the Presidio on the far horizon. Was there a quirk of humor about his mouth? Or did he just find her amusing in general? "And yet, your grand-father was important enough to set up that museum over there. I take it your father prefers to stand on his own feet. Make his own way, as you Yanks say."

She leaped onto this. "That's my father, all right. But we're a close family. And speaking of families, where is yours? Do you see much of them?"

"No." The word was clipped, tight. She wondered if she had offended him. Maybe he and his family were feuding. She could see them now, elegant, reserved, perhaps titled, turning away from Leland because he hadn't lived up to their stuffy expec-tations. She studied him while drinking her drink. She was usually comfortable enough with young men, but Leland was far more mature. He had a look about him, a hard edge to all the surface charm that made her wonder if his past had been dangerous.

"Were you in the war, by any chance?"

"Mmm."

Whatever that meant. She took it to be a yes.

He took a long swallow of her combination of chocolate and coffee and grimaced.

"What on earth—what *is* this?"

"Coffee, chocolate and brandy. What did you do? In the war, I mean."

He set aside the drink, a particular favorite of hers on windy, salty days, and signaling the waiter ordered another scotch. When he answered her his tone was light and indifferent. She suspected it was put on, which made his quizzical answer even more harsh.

"Ever hear of the Commandos?"

That was almost twenty years ago. He couldn't be old enough for that war. The wind off the Golden Gate whipped his hair and made him look younger, she decided.

"Yes. I've seen the movies. You must have been very young then."

"Thank you." This put him back in a good mood again. "I was sixteen in forty-one. I lied a little. Stretched a point."

"But nineteen forty-one is the year..." *The year I was born*...Thank heaven she hadn't blurted that one.

He grinned, reached across the table and took her hand.

"I'll make it easy for you. I'll be thirty-seven next month. October twenty-fifth, to be exact."

She looked around, suddenly aware that they were the last pair of diners on the deck and getting impatient attention from the waiters.

She sighed. "I'm afraid we're being invited to leave."

He looked around, shrugged, and finished drinking his scotch. Then he signaled for the check and laid down two bills on the table. He helped her out of her chair.

"I'll get you a cab."

She was afraid he would ask her address. She still wanted to hold tight to this romance between Eve and Leland, an affair that had nothing to do with Andrea Lombard.

"Never mind. I'll take the Hyde Street cable car. It's only a few blocks away."

They walked out and down to the street, into the bright afternoon. The day was as perfect as it ever would be in San Francisco for being swept along by the wind, heavy with salt and moisture.

In the distance, beyond the many seafood cafes, several brave characters were playing in the surf. With toes dug into the wet sand further along, three young boys with long hair bound by rawhide thongs were tossing a volleyball back and forth. Leland pretended to shiver.

"They must be polar bears." He looked down at her and smiled, noting her surprise. "I'm not one of your western cowboys, you know."

Feeling wonderfully confident, she teased, "Somehow, I got the impression you were an an outdoor man."

"You mean the tan? Nothing but sun lamps," he joked.

She kept waiting for him to mention seeing her again. He

didn't touch her but she was intensely aware of his body. Walking beside her, he seemed uncomfortably silent, even moody. She wondered if she had said or done something to put him off.

He walked her to the Buena Vista Cafe in its old Victorian house on the corner of Hyde Street.

"I'm afraid this is good-bye."

She didn't need to be told that this meant good-bye for good.

Pride came to the fore. She put on a quick, flashy smile. "Traveling on, I take it."

"I'm afraid so. I fly out tonight."

She was beautifully casual. "Isn't it lovely to be on the go! Free as the wind."

"I wish—" He broke off. He hadn't released her arm yet. "I'll walk you across the street."

She wanted to tell him not to bother, but it would be too flip. Her tone would betray how much she cared.

"Thank you. You can help push the car round the turntable. It's fun." Her voice sounded normal. She was proud of it.

The cable car rattled around the turntable and several passengers leaped on. Leland held her back, but she pulled away. He wrapped his free arm around her, pulled her to him and kissed her. It was just a brushing of lips, but no one could deny the tenderness there.

The car bell rang loudly and Andrea broke away, red-faced, and climbed quickly onto the rear platform. A boy in a crimson and white Stanford sweater pulled her inside. When she looked back to wave to Leland he was halfway across Beach Street. He didn't see her.

She went inside the car, sat down on one of the long seats that faced each other across the central aisle and thought about him. She decided Leland must be married. He must have a wife and several children whom he was now returning to. In his old age he would always remember the girl he kissed one sunny September day in San Francisco, long ago.

She was still dreaming when the car started to climb the Hyde Street hill and the Stanford boy lost his balance, falling into her lap.

"Sorry."

"Sure."

He shifted to the place beside her, but he kept looking.

"You're Andrea Lombard, aren't you?"

Oh, damn! "That's right."

"Then I *am* sorry. I mean, really sorry. It was a big shock to see you and, uh—"

She looked back toward Beach Street, barely catching Leland's tall figure as he vanished behind the Bay side of the Buena Vista Cafe. She felt suddenly drained. Beside her, the boy seemed to feel she had rebuffed him and turned away.

A big shock? What on earth did that mean, anyway?

CHAPTER
FIVE
___

THE BOY'S remark was soon forgotten as she became en-
grossed once more in deciphering Leland's strange behavior.
By the time the car crossed the northerly crest of Nob Hill she
had made up half a dozen explanations, all with a tinge of
melodrama. Through each of them she saw herself in a romantic
light—Leland's unattainable woman.

Unless, of course... she sat up straight... he had simply
walked away from her because he wasn't interested. Obviously
she lacked the enchantment and appeal of women like her
mother, her stepmother or Faith. In Andrea's eyes even Aunt
Brooke had a brighter image to offer men.

That must have been it. Leland found Andrea a bore. She
should have borrowed some of the sophistication that made
Faith such an alluring woman. Andrea wished that she could
relive the last hour so she could do it all differently. She would
sparkle with wit and a more worldly air. Too late now. Her
one opportunity was gone.

She looked up, discovered they were approaching Jones Street
on Nob Hill and decided to walk the few blocks home. She
pushed her way out to the platform and jumped off before the
car came to a grinding halt. She walked up the street wondering
if she would ever again meet a man as appealing to her as
Leland. That is, if she didn't cross paths with him again some
day, somewhere. The more she thought of it the more she
convinced herself that it was not impossible....

In front of an expensive new condominium she almost walked
into a young man setting out the early evening newspapers.
The headline was so bold on the top page she wondered if war
had been declared somewhere.

The newspaperman finished stuffing papers into the rack and drove away.

Andrea glanced at the headlines as she passed.

STEVE AND RANDI IN JAPAN CRASH

There was no immediate horror. The thing was too incredible. A coincidence. Two people sharing the nicknames of her grandparents had been in a crash of some sort. She fumbled for change in her coin purse, finally got it into the coin slot and grabbed a paper.

Lombard. Stephen and Mary-Randal Lombard...taking off from Tokyo to San Francisco via Honolulu...Not known whether there were survivors...Reports fragmentary.

Fragmentary. The word brought up hideous pictures. She began to run, dangling the paper in her free hand, raising it every few seconds, hoping to read that *among the survivors were Stephen and Mary-Randal Lombard...*

Please, God...*among the survivors.*

Her grandparents were born survivors. They had survived two World Wars, a depression, two major earthquakes. A little thing like a plane crash wasn't going to stop them. They were too alive, too vital. They were needed by countless people besides just her.

As she ran toward the solid stone Lombard mansion amidst all the high-rise hotels and elegant apartment houses on Nob Hill, she shifted suddenly, crossed in the middle of the street and headed east toward the back entry and kitchen area of the house. The sooner she reached home, the sooner Steve and Randi would be found safe.

The kitchen was deserted. A pork roast in the oven exuded savory odors and several salmon fillets had been spread on waxed paper, left untended. Mrs. Trentini, the cook, and the young Korean girl whom she was training were nowhere in sight. Andrea thought that odd—they were always in the kitchen area at this hour.

Otherwise, there was a terrible emptiness. Silence. Even the pillars and the archway between the living room and the front vestry no longer creaked. Andrea rushed through room after room before she realized no one was downstairs.

All her nervous haste dissolved into an icy numbness. She climbed the back stairs. The servants were at the doorway of the family's favorite spot, the sunroom at the back of the house. In silence they made way for Andrea.

Sam Liversedge was at the telephone extension in the corner, one of his hands resting protectively on Aunt Brooke's shoulder. She was crying. Faith, sitting next to her, got up when she saw Andrea. Wordlessly, she shook her head. The implication was clear but senseless to Andrea, who heard herself babbling.

"You'll see. It'll be a mistake. They're survivors, don't you know that?"

Her trembling legs gave out and she went down on her knees before Aunt Brooke whose round, almost childish face was mottled with red. Her eyes brimmed with tears.

"We tried all over town. Where were you? We've been trying for hours... But never mind that. You always were a brave child... Oh, honey, Randi was like the sister I never had. And Steve!"

She turned away from Andrea, clutching at Sam, who patted her shoulder absently. "Sam! What will I do? Who shall I turn to? Steve was my very own brother. My dearest relation in all this world."

Faith's voice lent a cool sharpness to the moment.

"There is your son, Mrs. Lombard. You've still got him."

Brooke shrugged and blew her nose into a wisp of pink tissue offered by Faith. "Oh! Alec has no feelings for his old mother. Hiding away in New York, what does he care?"

No one said what they all thought. As an executive of Universal Broadcasting Corporation in charge of television news, Alec Huntington was scarcely hiding away.

Sam Liversedge put his hand over the phone. "The loss will be Alec's too, my dear. He was very devoted to his uncle, and especially to Randi."

Andrea was desperate. "They don't know for sure. The papers said—"

Sam spoke into the telephone. "Thank you, I'll relay it." He set the phone back, and suddenly looked very old. Andrea had never noticed before how old he really was. "The papers have only the first reports. I've been talking to Tokyo. The plane—" He cleared his throat. "It didn't clear the ground. Some malfunction." His voice dimmed. "No survivors."

"Not—"

"Not one."

Andrea got up shakily. Both Sam and Faith reached out to grab her as if she were going to faint. She shook off their hands and made her way to the doorway. The servants stood aside silently, letting her pass among them and into the dark upstairs hall. None of them took their eyes off her and for this she felt suddenly enraged at them.

She got to her room near Brooke's at the front of the house, a sunny, ruffled room done in pink to please Jany. Outside the California Street cable car clanged past. Several passersby had stopped on the sidewalk. They were staring through the wrought-iron railing, hoping to catch a glimpse of someone in the family.

Through her closed door Andrea became aware of the shrill ring of telephones that cut the eerie silence of the house. One ring after the other. They never stopped.

There was a knock on the door, but she ignored it. She had to be alone, at least for now, as if by avoiding the family's grief she could keep grandpa and grandmother alive.

Whoever was at the door must have given up. Andrea had been sitting on the high four-poster bed under its frilled white canopy. She got up and smoothed the dotted swiss coverlet. A small tribute to Gran Randi.

But for Grandpa Steve?

When he kissed me good-bye at the airport that day, was it for the last time?

She closed her mind to that horror. Any minute the good news would come. There had been a mistake. The Lombards were safe, like the survivors they had always been.

More phones ringing. She shuddered. The next time someone knocked on the door the sound was drowned out by that hideous jangle. The door opened in a gingerly way. She saw Sam Liversedge's face.

"You mustn't cry all by yourself, honey. Come and sit with the others."

"I'm not crying. Why should I? We'll hear the whole story any time now."

Instead of showing relief he looked more worried than ever.

"They had a beautiful life. You've got to look at it like that. And they went out hand in hand, you might say."

She knew she was behaving childishly but couldn't stop herself. She pounded her fist on the three-mirrored French dresser so hard it made him wince.

"They didn't go out. We don't know that yet." She took a breath, calmed down and pleaded. "Can't we just go on hoping...for a little while?"

The old man felt helpless before her obstinacy. He tried to pat her shoulder but she shrank away from him and moved out of his reach.

"When he heard the news your father tried to telephone you several times."

"I was having lunch at Ferrante's." Was that only a few hours ago?

Had that girl really been Andrea Lombard, feeling secure and loved, constantly taking her cue from what Grandpa Steve would do? Even her attention to Leland was partly rooted in the qualities of Steve Lombard that she saw in the tall stranger. And all that time when she had been so happy, Steve and Randi were already dead.

It hit her then, the awful thought that at the very minute she was laughing, flirting, enjoying herself today, that *thing* had happened in Japan.

A hot stab of pain hit her eyes. She covered her face with her palms. It hurt. It hurt so much...

Sam tried his best to comfort her.

"There, there, honey. I'm here. You just cry it out."

Despite his efforts to console her, she knew with a twinge of bitterness that he was relieved because she finally accepted their death. But she didn't accept it. She felt that she couldn't face the ordeal ahead if she didn't keep a place in her memory for the living pair, Steve and Randi.

They would be her mentors. She decided that at every turn she must ask herself, What would Steve do? How would Randi react? And above all, what could Andrea do to bring Steve's quick, spontaneous grin, or Randi's slower, quieter look of approval? They would be watching her. She must not disappoint them.

The plane which had crashed on takeoff at the airport outside Tokyo was an American airliner on regular schedule. The investigation into the crash, which determined that there had been an engine malfunction in a high crosswind, prevented the immediate return of the bodies of the eight Americans that had been on board.

They were the longest hours of Andrea's life. She was not allowed to accompany her father to Japan and could only wait for the arrival of the bodies and the all-too public funeral that would follow.

The memorial service at San Francisco's Masonic Temple attracted such a crowd, both inside the auditorium and out on the sidewalk, that the whole thing was frighteningly impersonal. When the procession left for the Woodlawn Memorial Park down the Peninsula it looked as if half of San Francisco might be following them.

The tribute to Steve focused on his strong sense of civic duty, his brilliant organizational ability and his unmatched skill in successfully negotiating difficult treaties, but nothing was said of Steve the family man, the Grandpa Steve Andrea knew.

It was hard to indulge any of the family's private grief when they were surrounded by so many people who had come to pay tribute. Andrea was introduced to numerous dignitaries who praised Steve Lombard as the special friend of their country. Each of them mentioned Steve's only son as his natural successor. None of them spoke of Tony Lombard's own work. It was doubtful if some even knew what he did.

Andrea could see how this troubled her father. All his life Tony Lombard had lived in the shadow of his father's accomplishments. Even during the war when he behaved with exemplary courage, joining Jany's brother in the fight to retake Occupied Paris from the Nazis, his father had still managed to arrive in triumph, expecting to "rescue" Tony.

Andrea knew all this, but as the special favorite of Steve Lombard she had seen his side as well in the rivalry. It troubled her now that Tony was already talking within the family about how he could save the next production season, how his control of his father's stock in Prysing Productions would give him free rein to do all those films he wanted to do.

Everyone listened to him as if to assuage a personal suffering. There was Jany, of course, with sweet, eager love for him shining in her eyes. Aunt Brooke was nodding; even Eden looked relieved. Only Aunt Brooke's son, Alec, was wrapped in his private grief. Randi had been more of a mother to him as a child than his own, and her death cut through him deeply. It had always seemed incredible to Andrea that this plain, quiet man could be Brooke's son.

Alec pulled Tony aside. "Tony, if you don't mind, I wonder if I can have a few minutes of your time. It's about some plans UBC has for doubling our on-air news time and I could use your help."

From the back Tony and Alec looked like brothers. Their interests as children, however, had diverged, due to the problem which Alec had learned to camouflage successfully. He had been born with one leg slightly shorter than the other. Operations did nothing to correct this, but an iron will had given him the skill to walk with a deliberate stride that fooled most people.

Tony looked up. To Andrea's eyes he seemed dazed at Alec's introduction of the subject at this time. But she saw he must have realized why Alec had raised the matter. He needed something to take his mind off the tragedy that absorbed his mind. He had resented his father, but he had also loved him and admired him. If Alec could get him thinking about matters outside his previous range it might raise his spirits....

Andrea's earliest recollections of her father before he married Jany were full of fun memories, of a playful young man, handsome and full of love. But when he married Jany he also assumed control over the major independent studio her first husband had owned.

The responsibility changed him. Nowadays, all he ever

seemed to think about was the success, or more often, the failure of his productions. Andrea knew, as his two wives knew, how deeply he had loved his mother, and his father, too, beneath all the rivalry.

It had always shocked Andrea's school friends that her mother and stepmother got along so well, but to Andrea it was the most natural thing in the world. Andrea knew that Tony and Eden had been incompatible. The fact that Eden's star was rising at a time when Tony was merely a rich man's son hadn't helped matters. He needed someone to adore him, to need him. That need Eden Ware could not fill. And Jany Friedrich Prysing had been the answer.

Eden mused, "I wonder if Steve would have come to Tony's rescue if this hadn't happened. He controlled quite a chunk of Prysing stock." She glanced at Brooke speculatively. "I suppose there is no doubt Tony will inherit."

Brooke's auburn eyebrows went up at this odd remark. Jany was indignant, her low voice almost inaudible over the telephone ringing in the hall.

"But Tony is the only child of Steve. The law is precise on this, *naturellement.*"

"French law. This is California."

Maria Trentini, the cook's daughter, looked in on the three women.

"Excuse me, Mrs. Lombard. Mr. Liversedge on the phone."

Brooke sat up and the girl plugged in the extension behind her chair. Brooke was uncharacteristically abrupt.

"Okay, Sam. Shoot." She listened, then, "Not ten, honey. I'm not even up until ten... Thank you. We'll be there."

She hung up in what looked like slow motion.

"For God's sake, Brooke, what next?" Eden muttered.

"That was Sam Liversedge. He wonders if we can come down to his offices in the bank tomorrow. About eleven."

"What—"

"About the will. Steve's will."

Jany and Eden looked at each other. Jany said, "I must tell

50

Tony. It is Tony who is concerned."
Brooke said nothing.
Andrea remained numb.

CHAPTER SIX

ONE WAY Andrea kept her grandparents' memories alive was by filling new scrapbooks with articles that had been written about them. There was the story of what Steve had done in the First World War, along with his friend André, the Comte de Grasse, who died many years later in Dunkirk, while rescuing his wounded men.

Tony Lombard walked into her room that evening and found her reading one of the stories. He looked tired and there were dark hollows under his eyes, but his smile was warm as ever.

"Hello, sweetheart. We haven't had much time for each other lately, have we?" he said, boyishly straddling a little slipper chair that he pulled up to the vanity where she sat.

Despite all the recent shocks, he still looked younger than his years. Although he was more than forty, his hair was dark as ever, his smile as winning as it had been when he used to clown with Andrea back in his younger days.

Andrea shook her head. "We were going to go to Mount Tamalpais when grandpa got back from the Orient. Picnicking in Muir Woods. All that."

"I know." He reached out almost tentatively. With his arm around her she felt like the child whom he used to comfort over minor hurts. She hadn't gotten much sleep lately and here was her father's shoulder, the satin lapel of his elegant dinner jacket smooth against her cheek.

"Daddy, I don't suppose you'd care to take that hike with me, you and Jany?"

His arm shifted, but he tightened his grip on her a few seconds later.

"Sweetheart, I'd like that better than anything I can think of."

"But?"

He hesitated. "But I'm in big trouble with the minority stockholders at Prysing. I'm afraid I'll be terribly busy for a little while." He felt her withdraw and went on hurriedly. "Wait. Pretty soon. Just give me a little while. And we'll make that hike, right through Muir Woods. Or anyplace else. You just name it."

It wasn't very satisfactory but it was good to have him here beside her, anyway. After what happened to her grandparents she must treasure all the more those who remained.

Tony changed the subject, pointing to a blurred black-and-white snapshot of two men in the curious old uniforms of the First World War.

"Father and his friend André. You were named for him. Eden wanted it that way. André de Grasse was a real hero, all right."

"Mother named me after a friend of grandfather's? How could she know this André what's-his-name?"

She had heard something of this before but wanted to see what her father would say. He seemed very open about it.

"It was before your mother and I were married. She and the count were—well, very good friends in Paris before the war."

"And you weren't jealous?" She had seen him intensely jealous of men in his own profession, even of men who monopolized Jany at studio parties, which was ridiculous, because Andrea knew that Jany never looked at another man. Now he dismissed the Comte de Grasse with a curious inflection that seemed to have some meaning.

"Of André? God, no!"

But of someone else?

Andrea had once overheard a conversation between her mother and Brooke that might have hinted at the truth.

"Jany seems to know how to rub Tony the right way. You found him a bit more difficult, didn't you, Eden?" Brooke had asked.

"Well, no wonder," Eden had dismissed the slur breezily. "I don't think Steve has said two words in private to her since she married Tony. I'm sure he likes her, but they have nothing to talk about. I'm afraid Steve is the problem when it comes to Tony. There was never anything between Steve and me, but try and tell Tony that. He and his father were always bitter rivals. In every field."

"Inferiority complex, my dear. Pure and simple."

Eden ended the unpleasant gossip. "Steve's money and power will make Tony one of the richest men in this country, and he'll probably throw it all away on some damn fool projects that are twenty years behind the times. If all that money doesn't solve his complex, nothing will."

So the moment had come. When Steve's will would be read, Tony, his only child, would wear Steve Lombard's mantle. Andrea only hoped the money and the responsibility for it all wouldn't destroy him... With Steve's death Andrea was afraid that her father was now going to throw away years of his life trying to be someone else. Having failed to be Leo Prysing, the movie mogul who was Jany's first husband, he would tackle the man he had always envied and wanted to be—his father. Meanwhile, the real Tony Lombard, exciting and talented in his own right, would go down the drain...

Andrea hugged him, wishing she could warn him but knowing it was impossible. She felt his tight embrace as he returned her love tenderly.

"Daddy, don't be anybody but yourself." He broke away, staring at her, not understanding. She couldn't explain. She murmured, "You're so wonderful. Don't let them change you."

He must have thought she referred to the inheritance that he would hear about tomorrow. His voice was hoarse with emotion.

"I won't, sweetheart. You're my girl. You and Jany. Pretty soon you two will see just how high I'll climb. And you'll be beside me, all the way."

It wasn't quite what she had meant.

A little before eleven the next morning Faith came into the living room in time to hear Andrea asking not to be included in the family group at Sam Liversedge's office.

It was Brooke who overruled Andrea's peculiar squeamishness.

"You are an important part of the family, young lady. All the Lombards are expected, every last one of us." To make Andrea feel better, she added, "Sam says it's all right if Faith Cortlandt comes along. She can wait in the outer office."

"Faith has a date with Professor Kelly. She may not want to kill her day like that," Andrea said.

Faith turned to Brooke. "Your brother and his wife were awfully nice to me, Mrs. Lombard. They made it a lot easier for me here. As you all did."

"Naturally, dear," Brooke said. "We are all fond of you."

Andrea's voice was quiet. "We need you, Faith."

Faith couldn't resist that. "I'll tell Frank to meet me at the Eastbay Terminal. I'm helping him with some research at the Berkeley library."

Going upstairs with Andrea to get their jackets, Faith remarked casually, "You'd never guess who passed me on Mason Street the other day. He was headed for the airport limousine."

"Who?" Andrea's mind seemed to wander, perhaps, Faith thought, to the meeting in Liversedge's office, but she feigned an interest. "One of your boyfriends?"

"No such luck. Remember the night we ate in the Ruby Room at the St. Francis? Remember that man with the English accent opposite us? The one who stared at you?"

Andrea's effort at calm didn't fool Faith. "Vaguely. So you saw him leaving town. How long ago was this?"

Faith shrugged, wondering at her curiosity. Andrea had hardly looked twice at the fellow. "It was the day after the news came. The headlines were all over the place. I passed this guy on the street. A real looker, but tough."

"Tough? He didn't look tough to me."

"You know. Been around. Very sophisticated, kind of steely. I wouldn't mess with him."

"For heaven's sake, Faith. Who's messing with him?"

Faith was amazed at all this passion over apparently nothing. She wondered if it could be part of Andrea's strange moodiness lately.

"Take it easy, Andrea. Your folks are worried about you, you know."

They went downstairs and joined the others. As usual, everyone had to wait for Brooke, which struck Tony as ironically amusing.

"Here is Eden, Prysing's number one star—eighth in the polls last year—and it doesn't take Eden more than ten minutes to throw herself together."

"That's me," Eden agreed cheerfully. "Thrown together."

"You look lovely, Eden," Jany assured her.

Faith thought the Frenchwoman could afford to be generous. Tony's golden-haired wife always appeared in public dressed with Gallic elegance, devoting all her energy to pleasing her husband. The perfect wife.

When Brooke finally appeared she was in most elegant mourning attire, her simple black dress enhanced by a large-brimmed, black silk-straw hat and black kid gloves. The family all poured into her black Rolls-Royce, except Tony, who drove alone in the Mercedes he had bought in Jany's name.

No one had notified the newspapers about the hour of the reading of the will—a subject which had aroused speculation since the moment the news of Steve's death hit the wireless—so the family hoped to get through the morning's business without publicity. But what they did not allow for was the gossip of Sam Liversedge's receptionist. About the time the Lombards were ushered into Sam's spacious, high-ceilinged office facing Market and Kearny streets, the *Chronicle* had already been notified that "they're cutting up the Lombard pie."

Sam's assistant, a competent middle-aged woman with an effusive manner, rearranged chairs for everyone but hesitated over Eden.

"Miss Ware, I was so sorry a couple of weeks ago when you called. I hadn't a notion in the world that Mr. Liversedge had gone off to Pebble Beach. Playing hookey, the naughty man."

"I understood perfectly," Eden said, and gave her the famous movie-star smile. The assistant did a double take but decided to leave the remark alone.

"Mr. Liversedge will take care of you from here on. Good luck, all." She went out with Faith, who looked as if she would love to stay.

56

Sam's face seemed drawn and his manner tense. He was so often at the house and so much the friend and confidant of the Lombards that everyone felt the sharp difference in his present state. He squeezed his corpulent body behind his desk and sank into his swivel chair.

He seemed rather officious sitting there in front of them like that, and Andrea suspected her family was a little intimidated by him at this moment. Brooke and Jany settled somewhat stiffly on the heavy, worn leather divan. Tony sat on one arm of the divan beside Jany and the other three, Alec, Eden and Andrea, had straight chairs. Sam cleared his throat and tapped the blue legal cover several times on his worn desk.

Andrea could sense the tension in the room. Only Eden could feel free of it. She had nothing either to lose or gain. Though interested, she seemed almost amused. Andrea was sure her mother enjoyed the drama of the moment. Eden Ware had played scenes like this before.

Brooke's sudden burst of speech made them all jump.

"Sam, I do wish you wouldn't play cat-and-mouse with us. Get on, for God's sake."

"Sorry, folks. I don't mean to be melodramatic. But I guess you wonder why I didn't boil all this legal stuff down and tell you the gist of it up at the house." He sighed, got out his handkerchief and wiped his forehead. Tony, who was holding his wife's hand tightly, started to say something, but Sam waved him to silence.

"I know. It's just that Steve was a funny kind of guy. And he wanted things done his way. He had legal counsel—Bursten & Rafael. But as administrator, and if I may say so, as adviser, I find I'm stuck with the core of the thing. Do you want all the legal business? Here it is."

"No," Tony said hoarsely. "Leave that stuff for later. Tell us the facts. Straight."

"Fine. First, Randi's—that is, Mary-Randal Lombard's will. She seems to have had stocks, a few bonds, her checking account and real estate. About eighty thousand dollars. She leaves it all to 'my beloved son, Anthony Lombard, free and clear.'" He read this from the top page under the blue cover.

Tony closed his eyes. They all sensed that his relief was not over the money. It would be a drop in the bucket of his 1962-63 production budget. But it proved to them all that despite Tony's ambivalent relationship with his father, his mother's last thoughts were of her son.

Sam dropped the three-page blue file and took up the heavier one belonging to Stephen Lombard.

"We come to Steve. He laid it out very clearly." Sam flipped over a page. "Blocks of stock in various real estate operations are left to business associates listed here."

Watching Tony, Eden asked, "The Prysing stock?" Sam frowned. "Skip it," she said. He reached for his glasses and stuck them on his nose, but didn't read from the crucial pages. Apparently he knew their contents by heart.

"In the course of time, this list of legatees would have changed as Steve outlived them or other changes occurred. For example, Steve leaves his widow, Randi, trust funds roughly totaling between seventy and seventy-five thousand dollars per annum, depending, of course, on the fluctuating value of his stocks. In the event of Randi's decease within thirty-six hours of his own, her inheritance goes back into the estate."

He nodded to Brooke and then to Alec. "To his sister, Brooke Lombard Huntington Ware Friedrich—known herewith as Brooke Lombard—and to his nephew Alexander Huntington, he leaves shares in Universal Broadcasting Corporation. These shares will give his nephew what he also calls 'greater clout' in the corporation."

"Dear Steve," murmured Brooke. She groped for her lace-trimmed handkerchief. Alec ran his hand over his forehead and eyes in spite of his cool outward demeanor.

"To his ex-daughter-in-law, Eden Ware Lombard, as a mark of affection, he leaves the sum of ten thousand dollars." Sam smiled at Eden, then breathed deeply, wetting his lips.

"Now. Trust funds have been set up in the total amount of seventy-thousand dollars per annum..." Andrea saw the faint swiveling of heads toward her. She flushed hotly. They would never understand, none of them, that receiving Grandpa Steve's money was like being paid for his loss. In that moment she resented them for thinking she would be pleased.

"...To my beloved son, Anthony Redmon Lombard, in token of my love and regard."

There was general surprise but everyone assumed the trust fund was a featherbed for Tony to fall back on. He certainly wouldn't need it. Not after the Prysing stock and the remainder of Steve's estate still to come.

In a voice so low they had to strain to hear, Sam finished. "In brief, the remainder of the estate, with a half dozen minor exceptions, he leaves to his granddaughter, Eve-Andrea Lombard, who...I quote Steve, 'will understand all that she owes to her beloved parents and to those employees and subordinates whose fidelity is unquestioned.'"

There was a shocked silence. No one believed what had been said, least of all Andrea.

Alec Huntington was the first to speak.

"There was stock in Prysing Productions. That will naturally go to Tony."

"I'm afraid not. The stock is listed among the assets of the estate which go to Andrea."

"I don't want it," Andrea burst out. "It belongs to my father. Grandpa Steve got mixed up. There's been a mistake."

Sam coughed. "I'm afraid there was no—"

Tony waved his arm in a sharp slashing motion.

"Don't you understand yet, any of you? He hated me. My own father. This is his final kick. His final belly laugh."

Eden protested. "Don't you see, Tony? He knew you had a big studio in your hands. Properties. He figured you wouldn't need his estate."

Jany fussed around her husband, trying vainly to soothe him. "He loved you. He did not mean it as you say."

Andrea was afraid to look at him, but she reached for his hand. His face, crumbled with suffering and humiliation, broke her heart.

"Daddy, it's yours. Don't feel bad. What's mine is yours. You know that. Please, daddy, look at me."

Brooke and Eden were whispering. Had they no feeling for her father? The loss of the estate, the loss of the Prysing stock, were calamitous to all his hopes and plans, but there was more involved. He felt the cutting humiliation deeply, certain that

59

what he had always suspected was true. No matter how high he had climbed, no matter what courage he had shown during the war, not even the fact that he was head of a large independent film studio could change the terrible reality. His own father had despised him and had used this frightful public humiliation to tell him so.

Sam Liversedge tried to call them to order. Andrea was still fuming, wondering if he had been involved in any way with this preposterous will.

"Give us a little time, for heaven's sake," she pleaded.

But Tony had recovered his composure. He waved his daughter away at the same time that he shook off his wife.

"No. Go on, Sam. I assume that my twenty-one-year-old daughter is not expected to make all her decisions without the help of an adult. Let's see if he names a member of the family."

Sam was hesitant again. "He names me, along with Abel Bursten and Eugene Rafael as her... advisers." Tony smiled grimly. Sam hurried on. "You must remember. He expected to live many years, during which time he would train your daughter to her position. And he expected his wife to survive him."

Still smiling, Tony said, "Of course. Are you coming, Jany? I've had enough of this place."

His eyes fell on everyone in the room and finally on his daughter. The bitterness she read in his eyes seemed to be directed at her personally.

Andrea tried to follow her father and Jany but was stopped by Sam's sharp order.

"Wait, Miss Lombard. Andrea!"

With the others staring at him, he leaned across his desk toward her. "Andrea, please remain." He nodded to the others, who got up awkwardly and began to shuffle out.

"May we have copies of the wills to study?" Alec asked.

"Certainly." Sam offered him two folded blue sheaves of paper.

Alec thanked him, accepted the copies and hustled his protesting mother out. Before she too left, Eden touched Andrea's hand tentatively.

"Honey, if you need me... you know."

"No. Thank you, mother. I'll handle this thing. I'll settle it with daddy."

Eden kissed her on the forehead and left.

Andrea's own guilt weighed her down. Had she somehow cut out her father? Maybe by allowing the close relationship with Grandpa Steve to flourish—and by remaining his willing student—she had elbowed her own father out of his rightful inheritance.

Sam's sympathetic gaze helped her to open up.

"Don't you see, Sam? They say a cute baby can wheedle a fortune out of a wealthy man. It has nothing to do with intelligence or worth. I came up here and laughed at Grandpa Steve's jokes. I liked his company. I was a good audience. And he got carried away. It wasn't fair to my father."

Sam sat there shaking his head.

"It's true," she insisted.

"My dear girl, Steve and I talked this over with Eugene Rafael about two months ago when the Japan trip first came up. Naturally, Steve expected to live a good long time, but there had been those riots and the business when President Eisenhower had had to cancel his Tokyo trip, so Steve brought his will up to date. He told me he'd already begun to train you so that ultimately you would be able to handle it, with guidance from Randi and me."

"No. I couldn't do that to my own father."

He slapped the desk with the pages in their blue cover. She started nervously. People didn't often see Sam Liversedge showing a temper. He usually played the friendly, avuncular adviser.

"You can, Andrea. And you will. It's all in your grandfather's letter to you. Yes. He left a letter to you. I want you to take it home, say nothing to anyone including your parents and read it in private. Steve explains why he chose you instead of Tony, over his own wife's objections. Though I'm sure Randi knew in her heart he was right." Before she could protest, he held out a sealed legal envelope addressed to her.

The sight of her name scrawled in Steve's well-remembered hand made her throat close painfully. Her eyes burned. She managed with difficulty to blink back the tears.

She had Steve Lombard's blood in her. She would prove her strength.

"Thank you." She took Steve's letter, slipped it into the outside pocket of her handbag and, reaching across the desk, offered her hand to Sam as if she were already in business. "You've been a big help. But I expect you'll be even more help in time to come."

They shook hands. Then Sam changed the subject. "My nephew Herbert is coming into the bank very shortly. Starting to work his way up. I hope he'll land in this chair in the not-too-distant future. Keeping it all in the family, so to speak. But you know Herb. He tells me you and he are going together. Nice boy."

It was crude but she laid it to family devotion. Something her beloved Grandpa Steve didn't seem to have. She left Sam there watching her. She was proud that she could leave with head high and a certain illusion of calm self-confidence in her walk. Because inside there was nothing but turmoil.

SEVEN

WHILE ANDREA was with Sam Liversedge, Faith accompanied Brooke and Alec to the limousine. In defiance of all parking laws the car was parked on one of the busiest corners in San Francisco. Tony and Jany had already gone off somewhere and Eden Ware was besieged by fans. She stopped often to sign autographs. After some time she waved to the limousine.

"Don't wait for me. I've got plane reservations to look into. The Klondike epic is still waiting to get started." To a reporter she added, "After that, it's the New York opening of my latest from Warner Brothers."

The reporter asked her about the Lombard will, but she shrugged. "I wouldn't know. We've all lost a great man and a great woman. We must remember that."

Brooke Lombard spoke Faith's thoughts aloud. "I suppose that's what they call public relations. A word for my brother and a word for her movie opening. She's a dear girl, though. Despite all that tireless ambition."

The reporter mentioned that a new park in the Mission District would be renamed the Stephen Lombard Park, and a subscription had been started to form a collection entitled "Early California Artists" in the M.H. DeYoung Museum, to be named for Mary-Randal Lombard.

"I'll be here for the dedication," Eden promised. "And put me down to open your subscription."

"Can't open with your subscription, Miss Ware. The story ran in the morning edition, and the contributions are already pouring in."

Alec suggested, "Mother, why don't you and Miss Cortlandt get into the car. I'll get Andrea out through the vault room and the car can meet her in the alley."

Faith reached for the car door. "Excuse me, Mr. Huntington. I should be the one to get her. She relies on me."

"Yes, of course." They changed places.

As Faith got out of the limousine, Brooke called to her. "Tell Andrea I'm going to take her to New York with me. Take her mind off this sadness and all these responsibilities for a few weeks."

Faith walked quickly through the crowd still surrounding Eden and went into the lobby beside the main bank entrance. Andrea was just stepping out of the elevator. She looked grim, Faith thought, not at all like a woman who just received a down payment on the moon and stars.

"Reporters and a crowd of nosy fans," Faith explained, pushing her toward the steps beside the elevator shaft. "This goes down to the office supply room. I worked here two summers ago. There's a rear door for deliveries."

Andrea said nothing. She was clutching her handbag tightly, and Faith noticed at the same time that a long white envelope with Steve Lombard's well-known return address was sticking out of it.

The two women crossed the big room between ill-lighted shelves full of the normal office paraphernalia. A young male clerk rushed over as if he recognized the Lombard heiress. Faith hurried Andrea through the alley delivery door.

"There's the limousine. I'll be off to the Eastbay Terminal if it's okay with you."

"Sure. Run along. Give my best to Frank." She still seemed preoccupied as she started up the alley to the car.

Faith turned around and started toward Market Street. She was a good walker. It would be quicker than trying to hail a cab.

She made it in record time, reached the semicircle in front of the terminal and stopped to straighten her dress out and smooth her hair.

Frank wasn't inside the terminal, however. She killed some

time daydreaming about how she would spend a windfall inheritance if she were to get so lucky.

She stood around for more than half an hour before she decided that Frank must have misunderstood either the time or the place of the meeting. He was probably at the Berkeley library. That had been her first suggestion for their meeting, but he had suggested the terminal.

She got the Berkeley bus and sat down, tired. The man sitting next to her appeared to be reading his day's mail. The envelope reminded her of the letter from Steve Lombard to Andrea. She would give a lot to know what he had had to say. What family secrets had Steve confided?

At the Nob Hill house only Brooke and Alec were in that afternoon, which meant Andrea had to put off the confrontation with her father. She wanted to get the problem settled so they could be friends again.

She was curiously ambivalent about reading Grandpa Steve's letter. She took the envelope out of her purse, almost ripped it open but decided to save it. She knew that reading it now would bring back too much anguish.

Maria Trentini rapped gently on the door.

"Miss Andrea, your aunt wants to know if you'll be down to lunch. It's a little late, but..."

They must be waiting for her, she thought guiltily. "I'll be right down," she called out.

She stuck the precious letter under one of her pillows, washed up hastily, then hurried downstairs.

Aunt Brooke and Alec were at the table in the breakfast room. Aunt Brooke looked her up and down, smiling strangely.

"Well, dear, this must be a red-letter day for you."

Alec's voice was quiet. "Mother, don't."

Brooke was upset. "I didn't mean anything. I always speak my mind. I pride myself that I never hide my true feelings."

You're lucky others don't speak their minds about you, Andrea thought.

"Grandfather didn't expect anything to happen for a long

time. He would never have made that awful will if he had even suspected," Andrea said.

"What a shock for Tony." Aunt Brooke sipped her coffee and sighed.

"It was a mistake. I wish he'd come home. I want to see him as soon as possible." Andrea looked up anxiously. "Suppose he won't talk to me."

"Oh, he will. He darned well has to."

"Mother!"

Alec's voice was like a crack of a whip. Andrea jumped, but Aunt Brooke paid little attention to him. "It's no use blinking at facts, dear. We all know poor Tony is on the rocks. His precious studio is going to be in the hands of receivers within the year. Wait and see."

"It's not true. Daddy has made some wonderful pictures."

"He has. But nothing he's made has succeeded for a long time now."

The phone rang and Maria Trentini stuck her head in from the hall.

"Reporters again, ma'am. They're after pictures of Miss Andrea."

Andrea panicked at the idea. She could see it all spread across the front page, her picture and the bold claim that she was the luckiest girl in the world. It would be like wishing for the plane crash that took Steve and Randi from her and from all those who loved them.

Maria added, "By the way, Miss Andrea, there have been two calls for Miss Cortlandt. From Berkeley. The last one came just after noon."

"That nice-looking young professor, I'll bet," Brooke said.

Brooke speculated on the reasons for the phone call while Alec gave Andrea a breakdown of some details in the will. He mentioned that the servants, including several ex-employees, were left annuities.

"Actually, there isn't a lot of cash. It's all invested, turned back into the different enterprises. Every month you will receive reports from the trust department of Con-Mercantile. These give you an idea of your income from stocks on the big board. There will be similar bond reports. Steve's own personal in-

66

vestments, mostly with real estate bases, will probably he handled through the offices of Sam Liversedge."

"I've been getting an allowance of two hundred dollars a month. How do I get cash?" It was embarrassing to have to ask.

"Very natural question, Alec. How does she?"

But Alec had no information on this matter. "I'll ask Sam, if you like."

"Oh, please do, Uncle Alec. I'd hate to have to ask him myself."

Brooke changed the subject. "I'm so happy Andrea is coming to New York with me. We're going to do our best to have a good time."

Andrea wasn't in the mood, but she felt the trip would help her make a break with the past. Perhaps when she returned to California she could better cope with reports, corporate responsibilities and endless new problems.

"Of course, I may send you off on your own occasionally," Aunt Brooke added with a sparkle, as if considering some delightful event that only she could envision.

Alec rolled his eyes. "Mother, stick to men whose background I know. Those others are pure gigolos."

Andrea was intrigued. It was the first time all day that she smiled.

"Auntie, don't tell me you know a gigolo!"

"Dozens, darling. Absolutely dozens. And every one of them more charming than the other."

Alec got up. "Don't be ridiculous, mother." He threw down his napkin and left the room to the sound of his mother's light, tinkling laughter.

"Poor Alec! He's always been such a prude."

Andrea wasn't surprised. Alec's wife, whom he had known since childhood, had died in 1945. He'd lived alone since then, and Andrea doubted if he ever bothered with other women.

The telephone rang every five minutes during the next hour until finally Aunt Brooke ordered that the main line be left off the hook. It was less easy to get rid of the people who came to the front doorstep or the big iron fence, some with cameras, some just to gawk.

67

The doorbell rang, and in came Frank Kelly. He looked wind-blown and to Andrea rather like a breath of fresh air. Faith was a lucky woman.

Andrea explained that Faith had gone to the terminal to meet him.

"Not when I got there. She must be on her way back here to the house. I wonder if—" He approached the matter hesitantly. "Would you mind if I waited here? Otherwise, we're liable to miss each other again."

Brooke and Andrea welcomed him in. Both women were relieved to have someone else to talk to after the gloom of family, servants and the press. Andrea reassured him that Faith would be bound to come home when he failed to show up.

Frank looked uncomfortable in the cluttered Victorian surroundings. Remembering how he had described his past, the early years in North Beach and how he had learned to fight and survive, Andrea tried even harder to make him feel at home. She talked about football and the racing sculls with which Cal had achieved national fame, then it occurred to her that he might be interested in her grandfather's billiard room. She guessed right. In no time he was racking up the balls and breaking, demonstrating his prowess to both Andrea and Brooke.

Having volunteered to give the ladies a lesson, he delighted Aunt Brooke by standing close and guiding her arm as he showed her how to shoot.

Then it was Andrea's turn. It was with newborn confidence that she let him encircle her with his arms to correct her handling of the cue. She enjoyed his closeness.

Nevertheless, she was relieved when he moved away from her, remarking that he had stayed too long and would have to go out and look for Faith. She respected fidelity.

"Faith should have been here by now. I can't figure out what happened." He was clearly anxious about Faith.

Frank was just leaving by the kitchen entry, hoping to avoid the press and the curious bystanders when Steve's private phone rang.

"Faith Cortlandt is on the line," Alec told them.

Remembering Faith's jealousy the night they went to the Wharf, Andrea asked, "Did you tell her he was still here?"

"Yes. Shouldn't I?"

Both Frank and Andrea got on downstairs extensions at the same time. Faith's voice was unusually sharp.

"Where have you been, Frank? I've been over half the city looking for you."

Andrea hung up quietly. She knew her name would come up, and felt sorry for Faith.

"She lives here, after all... Anyway, I was supposed to meet you here at the house." And then, "Yes. I *am* sure...Okay. Wait right there. I'm on my way."

He hung up.

"I'm sorry it turned out this way, Andrea. But I can't remember when I enjoyed myself more."

She liked his honesty. When they shook hands again she put her other hand over his rough knuckles.

"Friends are terribly rare. Let's be friends."

"You've got a deal." He grinned. "'Bye... *friend.*"

His departure left the household uncomfortably quiet. Even Eden's arrival, usually a lively event, failed to relieve the tension.

Tony and Jany returned too late for dinner, though Brooke ordered Mrs. Trentini to wait as long as she could. When Tony did show up, Brooke had gone with Sam for a nightcap at the Top of the Mark, Eden was packing for departure and Alec was giving Andrea a crash course in the control of corporations by stock manipulations.

Andrea was thinking of Steve's Prysing Productions stock, of which he owned approximately 50 percent. In itself it was not enough to veto any move by Tony, but *added* to Tony's 28 percent which remained out of his original 35 percent, it would be enough to give her father a majority over any move by the other stockholders, even if some of them worked in collusion. Without Steve's shares, Tony could easily be outvoted.

Andrea was enormously relieved when Tony greeted her with a kiss on the forehead. "Don't look so worried, sweetheart. I've recovered."

She hugged him and started to tell him he could have the whole of Steve's estate, but Tony shushed her.

"Alec, tell this female tycoon to hold on to it. Don't go around giving away your fortune so recklessly to every hardworking movie mogul you see."

Alec smiled faintly. "Don't worry. She'll do all right. And Tony, don't play down the UBC thing I was telling you about. The studio rentals could provide a nice revenue right now, with the industry in the doldrums."

"Not my studio in the doldrums. You wait 'til *Klondike* hits the screens. It'll clean up. The scope. The color. The stars... Speaking of scope, I'm going for VistaVision, the Paramount gimmick. I like the proportions better than Cinemascope." Carried away by his own vision of splendor, Tony went on. "Or do you know what I'd really like? Too late now, but I want to try it on my ancient Greek epic. Cinerama."

"My God!" It was unlike Alec to let such feelings escape him.

"Well, maybe VistaVision would do it. We'll see when the profits come pouring in on *Klondike*. I'm not doing a cloak-and-toga thing on the Greek story, you know. It's going to be authentic. Just the way the retreating Greeks went across Asia Minor. Anatolia, Iran, the Caspian Sea, along the Russian border."

"The Kremlin will love you."

"Never mind the Kremlin. I've got the shah of Iran on my side. He'll put up some of the cash, if we iron out a few details. You see, it makes heroes of the ancient Persians as well. Like showing our Civil War with both sides heroic."

"It sounds... exciting," Andrea murmured, trying to drum up enthusiasm.

"It will be, sweetheart. It will be. Well, excuse us, all. We've got to go up and pack. Jany wants to get back to Hollywood and her beloved old Bluebeard's Castle." He kissed his wife's neck playfully.

Tony was making a good try at being light-hearted. They watched him leave the room with Jany, laughing over some incident that had disturbed their dinner at a downtown restaurant. Whatever it was, Jany obviously didn't think it was funny.

70

"I hate the press," she burst out. "I hate their sly looks and cameras and all the flashing in the face. What do they expect of us?"

They went up the stairs, out of hearing. Alec and Andrea looked at each other. "He's handling it well," Alec said. "Better than one might have expected. It should not have been done that way. It wasn't like Steve."

"I think it was only a temporary will. He must have intended to do something for father when he came back. Or Gran Randi. She would certainly have seen to it that father got more out of the estate." Andrea started to leave but stopped. "Anyway, I intend to change all that."

Alec caught her hand. "Be very careful."

She stared at him, annoyed that he should add to her uneasiness. "Careful of what?"

"Be wise, Andrea. Be generous, but wise. Always consider your father's temperament, his business ability. The power that Steve's money gives you can be a drug. To you, and to Tony. Tony reminds me of Steve's father. Be very careful before you give a man such a drug."

"Let me go."

"Certainly. But Andrea, even if you hate me for saying it, remember what I say. Remember the analogy. A drug."

She jerked her hand away and ran out of the room. Not only was it downright shameful to discuss her father in this way, it was even more so because she had been thinking thoughts very similar to Alec's warning.

On the way to her room she realized that if her father was returning to Los Angeles tomorrow morning, she would have to let him know what he could count on immediately. The other officers and stockholders would be waiting like vultures once the terms of the will became known.

Throughout the sleepless night Alec's words haunted her.

CHAPTER
EIGHT

ON ANDREA'S right as she reached the second floor was Steve and Randi's suite. Her first unthinking reaction was to go in and ask their advice as she always had. She stood there a minute, brought back to the present by the pain of her loss. She ran her fingers over the doorknob, hesitant to enter their private domain.

Steve and Randi had occupied a suite of two rooms, including a large, rather masculine bedroom with heavy mahogany furnishings, a bathroom installed in 1940 and Steve's cluttered little office with a dilapidated couch, a desk and chair and a four-drawer file cabinet badly in need of paint or replacement. This was the throbbing center of Steve's one-man empire. All the splendid suites in cities all over the country were strictly for show. The threads wound back to this little cubbyhole of an office.

Andrea had gone into that office hundreds of times to ask advice of her grandparents. Randi was quick, decisive, no-nonsense. She solved every problem Andrea presented. Steve, perhaps enjoying a break from heady responsibilities, would also talk with her, draw her out, for hours.

She had only just begun to learn when all that education ended and she was left with nothing but a final word of instruction from Steve. She had years of training ahead before she could handle even a hundreth of what Steve Lombard had known and accomplished in his sixty-eight years. It was all wrong. The fates that caused that plane to crash were wicked, evil. She touched the doorknob again, tenderly. She knew it would be a long time before she went into a church again without asking that unanswerable question: *Why?*

What would Steve do in this spot? she asked herself. He would square his shoulders and cross the hall. She had to confront her father, who hadn't fooled his daughter with his easy, casual manner tonight. He had to be very bitter, and justifiably so.

She raised her hand to knock on Tony's door but the door opened. It had been ajar. She felt that somehow her father must have seen her hesitating across the hall and remained silent, watching her. It was a disturbing thought.

"Hello, sweetheart. I figured you'd have something to say to me. Want to talk in your room? Jany is bathing and I don't want to bother her with business."

He must be very sure that it would be business. Andrea knew he was counting on her offer.

"I'd like that, dad. Please. Come in."

He sat down on the edge of her bed. "I looked over a copy of the will. Steve's half of this house went to my mother. Brooke keeps her half."

Andrea was delighted. "And from grandmother to you, father."

"That's right."

He smiled. Andrea knew his half-ownership of the Lombard house meant much more. He had been denied by his father but Randi, cool and unemotional as she seemed, had saved his pride and perhaps more.

"Nobody thought it was important enough to tell me. But it doesn't matter. You wanted to talk to me?"

It was an awkward moment.

"At the studio you need Grandpa Steve's stock, don't you?" she blurted out.

For an instant he looked surprised, which puzzled her. But he stood up and went over to sit in her slipper chair. He agreed emphatically.

"Definitely."

"Well?" She threw her arms in the air. "The Prysing stock is yours. I'm signing it all over to you first thing in the morning— that is, if you can take a later flight."

She didn't know exactly what kind of reaction she expected.

She waited. He looked up, his eyes warm with gratitude and with love.

"That's all right. I made the reservation for a noon flight."

"Good. Then, daddy, you're all set. Wait 'til the board hears that you can outvote them. Aren't you pleased?"

He touched her arm. "Andrea, it did my heart good, believe me."

"Did?"

He avoided her earnest gaze.

"I had to counteract the news in the evening papers. Not only with the board, but especially with the banks. I knew you wouldn't let me down, honey. I simply let it be known in the right quarters that the extra shares were already in my hands." He shrugged and got up. "I only preceded you by a couple of hours. Now, honey, I think I'll be off to a shower and bed."

Andrea nodded, but her face betrayed her disappointment. Tony looked at her and all his careful reserve broke down.

"You do know how deeply grateful I feel about this, don't you?" He hugged her, and she could sense his relief.

He went across the hall, hesitated, then went into Steve's small office. He remained there so long she closed the door and slipped her hand under her pillow. Steve's letter was still there. She began to undress for her bath, not exactly sure why she dreaded reading that letter.

Perhaps she was afraid it would be an attack on her father. Remembering that he was across the hall, she wondered what he could be doing.

He was there for an awfully long time. Steve's office wasn't at all the sort of room Tony would frequent. His own office, which he inherited with some reluctance from Leo Prysing, was enormous and imperious—a far cry from the closet that had been Steve's real haven.

Andrea wondered whether Tony was examining and checking Steve's business files.

Suspicious, and feeling guilty for it, Andrea tied her robe around her and with her hair still piled high on her head after her bath she went silently across the hall to Steve's office. The door was closed. She pushed it open. She had expected it to creak, but it made no noise and she thought it must look as if she were sneaking up on her father.

He was kneeling beside an old candy box, turning over snapshots taken long ago, black-and-white, postcard size, mostly taken by his mother. He had put some of the snapshots aside in a neat little pile.

Andrea felt shattered by her own suspicions. She cleared her throat. "Daddy?" she whispered.

He looked up. His eyes were swimming with tears, but he managed a smile.

"I thought I'd take these. Just for old time's sake. She . . . she was always good with that old Eastman of hers." He thumbed through the pictures. "I wish she was in more of them herself." Like his cousin Alec, he had always adored Randi.

The sight of her father's sorrow made Andrea aware once again of their terrible loss. The tears stung her eyes yet she didn't bother to wipe them away. She managed finally to speak.

"There must be lots of albums. We could look through them tomorrow."

"Yes." He began to straighten the pile of snapshots, his thoughts miles away. He came to a photograph of Steve and Randi taken long ago in front of the Hawaiian beach house belonging to Eden Ware's father.

"We never really liked each other, you know, father and I. I got along better with Red than I did with father." He studied the picture. "Maybe because Grandpa Red was jealous of him too. I guess we all were. How can you fight a legend?"

"Grandpa Steve loved you, daddy."

He laughed shortly. "I don't doubt it. But he didn't *like* me. That's the thing. And he never respected me. His will proved it." He clenched his fist but then opened his hand and reached for Andrea's. "Don't look so unhappy, honey. It's not your fault." He got up in one swift, graceful move. "Let's get out of this room. Jany will be worrying about me."

He dropped dozens of snapshots into the nearest file cabinet but kept a dozen or so in his hand. He put his free arm around his daughter, and the two of them left Steve's little study together.

In front of his bedroom door he stopped. His eyes were bloodshot. He wouldn't fool Jany, but at least he was in better spirits.

"'Night, honey."

"Goodnight, daddy."

It was almost midnight when Andrea climbed into bed, took a couple of deep breaths and pulled out Steve Lombard's envelope. The pages were handwritten—Steve hadn't trusted them to a typist.

Andrea,

This letter may be an exercise in futility, as the fella says. I don't figure to pass out of the picture for a long, long time. But Sam Liversedge and Gene Rafael tell me I can't go running off to the ends of the earth every week or so without bringing my will up to date. So here goes.

You must have found out by now that you're my choice. I've been mulling it over all year. You have been an exceptional student. Of course, you've only just begun to learn what you need to know. But allowing for a reasonable life span and my proverbially good health, I know I can make you the biggest, brightest Lombard of us all.

Besides, you'll have my Randi, and if you have Randi at your side, you won't need hordes of business advisers, not even Sam.

Now for the bad part. Why have I chosen you when I have a brilliant, if slightly erratic and very stubborn son? I realize what I am doing to your relations with the family by choosing you to follow me. But I don't have many options. I believe that by the time I go you will be a mature woman, well versed in handling your fellow men. I'll see to that. If life should play us all a rotten trick and I go before I finish schooling you to handle these responsibilities, there will be Sam Liversedge and above all your Grandmother Randi.

I chose you because there is a great deal to learn and Tony, for many reasons, would never accept any schooling or advice from me. You didn't know your Great-grandfather Red Lombard, my father. But Tony is a throwback to him, and I'm afraid Red and I got along about the way Tony and I do. Maybe it's my fault. Very possibly it is. But I am what I am and it's too late for me to change. You made allowances for my shortcomings.

Tony never did. Tony and I love each other, but we never have seen eye to eye on our work.

I expect you to use long-range vision when Tony demands that you invest in his schemes. During past production seasons Sam and I have backed Tony's overblown features to the tune of nearly forty million dollars, some of that bank loan guarantees which we made good. It is merely throwing good money after bad.

It is my belief that if Tony had a small organization, say B-films or a television showcase, he could produce small, low budget films for Warners or RKO. But Tony has gotten out of his element in those Prysing biggies.

Andrea, think very carefully before you contribute to Tony's destruction by pouring more fortunes into his dream machine. Actually, if the fates are kind, you won't have to make any of these painful decisions until some future date when Tony has discovered his real talent for small films such as he made at the beginning of his career, not the old-fashioned epics that have put Prysing Productions on the brink of bankruptcy.

Well, Andrea my dear, until I have time to write a codicil to this volume when I return home, just keep in mind all our conversations, all the matters we discussed on those great afternoons when I made you hover so long over Standard and Poor's and you yawned a bit, but you kept plugging. I hope you will say it was all worth it, to prepare you for today.

If, by some idiotic trick of fate, this should be good-bye, go to Randi at once and show her this letter. Between the two of you I know you will keep Lombard Enterprises on an even keel. It wouldn't surprise me if you eventually bring the business to new heights.

Someday I hope Tony will understand that despite what seems like my denial I love him very much. He can make a brilliant success, but he needs to be held strictly accountable.

As for you, my lovely girl, bless you—I love you.

GRANDPA STEVE

"Bless you, too, Grandpa Steve," she whispered, folding the letter and lying back to think about its contents.

She was sure many people would call him hard, unfair to his only child. But she had been present at any number of her father's discussions about his film productions during the past

77

six or seven years, and in every case he sounded as he had early tonight when he talked about his ancient Greek film, based on an historian most people had never heard of, about a subject that could hardly have universal appeal. That was bad enough, but then he had begun to talk about the fantastically expensive Cinerama which would add a fortune in costs all by itself, and was besides a projection method impossible in all but a handful of theaters.

The enormity of her job in trying to carry on for her grandfather was too much to worry about tonight. She had to put it out of her mind for the time being. Maybe after she and Aunt Brooke went to New York.

This brought her back to the crucial matter that couldn't wait until after a New York break. Her father clearly needed to be bailed out of his company's present hole. She had to do something about it before Tony and Jany left for Los Angeles tomorrow.

The time for decision was upon her. She knew that if she hurried, though, she could make a serious mistake. She couldn't ignore Steve's letter. But after the blow her father had received today the least she could do was help him now. Her deep sense of guilt caused her to wonder if she had maneuvered her grandfather subconsciously? Maybe his belief in her was nothing more than the reaction of a mature man flattered by the adoration of a young girl, even if it was his granddaughter.

She owed her father the help he would almost certainly have gotten from Sam Liversedge if Grandpa Steve hadn't vetoed it.

So she had decided. She felt much better after making that first decision on her own. She had even overruled Steve Lombard, her mentor. That took courage.

Faith Cortlandt had her hands full the next day. The phones never stopped ringing. The second-floor maid was assigned to take messages, and even Alec Huntington postponed his New York flight to handle some of Andrea's more technical problems.

But for Andrea the great moment came when she stood in Sam Liversedge's office and announced that the new Prysing production year would receive Lombard backing. It had taken her much of a sleepless night to make her decision and she had no intention of letting Sam talk her out of it. Sam was still trying to catch her eye for a little private conference when Jany mentioned that they would be late for their flight and all three of them left Sam's office, Tony happily putting an arm around both of his women.

In the corridor while they waited for the elevator, Tony hugged Andrea close.

"I know it wasn't easy, sweetheart. Believe me. For you or for me. I thought I'd lost you, and Steve had won."

"Never!" She said it quickly, too emotional to say any more. But then, emotion had influenced her decision. It certainly hadn't been common sense.

He explained. "It hurt, honey, when I thought...well, all kinds of things. But you're back again, my own little girl." He embraced Jany. "We're a family again. Wait 'til I notify Eden. She said you'd come through. And so did Jany. You told me she wouldn't betray me when it was a matter of survival. You were right, darling."

"Naturally I was right. Andrea is your daughter," Jany said softly. "What is hers is yours."

Andrea had already told Eden what she was about to do and as she had expected, Eden endorsed her action 100 percent.

"Honey, your father has worked pretty damned hard to get where he is. You couldn't sit by and watch the whole house of cards come tumbling down now. I know you."

House of cards. It had been an unfortunate comparison. But Andrea wondered also if *betrayal* wouldn't have been a pretty strong word for a refusal to pledge between fifteen and twenty million for one season of badly planned movies. She knew she had acted hastily and almost purely from the heart when she went against her grandfather's judgment. Already she was wondering if she had done her father a long-range disservice. Nevertheless, it was good to see the warmth and affection in his eyes. His freedom from that haunted look was reason enough.

"I'm glad, daddy. You go back and show those stockholders."

Andrea drove them down the Peninsula to the airport. It was

here, as she kissed them good-bye and watched them on their way out to the field where they turned to wave, that she felt her first surge of terror. She tried not to think of another airfield half a world away, of a terrible, howling wind and the crackle of flames...

The engine roar out on the field twisted in her stomach like a corkscrew. Nauseated, she made her way back into the terminal and sat down in the nearest lounge.

Gradually, she became aware that she was the object of considerable attention. She glanced around, hoping it was only her overcharged imagination. But many faces were turned toward her, and the whispers had begun. The young man sitting across from her leaned forward.

"Excuse me. Are you really the Lombard girl? I mean—the one in the papers? I saw your picture. I guess it happened kind of suddenly."

"Yes, it did."

She stood up, pulled herself as straight as possible and walked away. It was not flattering to be gawked at so.

Once out of the terminal she began to run to her car to avoid the roar of planes and the memories they evoked.

She was surprised and intensely relieved to see Faith Cortlandt waving to her from the parking lot beside Andrea's white Thunderbird. She must have come all the way out here in the airport limousine.

"Hi." She had evidently gotten over her pique about missing Frank Kelly yesterday. "Brooke gave me the afternoon off. I'm to keep you company on your way home. Mustn't let anything happen to our heiress, Brooke says."

Ignoring the dig and wondering if it actually came from Aunt Brooke, Andrea hooked her arm through Faith's.

"You're a welcome sight, believe me." She was still shaken by her reaction to the plane noises. She slid over. "Mind driving? I've had it with engines for a while."

"No problem." Faith got behind the wheel. Andrea settled back and tried to relax.

Faith pulled out onto the busy highway and zoomed into line before glancing sideways at Andrea.

"What's the matter, Andrea? You look terrible."

"It's those planes. I kept seeing Grandpa Steve and my grandmother...you know." Andrea covered her mouth with her hand.

"You know what they say—fall off a horse, swing up into the saddle again."

"That's all right for you, Faith. You're braver than I am. Even going into the airport gave me the creeps. That noise!"

Faith pulled out of her lane, zoomed in ahead of a Chevrolet and raced along toward the San Francisco skyline.

"You're going to have to get over it the best you can, Andrea. You'll have a lot of pressures from here on in." She let this thought soak in and then went on. "Just assert yourself. You're stronger than those damned plane noises. They're kid stuff."

Andrea sank lower in the seat.

"Not for me."

"Okay. Start small. Seems to me you let old Sam walk all over you yesterday."

"Not this morning," Andrea said, stiffening indignantly. "I stood up to him. I got my father the backing he needs."

Faith's eyebrows rose. She was impressed.

"Good girl. Now that you've got your foot in the door, keep it there. Don't let him get away with it."

"With what?"

"He seems to be running Lombard Enterprises. It's your show, isn't it? I just hope he's not feathering his own nest, if you know what I mean. He's got a nephew, don't forget. Herbie might like a sample of Steve Lombard's estate." Andrea shook her head, but Faith persisted, apparently trusting no one. "How would you ever know, if you relied on Sam Liversedge all the time?"

Andrea thought this over. She remembered Steve's old beat-up file cabinet back home. That would be her first project, getting to know those files.

She was grateful to Faith for her forthright honesty. It was good to talk to one person who was making no demands of her.

CHAPTER
NINE

FOR FAITH Cortlandt the campaign to make Andrea stand up to Sam Liversedge began as a challenge. She wanted to see if she could toughen Andrea up. She didn't want to see her get pushed around.

Faith considered, then, that she was offering advice for Andrea's own good when she reminded her that men like Sam Liversedge took advantage of their position. They had too much power over riches that didn't belong to them. It took nearly a month but she finally got Andrea to the point where she spoke up for herself. Although Andrea had been unable to visit the airport again, even to see her mother off for Vancouver, she was beginning to show a certain courage with the men who handled Lombard Enterprises.

Andrea's performance surprised even Faith.

Andrea was in Sam's office one late September morning when she remarked quite unabashedly that she saw she wasn't wanted there, particularly with her opinions about Lombard programs.

Sam was left stammering. "I must say, Andrea, I kind of thought you'd be easier to...to—" His voice drifted off.

"—Handle?" Andrea finished for him. Andrea had saved up her small store of independence for this moment.

"No, to reason with," he explained. "I'm sure Steve did too. You've only had three weeks to understand what it's taken older and more experienced heads twenty years to learn." He shifted paper clips around his desk nervously. "I still think you've worked too hard to learn everything in a few weeks. You deserve a vacation. Time to spend a few of those big dollars. It won't hurt you to play a little."

Sam was taking too much for granted. Almost every business

move connected with Lombard Enterprises had been made lately without even an effort to contact her. She had hoped to sit in and learn from these advisers. In the dark hours of night she sometimes wondered if there were reasons why she was not meant to know what went on. She understood very well why Sam wanted to ship her off to New York to join Aunt Brooke—she was in the way.

"I'm going, Sam. Really, I am. Don't rush me." She tried to make her manner light and teasing. "You wouldn't shunt off my grandfather like this."

"Your grandfather listened to me now and then."

She leaned across the desk, flipped a paper clip at him and joked, "So do I."

"Ha!"

"Now and then."

He laughed. "Okay. You're a chip off the old Steve. But for God's sake, go to New York. Better yet—Paris. Get some rest."

"How about Moscow? Is that far enough? I certainly won't get any rest in Paris."

He threw the clip back at her. She caught it, stuck it in the pocket of her new suede coat.

"First lesson, be frugal. I'll save the clip. Tell you what, Sam. I'll leave tomorrow for New York. I'll find a train with a bedroom and take a little homework with me."

"A train? These days? You must be out of your mind."

"I'll take with me the files on a lot of Lombard properties. I'll leave the stocks, bonds, Treasury notes, but I want to take the loans, the investments, escrow details on some of the older Lombard properties, and some detailed maps. City. Topography. The works."

"Afraid I can't help you on that just yet. I'll have to get copies from the various corporations your grandfather set up. They're mostly on the coast. A few in Nevada."

"No, Sam."

His eyes narrowed. "What do you mean—no?"

"I already have the originals. They were in Steve's office files." She smiled at his shock. "How do you think I've been spending my nights, Sam? Throwing the family fortune away?

83

Aunt Brooke is in New York and I can't wait to meet her there. But here at home I'm trying to fit into Steve Lombard's shoes."

"Well, I'll be damned." Sam gave her an impatient glance.

It wasn't until she got to the outer hall where Faith was waiting that Andrea let herself go and allowed her knees to shake. But she looked at Faith and winked. Faith grinned back and gave her the thumbs-up sign.

Andrea had succeeded in asserting herself. Maybe now Sam and the others would take her seriously when she came back from New York. She suspected Steve would have been proud of her.

But she still couldn't get on a plane—she wasn't that brave yet. Andrea planned to take the transcontinental train, leaving Faith to handle the phone calls and the press until she and Brooke returned from New York.

By the time Andrea left, Faith had fairly well drummed into her head all that she felt her friend needed to know about men and how not to get burned.

Andrea hugged her. "Have Frank over to the house. Okay?"

After a slight hesitation, Faith returned her hug. "I think I will. But don't you worry about me. Take good care of yourself. Live it up a little. Find yourself a nice guy. But stay away from Brooke's gigolos." Andrea laughed at the preposterousness of the idea.

When she reached Oakland and got on the train, she felt that this was her first real step to independence.

There were moments on the three-day trip to New York when Andrea envied her friend Faith. The longer she knew Frank Kelly the more she liked him. He was honest, up-front—not at all like her mysterious friend, the vanished Leland.

But Frank Kelly belonged to Faith.

The train was shabby—unlike those she remembered from her childhood—but at any rate, it served its purpose. By the time she transferred in Chicago, barely making the switch from the City of San Francisco, which had arrived two hours late, to the Broadway Limited, leaving on time, she had read through the stack of files she carried in her old Vuitton case and had some solid opinions on a number of real estate properties Steve had intended to trade off. As nearly as she could make out, these pieces of acreage were being held by Steve for tax losses.

She hated the idea. They were like living beings to her, wasting away. Steve wouldn't let these parcels of land just sit there. Some could be developed. A desert strip within city transportation of Los Angeles could bloom as a suburb, with greenery and gardens. On the other hand a strip of redwood and brush just off Highway One on the northern California coast should be kept in its primeval splendor.

A series of shabby stucco buildings on the rocky coast between Laguna and Seal Beach had been left to ruin. They should be rebuilt, reinforced.

She had a great many ideas. She was sure Sam and Gene Rafael would disagree. She would have to show some of Steve's strength, and prime herself with knowledge of the subjects. On the other hand the losses by Prysing Productions for four consecutive years shocked her. Hundreds of people could live on the amount of money washed down the drain by the film studio. Only Eden Ware's films managed to show a profit, and these were feeding off her big successes at other studios. Lombard Enterprises simply couldn't go on bailing Prysing Productions out. There had to be an alternative, but one which would allow Andrea to help her father.

She arrived in New York and found Aunt Brooke staying with Alec in his twelfth-floor apartment on Central Park West. It was an old landmark building with breathtaking views of Central Park, and Brooke loved staying there.

But Andrea was determined to be on her own. She took a mini-suite high up in the Plaza Hotel. It was a small, enchanting round room with an adjoining bedroom on the Fifth Avenue side of the hotel. She had always wondered what was within those corner towers that had looked so medieval when pointed out to her as a child.

Today, one of those tower rooms belonged to her for as long as she could pay for it. It was nice to know that she need no longer depend on an allowance from her father.

The limousine service which Aunt Brooke had employed to pick Andrea up from Pennsylvania Station delivered her to the

Plaza's front door. She walked up the steps and inside, past the desk, hoping someone would follow with her bags. She had never thought about this before. Her father had always been there to register her. She stopped at the desk, fumbled in her bag for her American Express card and couldn't help thinking that it had been easier when she was just Tony Lombard's daughter and not a grown-up woman.

Behind her as she stood at the desk she heard music unlike that which she was used to back in San Francisco. They must be playing the "Merry Widow Waltz" in the central Palm Court, she thought. The place had changed little in the years since Grandpa Steve and Gran Randi first took her to tea here. The court, looking very like an old gouache of a nineteenth-century *wintergarten*, was filled with afternoon shoppers, romantic pairs, a few men with attaché cases and business on their minds. Between the potted palms, Andrea was surprised to see that some of them were drinking tea.

She was glad Faith was back in San Francisco. Faith would have laughed at all this, called the scene and the music corny. But Andrea, who hadn't waltzed since she was a little girl, suddenly saw herself in Leland's arms, swinging, dipping, swaying around a huge ballroom. The vision was something like those castles her father and Jany had taken her to see in Europe. She wished only for a handsome man—a man like Leland—to perfect this romantic image...

The desk clerk broke the spell. He handed back her card, hoped she would enjoy her stay and turned her over to the bellman. She found it odd that she had never really noticed a bellman until she was out on her own. With independence a new world opened up for her. She was beginning to enjoy her freedom as she had enjoyed defying Sam Liversedge. But to do either, she knew she must acquire knowledge. That was part of the challenge.

Andrea Lombard was going to show the world.

Her confidence ebbed slightly when she started to follow the bellman to the elegant old elevators and caught a glimpse of a dark-haired man in the Palm Court drinking an aperitif. When she saw his profile in the mirrored back wall of the court he was completely unlike the handsome Leland. At this moment Leland was probably cuddling up with his wife and children in some London suburb.

She told herself she couldn't care less about Leland when she saw her mini-suite and actually stood in what she thought of as her very own tower room. The bellman pointed out the view of churning traffic on Fifth Avenue which fascinated her. She opened the curtains and looked out each window. The bellman watched her with some interest. He had probably seen her face in the papers. She gave him a five-dollar bill, decided he would expect more and drew her hand back just as he reached for the bill. She pulled out a ten. It had been an awkward moment. She still had to learn to be smooth in all her actions, even when she was wrong. Confidence was everything.

The bellman left, and she turned to unpacking. She was in the middle of hanging up her dinner outfits and suits, smoothing her sweaters into drawers, when the phone rang. A newspaperwoman from Washington, D.C., wanted to reminisce about her "flirtation" with Steve Lombard during World War II.

Andrea put her off, but unfortunately, the Washington woman was only the first. Four more calls came in the next half hour before Andrea admitted to herself that traveling with an entourage wasn't a bad idea.

Another bellman delivered her mail soon after, along with a vase of long-stemmed red roses and an orchid plant. There was also a basket of autumn leaves, blazing with colors from golden yellow to scarlet red. The roses were from Frank Kelly and Faith, but she had a feeling that Frank was behind the gift. It wasn't Faith's sort of gesture.

"Welcome to the Big Town," the card read. "We're thinking of you."

The orchid plant was from her father and Jany. A beautiful thing. Long, pliant stems with delicate blossoms of mauve and white. They made her think of Hawaii.

More flowers came from people she had never met, including the senior trust officer and vice-president of a New York bank.

She had the flowers set around the two rooms but decided that people were getting carried away by her sudden wealth.

Nor was the mail much better. A dozen plaintive letters already.

Disillusioned by her sudden and mercenary popularity, Andrea soothed the burning tightness inside her stomach with an ulcer pill. In a while she began to feel better. The sensation of a drill running through her stomach soon faded and finally disappeared.

She walked over to the basket of leaves in all their radiant fall shades. Someone had great taste. She looked for the card but couldn't find it. She even searched the fake fireplace.

"Tough luck, whoever you are. You created something special to get my attention, but I can't give you credit. I hope you didn't spend too much."

Aunt Brooke arrived to find Andrea on her knees, with her hands in the grate. Brooke was amused.

"You can't light those things, dear. Against the fire laws or something."

Andrea hugged her aunt, then explained about the anonymously sent basket. Brooke's eyes lit up.

"Secret lover?"

"More like somebody wanting something. Who cares?"

"My sentiments exactly." Brooke snapped off a red rosebud and sniffed it. She was looking marvelous. Andrea had never seen her more radiant. She could almost be the young redhead Brooke Lombard...

"Hurry, now. Fix yourself up."

"Why the hurry?" Andrea refreshed her makeup but didn't bother to change. She was still wearing the same wrinkled skirt and jacket from her morning on the train.

"Okay. I'm ready."

"Like that?" Brooke threw up her hands. She herself was no longer in deep mourning. Tonight she was a vision in green, a new, sleeveless silk sheath, with a Jackie Kennedy pillbox hat. "I hurried right over because I want you to meet a particular friend of mine."

Why not? Andrea asked herself.

As they left the suite, she thought of her business on the train. "What do you know about any undeveloped area behind North Hollywood, Van Nuys and Tarzana?" she asked Brooke.

Brooke passed regally through the glass doors to the elevator banks.

"If there is one thing I can guarantee through a long and reasonably varied life, it is that I have never had the misfortune of finding myself in Tarzana," she said, marching into the elevator.

Andrea sighed. She wouldn't have much help from Brooke when she tried to fit into Steve Lombard's shoes.

They arrived on the ground floor. Andrea heard a toe-tapping Strauss polka, and hoped Brooke was headed into the Palm Court for her rendezvous. Aunt Brooke nudged her along past the mouth-watering pastry tower at the court entrance.

"The bar. Keep going, around the corner."

At the dark entrance to the bar, jammed with men bellowing loudly to each other, Brooke poked Andrea in the ribs, excited as a girl of fifteen.

"My friend is over there, to the right. At the end of the bar. Isn't he divine?"

He was all of that.

He was also the man who called himself Leland, and he was looking along the bar at the two women as if he had never seen Andrea before. His glance reminded Andrea very forcibly of his expression the first time she saw him, in the Ruby Room. Polite but noncommittal.

CHAPTER
TEN

"ANDREA, THIS is Dexter Cartaret, a friend of Alec's from when he lived in London."

Embarrassed by her wrinkled skirt and baggy jacket that didn't fit her figure properly, Andrea pulled her hand back when she saw Dexter Cartaret smile. It was that damned winning smile she had dreamed about for the last month. He reached again for her hand and held it so tightly it hurt. But Andrea couldn't bring herself to protest.

Angry as she was at his deception, she was more furious at her own reaction. She found herself falling under his spell all over again. Her knees shook and her voice quavered; she was afraid he would notice, and forced herself to recover.

Then she raised her eyes, saw his strong, sensuous mouth and had to look away again. She remembered that parting kiss in San Francisco far too well.

"You said Mr. . . . Cartaret?"

"That's right, honey." Brooke put an arm around Dexter Cartaret.

He signaled to the man behind the bar for some drinks. With great familiarity, he ordered a manhattan for Brooke and scotch for himself. With a spark of humor that infuriated Andrea, he suggested, "Shall I make that chocolate and brandy?"

Her reply was in keeping with his remark.

"Good Lord, no! The last time I drank that I was with a real Jekyll and Hyde. Awful man. Better make that a martini."

"Dex, Andrea just graduated from Cal."

"Oh my, that young," he said, his voice patronizing.

She could have hit him. What was his game, anyway?

She studied Dexter Cartaret furtively over her chilled martini and he caught her at it.

"Yes, Miss Lombard? You were about to say—?"

"Nothing." She shut her mouth haughtily, debating with herself whether to betray him to her aunt. But betray what? That he had been in San Francisco a month ago and met a girl named Eve? Probably he had been there to see Aunt Brooke in the first place.

Brooke watched the two of them, amused at Andrea's surly attitude and not averse to getting a few sparks.

"Did I forget to tell you, Dex? This young lady is my brother's heiress."

Andrea shrugged and finished her cocktail in one gulp, only just catching the olive before she choked on it. The martini and the all too familiar "heiress" label added fuel to her fire. When she spoke her voice was angry and bold.

"The New York *Daily News* says I own half of California." She leaned off-balance toward Dexter Cartaret, gave him her sweetest, broadest smile. "It's not true, you know."

He caught her in the hollow of one arm. "It's not?"

"No. It's Oregon. I own most of Oregon."

Aunt Brooke chuckled and ordered another round.

"Lovely country," Dex said.

Still in the crook of his arm, she turned her head, looked up at him.

"You've been to Oregon."

He nodded.

"Have you been everywhere?"

"I sometimes think so. But I recently became a citizen of your beautiful country."

Andrea wished she could break her fascination with his mouth. "Ever been to San Francisco?" she asked suddenly.

Aunt Brooke turned around and looked at them.

"Yes. Among other places. I have several friends out there."

Brooke took a sip of her manhattan. "Anybody I know?" she asked.

"I doubt it. A girl whose father owns a diner? Doesn't appear to be your style."

Brooke lost interest but Andrea wanted very much to laugh.

He really was a rogue. No question about it. Yet she remembered his moodiness during their last few minutes together at the Hyde Street turntable. He had seemed to care a little. When he kissed her it was full of a sort of bittersweet passion—not at all one of those everyday, see-you-again kisses.

She wondered just what, if anything, Dexter Cartaret had left of that feeling today.

Faith Cortlandt would have good advice in a case like this. But before she could imagine what her friend would say, Brooke surprised her by inviting both Andrea and Dex Cartaret back to Alec Huntington's apartment.

Andrea saw that Dex had moved to the other end of the bar where he was greeting an obvious acquaintance. Andrea was relieved to see that it was a man.

"What will Alec say about—you know?"

Brooke shrugged. "Alec introduced me to Dex. He knew Dex and his wife a long time ago in London."

"His wife!"

"Ex-wife, I should say."

Andrea was dying to find out more but Brooke reminded her of the time by glancing at a tiny gold watch with emeralds marking the hours that Andrea hadn't seen before.

Dex Cartaret got them a taxi, and the three of them crowded in. Andrea was still eying Brooke's watch when Brooke noticed her interest and flashed her her hand proudly.

"Isn't it adorable?" She wrinkled her small nose at Cartaret. "Don't be modest, dear. I want my niece to know how crazy I am about it. Andrea, Dex gave this to me."

Andrea stared at Dexter Cartaret. Brooke was almost twice his age. Was this bracelet a gift of affection—or was it his investment in the pursuit of a rich woman?

He's really got me going, Andrea thought. She didn't know quite what to believe about him...

When the cab pulled up in front of Alec's apartment house on Central Park West, Andrea noticed that Brooke, not Dex, paid for the cab.

Even in the dark blue of evening the building held its own with the elegant skyscrapers across the park on the east side of Fifth Avenue. Alec's own big, twelfth-floor apartment was not furnished according to Andrea's taste, though it was much like Cousin Alec. The foyer was brightly lit with twenties-style ceiling globes. The apartment itself had long, narrow windows opening on a view of Central Park. The rooms were big and high-ceilinged, their barny look camouflaged by subdued lamplight and Jacobean furniture, heavy and dark but unexpectedly comfortable.

Guests straggled out of the living room. Alec introduced them to Andrea. They all knew Dexter Cartaret, of course, having encountered him in many of the international haunts of the rich and the famous. The women were asking if they were to see him at Longchamps or the Tour d'Argent or, as one sporty young woman wanted to know, at some new resort in Sardinia. The conversations were a potpourri of racing, restaurants and hideaways.

Brooke was soon surrounded by talkative admirers who separated her from both Andrea and Dex. Andrea shook dozens of hands and gave up trying to remember the faces that went with them. She accepted some hors d'oeuvres from a passing tray but declined another cocktail.

"Smart girl." She turned around to find Dex Cartaret standing next to her. "But you took the very cracker I had my eye on," he said, feigning displeasure.

His charming impudence had the desired effect. Andrea burst into a laugh, and they were friends again.

Andrea seized the moment to satisfy her burning curiosity. "Have you known Aunt Brooke for long?" she asked him. The unspoken questions were somewhat more personal. *How far does this relationship go between you and my aunt—my great-aunt, that is. Do you really care for her?*

He said, "Oh, we've known each other eons. Tell me, what do you plan to do after you leave New York? Go home to San Francisco? Or will you become yet another beautiful jetsetter?" Dex's face was smiling, but his eyes seemed serious, interested in her reply.

Andrea was taken aback by Dex's blatant reference to her wealth. She decided, however, to keep her response as naive as she could. "Now that I can afford it, yes, I'd love to travel, see a lot of touristy things in the world. Then I'm going home to go to work."

"Work?" He was amused now. "What kind of work would you do? Besides counting coupons, that is."

Andrea ignored the dig and instead described some of the problems that awaited her. She told Dex about Sam Liversedge, Gene Rafael and the others—all those who she suspected might wish to take over what Steve Lombard had spent a lifetime building.

She stared out at the faint green halos where the park lights illuminated the shrubbery. It did look dangerous and spooky out there, but she knew there was a different kind of danger awaiting her back home...the danger of being smothered, maneuvered by old men who thought they knew best. Faith Cortlandt had been right. Andrea intended to assume her responsibility.

"You may share Sam Liversedge's opinion of me," Andrea said, staring at Dex defiantly. "But I promise you, someday I'll show them all."

"Someday."

He was leaning slightly toward her, his arm outstretched, his palm flat against the wall beside her head. *Someday.* The expressionless way he said the word puzzled her.

"Well, it takes a little time," she reminded him defensively. "But you wait. I'll show you."

"I'll wager you a tenner you won't." Before she could get angry he put his hands firmly on her shoulders. "Because you are a very nice young lady. And nice young ladies don't run enterprises with the ruthless hand of a Steve Lombard."

"I'll have you know I can be just as ruthless as the next man. Or woman. As the case may be."

He laughed. "Naturally. I never doubted it. However, I suggest you make one rule. Ask yourself the motive of everyone who offers to advise you."

"Including yourself?"

He didn't seem offended.

"Including myself. I must have a motive, somewhere down the line." He began touching her hair, running his fingers through the curly strands down the nape of her neck. She looked around the room nervously, hoping Brooke wasn't watching them.

"Are there motives for that?" she asked, trying to sound sophisticated.

"This is my motive." His fingers closed around a handful of her hair. He pulled her head close, and his mouth found hers. She was trembling, afraid of him and yet wanting him, wanting more...

Suddenly a man's voice boomed out behind Dex. "In here, sweetie. Let's find us some privacy—"

Startled and embarrassed, Andrea broke away from Dex, who muttered, but let her go.

The intruder, a stout man with curly white hair, stopped when he saw Dex.

"Well?"

"Oops. Sorry. Never mind, Amy. This pew is occupied."

Andrea began to laugh. "I think you scared him."

"Me? I'm harmless."

That made her laugh again. "Oh, sure. Who was he? Poor man."

Andrea went into a fit of giggles, but Dex put his hand over her mouth and shifted her further from the library. They stopped before the wide double doors opening on the foyer.

"That gentleman merely happens to be a senior vice-president of UBC. Need I remind you, Alec is a junior V-P."

Her eyes sparkled and she made muffled noises. He removed his hand from her mouth.

"Not for long. Grandpa Steve left him some UBC stock," she reminded him.

"Ah, the power of nepotism."

Two women came out of the little powder room opening off the entrance foyer. Andrea caught only a glimpse of them and didn't remember meeting them earlier, but they certainly knew her. They were fortyish, beautifully dressed, with hair bubble-coiffed like Jacqueline Kennedy's. They were deep in a back-stabbing conversation.

"...One of those dreary little creatures who always inherit money unexpectedly. Brought up in Hollywood, of all places. Did you notice that ghastly outfit she was wearing?"

"Supposed to be a suit, I should imagine. It looks as if she's slept in it. And those shoes—*really*—unspeakable. And with all that Lombard money." The woman shook her head and the two walked out of earshot.

Dex had tried desperately to shift Andrea out of hearing but she had resisted. She shook now with anger and shame. Dex's arm was tight around her waist.

"Why did you stop me? At least I could have kicked their shins."

He laughed, and she felt his arm, which had held her waist so securely, move. He hugged her shoulders.

"You could show them a thing or two."

"I'd be happy to show them. If I knew how."

"Leave that to me."

This was the last thing in the world she had expected of him—he had acknowledged the women's comments rather than denied them. She stiffened, released herself from his grasp.

"Thank you, but *I* personally am quite satisfied with my wardrobe. And I don't give a hoot about what two old crows say about me or my clothes."

Dex made no more efforts at familiarity, but walked silently beside her through the room. Andrea studied the women standing in groups around the room. She had to admit, they did look chic. Their clothes, mostly suits or dresses, shimmered and rustled in a rainbow of subdued colors. As they spoke and laughed with those around them, these women seemed to Andrea to radiate grace and elegance. She looked down at her own rumpled gray suit and felt miserable.

It was like a blow in the stomach when she saw Dex glance across the room at Brooke. She was at the center of a group, but she was staring at Andrea and Dex. Andrea couldn't tell whether she was angry. How long had she been watching them? When Andrea caught her eye Brooke smiled, saluted her niece with her cocktail glass, then turned to answer one of the men standing by her. Andrea felt uncomfortable. And desperate enough to do something about it. Mustering her courage, she took another drink from a passing tray.

"Dex, you know back in San Francisco the women just don't deck themselves out the way they do here in New York. Here all I see is Chanel suits, Dior dresses and, well, I just don't know too much about it all." She stopped, fidgeted with her drink, then went on. "Do you think—do you think you could help me look like these women do tonight? Unless you're busy somewhere else." She tried to make it sound careless.

"Not that I know of." His own casual air about it hurt her. "You really want to go through with this personality change-over?"

"Why not? Think you can help me bring those two old hags to their knees?"

He tilted her chin up.

"If that's what you want."

"Passionately. Then I'm going back and show my grandfather's trustees who's boss."

"Bravo. And you'll do it, too. Leave it to me."

She thought he was about to kiss her again and turned her face away quickly, surprising herself as well as him.

"Shall we have breakfast tomorrow? Then we can make our plans for shopping."

"Sounds fair enough." To her annoyance he seemed amused by her manner. He took her hand and shook it politely. "I'll be leaving now. Your family will want you to themselves this evening."

"Not much chance of that," Andrea said. "Until the party decides to go home."

He looked around and laughed. "Don't worry. In a few months you'll be queening it over a party like this and loving it."

"No chance."

He held her hand as they walked to the door as if she were a child. He rang for the elevator and got out his cigarette case. It looked like gold, heavy and expensive. He offered her a cigarette, but she waved it away.

"Why were you out in San Francisco?" The question had plagued her since she first saw him in the Plaza bar. He was quiet for a moment as he tapped out a slim cigarette, lit it and inhaled.

"Looking over the prospects," he said finally. "Why did you think?"

She was embarrassed for him and couldn't understand why he joked like this.

"Was I a prospect? Or Aunt Brooke?"

"Do you really want to know?"

She was about to say yes but the elevator doors opened and Dex got in. She watched as the doors closed, thinking that she would always remember this moment. Was he being sarcastic, she asked herself, or did he hide his shame behind that swaggering manner?

"What are you thinking about, Andrea?" Alec came up behind her so quietly that she jumped.

"About Aunt Brooke's boyfriend."

To her surprise he laughed. "Oh, you mean Dex? Mother is safe. Matter of fact, I introduced them." He added wryly, "I haven't decided whether I'm sorry or not."

"But he's a gigolo."

Andrea hoped that he would deny this.

"Not really. He takes after his father. I knew Rolly Cartaret pretty well during the war."

"Rolly?"

"Roland. Very old family. Roland lost the estate some time before the war but I know the place in Wiltshire. Worth a quarter of a million pounds, before devaluation."

"But Alec, did this Roland take money from women?"

"That isn't the way it's done, Andrea. Rolly was a mighty decorative fellow. Good company, you know. It wasn't a case of his accepting money. He was an invited guest. Payment was made offstage, so to speak, and not to him. Bills were paid at the end of the month by the friends who enjoyed his company. Everyone welcomed Rolly."

"Women?"

"Sometimes. Tell you what, as soon as we get rid of this crowd, we'll have dinner. We can talk about the Cartarets some other time."

"No. Please. I'd like to know more—"

Their conversation was interrupted by a heavy-set woman and an older man in a dinner jacket who wanted to say goodnight to their host. They shook hands with Alec, went on as if Andrea wasn't standing right there.

"A dear child. Let's hope it doesn't just ruin her life. I don't know what poor Steve was thinking of."

Andrea could hardly wait for Alec to pour his guests into the elevator. When he returned to her, his usually grave face was almost cheerful.

"All right, Andrea. Stop frowning. Are you still worrying about mother marrying a gigolo? I've known Dex since he was fifteen and making a damn fool of himself trying to be a commando. But he made it. He has a mighty good war record. He was doing incredible things—raids on Europe that you wouldn't believe. But he's not about to marry mother."

She suddenly felt much better. "Go on," she urged him. "Tell me about the war record."

"Well, Dex ended up with a plate in his head. Recovered perfectly, far as I know. While he was in the hospital, though, I used to see him making his way around the corridors when I visited my wife. Heather had a brain aneurism, you know."

She nodded, though she knew little about the woman. He never talked about her. Alec finished in a rush.

"He was still in the hospital when Rolly and Dex's little ten-year-old sister, Deirdre, were wiped out in a fire raid on London."

She didn't know what to say. She felt sorry for Dex's tragic loss but at the same time she couldn't help being glad that Dexter Cartaret had a sympathetic background. She tried to ask Alec what kind of women this war hero sought.

"Well, he doesn't court just anyone..." He hesitated, attacked by an unpleasant thought. "Anyway, Andrea, you're much too young and pretty to need escorts of the kind my mother requires."

"Why won't he? I mean, get involved with just anyone?"

Alec considered the question. "I imagine he still remembers his little sister. A sweet child. But how he feels about older women like my mother, I've no idea. Whatever the case may be, mother seems little the worse for it."

"Horrible." Andrea said emphatically. "How can women do it?"

"I couldn't say. Except that I've never heard any complaints, and I long ago gave up trying to regulate mother's life. One thing I do know. Dex doesn't get paid for seductions—not like some of them."

"You mean he doesn't seduce *old* women, don't you?" Andrea asked.

"Who doesn't seduce old women?" Aunt Brooke wanted to know. She had returned from the foyer after sending off the last of the guests. Her gaze went quickly from her son to Andrea.

"You don't mean Dexter L. Cartaret. My God! As for seduction, I wish he wasn't so damned scrupulous. And why would you care anyway? He's not interested in younger women. Didn't you know that, dear? But your new status certainly attracts men on the lookout for Steve's money."

Andrea quickly diverted the conversation away from herself.

"What does the *L* stand for?"

She should have known. "Leland. Dex's middle name." Brooke had given her the last link to bring back memories of Andrea's little romance. Brooke went on. "Now, don't worry about bills here in New York. Just sign for everything, the way I do. Sam will handle the bills."

All that night Andrea thought about how much happier she had been twenty-four hours ago, when, in her fantasy romance, Leland had been an unhappily married man who sacrificed his great love for Eve out of family loyalty.

They didn't make heroes like that any more.

ELEVEN

ANDREA LAY awake a long time that night. She enjoyed her warm perfumed bath, followed by the comfort of her bed, but she had made the mistake of stacking some of Steve Lombard's files on the nightstand. Each of the files had an exciting story to tell, and she knew instinctively that delving into them would take her mind off the events of the evening.

Like Steve she was particularly interested in land acquisition. She read about farm acreage, riparian rights and highway frontage. Then she ran into something about Northern California ranch land. It seemed incredible to her that a person could own a five hundred and seventy thousand acre ranch, but here it was, named the Modoc, and the Lombards owned it.

The Modoc was named either for the Modoc Indian tribe or for the county containing the ranch house, outbuildings and bunkhouse. In either case, the Modoc's rangeland included a sizable corner of Lassen County and even spilled over into Nevada's neighboring Washoe County.

The ranch ran several thousand head of cattle even during slow years, and to Andrea's surprise much of that open range was under control of the Bureau of Land Management. If those half-million acres were considered government land, why was the Modoc listed as a single Lombard asset? Andrea read further, interested in the fact that the Modoc still complained of cattle rustling, especially near the border range between California and Nevada. But when she got into complicated legal jargon, she discovered that Lombard Enterprises was the legal owner of every water hole in the huge Modoc spread.

Lombard Enterprises seemed to get along well with its neighbors—some of whom, for all she knew, were the rustlers. The files contained personal letters stuck in haphazardly, some poorly written, few of them typed. But a glance at their contents showed an excellent working relationship with the Modoc neighbors. Many of the letters thanked Steve for a favor.

It was something to remember, something Andrea resolved to live up to.

It was harder to get interested in the geological reports. No exciting gold discoveries. Nothing about uranium nor plutonium. But one of the other parcels of acreage interested Andrea. It seemed to her that this piece of land, which had proved unprofitable for farming and unfit to raise cattle or even sheep, was nicely situated between two towns on the Redwood Highway. This was an area that saw busy traffic between San Francisco and Southern Oregon.

Excited by the idea she was formulating, Andrea got out of bed and walked into her little semicircular tower room. She stood there looking down on Fifth Avenue, not as busy at this hour, but not completely quiet either. The lights fascinated her. She studied the skyscrapers, where the lights were still on.

She couldn't see herself building a skyscraper—not just yet, at any rate, and certainly not on that abandoned acreage between two modest-sized towns in Northern California. But what about a place, full of shops, perhaps even including a restaurant? It would be a shopping center that provided the kinds of things people couldn't get in their small towns. By drawing customers from each of the two towns as well as from those cars just driving through, the businesses could succeed where they might have failed in each separate community.

She hurried to the desk against the inside wall and felt around for a pen and pad. She couldn't find the pad, so she jotted down "shopping center" on the hotel directory and returned to bed, by now wide awake. She hadn't thought of Dex Cartaret for more than an hour.

The next problem that captured her interest was a hotel nearly completed on the bank of the Truckee River in Reno, Nevada. It appeared to be within a block or two of the little city's leading hotels, the Mapes and Riverside, but was not as yet licensed by the Nevada Gaming Commission.

What a natural site for a luxury hotel that catered to women

102

and children without the hurly-burly atmosphere of gambling! Andrea remembered her own visits to Reno with Steve and Randi. She had felt left out because there was no entertainment for a teenager and she wasn't welcome even near the slot machines.

Andrea closed her eyes, picturing the city, with its charming tree-lined streets and the picturesque river which had gone on its latest rampage this very year and flooded half the city. Grandpa Steve had told her once that if some cataclysm ever destroyed Reno, half the wealth in Northern California would sink with it, since so much West Coast money was deposited in Reno banks to avoid the California taxes.

Andrea remembered the two reasonably prestigious hotels in the city. There was certainly room for a nongambling atmosphere, she thought. The new hotel they were building was more modern, with lanais outside almost every room and a choice between a river and a desert view. The hotel, she reasoned, could make its reputation on good food, comfortable rooms and a peaceful atmosphere. Those women who didn't gamble with their men would love it, and they could of course bring their children. The guests who wished to could walk a mere block to do all the gambling they wanted.

She jotted the idea down on Steve's file folder, and wondered why Grandpa Steve hadn't thought of it. She finally wound down and got to sleep, convinced that Steve Lombard had done well in naming her his successor.

The jangle of the telephone shook her awake. It was Dex Cartaret, wanting to know where they would have their breakfast meeting. He sounded awfully businesslike, Andrea thought dismally. But even so, he might get the wrong idea if she invited him to breakfast in her suite. She wanted to make sure everything was on the up and up—at least for now.

She wanted to ask him if Aunt Brooke had let him off the string, but didn't want to appear too interested. So she suggested casually that they meet in the Palm Court . . . with every eye on them, including those hotel guests passing back and forth between lobbies, Dex wasn't liable to tempt her with his powerful charm. Even so, she wasn't at all sure how to behave with him. . . .

Andrea had grown up as an eager, slightly spoiled child in the material sense, but with a need for love and attention that grew out of loneliness. Her mother was off chasing her dreams, and her father was all too often caught up in his various business successes and failures. If Dex were more like Frank Kelly, simple and homespun, she could be honest. Nothing put-on. But she didn't dare let Dex Cartaret guess how deeply she wanted him. She had no intention of becoming just another one of those headline heiresses who kept marrying and paying, never able to find their genuine love....

Dex stood up from a table behind the potted palms and waved to her. His coffee had already been poured and he had eaten half a croissant—not especially polite, she thought, considering that she had invited him to breakfast. However, his compliment when she was ushered to his table so pleased her that she forgave his lapse in manners.

"Anyone who looks like you do at this hour doesn't need my advice."

All her careful efforts to be cool and sophisticated fell apart. She beamed.

"Do you like it? Faith said it was old-fashioned, but I love it."

The suit was a deep blue knit, with an Eisenhower jacket. Her velvet pillbox hat matched it exactly.

"Not the suit. Lord, no! Almost ten years out of date. It's you. 'Mine eyes dazzle,' as somebody said."

She covered her disappointment with a faint note of sarcasm. "Probably Shakespeare. He had good taste, too."

"At least the color suits you." He must have sensed that her feelings were hurt and he added whimsically, "Anyway, if you came in looking like our fashion-plate First Lady, I'd be out of a job."

"That's all right. It's to be a job like any other. You'll be paid for your time."

The shot was so blunt and so unexpected that he stared at her for several seconds, apparently unable to respond. She was instantly sorry she had said it, but it was too late even for a lame apology. His face was flushed and he bit his lip, but he did not say a word. Quietly he pushed his seat back and stood up.

"Please, that was just a joke. Dex, please don't leave."

He sat down, broke off another piece of the croissant and buttered it. She wished he would say something. When he did, though, she felt even more uncomfortable. He was much too casual.

"Have you any ideas about where you want to go? Specialty shops? Most of the designers are off on their pilgrimage to Paris and Milan. But how about Bergdorf's for a start? That's handy. Just across the street. And then Bonwit's, Saks."

Her guilt over the crude remark forced her to be as obliging as possible. Since Bergdorf's was closest, she agreed to visit their designer rooms first. When he asked what she would like for breakfast, she said she wasn't hungry. Before they left, Dex signaled the waiter to their table and over Andrea's protests signed the check himself.

As they went from store to store she discovered what she had suspected all along. His taste was impeccable. She had half hoped he would go into raves over the mini-skirts; after all, her legs weren't that unworthy. But when Andrea paraded before him he just yawned.

"Remarkable how those styles age a woman. Every fifty-year-old female on Fifth Avenue is wearing them. However, you certainly look as good as they do."

"As good as they do! You louse!"

She caught his eye and they both laughed. But the moment still couldn't wipe out the memory of their earlier exchange.

Her purchases were all off-the-rack—she couldn't wait to get into all this glamorous clothing that would entice Dex Cartaret. She hadn't minded his criticisms. As a matter of fact, he had certain qualities that reminded her of Faith Cortlandt. Faith, too, was pointedly direct when she disapproved of something. Unlike most of Andrea's acquaintances, Faith had never let the heiress legend interfere with her honest evaluations. Andrea respected that.

Her respect for Dex went up, too. She had told herself that if she spent a lot of time with Dexter L. Cartaret, some of his romantic gloss would wear off and she would see through him. It didn't. The infatuation that had obsessed her changed its direction that day. They became friends.

For a while she kept wondering how Aunt Brooke would feel when she called Dex and found him not available. But gradually, as the day progressed, in the sheer joy of his company, Andrea stopped caring about Aunt Brooke's disappointment.

By evening, when they were leaving the hotel for dinner, Andrea even brought up the subject of her business plans with Dex. She described her ideas for the shopping center in Northern California, and nongambling hotel in Reno, and how she was going to keep an eye on her grandfather's stocks.

"Grandpa was so busy he didn't notice their daily ups and downs."

"And you, of course, will pay attention." Dex was, as always, amused by her seriousness.

"You bet I will."

They waited for a limousine he had hired for her New York stay. It upset her when he billed the car's rental to himself, but he wouldn't discuss it and ignored her protests.

Dexter Cartaret seemed determined to set himself apart.

"You look sensational," he told her with every evidence of sincerity. She was wearing one of the dinner dresses he had picked out for her today, a black taffeta Givenchy with a balloon knee-length skirt and a wide Sabrina neckline. She wore an exquisite handmade shawl that her mother had brought her from Thailand. Bits of silver had been sewn into the heavy lace fabric, creating butterfly designs that sparkled under the marquee lights of the hotel. With her thick black hair the shawl made Andrea look dazzling and exotic.

It also attracted stray passersby who stopped in front of the Plaza to stare at this stunning, obviously aristocratic couple. Andrea noticed none of this. She was with Dex and she was happy.

She beamed at Dex's compliment. Surely, he meant it. Looking up into his sensitive brown eyes, she was persuaded. She read warmth there.

He helped her into the limousine, draping the heavy shawl

over her shoulders. As his fingers brushed her skin she felt the same dizziness she had known the day he kissed her for the first time.

Dex reached for her hand and patted it in a fatherly way. She smiled but looked away, embarrassed by her own wish that he would behave less like a relative, more like a lover. But she herself had set the rules.

She saw New York's varicolored evening lights blur as the limousine rolled smoothly along Fifth Avenue. Deeply aware of his body beside hers, she looked out at the city and fell in love with every skyscraper, every stranger who glanced up when the car passed. Tonight she was convinced that because she was happy, every pair of eyes that followed her was friendly. Nothing or no one could threaten her. Not so long as she had the Lombards' heritage of power that went hand in hand with their wealth.

Faith Cortlandt was awakened by the sound of a bell ringing somewhere. Probably a cable car approaching Taylor Street, she told herself. She had never thought she would find the Lombard house too large and a little scary, but the loud sound upset her. She glanced at the glass clock on the nightstand, running her fingers over the delicate gold banding. Six A.M.

She sat up and listened, wishing she hadn't left the bedroom door open. The sudden creaking of that staircase couldn't be caused by one of the servants; only the second maid slept in while Brooke Lombard was away. Surely, the noise must be the wind.

"If I owned this mausoleum, I'd do some repairing,"

Sometimes Faith thought she wouldn't be caught dead in this old mausoleum if *she* owned it.

The creaking was not the wind.

She put one long, shapely leg out of the bed and then the other. Her blonde hair hung loose around her shoulders. She tied her filmy white bathrobe around her, and remembered that today was Saturday and she had invited Frank to have breakfast with her.

Maybe Frank had come in early and had been let in by the maid. She felt under the bed for her slippers. Just then someone

107

passed the open doorway. She straightened up and stared. Frank knew where she slept, but this intruder had gone past her bedroom without even looking in.

She slipped across the room and looked out into the hall. Whoever it was had gone into Steve Lombard's study. The door was still open.

Faith wished now that she had kept a gun handy. In the hall she reached for something heavy and came up with a marble trophy on the hall table. The brass plaque read: "TO STEVE LOMBARD, HUMANITARIAN, FROM THE PRESS AND UNION LEAGUE CLUB."

So much for humanitarians. She had a better use for it. Holding it behind her, she moved to the study door. She couldn't make out anything until she pushed the door open quietly.

There was Sam Liversedge, kneeling before the open drawer of Steve's file cabinet. He looked up, startled, and stared at her sheer robe and disheveled hair.

"Why Miss Cortlandt, you are a vision. Didn't you hear the bell ring? One would think it would have woken up the entire household. The maid let me in."

She tried to ignore his glances at her body.

"What are you doing here at this hour?"

He waved manila folders at her. "Recovering Steve Lombard's bank records for tax purposes. Doing my job. I didn't know you were here, Miss Cortlandt, with Brooke in New York."

It was hard to remain dignified when she was half-naked. Why hadn't Andrea told him she would be here? Also, how did he assume that it was all right for him just to march upstairs alone and come into Steve's bedroom?

"*I* was asked to stay here, Mr. Liversedge."

She had him there. She saw his mouth twitch. He glanced at the files and then at the cabinet, now looking angry.

"May I remind you that I am an executor of Stephen Lombard's estate? It won't be out of probate for two years. Eighteen months at the least. What do you think can happen to his properties and his banking records in two years? They have to be worked up, month by month. Day by day."

She laughed and hoisted the trophy.

"Well, this is your department, Mr. Liversedge. I guess I won't need this."

He gave the heavy chunk of marble a startled look, shrugged and began to riffle through the files in his hand.

"Miss Cortlandt?"

"Yes?"

She had thought for a brief instant that it would be a better idea to be on Sam's good side, and decided to invite him to breakfast. Mrs. Trentini would be arriving any minute.

"Have you been at these files?"

Her surprise at his question turned to anger. "Me? What the devil do I want with that dusty mess? Do I look like a file clerk?"

He looked her up and down.

"Frankly, no. Not at all. But an entire drawerful of files is missing. You don't know anything about it?"

"No. I don't," she said, but she had a pretty good idea. After her pep talks to Andrea, her friend had mentioned that she would do some work on the New York trip. Faith had thought then that it would be a good joke on Sam if Andrea boned up on Steve's affairs and could handle some of them herself.

Sam said, "Well, I've got most of the years the IRS is interested in. I'll be on my way."

She followed him to the stairs, watching him leave. Then she went down the hall to the bathroom. Under the icy tingle of the shower she did some thinking. Maybe Sam Liversedge was up to something. That could explain his pointing the finger at her.

There was something about Sam Liversedge that Faith had mistrusted from the beginning. She had noted his patronizing attitude not only toward Faith herself, but to Andrea as well. He was probably delighted to send Andrea out of the state for a little fun in New York while he no doubt manipulated her property. Andrea was far too trusting, Faith thought. Someone had to steer her in the right direction—but definitely not Sam Liversedge. She knew, though, that her dislike of him was matched by his distrust of her. . . .

She was relieved when Frank showed up half an hour later. Mrs. Trentini arrived as well and set to work preparing breakfast. Frank agreed to join Faith at the breakfast room table, but only after he went to the kitchen and apologized to Mrs. Trentini for the extra trouble he gave her.

Faith was annoyed by his effort to placate the cook.

"She's being paid while Brooke is away. Don't worry about her."

Frank took a biscuit out of the electric warmer and split it, covering both sides with butter and guava jelly. He wasn't too happy being here while the family was away, she could see. Faith thought it strange how the very qualities she loved in Frank were those most unlike her own. She knew she was jealous of those who now possessed what she had enjoyed as a child, and that there was a selfish streak in her. Frank also knew and understood. Sometimes she wondered why he wasted his time on her.

He saw her glance up nervously at the old-fashioned crystal chandelier with its dangling prisms.

"Breakfast room with a chandelier. How do you like that?"

"Corny. Typical of Mad Tony Lombard. Did you know that at the time he was putting up his tent here on Nob Hill back in the eighteen fifties, the Cortlandts were building the biggest, most respectable hotel in San Francisco?"

Frank studied the eggs, country-fried potatoes and the thick slice of ham on his plate before he spoke.

"In those very years my people were pulling up blackened potatoes in the fields. You must admit there are more opportunities for some of us today."

She threw up her hands. An associate professor's position with a dingy one-room flat in Berkeley wasn't exactly her idea of ambition. But something else was disturbing her this morning.

"Frank, it wasn't the chandelier I was looking at. I was thinking of that old crook upstairs prowling through Steve Lombard's files. If he can do that, so can we."

"Do what?" Frank stopped chewing and looked up from his plate. "What are you talking about?"

Faith described what had happened.

Frank continued eating for an uncomfortable minute or two. Without looking at her he said. "We wouldn't be robbing Sam

Liversedge. And we wouldn't be fooling an innocent child, either, if we took advantage of this opportunity."

"Innocent child!"

"Andrea is hardly up on the stock market and land manipulations, as we both know." He looked straight at her, and she was very much aware of his steady, blue-eyed gaze. She wondered if he were able to read her thoughts. "If you want to help the girl, count me in."

"It *is* Andrea I'm thinking of. If we knew something about her property, we could give her a little honest advice. Protect her from Sam and his gang."

He looked puzzled.

"Some of the files have disappeared already. He practically accused me of taking them. But if you ask me, he said that to cover his own tracks. He probably took them himself. I think he sneaked upstairs, you know. I was pretty scared when I first heard him."

Frank leaned over the table and kissed her. Then he reached for her hand and brought her around to him. He drew her close, buried his face in the sweet mass of her loose hair. Faith felt his solid, muscular strength and smiled.

CHAPTER
TWELVE

AFTER ALMOST a week of seeing each other constantly, Andrea grew more and more certain that Dex really cared for her. It pleased her that he listened to her ideas about the Lombard properties. He then presented suggestions about which they had heated discussions, especially when those ideas seemed to be more sensible than her own. But beyond his greeting and parting kisses—which seemed to hide or suppress his passion—he was utterly the gentleman, proper at all times.

This curious ambivalence about Dex's behavior climaxed the day he took her up to Connecticut to see the autumn foliage. Dex drove a slightly beat-up Corvette that he said was borrowed from a friend. Afterward, she would always remember one particular maple tree that she saw overhanging a neat white fence. The house beyond the fence, built in the saltbox style, was set on a knoll a good quarter mile from the entrance gate. Dex pulled up under the flaming maple to get a better look at the house. One huge scarlet leaf fluttered down through the window and into his lap.

"Autumn leaves. My favorite colors. From gold to russet and all that shading in between. More beautiful than any painting."

She slowly remembered her "mystery" admirer, and stared at him in the passionate hope that her guess was the right one.

"Did you send that basket of autumn leaves to my suite at the hotel when I arrived?"

She thought he was going to ignore her question, but he turned to her determinedly as if he had made up his mind about something.

"I wanted you to have something different to greet you."

"It was. I loved it. I still have the basket."

He studied the saltbox house. "Reminds me of my happiest days at home."

It was not nearly so imposing as the stately home Alec had described. He must have guessed why she looked so surprised.

"Not Cartaret Hall. I spent my best times at the gatehouse with old Cyril, the gardener. He took me fishing. And I'll never forget the walking tours. We went everywhere. Over to Cornwall, and the coast. We cut across a corner of Dartmoor Moor. Great place for mist and murders. And we even walked to Stonehenge. Cyril was a rugged soul. But he was gentle as a lamb to Deirdre, my little sister."

"Was it Cyril who gave you the commando idea?" she asked softly.

He considered. "Probably." He drew her to him and kissed the top of her head. "You're a funny little thing." She tried to sit up straight, pretending indignation, but he held her close to his body, her head against his throat.

"I mean, you care about Cyril. And even Deirdre, and you never knew them. But I can see it in your eyes. You even care about me."

She twisted slightly against the pressure of his arms and touched his neck with her lips. She couldn't be wrong about him. She felt such tenderness in the way he had held her just then.

But his voice was harsh, unlike himself. "Don't. You know this is no good." He grabbed her arm.

His words terrified her, but she decided to be light.

"Don't be silly. I'm over twenty-one."

He gritted his teeth. "You are an infant in this game. Now, stop playing. You think you can turn it on and off like a water tap?"

"I don't want to turn it off. I didn't want to turn it off that day in San Francisco. You left me alone then. Remember?" She was getting worked up now, but couldn't seem to snap out of it.

"Yes. I remember. I left you for the same reason I am trying to set you straight now. Don't let's go into it, shall we?"

"Suppose I don't care?"

He gave a great, exasperated sigh and finally removed his

113

hand from her arm, leaving marks on her flesh where his fingers had gripped her.

"The only possible thing that can happen between us," he said, his mouth tight, "is that I become your paid puppy dog. Or at least that's what everyone will think."

He waited for some reaction from her; when he got none he started the car and made a sweeping turn into the highway, just missing an oncoming car. After a loud honk from the horn, the other car vanished northward, leaving Andrea stiff with fright. She tried to laugh it off.

"That was a close one. I know you're mad at me but this is carrying it too far."

She expected him to ignore her levity. Instead he quickly pulled the car over and drew her to him. She opened her lips to protest but his mouth silenced her. She was breathless and about to panic but her own desire responded, and the struggle became a hungry passion for them both. It was as if he wanted to devour her—with his eyes as they drank her beauty in, with his hands as they caressed the silk dress she wore.

Suddenly it was all over. He backed away, let her go, his eyes masked by his dark lashes. He settled back behind the wheel and started the car.

He tried to make a joke of it. "Well, that was hardly the way to *end* this." But his words could not deny the tension she saw in his face, the way a small nerve or muscle twitched along his jaw.

"Maybe it means we shouldn't." She added after a breath or two, "End it, I mean." She gave him a smile that was fitful and nervous.

He laughed. One hand reached out to her. She put her hand in his and they drove back to the city in silence, each thinking their separate thoughts.

"Don't let me off in front of the hotel," she said when they were about to make the circle around the Plaza fountain. "Down the street. I'll walk back."

"Hiding me?"

"No. It's just that I'm going to a musical tonight with Aunt Brooke and Alec. They might get here early."

He said nothing. She was sorry she had mentioned Brooke. He let her off on Fifth Avenue in front of Bergdorf Goodman. She leaned over to kiss him as she left the car but he turned away and drove off almost before the door slammed...

It had been a tumultuous day, if slightly confusing. Andrea was thoughtful that night as she went with Alec and Brooke to the theater. All during the show she was mentally reliving the day with Dex, and afterward the three stopped at Sardi's for a late supper.

One of Brooke's gossipy girl friends, the latest wife of Alec's immediate UBC superior, stopped by the table, interrupting Vincent Sardi himself as he and Alec exchanged current television news. Sardi, being a gentleman as well as busy, bowed out and went on his way, leaving the stage to Brooke's friend. Andrea was disappointed. She had found Mr. Sardi far more interesting.

But her curiousity was piqued when the woman lowered her voice confidentially to Brooke, though she was audible to Andrea and Alec.

"Darling, if I'd only known you were going to drop that divine Englishman of yours, I'd have snapped him up."

Brooke's hackles seemed to rise. Andrea didn't blame her. Worse—she had never felt so guilty. She studied a distant table where a first-night cheering section waited noisily for their special star, but it was to avoid the gossip about Dex.

Brooke was too elaborately casual. She must care more than Andrea had suspected.

"My Lord, Lila! The poor man has to get on with his work some time."

"Of course...darling, I've always meant to ask you, just what is Dexter Cartaret's work?"

Alec stifled a laugh, and Brooke gave him a disapproving frown.

"He is an absolute genius in the stock market. Alec threatens to turn over his portfolio to him."

Alec tempered her enthusiasm. "Not my entire portfolio. But Dex does have a talent for picking the crucial moment to sell, I'll say that."

115

Lila said, "If only he could tell me when to buy. I suppose that's what he's up to with that young girl."

Andrea avoided the woman's eyes, afraid of what was coming. Brooke seemed abnormally calm.

"What else? Young girls aren't his type."

"I wouldn't know. I didn't see him myself. My friend Corinna told me about it. She's seen him with the girl twice, hiding away in some little Italian joint on First Avenue."

Brooke shrugged. "I'll ask him about her tomorrow morning. We're invited to a bon voyage party on that fabulous French liner. The commandant of the French line is a friend of Dex's, you know. They were wartime buddies."

Lila looked slightly chagrined but the news hit Andrea harder. Dex hadn't said a word about it. She had grown too confident, almost forgetting that he was still Brooke's "gentleman friend."

Lila leaned over and let her cheek linger briefly against Brooke's. "Well, so long, all of you. See you at that Philharmonic thing next week. What do you think of our precious new Lincoln Center?"

She waved away their replies. "Never mind. Some other time. There comes that awful Hollywood cow. Thinks she owns Sardi's because Broadway actually let her walk onstage. Listen to the applause. All of it from those poor creatures she's bought. 'Ta, folks."

Alec and Andrea took care not to look at Brooke.

"I never dreamed that actress was so popular. Look at the way they're clustering around her," Andrea said with forced gaiety.

"Paid for, as Lila says." Brooke gave the proceedings a sour smile. "Everything in this cockeyed world is paid for."

In her hotel that night, Andrea realized suddenly that his date with Brooke tomorrow must have been on Dex's mind when he behaved so oddly to her. She was sure he wanted her and that it was more than just momentary desire. In his eyes she believed she had read love.

She knew she would have to do the pursuing in this bizarre courtship. She wanted him more than anything. She had to make sure—and quickly—that he felt the same.

She didn't even know where he lived. She vaguely remem-

116

bered him saying it was somewhere in the East Forties, beyond Third Avenue, but he hadn't been clear about it. She supposed he was embarrassed because of its contrast to the Plaza. Dex was obviously meant to live well.

On the other hand, he hadn't told her about his date with Brooke. She considered Brooke a rival, though for precisely what she wasn't sure. Certainly Brooke had no intention of marrying Dex.

In that moment, Andrea knew her plan was to marry Dex. Other heiresses did things like that, and for less reason. They married for a silly, meaningless title, and never married anyone as fascinating, as companionable or as intelligent as Dex Cartaret. Of course, it hadn't worked for them. None of those heiresses stayed married. But Andrea was different. She would make it work.

But she had to get him before it was too late.

Waking up early to a rainy fall day, Andrea hoped that Dex would call her before he went down to the bon voyage party on the *France*. At eleven o'clock, after having looked unsuccessfully for his number in the phone book, she took a pill to calm the nervous flutter in her stomach and called Alec at his midtown office.

"I'd like to get hold of Aunt Brooke. It's about a shop she mentioned. They have some lovely Limoges china that I'd like to get for Jany's collection. Dad and I add to it whenever we can."

If Alec was surprised, he didn't sound it.

"She has a luncheon at the St. Regis at one, but I'll leave a message there for her to call you."

"I'd appreciate that." She needed something else. "But she may go on to Mr. Cartaret's apartment first, to ... to touch up her makeup or something. Let's see ... That's on Forty-fifth? No. Forty-sixth?"

Alec took all this fumbling at face value. "Dex has a little place on Forty-seventh. East of Third Avenue. A three-story brownstone. Near a sidewalk cafe, if you can believe it in this weather. Why?"

117

"No reason. It doesn't matter. I'll call later today. I have a fitting in about fifteen minutes. 'Bye."

She decided to wear one of those glamorous outfits Dex had helped her buy. The Givenchy would be perfect. An elegant beige knit, which clung to her figure as if it were made for her. She put it on, smoothed it over her hips and adjusted the low neckline. She stepped back to look in the mirror. A dress fit for a seduction, she thought. If this dress didn't help to win him, nothing would.

Feeling courageous, she swept past the hotel doorman and signaled a taxi on Fifth Avenue.

By the time she got out on Third Avenue, after glimpsing the sidewalk cafe in the distance, she found that some of her confidence had evaporated. It was raining hard and she had to hurry along against the blinding spray. She passed the empty sidewalk cafe.

At least she knew she had come to the right neighborhood. With her feet squishing in her rain-drenched high-heeled alligator pumps, she made a dash along the street toward a three-story brownstone with a narrow front.

The forbidding front door was locked. She knocked. Nothing happened. Dark strands of hair lashed across her cheek and she pushed them away. She was going to be a real sight when Dex saw her. Would he think her worth having?

The woman who finally came to the door in answer to Andrea's banging looked her up and down suspiciously. The lanky woman was dressed neatly, and her hair was pulled back in a bun.

"Are you looking for someone?"

"Yes. My cousin, Mr. Huntington, sent me over. I have a message for Mr. Dexter Cartaret. Is this the right house? I could hardly see the address through all that rain."

The woman looked at her without enthusiasm.

"He isn't here," she said, "but if you want to leave a message, I'll give—I'll be happy to give it to Mr. Cartaret."

Andrea stood her ground on the top step. She sounded more self-assured than she felt.

"Thanks a lot. I appreciate that. But you don't know my cousin. I'll just stick around. He should be back here any minute now." She only hoped Aunt Brooke didn't show up with Dex.

The woman looked as if she would object but another voice called to her from the front room near the street door.

"There's a draft, Hattie. I'm getting a draft."

"All right, mother. I'll just be a minute." The lean woman looked understandably flustered. She started toward the apartment, stopped, gave Andrea another quizzical look. "If you want to wait here in the hall, you're welcome." As she went into her own apartment, she gave Andrea a parting shot. "All the apartments are locked."

"Hattie!" the old woman called again and the harassed landlady closed the apartment door.

Andrea took a breath, looked around and saw a stiff, uncomfortable ladderback chair opposite the newel post of the narrow staircase. The blue carpet runner seemed fairly new, and so did a similar runner lining the staircase. The overhead light fixtures were frosted globes, and there was a Tiffany-style lamp perched on a tiny round side table beside the chair.

Outside, the rain slackened and then stopped altogether. Two figures came up the front steps.

"Please, not Aunt Brooke!" she prayed silently.

Through the small etched pane of glass in the door she saw Dex's face clearly as he stopped to get out his keys. The person behind him, thank God, appeared to be a man. Dex's expression was thoughtful, far from lighthearted, with a gentleness in those somber eyes.

He opened the door, stood aside and a stout, elderly man with a bushy white mustache thanked him for unlocking the door and started for the staircase. Obviously another tenant. The man gave Andrea a faintly surprised glance, murmured, "Mornin', ma'am" and went on up the stairs.

Dex had taken several steps before he noticed her. He stopped in his tracks.

"Good God!"

She didn't know how to take that. She stood where she was and smiled shyly.

"Would you be a good Samaritan and take in a drowned cat?"

His face relaxed and he took her arm.

119

"Drowned kitten, you mean. Come along." On the way upstairs he shook her arm lightly. "You really shouldn't be allowed up here alone. You know that."

"Why?"

"Forget it." They reached the second floor but he kept going. "Third floor, front. When you visit a man's rooms you must accept all the unpleasant surroundings."

"I think this is a very nice house, if you live alone." She added on a sudden half-humorous, half-panicky note, "You do live alone, I hope."

He didn't answer her but instead hustled her along the third-floor hall to the door of an apartment overlooking the street.

It was a surprisingly pleasant studio, with a small dressing room and bath, and a kitchenette. The room itself, lighted by three long windows with an eastern exposure, was furnished like a London men's club, with leather couches and lots of bookcases. There were two prints of Turner landscapes on the back wall.

He let her go. "Seen enough to make up your mind you've come to the right place?"

"It's just as I pictured it. Except more comfortable." She went around admiring the pieces of furniture, the big, worn leather chair that must be his favorite, a stock of *Country Life* magazines beside the chair, a London *Times* and a Paris *Match* lying on the couch.

Andrea heard the click of the lock as the hall door closed behind Dex Cartaret. She then realized that she hadn't prepared herself for this moment, and didn't even know what to say.

Dex crossed the room toward her with a slow stride that made her more nervous. She had come here hoping he would try to make love to her—now it looked to her, judging by the light in his eyes, that he might simply assume this was all she wanted. It might even be all *he* wanted. Ever.

Her boldness disappeared, and she began to back away, laughing nervously.

"Now, hold on."

"Oh, I will. *I will!*"

He was laughing now.

He reached for her, caught her around the waist and neck

and tilted her chin up. The pulse-pounding excitement of his touch affected her more than his strength. She felt herself falling under his spell.

Then something clicked inside of her and Andrea yanked herself away from him. Now it was *his* turn to look hurt and amazed.

He stared hard into her eyes. She thought he was going to shake her any minute.

"Just what is it you're after?"

"I'm in love with you. Can't you tell?"

He did shake her. "There is more to it than that. I've heard that line before. If that's all you're after, let me know. The couch is behind you."

She was hurt, puzzled by his coarseness and his rejection. But she gathered her wits together and looked at him as she spoke.

"I *did* come here originally hoping to seduce you. But as you saw just now, I couldn't go through with it." Andrea willed herself not to cry. "Damn it, Cartaret, I *do* love you. Enough to want to be your wife."

He stood there dumbstruck for several seconds. Even Andrea herself was now speechless. Dex let her go, turned away from her and stared out the window. Outside, double-parked trucks blocked a line of traffic and the honking began.

For once, she felt that she had the upper hand in their so-called relationship. She regained her composure and needled him lightly, "I know the streets of New York are endlessly fascinating, but I'd be willing to bet that San Francisco could be just as exciting." She watched him turn to face her. She couldn't believe that what she saw in his eyes was pain. He must be just surprised. There was also tenderness, and now as he looked searchingly into her eyes she knew he loved her.

"Dex, my mother left my father when I was a child. She ran after a dream—and found it, I hope. My father wasn't so lucky. His struggles with the studio are far from over. But I think you'll love them both."

"I know." His tone was grave but she hoped her honesty created a lightening of his mood. After a moment, she thought she saw his lips twitch, as if at the memory of some private joke. "Then it must be your grandfather who ran the diner." With one finger he traced her profile from forehead to chin. The feathery touch made her shiver and he seemed to relax.

She remembered those lovely hours before she knew her grandparents were dead, before everything changed. She smiled. "I know you're making fun of me. You think I'm young, just a silly schoolgirl. But that doesn't matter, I've grown up a lot in the past few weeks. And I've learned a lot about myself. Enough to know that I don't want to be just another woman in your life. You're free, aren't you? You're not married or anything?"

He felt for the rolled leather arm of the couch as if he needed the support of something solid. She still couldn't guess whether he would take her up on her offer or not. His lips were on the verge of smiling, but she was troubled by the somber look in his eyes. He held out his hands, both palms up, as if he were seeking forgiveness.

"No. I'm not currently married. I was, once. But we proved too expensive for each other. Terri lives in Mexico somewhere. So it looks as though you and I will have to have a serious talk."

She put her hands in his. "You do love me a little bit, don't you?"

He sounded matter-of-fact. "Oh, yes. I think you could safely say I love you." He added, "You might even say more than a little bit." She preferred the reassurance in his eyes. Their gaze held hers in the silence that followed, until his fingers curled around her hands, tender and warm. Still he kept looking deep into her eyes.

"Is it because you think I'm buying you?" she asked, her voice a hoarse whisper.

He gazed at her hands in his, brought them to his lips and kissed them softly.

"I don't intend to be bought by you, my darling."

My darling ... the words brought a rush of warmth.

"Is that a rule you just made up for me?" she asked, smiling now.

"Righto."

122

"Is it why you walked out on me that day in San Francisco?"

He said nothing. She read his answer in his troubled gaze, and assumed her most businesslike tone.

"If you're worried about being 'bought,' then think of our relationship this way. I need you. I never expected to come into any of my grandfather's property until I was much older—past forty, anyway."

"Older," he murmured. She felt touched and saddened by his smile. "My darling child, have you ever asked yourself how old I am? I will be forty years old in three years. To you, that's *old*."

She had asked for that. She rested her cheek for an instant against his hands. She felt him kiss her rain-spattered hair. Very slowly, she turned her head until his mouth was on hers, hot and demanding. He was rough with her, as if he were releasing some hidden demon.

They broke apart, breathless. Somehow, all the tension in the room had vanished. For some reason they began to laugh. It was the right moment to go on. Andrea cleared her throat.

"Well then, Dexter Léland Cartaret, my cousin Alec thinks you're terrific with investments."

"Just lucky."

"Okay. But I've got lots of investments. Couldn't you be both my husband and my counselor? My business manager. With a salary."

"My sweet child, are you buying me?"

She refused to be deterred. "Did Grandpa buy Sam Liver-sedge?"

"Well..."

"I desperately need a business adviser of my own. I just don't trust Sam or the rest of them. Faith says—"

"Faith?"

"My friend, Faith Cortlandt. She doesn't let my money scare her. She tells me the truth, straight out. Can't you be like Faith? I need honest people around me."

"My darling, love sometimes makes lovers dishonest. All right. Let's suppose I'm like Faith, whatever that means."

"Don't tease me. Listen." She shook his hands excitedly.

"You would make a percentage on the profits you make in handling my affairs. Other people make prenuptial agreements. Why can't we? What do you say?"

He had settled on the arm of the couch and she knelt before him, watching him, her eyes wide and hopeful. He waited so long, just studying her face as if he would memorize it.

Suddenly, moving fast, he stood up and raised her to face him.

"Andrea Lombard, will you marry me? There, *that* makes it official."

She put her arms around his neck and kissed him.

"Does that mean yes?" he asked, smiling.

"Oh, Dex, I love you. Of course it's yes."

"Now," he went on in a conversational tone, with that humorous twinkle in his eyes, "Where do we go from here?"

THIRTEEN

THE PHONE kept ringing until finally Faith rolled over to the side of the bed where Frank lay sleeping.

Frank had been spending the nights with her there ever since the episode with Sam Liversedge. He was used to getting early calls here from his students, but never this early... Wondering who it could be, he pulled himself together and reached across the bed. He tipped over the cream-colored phone and managed to get hold of it.

"Hello? Me? Who is this?"

It was Andrea Lombard giggling and slightly hysterical.

Frank could have kicked himself for answering the phone this time.

"Is it you, Frank? How romantic! Are you and Faith enjoying yourselves in the old mausoleum?"

Faith was listening in now, with her head close to the earpiece. She grinned at Frank. She knew Andrea's question had embarrassed him.

"Uh—very much. I, uh, just dropped by before classes began to see Faith, check up on her, you know—"

"Frank, it's five A.M. in San Francisco." Andrea laughed. "Anyway, it doesn't matter. I just called to let you two know I'm getting married."

Faith didn't miss Frank's reaction, and it annoyed her. Just when things were going so well between them. He hesitated, then asked in a strained voice. "Isn't this a little sudden, Andrea? I hope it's someone you know. Not some guy who just read about your...well..."

125

"I know what you mean, Frank. It's all settled. I'm going to have a contract drawn up. A prenuptial agreement, and Dex is perfectly willing to sign it."

Frank persisted. "I just hope you're not falling into a trap. Listen, kid, things aren't always what they seem."

"Don't worry, Frank. I appreciate your concern but he's wonderful, believe me. Let me talk to Faith."

"Sure thing." He handed over the phone, covering the mouthpiece with his palm. "I told you that girl would fall into the first trap that presented itself. She's a babe in the woods, poor kid."

Poor kid, my eye! Faith laughed to herself.

"Hi, Andrea. What's this about you falling into traps? 'Things aren't always what they seem?' Frank is full of clichés this morning. Maybe because it's five A.M."

"I know. I hadn't realized until I called you. No wonder father blew his stack. Oh, Faith, I'm sorry. Listen. I'm getting married."

Faith rolled her eyes. "Not two months into multimillion-airehood and you've already bought yourself a peck of trouble."

"Don't, Faith, I wanted to ask your advice. I just called father and he's furious. He says he'll stop it if it kills him. Or me. Jany says I ought to be ashamed of what I've done to daddy. Can you beat it?"

The news was shocking, both the marriage idea and the violently negative reaction of her father and stepmother. Faith had no doubt Jany Lombard was thinking of the money. They wouldn't be able to tap the till so easily, Faith presumed, with Andrea being advised by a man she clearly adored.

Andrea went on. "I wondered if you have any suggestions."

"Number one, get a food taster. And stay away from high places."

"Faith, that's not funny."

"It's not meant to be. Wait 'til you hear the wrath of old Sam Liversedge. Well, who's the lucky entrepreneur?"

Andrea's spirits rose. "You're actually responsible, Faith. You called my attention to him."

"Me!" It was the last thing she expected. "You mean he's a friend of mine? Who?"

"I hope he'll soon become your friend. Remember the last time we had dinner in the Ruby Room?"

Faith's attention was momentarily distracted as Frank got up and began to dress quickly. He would soon be headed for Cal to get ready for his eight o'clock class.

"Yes, yes. I remember. Don't tell me it's that insolent maître d'."

"Don't be silly. Do you remember the dark-haired Englishman who sat at the banquette opposite us? You said he was looking at me. He was."

"Oh, my God!" From a tiny flirtation to have this grow! "So he followed you to New York and latched onto you. Honestly, Andrea."

"I followed him. He was in New York. Alec knew him in London during the Blitz. He's quite respectable, believe me. In fact, Aunt Brooke knows him too."

"That's no recommendation." Faith became aware of an offended silence on the other end and softened her tone. So much for the honesty that Andrea Lombard professed to admire. "However, you know what you want. Whatever else he may be, he certainly looked presentable. Why don't you bring him home and let us all meet this wonder?"

"Oh, Faith, if I could count on you and Frank. Do me a big favor. Persuade Frank to be nice. Only you can do it."

Faith wasn't averse to flattery. "I'll do my best, but you know Frank. But what were you going to ask me? You said you wanted my advice. Not, surely, about marrying this joker."

Andrea laughed. "We're getting married, all right. I proposed first, as a matter of fact."

"You're kidding!"

"What's good enough for Queen Victoria is good enough for me. No, Faith, this is serious. How can I bring daddy and Jany over to my side? I think mother would take it in stride, but it's so soon after my grandparents'... you know. Think, Faith. Help me out."

Faith's instincts had been appealed to. "Alec Huntington is this guy's friend. That ought to help you out with your father. Wasn't he in the Blitz too? You know. Brothers-in-arms. All that."

"Well, maybe. I'll talk to Alec first. He can help me with Aunt Brooke, too."

"A man who looks like the fellow I saw should be right up Brooke's alley. You shouldn't have any trouble with her."

"That's what you think." Andrea didn't explain further. "Okay, anyway, you're invited to the wedding, wherever it's held. I'll let you know soon. 'Bye now. Give my love to Frank and take care of yourself."

The phone connection went dead.

Frank came into the room, fully dressed now. His sandy hair hung rakishly across his forehead, and Faith thought she had never seen him look so handsome.

"She's really going to marry the fellow?" he asked.

"I think she is. But who knows how long it'll last? She's young still."

He grinned. "Don't be cynical. Some day you may be a bride. You want people to talk about your marriage like that?"

"Is that a proposal?"

"Not on my salary. Now, stop scowling. I had lunch with the chancellor yesterday. He thinks I have a good chance of making associate professor. Give or take a year. What are you thinking about," he asked, noticing that she'd suddenly become quiet.

"Nothing."

What they couldn't do with just a little of Andrea Lombard's fortune...

Frank picked up his lecture notes for his eight o'clock class and sat down on the edge of the bed to read them. Faith hopped out of bed and hurriedly slipped a skirt and blouse on and ran a comb through her pale blonde hair.

"How about breakfast?" she asked.

"Sorry, I've got to get going."

She reminded him, "It's early. You've got time before you have to go."

"Look, Faith, I've got to go. I didn't get where I am by being late for classes." His voice was abrupt.

"And where is that, Frank?" Faith was hurt. "You're the guy who wastes his time feeling sorry for poor little rich girls." She knew she sounded awful but couldn't help herself.

"So do you," he remarked mildly. "I saw you tiptoeing around Steve Lombard's study last night. You couldn't bring yourself to foul the girl up by stealing those property files, could you?"

The truth was, she couldn't. At the last minute she had told herself she was bored by the whole sneaky business.

Faith had been horribly afraid of the possibility that Frank would himself fall in love with Andrea—the girl who possessed everything in the world Faith wanted. It would be just like Andrea to wind up with a mountain of money and Frank Kelly, too. And it was this jealousy that prompted her to go into Steve's study, even if she couldn't go through with taking the files.

I wish I could hate our lucky heiress, she thought. What had made her respond when Andrea called for help? At least now she didn't have to worry about Frank...

Faith walked Frank downstairs.

"I'd give a lot to know what all her relatives will do about this," Faith said, not looking at Frank. "Not to mention the Liversedge crowd. I'll bet every one of them will want to wring her neck over this. They all have their hands out in some way, you know."

"Do they?" Frank asked, smiling. He kissed her cheek and left.

Dex called just as Andrea hung up with Faith and Frank. Andrea felt a lot better just hearing his voice. It helped to diminish all the prickling little doubts that had come to her during her conversation with Faith and Frank.

"Dex, you've no idea how good it is to hear your voice."

"You'd have heard it an hour ago, sweetheart, but you have a remarkably busy phone."

"That was daddy. And then Jany. And then Faith and her boyfriend, Frank Kelly."

There was a moment's silence. "And do they all approve of me?"

"Well..." She rushed on guiltily. "They do and they don't. But darling, they will. They have only to get to know you.

Frank and Faith will come around right away."

"Good old Faith."

"What?"

He changed the subject. "I've been thinking, Andrea. This should be my concern, not yours. I'll talk to Alec and Brooke. I may even convince your stepmother. Though I wouldn't wager much on your father accepting me. Fathers don't look kindly on a son-in-law when they think he comes with a price tag."

"Don't joke."

"I'm very much afraid it's not a joke. Anyway, I love you, little one." He hung up.

He had said he loved her, even if he tacked on the little-one bit...

Dex showed up half an hour later, kissed her elaborately in front of everyone in the outside hall and pretended to be insulted when she laughed. He took her downstairs to breakfast, but despite his efforts to calm her during breakfast and later in the limousine, she began to get more and more nervous as the moments passed. She kept rehearsing aloud what she would say to Alec and Aunt Brooke.

"I'm the guilty party, sweetheart. I believe the expression is 'no visible means of support.' So why don't you let me make my pitch? I can defend myself, I think. Within limits."

"Oh, Dex, I know." She leaned her head back against his outstretched arm. "I need your help terribly in my business. You have to help me fight Sam Liversedge and the others. If not, they'll never let me assume control of my inheritance."

He drew her to him thoughtfully.

"Where did you get that idea about Liversedge?"

"He's so anxious to run things. He makes it seem as if I can't raise a finger, make a single decision without him. Faith says I ought to stand on my own two feet. Let him know the estate is mine. Not his."

"Ah, Faith."

"But she's right. Steve made his own decisions. He didn't have to come to Sam all the time. And I'm Grandpa Steve's heir. Sam should treat my ideas with more respect."

"I see. Your ego is fragile."

"That's not it at all."

"Never mind. Isn't this the UBC building? I'll try and handle Alec," he paused. "If you agree."

She did. He had hurt her feelings when he seemed to make fun of her business sense and her attempt to fit into Steve's shoes, but she knew this was no time to make a fuss about it.

On the eighteenth floor they were met by glass-block walls and a battery of secretaries. They were ushered through the office of Mrs. Munks, the assistant to the vice-president and on to Alec, the vice-president. His office was less impressive than his assistant's, though it did have two windows, one of which had a clear view of Radio City Music Hall.

Mrs. Munks, slightly breathless, tried to announce Andrea and Dex, but Alec waved her away impatiently. He was calm and businesslike as usual, although when he began to speak his tone was more brusque.

"Sit down."

Dex began. "I think you should know, Alec, I intend to go straight. Isn't that how it's put?"

Alec waved this aside. "It's irrelevant. I've heard from Tony. How old are you exactly, Andrea?"

"Almost twenty-two."

"Then that is one obstacle overcome. Your father thinks he can stop you legally. He can't. I must say, he doesn't sound like the devil-may-care Tony Lombard I grew up with."

"It's not my life he's worried about. I just know it's the money," Andrea said bitterly. The two men looked at her. She had a flashing memory of all the good times with her father when she was a child. Now it was a question of money. . . .

"She doesn't mean that," Dex told Alec, as though Andrea couldn't speak for herself.

Alec shrugged. "What Andrea means or even thinks about Tony's motives wouldn't matter at this point except for the fact that Tony expected to inherit and didn't. I know something of the financial structure of Prysing Productions. If Tony inherited Steve's estate he would plough it all back into a string of those overblown epics."

"Well then maybe I can *buy* his good opinion."

"No!" Alec's low-key voice was unexpectedly sharp. "Don't try to bribe him. You'll only be feeding a voracious appetite.

131

Not Tony's, but Tony's dream of rising above his father. Now, about this marriage. I know your word is good, Dex. No one knows better. But you are an expensive guy."

"Let's get one thing straight." Alec and Andrea both turned to look at Dex. Andrea saw that familiar nervous tic, the muscle or nerve that throbbed faintly in his left cheek. Despite his pretense, Dex was disturbed. "There is to be a contract. We both sign. I am employed by Miss Andrea Lombard, or Mrs. Dexter Cartaret, as business manager, with a limit to my bargaining power and two signatures necessary when I make any move over and above the amount the two of you agree upon. You, Alec, are the other signatory."

Andrea felt enormously proud of her fiancé at this moment, but Alec was matter-of-fact.

"That sounds quite satisfactory. If Andrea asks me, I'll sign. You two will make your official residence in California?"

Dex hesitated before Andrea piped up. "Of course we will." Alec smiled.

"I'm sure you both know that California has some very handy community property laws." Andrea sat there with her mouth open. Dex colored a little. Neither of them spoke. Alec shrugged.

"Just a reminder. I don't think there can be too much of a problem. Depending on how long the marriage lasts."

It took Andrea a few seconds for the words to sink in. She felt Dex become rigid beside her and this added to her own outrage. Very slowly, she got to her feet. She kept thinking of her mother's speech long ago in the movie *Journey*, based on Eden's own experience. It was 1938, and Eden had turned to the Nazi agents on the Zurich Express with the proud words: *"You've got the wrong party. If you think that, you don't know me at all."*

She heard herself saying it aloud. Alec stood up and tried to reason with her. But he had gone too far. They all had.

"For two months I've listened and listened," she thundered. "No one thinks I know what I want. I've got news for you. I do know." She shook her fist at Alec. "What we do is our business. You think it won't last. But that's our business, too."

She felt Dex's hand on her wrist but she shook it off. Apparently, he didn't understand either. "No. I mean it. It's perfectly clear to me that if Alec, of all people, thinks this way, everyone else does. When I get married, it's going to be a private affair. You'll see. All of you."

Dex reached for her but she snatched her hand away and started past Alec's neat mahogany desk. Dex got to his feet when they were both stopped in their tracks by Aunt Brooke.

She stood like a fiery-eyed goddess, shutting out Mrs. Munks with a kick of her spike heel against the closing door. Worse, she was smiling.

"If it isn't the lovebirds! I just had a call from Eden. She heard the glad tidings from Tony. I see I'm not the first to congratulate you." She stared over Andrea's head at Dex. "Darling, congratulations. How clever of you! I had no idea you were open for bids on marriage. Why didn't you let me in on it—"

"Are you coming, Dex?" Andrea's voice was cold. Before today she had never before shown this defiance of her family. But all she heard here were insults and humiliations.

Even Alec lost his temper. "Mother, for God's sake! You're only making it worse."

Dex had Andrea's arm by this time and was trying to calm her. "Listen, they have no reason to think otherwise of me. Or of you. It's up to us to show them."

"Nobody talks to me like that. Nobody."

Aunt Brooke's laughter tinkled after them. "Got your attendants picked out yet? How about letting me give the groom away?"

Andrea heard Alec's disgusted, "Mother!" Then she and Dex passed rapidly out of the office and into the hall, where Andrea refrained from tears with an effort.

Dex caressed her hair, holding her close, murmuring comfort. But gradually his manner changed. He sounded almost stern when he spoke.

"Look at me."

She looked up. He held her chin in his palm.

"I want you to remember something. I love you. Whatever you may think or have heard, I don't make love to women for money. I have a very small income which helps me exist. I have

133

a great many friends and they do expensive things...Let's say I *had* friends...But I never asked any of my rich lady friends to marry me."

"I asked you," she reminded him.

"Why do you think I hesitated? I knew how it would be."

She persisted. "What made you say yes, then?"

"Because you were the only woman I have ever loved who genuinely needed me. You may think that's funny, but it happens to be true." She wondered what he meant by that. His voice was utterly serious. "I wanted to be needed. So I'm willing to face these unpleasant suspicions because I know I'm not quite what they think I am. But you've got to know it, too."

"I do know, Dex. I trust you."

"I want you to know what my past history was like," he went on, his tone suddenly flat, lifeless. "I've been a professional guest. That is, I had my gourmet meals and my first wife Terri and I had the best guestrooms, so long as we provided entertainment for the other guests. Wit, I guess you'd call it. We had to be witty and slightly cynical, and flirtatious. In return, food and lodgings of the highest quality."

"Did you do that for very long? Didn't your wife feel that you ought to...to go to work?"

He smiled. "Terri called what we did...work."

She found all this perversely fascinating.

"Why did you and your wife divorce?"

He studied her dark hair and ran the soft, wavy strands through his fingers.

"Terri was an even more pleasant guest than I."

"She was unfaithful to you?"

He laughed hoarsely. "She wound up in Acapulco with a Formula-One racer she met in Monaco. After him she promptly took up with a Mexican industrialist. Neither married her."

"Is she still there?"

He didn't appear too interested. "Possibly. The divorce papers came from there. That was six years ago."

This was the excuse she had been searching for. His wife's infidelity. He guessed her thought and shook his head.

"No. It goes back further. I couldn't seem to settle down after forty-five. Terri was singing in a London club during the war.

134

We shared a few buzz bombs in forty-four. That's when we married. We were both nineteen. Then, after the war...as I said, it was all over. The gut fear...the dread...the way you made every minute count. Nothing was left, except drifting around all those manor houses, providing a few cynical wisecracks, being wined and dined...The only thing I really got excited about was when somebody asked my advice about something. Clothes or wine. Trivial stuff. Sometimes it was a stock or bond venture. When friends followed my hunch and made a profit, it was an accomplishment of sorts."

"You have a wonderful flair for things, Dex. Don't ever forget that."

He rang for the elevator, but his mood remained somber. "I meant what I said, sweetheart. I need your trust, and I honestly think you need me. Because it's all over if you share for one moment their belief about me."

She had never been so moved. She hugged him so hard he winced. As he held her tightly against him she began to get her spirits back. The world looked sparkling and glorious again.

"We've still got two that I think we can count on. My friend Faith, and Frank Kelly. You'll like him. And you'll like Faith, once you get used to her."

"She sounds dangerous to me," he observed, but he smiled and kissed her forehead. Then, as she lifted her face his lips moved gently to her mouth, just as the elevator stopped. They found themselves entertaining an interested audience of newsmen. One of them had brought forth a camera and snapped a picture of the radiant lovers—for posterity and the next morning's edition.

135

FOURTEEN

"I WANT to get married immediately. Today. I'll show them all," Andrea announced as they stood in the hall outside her suite.

Neither Dex nor Andrea had spoken about their plans during the ride back to the hotel. She had hoped he would say something before now but here she was, making the advances again, this time with the door of her suite half open and he hadn't come in with her.

He just stood there with one arm extended over her head against the door. That gentle, unhappy look in his eyes made her uneasy.

"I know. You'd rather not. You've decided you don't like my awful family after all."

He leaned forward, playfully rubbed his nose against hers. "No such thing. but we do have those few legal technicalities to take care of first. I sign a disclaimer to any and all of your properties. Remember?"

"But can't that wait 'til after—"

"No." His finger sealed her lips. "Just as you originally described: I keep half of any profits I make for you. That will be my income."

"I wish you wouldn't talk like that. When we're married what's mine will be yours. And vice versa."

He was patient as though she were a child.

"We've got to get these things out of the way now. You know that. I told you I have my pride, too. If I married an heiress and had acccess to her fortune, I'd be exactly what certain members of your family believe I already am."

"Not if I want to give it to you."

"What would be the difference?"

"Men! So technical."

"Do you have a law firm in New York?"

She didn't. "But daddy's studio has. Alec probably knows."

He smiled. "I still think I can make him see that I have your best interests at heart. Suppose I try again without the interference of women—that means you and Brooke."

She knew she had behaved stupidly with her cousin, but it hurt to find that for all Alec's worldly aplomb he shared the general idea that the marriage wouldn't last. Like everyone else he thought that no one would marry her except for her money.

"If you think it will help. But we don't need to go crawling to them."

"I'll try not to." He cuffed her under the chin, got her to smile, kissed her softly and started for the elevators.

She wished he would stop treating her like a child. . . .

That afternoon she placed a call to Prysing Productions in Culver City but couldn't reach her father. He was out, she was told, on the back lot, supervising scenes for *Klondike.*

Not getting through to her father was Andrea's usual experience—a far cry from the way it had been in her childhood, before Tony took control of the studio. In those days, while Eden Ware was working toward her first Oscar, Tony had been the one to keep their small daughter company, play with her, listen to her, care for her. As a writer and assistant director he could afford the time. He wasn't responsible then for hundreds of jobs and millions in borrowed money.

Andrea then tried her mother's apartment in Hollywood but the woman at the switchboard said that Miss Ware had hurried out early in the day, carrying a suitcase.

That was her mother. Probably in Hawaii or Hong Kong by now.

Andrea called the Nob Hill house but even Faith let her down. She was out shopping.

The incoming calls began shortly after. Newspapers, photographers, even two Washington, D.C., columnists wanted the rumors of her "elopement" confirmed. She took the phone off the hook and sat watching the clock, wondering why she hadn't heard from Dex yet.

137

Could they have talked him out of it, appealed to his "better nature," the way fathers and mothers-in-law were always doing in old movies?

When she heard the rapid knock on the hall door she rushed through both rooms and threw the door open. Eden Ware stood there with her arms outstretched and a big smile spread across her face. It was the smile—the sign of her approval—that got to Andrea first.

"Guess who?" the actress cried and wrapped her arms around Andrea.

"Mother! I never was so glad to see anybody in my whole life. Come in. You look so good to me."

"I certainly hope so. My Lord! Not a thing has changed. Good old Plaza. How I love this place! I never could wean your father away from the Waldorf. No matter. Here's my luggage. I haven't registered yet." She threw her dilapidated overnight case onto Andrea's bed and hugged her again.

"So you've fallen in love. And he's a perfectly lovely man who just happens to be—well, what?"

She hoisted herself onto the bed and patted the spread beside her. "Here. Come and tell me all about your beloved. Is he your first?"

"Don't be silly. We're waiting. I mean, things have moved so fast." Her mother gave no special reaction to that. Andrea sat down, wishing she hadn't been so frank. "There was a fellow at Cal. But that's irrelevant. I love Dex. And he's not after my money."

"Everyone is, darling. Even me, sometimes. It's human nature. Does he care anything about you? That's the key to it all. I couldn't stand poor Jany's whining this morning. And at practically the crack of dawn. All that la-de-da about how you're going to ruin Tony. I take it there's trouble on his ancient-Greece film and the company is rethinking the sets. Lord! It's a good thing my next is for Delorqua. All over France and Spain. The works. Imagine being paid to work in France!" Her lively eyes remembered days and times Andrea could never hope to live.

"Talk about first love. Mine was in Paris. A friend of the

family's—the comte André de Grasse. You were named for him, you know."

Andrea raised her head, suspicious of the implications. "Wasn't father jealous of him?"

"Heavens, no. Don't forget. I'm eight years older than Tony. He was too young when I knew André. Besides, Tony sowed his own wild oats. Anyway, André died getting his men out of Dunkirk." She shook off the painful memory. "So this Dexter Cartaret isn't the first."

"But he will be the last."

"Good girl. Remember it."

Andrea remarked to herself that her mother was as always showing herself to be a different breed from all others.

She got up and went to the phone.

"I'll send for some ice and stuff. What are you drinking now?"

"Something French, dear. Dubonnet. Martini...accent on the first and last syllables, not the middle one. It's an aperitif. Or Cinzano. When you're in Paris call it *San-zano*. Accent on the first syllable. Are you getting all this priceless guidance?"

"Yes, mother."

In her own sphere of knowledge Eden Ware was unsurpassed. Andrea finished phoning down her order and disappeared into the bathroom for her medication. Her ulcer had begun to act up this morning, and she hoped a pill would calm the twisting nervous burn in her stomach.

It was Eden who, assuming it was the liquor, answered the ring of the doorbell and almost fell into Dex's arms. Of the two of them he was more startled, but he recovered rapidly. Andrea hurried over to untangle things and saw that Dex had everything under control. He and Eden were shaking hands, but he turned quickly from her to take Andrea in his arms. She felt the warmth of his mouth and wondered if this was a consolation kiss. Had Alec talked him into the big renunciation scene?

"Where did you find him?" Eden asked Andrea. "Never mind. Here's the liquor. Darling, can you tip this young man?"

A bellman had appeared in the open hall doorway with an ice bucket and trolley. He assumed Dex was "darling" and turned to him. Dex gave him a bill and he vanished.

139

"Who's pouring?" Eden wanted to know.

Not used to mixing drinks, Andrea looked to Dex for help. He dropped an ice cube and lemon twist into Eden's Dubonnet and offered it to her.

"It suits you, Miss Ware. You are like Paris."

Eden sipped the drink. She had come straight from a long plane ride and an airport limousine, with barely any makeup and wearing an old suit. Yet she seemed to sparkle as Andrea watched her.

"Oh, Andrea, I like this man. How well he knows me! I spent my happiest years in Paris, poor as a church mouse, doing the damndest things to make a living. But I adored Paris."

Dex nodded agreement. He poured several fingers of scotch into his glass, more than Andrea usually saw him drink. She wondered if he was saving bad news.

"Now, Mr. Cartaret—Dexter," Eden began, between sips. "I hear you want to marry my daughter. I won't go into all the clichés about you and my little girl."

"Your big girl, mother."

Eden waved this aside as irrelevant but Dex smiled and reached for Andrea's hand. His other hand offered a folded blue packet to Eden.

"This is only a copy, Miss Ware. Alec Huntington has the original. It was drawn up by the solicitors who handle Alec's own will. They've done work for other UBC executives."

Andrea felt humiliated for him, although he himself didn't seem to feel it. The papers were undoubtedly his surrender of all her fortune.

"Dex, you didn't have to."

He ignored that. So did her mother, who actually read the document. She took her time, and when she got through she started to hand it to Dex, then thought it over and tapped the papers with her fingernails.

"Dexter, would you mind if I used this to smooth Tony Lombard's ruffled feathers?"

"Not at all, though I'd like Andrea to read it first. I'll ask Alec for extra copies."

Andrea waved it away.

"It doesn't matter," Dex said. "You'll have a copy in your safe deposit box, Andrea, any time you want to study it."

"And now for the fun part, the wedding details." Eden got up and strode back and forth, working out the entire ceremony and the honeymoon. "I don't suppose we can give you a true Lombard wedding. But that's no loss. Tony and I ran away to a funny little cow town called Vegas. Seems to be doing rather better for itself nowadays."

Dex agreed. "I'm afraid my background would make it a field day for the press. But I've given some thought to a quiet ceremony and then a long honeymoon in Europe. I know the Continent fairly well. And by the time we return, they will have someone else to gossip about. That is, if Andrea won't be disappointed."

"Not me." She tried to rid herself of a lifetime's worth of dreams about a white gown and veil... the stately walk down the Lombard staircase to Dex, looking so tall and handsome in his black tuxedo. The family would be gathered around the improvised altar in the ballroom, all of them still loving her. It would be like when Grandpa Steve married Randi Gallegher in 1918. And there would be a picture of Dex and his bride in Town & Country magazine. Maybe her gown would get a full page in Vogue....

Dex and Eden were both looking at her. She shrugged and played it lightly.

"It's much better this way. We'll be together sooner. And who ever turned down a honeymoon in Europe?" A few hours ago she had asked Dex to marry her at once. But the reality, in all its hurry and hint of disgrace, sickened her a little.

So it was settled that easily. Out went the bridal veil, the staircase and the loving family. She snapped her fingers, symbolizing to herself the popping of that childish memory-balloon. She had Dex and she loved him. She reminded herself that she had grown up an awful lot in two weeks.

FIFTEEN

IN THE end, nothing was heard from Tony Lombard, though Jany sent her love, along with a large package containing Andrea's remaining clothes, some of her jewelry that had been in the home safe and a refilled prescription for Andrea's ulcer pills. It was good of her, Andrea thought, and sent back her thanks. In her note she had asked for Tony's blessing and offered her own and Dex's love in return. There was no response. So the small, almost secret wedding went on without them.

Andrea and Dex were married in Eden Ware's spacious Plaza suite by a judge who was a friend of Eden's. The ceremony was so short Andrea was still staring nervously at the round face of Judge Mascogna when Eden gave a joyous "Amen!" and Dex lowered his head to kiss the bride.

Her lips were cool and trembling, but they warmed under Dex's touch. She threw her arms around his neck as he held her close.

"Our turn now." Andrea turned to find Frank Kelly and her mother standing behind them.

While Eden kissed the groom, Faith stood watching Frank, who gave Andrea a squeeze around the waist that lifted her off the floor.

"You've never looked prettier, Andrea. I wouldn't have missed it for worlds."

"I didn't want you to spend all that money making the long trip. I wanted—anyway, Frank, I wanted my friends around me."

"And Faith appreciates it, believe me." But as they both knew, Andrea had only been able to pay Faith's way for the occasion. Frank was as proud as Dex when it came to money.

"May you be as happy as you deserve to be," he said softly.

Confused and excited, she kissed his rough, sunburned cheek. "Thank you, Frank. I don't know about deserving, but I'll try."

The others were joking about the kiss Eden had bestowed on the bridegroom. Frank glanced over his shoulder.

"By the way, if you ever need anyone . . . well, as they say, you can count on us. Faith and I are both very fond of you."

Instead of pleasing Andrea, his remark saddened her. She didn't want to have to need anyone but Dex.

"Thank you, Frank. I do know. I'll remember."

"All right," Eden announced. "Where's my little girl?"

Dex surprised Andrea by correcting his new mother-in-law. "Your little girl is a grown-up married woman now, Eden."

"True. I'll have to remember. All right, darling, we've got to snap to it if you're flying out today. Somebody bring in the cake. And that reminds me. I set down a champagne glass that was half-full. Has anybody seen—Oh, Judge Mascogna, thank you. I think it's time to make a quick toast."

Everyone rushed to fill his or her glass. Andrea and Dex exchanged looks.

"We've got twelve minutes," he reminded Andrea.

Andrea knew her mother. "We'll make it, if we have to take off from the roof."

"Not this roof, I hope."

Eventually, everyone had a champagne glass and Eden Ware toasted. "Here's to this beautiful couple who have their lives before them. May they never lose that first, fine, careless rapture."

Andrea grinned. "Is that what we've got?" she asked out of the corner of her mouth.

"Let's sneak out."

"Can't. Have to cut the cake."

After this the bridal pair was allowed to rush out into the hall amid a trail of rice. Faith Cortlandt followed them out, and at the elevator she caught up with Andrea and hugged her.

"Honey, be happy."

"Thank you. And thank you for sending my things from the Nob Hill house. Dex is wonderful, isn't he?"

"He ought to be. I found him for you, remember?"

Then Eden gave her daughter one last kiss and her passport hurriedly acquired for her new name: *Andrea Cartaret.*

"Darling, have fun. Live a little. I'll patch things up with your father and Brooke. Don't you even think about it."

The elevator gave Dex and Andrea their first brief moment of privacy together since their return from Alec's office on the morning they announced their wedding plans. Dex seized the moment and drew her to him.

"God, I love you, sweetheart! Did I ever tell you that?"

She could only laugh shakily and urge him on. "Tell me more and I'll let you know."

He kissed her lips and murmured huskily, "I love your lips. I loved them the first night on the Wharf. And I love your funny voice."

"But what about the rest of me?"

"I'll take it if it goes with the package. I love your hair. Did I tell you—"

They had arrived in the Fifty-ninth Street lobby. She grinned at him. "Don't forget where you left off."

They got into her limousine and headed out for the airport. Andrea huddled down in the seat against the hollow of Dex's arm.

"I know we've got to fly. I don't want to be cooped up on board a ship for five days with people who stare and question us. We'd be prisoners." She sighed. "But I sure wish we didn't *have* to fly. I keep thinking of Steve and Randi."

He understood. On a sudden protective impulse he hugged her. "I know it's old advice, but it works. If you fall off your horse, you remount. At once. No time to think. Besides, there is one advantage to a jet. Before you know it, you're there."

"I know. Maybe if I were drunk it might help."

"With your wedding night in Paris waiting for you?"

"Not such a good idea. A drunken bride." She looked up, with a sensuous innocence that moved him deeply. "I wore a dress you picked out. Would you have liked me better in white, with a veil and all?"

Her wedding gown had doubled as a going-away outfit so they could make their escape before word got out to the press.

She wore a cream-colored wool jersey dress with a neckline that flattered her young, unlined neck and throat. Dex kissed her neck in approval.

She colored. "The chauffeur," she whispered.

But Dex was not moved by any concern for the chauffeur. He framed her face between his hands as if searching for something in her eyes.

She wondered what he hoped to see. Surely, he could sense how much she wanted him. She couldn't imagine anyone in the world who attracted and aroused her so much. Emotionally, she needed him. He had said he wanted to be needed. And she loved him. Surely, he could see that.

The champagne on board the Air France jet gave Andrea courage, and she was able to enjoy the thrill of arrival, if not the hours of en route flying. They were traveling as the unknown Mr. and Mrs. Dexter L. Cartaret and Dex thought it better to hire a taxi rather than an ostentatious limousine. He didn't want to tip off the European *paparazzi* who had certainly heard of Steve Lombard's granddaughter. For the same reason, the newlyweds didn't stay at either her father's favorite Hôtel George Cinq or her mother's perennial home away from home, the Crillon.

Somewhat wistfully, Andrea confided that she had always thought it would be nice to stay at the Ritz, but Dex laughed at that idea, pointing out that it was the quickest way to be hounded. She had to admit it was true, but unfortunately his own careful choice, the St. Jean Imperial, which sounded so nice when he described it, turned out to have deteriorated since his last stay.

They arrived at the St. Honoré *porte cochère* of the hotel about nine o'clock on an October night. The surrounding area of tightly shuttered stores presented a less-than-friendly atmosphere. The golden light over the gateway to the courtyard glowed in the darkness. Andrea felt chilled and apprehensive.

Overhead the sky was almost equally black. The night was moonless, starless and bone-chilling. Because he understood Andrea's depression after a wedding spurned by half of her closest relatives, Dex for the moment forgot about their plan

145

of not calling attention to themselves. He lifted Andrea with impressive ease and carried her across the ancient broken stones of the courtyard. The hotel's bellman, with their bags on his back and under his arms, seemed to find this American custom amusingly quaint.

The hotel lobby was modestly lit with one brassbound vitrine and a Tiffany-style lamp on a credenza. The concierge, who looked uncharacteristically friendly, watched the new arrivals with furtive interest. On the other hand, the woman behind the desk appeared harassed and eyed the Cartarets' five cases with grave apprehension. Andrea hoped Dex wouldn't have the heart to tell her that more was on its way, having been air-freighted separately.

"You are late, monsieur," the female clerk complained.

Dex had set Andrea down and was placing their American passports on the desk. He corrected her with perfect courtesy. "*Pardon*, madame, The plane was late. We are precisely on time."

She shrugged, looked down at her guest register.

"With the Automobile Show we are at capacity."

Dex persisted, quiet but firm.

"But you have reserved our suite on the *troisieme étage* as you confirmed in this letter. This is your signature, I believe."

The woman refused to look. "Perhaps. It is of no account. There are no rooms remaining. We are full."

"You must have something," Andrea pleaded, anxious to unpack and settle in.

"We are full. Nothing available."

"I am sure you have a room if you will give it a trifle more thought." Dex's voice was a shade louder, and very British, with a definite snap in the tone.

"Nothing. Absolutely, monsieur. Nothing. Except of course a double chamber on the *deuxieme étage.*"

Her blatant turnaround baffled Andrea. Dex, however, seemed used to this curious behavior.

"That will do nicely. May we see it please?"

"Certainly, monsieur. Nothing simpler." She signaled to the restive bellman who had been shifting his weight from one foot to the other. He hoisted the cases again, led Dex and Andrea to the elevator at the far end of the lobby, which appeared to Andrea to be a little in need of dusting and a change of drapes and the table runner for the elegant old pink marble console.

But it was quaint and probably would look charming by daylight, she thought, and was prepared to love it because it was Dex's choice.

The elevator evidently had been made to accommodate two and a half persons, and the three of them plus baggage proved a tight squeeze. Dex had one arm around Andrea but he looked very sober and avoided her amused glance. No humor there. The bellman stopped at the tallest door Andrea had ever seen. The doorknob was in the middle of the door, which she recalled from other visits to France, and above the knob the wood was split badly. When she heard the badly creaking floor underfoot she wondered if the St. Jean was actually a prerevolutionary relic.

The room overlooked the courtyard, and had two long windows. There was a huge gold plush armchair by one window. The dressing table with three mirrors was exceedingly French, as was the massive armoire. The worn carpet was a pale gold and the bathroom, with two sinks and a toilet in its own little stall was all that she might expect of a medium-priced Paris hotel room, including the bidet. She knew what that was, and said quickly when Dex looked as if he might explain, "I know. I know."

The bellman took his tip and went out, closing the door with a rusty screech. Removing his topcoat, Dex pointed to the twin beds, speechless at the idea of those two narrow beds for honeymooners. His expression of mock horror caused Andrea to burst out laughing and after a few seconds Dex joined her.

They clung to each other, still laughing, and finally sank together onto the closest bed, breathless and still joking.

Andrea loved his laugh and then, when he stopped, there was the way he looked at her, with that glittering hunger in his eyes. With their fully clothed bodies pressed hard against each other, their desire, which had been suppressed for so long, was now free.

She held out her arms to embrace him. Her hands slid under his shirt and she began to caress his back. With his fingertips he traced the outline of her mouh. Then he framed her face with his hands and began to kiss her hungrily—lips, neck, throat. She was aware of a growing passion as his hands moved with feather touches over her body. They undressed quickly, each unable to take their eyes from each other. The look of desire in her young face drove him mad with wanting her.

She whispered, "I love you so much."

He laid her gently back on the small bed. When he entered her he clasped her flanks close and she wound her legs around his hips, her throat arched back as she moaned softly with pleasure.

He was murmuring things. "Sweetheart...love me...love me...I need you so, my darling..."

She did love him. In many ways she needed him, and just as she had suspected, he was a perfect lover....

When they parted and lay back, breathless and radiant, they turned their heads to gaze once more at each other. They couldn't resist caressing each other's body.

Sounds of domestic argument in the hall outside their room broke the spell. A man and woman who sounded American were discussing at the top of their lungs just how many glasses of beer he had drunk at dinner.

Andrea grinned mischievously at Dex. "Not like us."

He laughed. "No, indeed. I seldom drink beer."

She pretended to pummel him but he defended himself too easily, holding her two wrists in his hands, surprising her with his strength. He drew her down onto his body until he was staring directly into her wide eyes.

"Are you happy, sweetheart?"

"Divinely. Are you?"

"My darling, I'll never be happier than I am this minute."

He said it so solemnly she felt she had to lighten the mood.

"Well then, prove it to me. I'm hungry."

"Hungry for my love?"

"Food. Cafes. Those wonderful, sneaky little places mother always talks about. Let's wash and change and go."

He struggled to get up, pretending she had exhausted him, but when he did get up he was ready before she was. She debated what dress to wear while she was opening the new

Vuitton case given her by Eden, and was unable to decide until Dex reached over her shoulder and took out an unobtrusive dress of black crepe with a grass-green roll collar and buttons down the back.

"But I thought I was supposed to show off in Paris."

"Not in Paris, my love, if you are going to a little cafe. And not at this hour."

"Okay, my wise old professor." As she spoke she had a sudden image of Frank Kelly, that wise *young* professor, and wondered how he would fit into this heady atmosphere. He had certainly grown up in an exotic enough way, judging by the places he pointed out in North Beach that night on the cable car.

She forgot Frank in the memory of that evening in Fisherman's Wharf when she thought she saw Dex in that shop. She had asked him about that night when they were in New York before the wedding, but he hadn't even known what she was talking about.

It remained a mystery. Someday she would find out about his feelings during those interminable days before they met again. Had he thought about her at all? Or had he really been in San Francisco to stake out Aunt Brooke?

I mustn't think of that. Forget it.

He buttoned her dress, nuzzling the back of her neck while he held up a layer of her thick hair. She reached over her shoulder and touched his cheek as he raised his head. He kissed her palm. She sighed.

"Oh, how I love you, Dexter Cartaret!" She gazed up innocently into his eyes. "I love you even more than the man I adored until a few weeks ago."

"Tell me more." There was a quiet tension about him. He must be jealous.

"I didn't know him well. But I had these fantastic dreams about him. He said his name was Leland, but I have my suspicions. You just can't trust characters like that. He was too good-looking."

His tension dissolved.

"Shall we?"

She knew he wanted to make love again, but she was also

149

dying to get out and see more of the mysterious Paris her mother had always told her tales about.

She took his arm. "After."

He pretended to be shocked by her choice.

"All right, then. Stand still, close your eyes and hold out your arms," he ordered.

She felt a curious strand of woven cords go over her wrist. It must be a bracelet. But something dangled from the cords. A purse?

"Now."

She opened her eyes. The cords she had felt were green silk and tasseled at the ends. The suspended weight was an elongated golden egg set with patterns of emeralds and diamonds. The clasp was one larger emerald. She was awestruck.

"It's—it's so lovely. Dex, it takes my breath away."

He was enormously pleased by her delight in it, the way she held it one way and then the other, flashing it in the light, cupping it in her two palms.

"I love it. It's the most beautiful thing I ever saw." She hugged him and kissed him in her enthusiasm. "What is it called?"

"It's called a *minaudiere*. You can use it as an evening bag. Open it."

Inside were a miniature powder compact and a tiny lipstick. Tucked in also was a green paper ball that proved to be a fifty-dollar bill.

"Your mad money."

"Oh, darling! I'll never be that mad. Not at you." More hugs and kisses. She loved it even more when he pointed out a scratch near the bottom of the egg.

"I didn't buy it, darling. My father gave it to my mother the night my sister Deirdre was born. If Deirdre were alive, it would be hers."

She was deeply touched. The sentiment made it infinitely more precious. It was a gift that came from his heart, and had nothing to do with money.

He started to remove it from her arm. "Shall we go to dinner before you starve to death?"

"I want to take it with me."

"Not where we are going."

150

"Okay. I'll drop it in my handbag."

It was a fair compromise. He got a good deal of pleasure out of noticing that she kept her hand in her open bag, constantly touching the golden egg.

She took the arm he extended with exaggerated courtesy, and they walked out into the dimly lit hall. The peeling door caught her attention. She ran a finger over the door just above the knob and then squinted her eye close to the door.

"Do you realize that if there was a light on someone could see us in our room? There's a hole clear through the door."

He laughed. "Looks as though we'll have to stuff it with paper." He dismissed her complaint lightly but she felt his disappointment and was sorry she had mentioned it.

In the lobby they were surprised and none too pleased when the concierge beamed and wished "Mademoiselle Lombard, a happy evening."

"Madame Cartaret," she told him, holding Dex's arm tightly.

"But yes, madame. However, a message has been delivered in the last few minutes. Special, I was told. Addressed to Mademoiselle—ah, it is Madame Lombard-Cartaret."

Andrea was delighted. "It must be from father. He's forgiven me." She ran to get the envelope, but the contents were disappointing. The cream-colored stationery was engraved in gold letters with the name: *Danielle deBrett Friedrich* with an address in the Fifteenth Arrondissement.

Andrea's stepmother Jany had a brother in Paris named Carl Friedrich. During the Lombard family's visits to Paris, Jany had made separate visits to her brother and his wife Danielle, but Tony and Andrea never went with her.

Andrea showed Dex the note. They read it together. It was written in broken English.

Ma chère Andrea,

I do so hope that the so-enchanting stepdaughter of our Jany has had a pleasant arrival in Paris. We write now to ask that we may welcome our niece Andrea and her new husband to our home. We have only heard of the wedding this evening by the radio.

Please call us on the telephone and we will drive over and take you up in our little car for a brief visit.

151

We extend our hospitality with great anticipation. It has always been a matter for deep concern to Carl that he has not seen you since your childhood.

What a delightful child he says you were!

I embrace you for your Uncle Carl.

Yours with sincerity,

TANTE DANIELLE

"Sounds like a bit of an opportunist," Dex remarked.

"I've always been puzzled about Jany's brother and his family. I seem to remember he was nice to me when I was about five or so. But Danielle—she did something. I'm not sure exactly what—I think she was a communist right after the war. She tried to get father in trouble. She made people think he was a communist when he wasn't."

The concierge was taking all this in with interest. Dex guided her toward the front doors.

"Does she have a telephone?"

"The number isn't in the letter, at any rate. Mother told me this Danielle was a beauty." She yawned, then stifled it quickly. "Do you suppose she's still a communist?"

He laughed. "Not in that district. If I know the type, she's turned into a very proper *bourgeoise* and wouldn't be caught dead with her old comrades. I wonder, though, what her husband's like."

Andrea reached into her purse and took out one of her ulcer pills. Her stomach was burning. She swallowed it quickly without water when Dex turned to drop off the room key.

"I'll tell you one thing, Dex. Danielle's got to have heard about the money coming to me. That's plain."

"Sweetheart, you're a worse cynic than I am."

"Well, she's harmless enough, I suppose. And she can't get anything from me that I don't want her to have."

They strolled out into the courtyard whose walls, the wings of the ancient hotel, shrouded the area in complete darkness at each corner. Only the lights on either side of the *porte cochère* across the cobblestones showed them their way.

Andrea could hardly keep her eyes open—the excitement of

the long day seemed to have been too much for her. She knew that Dex was watching her.

"Are you all right, sweetheart?"

She didn't want to give in to her weariness.

"Great. It feels wonderful to be in Paris at night. I love it." She felt the golden egg in her handbag and looked up at Dex. "I love you too."

"I certainly hope so." He held her close to his body.

They stepped out onto the sidewalk of the Rue St. Honoré. The ancient street had seen everything, including the tumbrels that had carried the condemned toward the tall wooden uprights and slanting blade of the guillotine.

They hadn't gone more than half a dozen steps before Andrea stumbled over a crack in the sidewalk. This time Dex paid no attention to her protests.

"We're going back. We'll order supper in. Shall I carry you?"

"Heavens, no! I'm just sleepy. That's all." But she welcomed the hard strength of his arm. "It's strange, I'm not usually so foggy."

"You're not foggy, my love. We should never have left New York right after the ceremony. It was too much for you." He kissed the top of her head. "You need someone to look out for you."

"I need a keeper?"

He pretended to be amused. "Don't be silly, sweetheart. All you need, I hope, is me."

"How true!" She sighed with pleasure.

CHAPTER
SIXTEEN

DURING THE next few days Andrea learned what autumn in Paris could mean. The weather was brisk and sunny. The embarrassing sleepiness of her wedding night hadn't recurred, nor had she been troubled by the heartburn that always brought on her ulcer attacks. She had been happy just spending her days alone with Dex.

One morning she woke to the ringing of the telephone, and when Dex answered it he held it out to her with a smile.

"Your father."

It was Tony Lombard and he had forgiven her. "Honey, it's me. I've been wanting to call. To let you know we all love you. And that I'm sorry. Are you happy?"

"Divinely. Daddy, it's so good to hear your voice. It's a great connection, considering. We're having a wonderful time."

His warmth and enthusiasm, just like the young, vibrant Tony Lombard she remembered from her childhood, capped the joy she felt.

"That's my good girl. The important thing is that you're well and happy. Jany was worried about you eating all of that great French food. All those sauces. How's the old ulcer?"

"Fine, daddy. Tell Jany thanks for filling the prescription. I still have some left. I got it sent on from Nob Hill."

"That's a relief. Honey, so help me God, I haven't had any sleep since you and I... well, since we had our breakup. But I've come to the realization that if you're happy, that's good enough for me. And from what I've been hearing from your mother, this husband of yours is a fine man."

"I am. It's perfect."

"What is?"

"Our marriage." She looked up, blew a kiss to Dex who was grinning at her.

There was a slight pause.

"Great institution—marriage. Look, honey, is there anything we can do?"

"Daddy, you're a jewel. You know, there is something. You can patch things up between us and Aunt Brooke. She's a bit miffed. She knew Dex through Alec before I did, you know, and..."

Tony laughed. "That's all settled. I had a call from Alec last night. He wishes you everything good, by the way."

"Oh, wonderful! Did he mention Aunt Brooke?"

"No problem. According to Alec, Aunt Brooke has decided to play her usual sophisticate, with all those flip remarks, mostly about what she calls the frailty of man."

"Then she's still angry. Dex was only a friend, but you know Aunt Brooke."

"I do indeed. Pay no attention. You should have seen Aunt Brooke when I refused to marry a protégé of hers who eventually married—well, that's another story. I'll let you go now, honey."

"No, wait! Dex wants to talk to you."

Dex was frowning at her but she handed the phone to him. He cleared his throat.

"Good morning, Mr. Lombard."

"It's still night here in California," Tony reminded him. A bad start.

"Sorry. I just wanted to tell you that I do love your daughter. And I think I can make her happy. I'm glad you've called."

The response came through amid crackling intercontinental noises.

"I hope so, too... er... Cartaret. May I speak to my daughter again?"

Without expression, Dex handed over the phone.

"I just wanted to be sure I sent you our love, Jany's and mine," Tony said to Andrea.

She felt let down at her father's quick dismissal of her husband, and she cut him off sharply.

"Same here. Is that all, daddy? I guess this is running your bill up. I'll give you a break and stop babbling. Anyway, thanks for calling."

"'Bye, honey. Keep in touch."

The line went dead.

At least they had made a start. She now had to worry about getting her family all the way over to Dex's side. She knew Dex would prove his worth. As far as Andrea was concerned, he proved it every day.

He held out his arms to her now, and she went to him.

"Darling, daddy is going to love you. Wait and see. It's ten o'clock at night in Hollywood, so he's probably tired. He's had a bad day at the studio, I'll bet."

"Very probably." He held her tight.

They had seldom been bothered by publicity during the first few days of their honeymoon but that morning when Dex opened the hall door he came upon a chambermaid with her eye to the warped panel of the door.

"Sorry. Did I disturb you?" Dex asked.

She seemed a trifle disconcerted but gave them an insolent stare before turning away without comment.

In the elevator Andrea was puzzled by such voyeurism. "Is that how she gets her kicks?"

"No, sweetheart. That's probably how she gets her pin money. You come from an internationally famous family. Some Paris rag will pay her for the titillating details of our marital life. Not to mention the German and Italian scandal sheets."

"How disgusting!" Her eyes opened wide. "Can they see us...you know...in bed?"

"No, sweetheart. All they can see through that door is a glimpse of a window and whoever happens to be sitting in that plush chair." He rang for the elevator. "Besides, as things are in the world today there are a good many more crucial matters to occupy the public."

"I know. President de Gaulle. And then, back home, there's Jackie Kennedy, of course."

He looked surprised and she had a feeling she said something wrong. "Have I missed something?"

"Only that the United States and Russia have been on the verge of atomic war over Cuba for the last three days."

156

She couldn't believe it. "Cuba! Who cares about Cuba?"

"We may. The Russians appear to have installed missiles of some kind in Cuba, within range of the United States."

But it was Andrea's unwanted publicity that met her around a newspaper kiosk near the Madeleine.

RICHEST GIRL AND MAN OF MANY AMOURS

Even if she hadn't understood French there was her photograph, a hideous black-and-white thing taken by a newsman on her eighteenth birthday.

Others might be afraid the world would blow up. Andrea was too outraged to notice that the newspapers also reported that the United States had set up a sea blockade between the Soviet ships and their Cuban ports.

"How dare they!"

"Khrushchev? Castro? Kennedy?"

"Those reporters, saying that about you."

He shrugged. "It was bound to happen. Ignore it. How would you like to visit the Phantom of the Opera?"

"The movie?" She was still angry over the headline in the newspaper, and concerned over the Cuban affair. "I saw the movie. I even saw the silent movie once. In West Hollywood."

"Then you ought to enjoy his habitat. An old friend of mine works at the Opéra and she's going to show us around from dome to—well, practically the cellar."

"A friend of yours? A woman?"

"Mariella, my love, is a woman, and I consider her beautiful. She was once very fond of my father... when I was about seven."

"I'd love it. There's just one thing. Are you armed?"

"Armed?"

They were strolling along the noisy Boulevard des Capucines, headed toward the Grand Hotel and the Place de l'Opéra.

"Armed to protect us from the phantom."

He laughed. Hand in hand, obviously lovers, they passed the *terrasse* customers of the Café de la Paix. As was so often the case at this legendary cafe they ran into someone who knew

157

them. A dark-haired woman jumped up from a sidewalk table and reached out to catchAndrea's sleeve.

"*Chèrie!* One would know you anywhere. Our little Andrea, isn't it so?"

Andrea gave Dex a side glance. This voluptuous woman in the chic suit had to be Danielle deBrett Friedrich. Andrea found herself trapped in a stifling embrace and nearly choked on the scent of Coty's *L'Aimant* which clouded the air.

"And this must be the lucky Monsieur Cartaret."

Danielle turned to Dex but he managed to hold her at arms' length while accepting her congratulations with smiling equanimity.

Andrea nervously glanced around to see if they were being watched, but she saw with some relief that the people at the sidewalk tables were deeply absorbed in the Paris *Herald* and *Figaro*.

"I remember you well," she said, not altogether truthfully, to Danielle. "Mother always told me how beautiful you were."

Danielle smiled, and revealed her not-quite-perfect teeth.

"*Très charmante*, your maman. Of a type uncommon even in Paris. Quite unique. *Mais oui.* And this truly gorgeous companion is the famous gentleman described so charmingly in the press. *Non?*"

"*Non*," Dex contradicted her with equal charm. "Not as described in the press, I hope." He looked at Andrea, then returned his attention to Danielle. "Perhaps we may get together for an aperitif later. I'm afraid we are late for an appointment now."

Danielle wasn't that easy to get rid of.

"Oh, but—I cannot bear it. You leave me desolate, just as we find each other again after all these years."

Andrea understood Dex's warning look.

"Our afternoon will be terribly dull. I'm afraid you would be bored stiff. We have to meet a friend of Dex's and listen to a lot of rehearsal stuff—one of those frightfully long operas we never heard of." She made an effort, squeezed Danielle's shoulders and promised her. "But soon. We must get together very soon... mustn't we, Dex?"

"Of course." He saw that this wasn't enough and proceeded with more enthusiasm. "I had thought of taking Andrea to Le Grand Vefour one evening. We've been lying low for a few days but I do want to treat her to some of the better restaurants. Won't you and your husband join us?"

Unfortunately, Danielle leaped to accept.

"Wonderful," Andrea said in reply. "Suppose you give us a call at the St. Jean Imperial. We'll get together about a convenient time. Now we do have to be going." She put a hand on Dex's arm.

Danielle saw Dex look over at the overwhelming presence of the great Opèra house across the square from the cafe. The square itself churned with activity. Cars, endless buses with their bouncing, open rear platforms, pedestrians, all mingled in a cacophony of sound and movement.

"I cannot believe it." Danielle gushed, delighted when she discovered where they were heading. "You are to visit the Opéra today, during rehearsals? How I envy you! I have always longed to see the interior. And you go this moment. What luck!"

Dex rolled his eyes, and Andrea giggled, imagining how annoyed he must be.

"Do come along, madame," Dex managed to say politely. "I'm sure my friend can accommodate three as easily as two."

"What luck, indeed!" Danielle clung to Andrea's arm. *"Chèrie,* we have longed to see you. My Carl adores his sister and Jany talks of nothing but her adorable stepdaughter. She writes often about her concern for your problem of the ulcers and the nerves."

They were crossing the Place de l'Opéra toward the Metro steps as Andrea corrected her irritably.

"There's nothing wrong with my nerves."

"But no, Andrea. Did I say nerves? How clumsy I am! It is my bad English. Only one may see that you are of a fragile nature. One must protect you from the harsh world and evil influences."

"Am I one of those influences?" Dex wanted to know. He smiled but there was a hard light in his eyes.

"Oh, no, no, monsieur," she protested.

Andrea remembered that it wasn't until last night that she and Dex began to use her money rather than his, and then only

159

at her insistence. She wished this silly woman hadn't reminded her.

They passed the elaborate Second Empire facade of the Opéra, which Dex explained gave an illusion of more space outside than the actual theater provided. Andrea wondered with a shudder whether the spirit of Lon Chaney, the phantom of the opera, still haunted this building.

Mariella was at the door to greet them and she ushered the three into a long, unadorned passage. As Dex had described, the woman was quite old, though her tall, straight-backed carriage and virtually unlined complexion tended to diminish her years. Though gracious, she had a cold reserve that made Andrea uneasy.

Nevertheless, she greeted Dex with an embrace and a kiss on both cheeks. He hugged her again before introducing her to his wife and Madame Friedrich.

"Madame Mariella Cavalcante. She is with the secretariat of the Opéra association."

Everyone shook hands. Mariella apologized for her haste but explained as they walked that she must be back at her desk for an important meeting within an hour.

The whirlwind tour followed. Mariella led the way with Andrea, leaving Dex a few paces behind with the willing Danielle. They walked through the back recesses of what would appear tonight as one of the world's most glamorous spots.

But before moving through uncounted attics, rehearsal halls, ballet barres and dark passages, Mariella brought them out on the dazzling splendor of the grand staircase. Andrea remembered attending a gala once with her father and Jany and walking up these stairs amid the wonderful glitter and magic of women's gowns, crystal lustres, and best of all, the polished cuirasses and helmets of the Garde Republicaine who lined the staircase. Jany had looked like a fairy-tale princess in strapless white chiffon with flashes of gold sewn through the gossamer folds. Even the gold in her skirts had not been as radiant as her cloud of pale golden hair. Andrea remembered feeling plain standing beside such loveliness.

At least today Andrea felt more confident in her mauve Chanel suit and matching suede pumps.

She saw Dex moving rapidly ahead of them up the broad staircase, trying to shake off Danielle chattering beside him.

Andrea seized the opportunity to speak privately with Madame Cavalcante.

"I understand you've known my husband since he was a boy."

"*Le petit* Dex? Ah, yes. I was a close friend of his father. What a charmer! Dex is a fine boy but nothing like the man his father was. His papa could charm me out of my last sou. Dex has more scruples, I think."

Andrea became courageous. "And his ex-wife? You knew her?"

Madame Cavalcante shrugged.

"Oh, Terri. Yes. We were great friends. I have not seen her in many years but we occasionally correspond. She prefers Mexico. She has her reasons, I am sure."

"She is beautiful...I believe Dex said."

Madame almost gushed. "Wonderfully so. These redheads, sometimes they have the—what you call freckles. But not Terri Cartaret. That flawless complexion. Not even the *maquillage* is needed. A true beauty, Dex's wife."

I am Dex's wife.

Andrea feigned elaborate indifference.

"I understand they were quite a pair, Dex and Terri."

"That and more. They were so young. Not yet twenty. They had been through a terrible war. They did all the expensive things. Those Savoy lunches. The welcome at every home, every estate. And here in France, as well. The comte de Paris once received them at a grand gala. A pity we must grow old..." She waved her hand in the air as if she were trying to wave away the past.

"But, Madame Cartaret," she went on, "That was long ago. When they were young. He is more sensible now. He thinks of the things that count, to an older man. He is wise. *Très practique.*"

So practical that he married lucky me, Andrea thought to herself.

When she looked up she saw Dex at the top of the right-hand staircase, holding out his hand to her.

She banished from her mind the troubling implications of the woman's words about Terri Cartaret, waved and ran up the stairs to her husband. *The warmth in his eyes has to be love, doesn't it? ...*

In the pink plush box overlooking the stage Andrea playfully pretended to be the "phantom"—clawing her fingers and peeking out around the drapery that half-concealed the occupant at one end of the box. Everyone laughed and Dex hugged her.

Mariella beckoned to them. "I believe your phantom would be more at home in the labyrinth of the house. Come. Let me show you."

Within minutes they were squeezing through a passage which seemed to have no doors and more than its share of cobwebs. The dim illumination came from behind the cobwebs. The place made Andrea and the others uneasy.

Suddenly a young woman opened a door down the corridor and dashed inside a room. The door remained ajar and a chorus rehearsal could be heard inside. Andrea had never heard such a deafening roar, and from an opera unknown to her. She put her hands to her ears and dashed past the door, leaving her companions to Mariella's careful explanations.

She ran into what looked like an open freight elevator and got in, calling to the others to follow her. She held the door open, waving to Dex, who was watching the chorus. He turned just in time to see the elevator close.

Someone had rung the elevator from above.

"I'll get off at the next stop," Andrea was screaming. "The next..." *Damn.* They probably hadn't heard her, but at least she had escaped from that chorus rehearsal.

The elevator stopped. She stood still, afraid to move. Through the faint twilight of the Opéra's backstage labyrinth she saw the most bizarre creatures push their way past her into the elevator. They were made up like mimes in ghastly whiteface, expressionless except for the glistening eyeballs.

She was soon surrounded by these silent beings. She looked down, recognized the long, muscular legs in black tights, leotards and knew then that she had walked in on a ballet rehearsal. But why on earth were they all painted up? she wondered. When they filed by her, still without a sound, she tried to follow them but the elevator door closed before she could get out.

She tried to press the right button to return to Dex, but she found herself still traveling upwards. She gave up and got out the minute the door opened. The elevator cage vanished behind her.

A draft of air met her. She thought she must be near the roof. She felt her way through semidarkness, aware that the wind made eerie, moaning noises through this passage, if it was a passage.

She laughed at a sudden ironic thought. What a place this made for an opera phantom, or something else...

Nevertheless, she hugged her shoulders against the chill of the October day. A few steps brought her to an open doorway. She looked in. The place was a pallid, fading green, a tiny amphitheater, the semicircle of seats rising above the miniature stage. At the far end of this semicircle Paris spread out openly below the windows. She looked out to the avenue bordered by hundreds of mansard roofs, to the distant Louvre and the domes across the river.

This little, open-ended rehearsal theater must be just under the round green dome, she reasoned, a small cap that sat atop the great, solid edifice. The wind whistled across and around her. She hoped Madame Cavalcante would bring Dex up to find her. The elevator hadn't returned yet, so at least for the moment she was stuck here.

The moaning of the wind raised in pitch until it seemed everywhere, like throngs of lost souls hovering just beyond the periphery of her vision, at the shadowed rear of the little amphitheater.

She thought about Grandpa Steve. Andrea had no clear idea of what she believed about death or the hereafter, but if ghosts did exist, maybe Steve was trying to reach her. The idea frightened her and she reached out to grasp something solid. Finding nothing but the edge of the platform, she drew her hand back quickly.

A thick coating came away on her fingers. Dust upon dust,

so thick it appeared solid and moist. She brushed her hand frantically on her skirt and started back to the doorway but stopped.

The passage beyond was full of whispers, papery little sounds. She let out her breath in a rasp of a laugh and stepped into the doorway. Out of the darkness she saw figures shuffling their way through the passage.

For a terrible instant she thought they were unreal. But then she heard Dex's voice, and the sound caught and held her steady.

"Sweetheart! Where in the name of God did you go? We've been on every floor in this bloody place. Are you all right? Darling, are you really all right?"

She nodded, wanting to reassure him and the two women.

"Of course I am. I just couldn't stand all that noise down below." She managed a weak smile.

Dex shook her playfully. "Don't you know how dangerous it is to get lost in this place? They've lost people for weeks in these caverns." He held her close and she recovered some of her humor.

"So very amusing," murmured Danielle. "But surely, you could not have been afraid. Of what possibly could you be afraid, *chèrie?*

Andrea started to answer Danielle, then stopped. She turned to Madame Cavalcante, who was staring out the window. The woman's gaunt face was impassive.

"Of course there's nothing to be afraid of. How silly of me," she said. "Come, let's go."

CHAPTER
SEVENTEEN

ONCE THE invitation had been made, they could not politely back out of the dinner engagement with Carl and Danielle Friedrich. After the experience at the Opéra, however, Andrea was reluctant to see Danielle, who had continued teasing her about her experience there.

And yet when Andrea and Dex met the man Danielle referred to as Andrea's Uncle Carl, he turned out to be totally unlike his wife. A trim, light-haired man with a cool, reserved manner and unreadable blue eyes, he could have been handsome but for that remoteness he showed everyone in the party, including his exuberant wife.

It had been arranged that the Friedrichs should drive by the St. Jean Imperial, pick Dex and Andrea up and drive on to the Grand Vefour, a classic restaurant hidden away at the far end of the silent, time-forgotten Palais-Royal gardens and behind the Comédie-Française.

By coincidence, President de Gaulle was appearing this same night for a gala at the Comédie-Française, so a good deal of manipulating was required before the Friedrichs could get their little car into the Rue de Richelieu and parked. *Sureté* men were everywhere.

During the walk to the door of the famed restaurant, the foursome began a heated discussion about the president of the French republic. Carl reminded Dex that de Gaulle was the first of the Western leaders to side with the United States in the Cuban missile crisis, a fact in which he justifiably took great pride. Danielle immediately vented her own opinion of the French president. As Andrea tried nervously to counter Danielle's hostile remark with a joke, Carl Friedrich silenced his wife with an almost brutal directness.

"Be silent! We all know you would have turned him over to the Boches."

Danielle shrugged and nudged Andrea. "We two fought beside your father to free Paris. Our politics differed, but we had a common cause. We loved Paris. Now we are free, but we make the quarrel over politics so important. It is amusing, *non?*"

"Here we are," Dex said. He turned to Andrea. "Don't worry, sweetheart. I expect it's a well-worn argument with them... Are you coming, Mrs. Friedrich?"

The women were ushered before him into the first of a series of rooms, small salons with panels of faded but exquisitely detailed classic scenes separating the mirrored walls. Andrea and Danielle were seated against one such wall. Andrea looked around at the other diners and was surprised to see that no one appeared to be in evening clothes. Now she felt more relaxed in the above-the-knee blue silk Cardin chemise that Dex had advised.

Danielle, too, wore a short dress, with fringes that rustled to great effect when she walked. She was busy pointing out the identity of at least half the diners.

"But Andrea, my dear, they point you out, too. You are a celebrity. The maître d' must have spread the word that the heiress of the Lombard fortune is dining here tonight. You see how they look at you?"

Andrea set the menu directly in front of her as a shield.

Carl was telling Dex how he had been with the Gaullist Resistance in the war, and Dex described once having been rescued by the Resistance after a commando raid north of Dieppe.

"I'm afraid my rescuers were with the *Franc-Tireurs*. The communist wing," Dex explained with a smile for Danielle.

Even Carl smiled at that. "It is conceivable. They cannot have spent the entire war plotting to give France to Stalin." He rapped his knuckles amiably against his wife's hand. It was the warmest gesture she had seen him make, Andrea thought.

Over the fish course Carl asked Andrea a great many questions about her father. His English was excellent. It was clear

166

that he and his sister Jany kept up a steady correspondence, but although he and Tony had been comrades in the fight to free Paris, they had nevertheless been alienated after the war, most notably because of Danielle's communist mischief-making. Carl's visitor's permit to the United States had even been revoked as a result of this activity, he explained.

"So you could never visit the States again? That's terrible."

Carl was cool; any regrets he had were not betrayed by his manner. "I deserved it. I was a fool. I believed what trouble-makers told me." He saw the glance both Andrea and Dex gave his wife and he laughed. "I don't mean Danielle. One knows what to expect with her politics. She is not subtle, my wife. We understand each other, isn't it so, Danielle?"

"You speak of subtle, *chèri*. Well then, I am not. But what I wish to know—" The waiter brought the meat course. "The Chateaubriand for me, *comme toujours* . . . What I wish to know is why your grandfather left you, and not Tony, his—how do you say? . . . his fortune?" She sipped her wine with moistened lips.

Andrea was speechless, outraged at the woman's crudeness. Carl was the first to speak.

"You need not answer, Andrea. I warned you about my wife."

"But we are all among friends, all family, so to speak," Danielle persisted. "When Monsieur Steve visited Paris I asked him how rich he was."

"What did he say?" Andrea was curious about Steve's reaction.

Danielle beamed. "He said, 'More than I can count, but not so much as I would like.' He was a man, this Steve."

Everyone smiled politely. Andrea hoped the matter had been settled.

Shortly after, however, it came up again, this time oddly enough from Carl.

"It is a great responsibility, this so-enormous fortune. Of course one wonders why Monsieur Lombard did not leave it to his son. Surely, Andrea, your father would then train you and in your time, you would succeed to the estate."

Dex agreed. "It is the usual thing, I believe," he said. "But

Stephen Lombard had no intention of dying when he left for Japan."

"Still," Danielle persisted, "it is a very bad thing, our Jany says. Poor Tony, he had plans."

"Danielle..."

"My father couldn't have had plans. He had no way of knowing grandpa would die. And grandmother with him."

Dex reached out, made a small gesture to calm her, but Andrea deeply resented these people who were not related to her by blood, yet who pretended to speak for her father. Most of all she resented the thought that her father's wife had complained so shamelessly about the will. Andrea still could not get over the guilt of having cheated her father, and this was just another painful reminder of that guilt.

Danielle rattled. "It is nothing, *chèrie*. You may so easily make it right—"

"You talk too much," Carl cut her off sharply.

"I say we have all talked too much on this subject," Dex said immediately. "Tell me, Friedrich, do you think the crisis will be settled peacefully?"

"I think the Soviets will back down. This time."

"Soviets! Missiles!" Danielle muttered. "Bah! Is there nothing else to discuss? Must it always be war?"

Andrea had to agree with her there.

The rest of the evening went reasonably well and by the time the Friedrichs dropped the Cartarets off at the St. Jean Imperial the earlier tensions had relatively relaxed. Danielle, Andrea felt, was so transparent that just being with her was a good rehearsal for more important and difficult characters that would come along.

As if by chance Andrea found that evening that she would need to develop a hard shell in dealing with the press. Shortly before midnight when Dex and Andrea crossed the hotel's courtyard after the Friedrichs let them out, they were startled by the flashbulbs of a photographer who leaped out at them. Andrea cringed but when Dex raised his arm to ward off the fellow, she recovered with a shaky laugh.

"Afraid we'll have to get used to it pretty soon. It won't get any better. Never did for my grandparents."

"Damn them!" Dex said, but he probably knew it was true.

The photographer called to them in English, "Is that a Cardin original, Miss Lombard?" A woman's voice.

"Mrs. Cartaret," Dex snapped. Andrea shook his arm.

"Honey, don't let them upset you. All they see is my money. It's not me. Or you." Seeing how the photographers had disturbed Dex gave Andrea courage. She raised her voice. "Sure it's an original." She knew she could beat them at their own game.

"Miss—Mrs. Cartaret. Do you think it's fair to American designers, you sporting the latest from Paris?"

Dex was impatient but Andrea had to finish what she had begun. "Don't think I sell the Americans short, my friend. I've got a whole trousseau of Norell."

"Can I quote you?"

"You darn well better."

The girl giggled. "You're very—Western, aren't you?"

"Just say I'm coastal."

"Which coast?"

"Pacific, of course. Is there another?"

"Wow!" the girl got her old-fashioned camera set up and blasted the night with another flash, catching Andrea provocatively as she turned to her husband with a big smile.

Dex waited until they were in the lobby before he made known his feelings.

"What's happened to you, sweetheart? You didn't seem to be yourself out there at all."

"I wasn't. I was playing their game. If I'm going to be in their newspapers anyway I might as well be running the show, right?"

"I'm not sure. I don't want to lose my little girl."

She hugged him, sensitive to what troubled him. "Don't worry. I'll never stop needing you."

"I devoutly hope so." He said it lightly but she suspected his tone was a cover-up for some deeper feeling.

She glided through the narrow hotel lobby now, though the woman at the front desk still greeted them with a supercilious look. Up to now the St. Jean Imperial had represented a haven from the notoriety that accompanied their honeymoon everywhere else.

But that was changing. First, the photographer in the courtyard and now the concierge met them with a stack of mail, Paris business invitations galore, many letters and manila envelopes with overseas stamps, as well as an impressive vase of salmon gladioli and a little bowl of hothouse Parma violets that gave off an exquisite scent.

Dex had also received some mail and glanced through it while Andrea looked for the cards on the flowers. The concierge explained that other flowers had been sent to their room, but the gladioli were from the hotel management and the violets had been originally ordered from San Francisco.

"I'll bet it's from Sam Liversedge," she whispered under her breath.

The violets, it turned out, were to her surprise from Faith and Frank Kelly and she adored them. They brought back memories of her Grandmother Randi, who used to talk about the violets that had grown wild on the hillsides of San Francisco when she was a girl.

Andrea thanked the concierge and took Dex's arm. He quickly folded the letter he had been reading and stuck it in the pocket of his topcoat. She could see that something had plainly upset him.

"Most of my mail is ads and people who want me to buy something." She fanned out her mail so he could see it. "What's yours?"

"Pretty much the same."

He didn't bother to show her what he had jammed into his pocket, but she had seen several business envelopes. Whatever his mail, it had put him in a thoughtful mood.

The answer was suddenly obvious to her. He must need money. It wasn't fair that she had let him pay for practically their entire honeymoon. She had done so because she thought it made him feel an important measure of self-respect, but she was sure he certainly couldn't afford to keep it up. Besides, she knew they were going to have to leave the St. Jean soon, and their next stop would probably be more costly.

She decided to come right out with it.

"Dex, we've simply got to use my money. Now that we're known over here we might as well do what's expected of us. Live it up a little, like my father."

"That's an alarming example."

"You know what I mean. Grandpa always said he took his European trips off his income tax."

"They were business expenses, sweetheart. We can hardly call our honeymoon an investment in business. At least, I hope we can't. As for using your money, if you want to live it up, as you say, then we must use it. My pride—as well as my bank account—doesn't go that far."

"Then what is it? You're being awfully serious."

They had reached their floor. He spoke carefully.

"I suppose I resent those damned hangers-on. That photographer. The Friedrichs. The trivial questions. Damn it, Andrea, we're on the verge of war. And our greatest worry seems to be that our life is lived in full view of strangers who insist on violating our privacy. The whole world seems to know who and where we are." He shook his head wearily.

Andrea was silent. She wondered if he might still be sensitive about the press's coverage of his own role in their marriage. She could understand that, but what puzzled her was the underlying sadness beneath his words.

In their room Andrea looked through her mail and came across a heavy manila envelope from the offices of Sam Liversedge. She straightened the clip and pulled out a sheaf of legal documents.

"Oh, no. Wouldn't you know it?" She showed the papers to Dex. "What does all this mean, Dex?"

She knew something like this would distract him. He looked over the report, read a number of the listings and nodded.

"The details ought to interest you. For instance, the big ranches you once told me about. Here it seems you are earning a sum for—what is a twenty-four sheet?"

"Those huge billboards you see along highways." She glanced at the page he indicated. She didn't like it. A ridiculously low sum of money gained for hundreds of miles of ranchland bordering the highways to Oregon, the Siskiyou and Modoc coun-

171

try. And for this piddling sum, the landscape was marred by unsightly advertising.

"Business is business, Andrea," he said after she described her feelings. "You can't let your aesthetic considerations get in the way of potentially lucrative business deals."

"But it's got nothing to do with the aesthetics of it. It's wasting valuable space. I'd like to see some kind of community go up to give those people a taste of city stores, city products." There. She finally revealed her long-simmering plan.

"A dubious theory, unless they want it. Sweetheart, it's getting late."

She looked at her watch. It was after midnight, and she knew it would be good for both of them to sleep. Besides, she looked forward to their time alone. Marriage to Dex, loving him and being loved, was always exciting, full of warmth and sharing. She was learning to open up more with Dex, to reveal more of herself and also to give more of herself to him. This made everything that much more exciting. . . .

"Business concluded, sir. It's bath and bed for us."

He laid her mail on the triple-mirror dresser and reached for her. Breathless, she felt his hands close warm and strong around her waist. He swung her out, her feet just missing the bed, and lifted her high. With little sounds she feebly tried to protest. He brought her down slowly against his body until his lips touched the hollow of her throat and she shivered with pleasure.

She knew he was hiding his worry in the act of lovemaking, but she had learned enough to know to let his emotion, whatever it was, fulfill itself with her. Later he could perhaps tell her.

They made love with a swift, hungry passion, forgetting even the lights. Each possessed the other as if to make up for fancied inadequacies in themselves. They were brought closer together than ever before, and this was a balm to Andrea's secret fears that the relationship could not last.

During the next few days Dex took the time on several occasions to discuss with her the long lines of figures, profit and loss, on real property as well as the trust reports of moneys coming in from various stock and bond investments. They also went over the Lombard expenditures, including their offices throughout the West.

The amount of money that was necessary to satisfy her father's problems at Prysing Productions shook her, but she had expected it. The upkeep of the house on Nob Hill seemed to be almost entirely paid by Alec, who was paying for both his mother's share and also a part of Tony's half-ownership, since Tony didn't live there and Brooke did.

"We should see to it that dad contributes to the upkeep, and that Aunt Brooke also pays her share during the time she lives in it," Andrea decided.

"She won't like it. And besides, your friends are living there now," Dex reminded her.

"I mean when Aunt Brooke goes back home. As for Faith, I'm going to see if she'll agree to take a job as my secretary. We could use her help as an assistant. She's very bright, and I trust her."

"I already guessed that." He said no more about it.

She was amused by his apparent jealousy of Faith Cortlandt's influence on her. As far as she was concerned, Dex was responsible for all major decisions, anyway. Faith was simply a good confidante.

Meanwhile, Andrea had gotten him to make a list of her inactive stocks and to offer suggestions for changes. The idea challenged him, as she knew it would, and sparked his enthusiasm. It also distracted him from the constant presence of Danielle Friedrich during the next days.

Danielle's conversation turned far too often to the needs of her "dear sister Jany and *le pauvre* Tony, who is in such great trouble."

"Not financial trouble, surely," Andrea insisted finally. "He was able to throw off that gang of board members who wanted to move in on control of Prysing."

"But Andrea, Tony is very proud. He does not tell all that he suffers."

"He certainly said nothing to me when we talked on the phone."

"And yet—" Danielle polished her long nails on her sleeve

and studied them critically. "They come from outside to buy the studio for television. They sell gas."

"Gas!"

"And oil. Century-Planet Oil. *Quelle horreur!* Jany is in such a state. She cries for poor Tony every night."

Andrea grimaced. She shared Jany's feeling for her father, but she hated to hear Danielle's relentless reference to him as *poor Tony*.

She would have to do something more. She wondered if she could buy up stock in Prysing Productions. But at the same time she knew it would mean that he would merely become more and more entangled in a business that was slowly destroying him. . . .

Dex understood, though. When Danielle had gone and Andrea was at Elizabeth Arden's having her hair done, he went on an excursion of his own. When he returned he presented Andrea with several travel folders and the announcement that they were finally moving on.

"You haven't said what you think of me."

She paraded before him, showing off her figure in a pair of tight slacks and a sleeveless shell. Her hair was fashionably piled high on her head.

He circled around her. "I think you are possibly the most beautiful woman in the world."

"Only possibly?" she teased.

He reached out, took a handful of gleaming strands of hair and mussed it up. He ignored her cries of outrage.

"Now you're perfect."

She couldn't resist that.

When he made his announcement about moving on she was relieved, anxious to get away from the Friedrichs at last.

"Where to?"

"How about a chateau in the Loire, with acres of woods and Mariella to receive us? She is to be hostess there for a month."

Andrea stiffened. "Oh?"

He went on. "She promises faithfully you can't get lost. The trails are all marked."

"Really? How nice of her."

174

"I thought so." But he read something else in her face. "You don't, though, do you?"

"Well...we've been in France a long time."

"Paris isn't France, sweetheart." He seemed to change his mind, however and picked up the folders. "Okay, the chateau is out. I had thought that from the chateau we might move on to Italy, Spain or Portugal. You've only to make the choice. Do you want to see the folders?"

She was torn between the desire to continue their enchanting honeymoon and her need to get to work on the business of running her inheritance.

Perhaps she could do both. In some quiet place, without the distractions of Paris, she could both work and spend time with Dex. It provided all the more reason, too, for bringing Faith over. But Faith would have to get by Dex, win him over. A word of warning might help. Andrea flipped through the folders.

"I've only been to Spain once, with my father and step-mother. We went from there to Lisbon. I loved both. But that was in nineteen fifty-six. Capri—oh, Dex! We missed Capri. There was a big storm and daddy decided not to take a chance. The waters were awfully choppy. Let's go!"

Dex laughed. "You are a born tourist." She frowned and he kissed her. "Nothing wrong with that, sweetheart. Capri it shall be for our next stop."

She threw her arms around him. "I do love you, Mr. Cartaret."

Andrea decided it would be better not to tell Dex just yet about Faith. She would make it a surprise, instead. It wouldn't be too hard to dig up a crisis that could bring Faith over. In the end he would be glad.

With Dex and Faith working together, she could check out the work of Liversedge and the others, make some changes in the estate, get rid of the deadwood properties and start to run things herself. This would also give Dex's life a direction, perhaps even keep him from looking the way he had that evening in Paris when he went through his mail and seemed so upset.

She hadn't forgotten that look.

175

CHAPTER
EIGHTEEN

AT LEAST, Andrea thought, they didn't have to fly to Capri. But in the bar car of the Express from Paris to Rome and Naples, Andrea recovered from a bad bout of burning ulcers followed by a night of such deep sleep that she felt doped up the next morning. Although Dex gave her the little white pill she always took to recover from her ulcer attacks, he still suggested that they ought to worry more about the cause of the attacks than the pain itself.

"That's easy for you to say," she had cut him off. But the next day in the bar car, sipping a glass of warm milk, she felt better and began to confide some of her plans to Dex. He listened to her carefully before he responded.

"Those are excellent ideas, as far as they go. You should know and understand every property you own. Every stock certificate. Everything. But you have lawyers and brokers. Their advice is bound to be better than mine."

"But I've already made changes, thanks to you. You seemed to think they were a good idea."

"Those were gambles I believed in. Liversedge has many business affairs. He can't be responsible for every single stock you own. Nevertheless, from what I've seen of your portfolio, he hasn't done badly for you nor your grandfather before you."

She swished the milk around in her glass and drank it down impatiently.

"That was entirely Steve's doing. All Sam had to do was clip coupons and collect dividend checks. Steve made the choices. The buys and sells. And I want to—I want *us* to do that."

She became aware of his deep gaze, and it made her nervous. Around them the Italian landscape was racing past, and as she looked out the train window she realized that this blurred morning world she was being whirled through was as foreign to her as the moon.

Dex sensed her uneasiness, though he did not know its source.

"All right," he agreed. "We'll tear it apart and examine every investment. Frankly, I'd enjoy it. But I don't guarantee to do better on the entire portfolio. I'm not going to set myself up against the investments that made your grandfather wealthy."

He finished his coffee in a gulp and gestured toward the train window. "We're coming into the Naples station. I have one piece of advice here, sweetheart."

"And what would that be, charming sir?" Andrea picked up her purse and smoothed her hair.

"Watch out for the Italian men. They're notoriously fond of beautiful women."

"I'll remember," Andrea promised with a laugh.

They were met as they descended the train by a small man who poured out a torrent of Italian to Dex. Dex introduced him as Alberto Lotti, explaining that he had been a liaison between the bank chain of Roma-Campania and the British Barclay's Bank.

Signore Lotti bowed to Andrea, then turned and slapped a copy of the *Wall Street Journal* into Dex's hand along with several fierce phrases.

"What is it? World War Three?" Andrea asked in a low voice.

Dex grinned. "Not quite. Planet Oil is up seven points. You recently acquired a thousand shares. Lotti is just congratulating you."

Andrea smiled, but did not reveal her surprise. Planet Oil, she reminded herself, was the company that was trying to push out Tony Lombard....

Dex took the *Wall Street Journal* and a pink folder from Lotti, shook hands and walked Andrea out to the curb where a uniformed chauffeur saluted Andrea. She had to admit, her husband was certainly efficient in running things.

"Are we in time for the Capri midday run?" Dex wanted to know when Andrea was in the Fiat and he was supervising the stowage of their suitcases.

177

"We will make the time, signore," the chauffeur answered.

"I'm afraid to ask just *how* we'll get there on time," Dex said, and got in beside Andrea.

The ride through the lively, crowded streets to the dock was predictably rough, and they left in their wake scores of cursing, fist-shaking Neopolitans. Andrea was both fascinated and appalled with what she saw of the streets of Naples. The war damage had pretty well disappeared but there was still all the rickety tenements with their colorful clothes flapping on lines over the narrow streets, straight out of a movie, Andrea thought.

The Capri ferry belonged to the same movie. The deck was crowded and since the season was well-advanced, most of the holiday-goers appeared to be Italian. While Andrea stood there on the dock, Dex made a deal with the sleek young chauffeur to help them get their luggage to Capri.

"My great pleasure is to serve the beautiful signora," the hot-eyed boy trilled.

"Can't ask for more gallantry than that," Dex said to Andrea, who was now busy having her hand kissed by the young man. The revellers on the deck above watched and cheered.

She hadn't noticed any of this lively atmosphere during her visit to Naples that one time with her father and Jany. Jany had had bitter memories about Mussolini and couldn't enjoy herself. As a result the family remained in the Excelsior Hotel during their visit, hurrying out long enough to show Pompeii to Andrea and driving back in their Mercedes to dine inside the hotel. As she told Dex, they never got to see Capri.

"Let's go!" She locked her hand in Dex's and they hurried up the plank onto the ferry. In another minute they were pushing their way through the upper deck crowd with the afternoon wind whipping in their faces.

The ferry pulled out. Andrea pointed out the wonders of Naples Bay, getting Sorrento mixed up with the still mysterious site of Herculaneum, but quite correct about Vesuvius. It was hard to mistake the broken volcanic peak with its ominous shroud of storm clouds, Dex told her later.

They drank Cinzano out of paper cups bought from a vendor and laughed about it. The sea was a deep piercing blue, choppy with the winds of early fall. Dex maneuvered her through the

178

crowd to the starboard side of the ferry and pointed out the lowering dark hulk of Capri on the horizon.

Since they were on a local ferry, they docked briefly at Sorrento. The delay didn't bother Andrea, who rushed back to the port side of the boat in time to watch newspapers, mail and other paper bundles from Naples dumped off at this resort town on the outer prong of Naples Bay.

A lean youth who had been lingering near them suddenly came up to Andrea and Dex with an ancient camera in his hands. He looked from one to the other with an expression of appeal. Andrea turned to Dex but he shook his head firmly. No photographs. The boy shrugged and walked away.

Andrea leaned far over the port side of the ferry. Dex put out a hand. "Careful."

"Is that how they'll bring us our mail at Capri?"

"In a manner of speaking. This mail business is new to you, isn't it?"

"The business part is." She jingled the gold charm bracelet that Eden and Tony had started for her long ago. The talk about the mail had made her suddenly thoughtful.

She couldn't forget the patronizing tone of the progress reports forwarded from Sam Liversedge.

"...We feel your interests are best served by...

...The Lombard policy has always been...

...You will observe that we have renewed all leases on...

...Your suggestion unfortunately conflicts with the actions of the committee who believe, after serious study of the matter that..."

In four deliveries of papers from Sam he hadn't taken one of her cabled suggestions. It was like arguing with a stone wall....

Together, she and Dex watched the approach to the island of Capri. He pointed out Ischia on the distant horizon. "The more elegant jetsetters are taking that over. Capri is becoming passé. Are you still game?"

"Look at those cliffs. I love it. The Blue Grotto must be somewhere along the cliff there."

He was pleased. "So you aren't a jetsetter. I hope you never will be, sweetheart. Don't lose your enthusiasm."

Their chauffeur came to join them at the rail.

"Signora, you wish I will make the landing with you at the Marina Grande, no?" His eyes were on Andrea.

Dex answered the boy impatiently.

"The arrangement was to the hotel. Then you may return to Naples on the night ferry. Is that satisfactory, Andrea?"

The liquid black eyes of the chauffeur gazing at her distracted her.

"I'm sure it will be satisfactory, darling," she said after a moment, then moved along the rail, closer to Dex.

The chauffeur understood. He bowed and retreated.

The ferryboat moved into its slip at a pier leading out from the Marina Grande, the port village of Capri. Andrea clung to Dex.

"Our ferryboats to the Oakland trains are a lot clumsier. They bang against the slip every time," she murmured. Oddly enough, the mere mention of those clumsy white Southern Pacific boats made her homesick. She blinked and changed the direction of her thoughts.

Whitewashed Mediterranean houses lined the colorful waterfront. A sharp series of cliffs rose up with breathtaking force from behind the greenery and the flat rooftops.

"I didn't know about the mountains," Andrea whispered. "Those sheer rocks. You mean this village is all there is? It looks like it crawls right up those cliffs." The sharp peaks looked to her like the Sierra range that separated California from Nevada.

"This is far from all there is. We won't be staying here. We stay above the central piazza. Then there is Anacapri, the other part of the island off to the right."

The car Dex had hired by phone from Paris turned out, much to her surprise, to be a big American Chrysler. While Andrea found it far more roomy and comfortable than the Italian car they had left near the dock in Naples, she would have preferred something that didn't hog the terrifyingly narrow roads of the island, with their hairpin turns and steep grade.

The island was, however, used to luxury cars. The smaller vehicles backed up or down and the danger passed. Andrea began to relax and to notice the beauty of the island, the perfumed air where the car passed late-blooming flowers and end-

180

less hedges of greenery, all under a windy sky with drifting clouds.

Dex and Andrea were deposited beside a narrow alley at the upper end of the piazza which seemed to be the lively heart of the island. At the lower end of another twisting, serpentine alley lined by delightful little shops was the famed Quisisana Hotel. Andrea expected that they would be staying here, and was surprised when Dex and the chauffeur loaded up the suitcases and started along the alley toward a distant white building on a higher slope. This hotel hovered over the piazza and the blue Mediterranean beyond.

It was hard to get to and when they did reach it they passed through a Moorish-style lobby with varying floor levels. The chauffeur from Naples left them at the desk where they checked in. Dex thanked him and paid him liberally. The young man kissed Andrea's hand and walked away, though not without a backward glance.

The single aging bellman on duty carried most of their bags up to the fourth *piano,* which turned out to be the entire top floor of the hotel. The suite consisted of a bedroom, living room, foyer and balcony. The furnishings were bright and colorful, and the wide, azure-tiled balcony looked out over the sea.

This view included the piazza below with its comfortable hum of voices and the rattle of silver against china at various sidewalk cafes. Now and then a phonograph or a radio played songs, and the sounds floated up gently to their balcony.

Andrea swung around, held out her arms to Dex.

"Thank you, sweetheart. This is a fantasy. I'll be forever grateful."

The businesslike mood with which he had handled the chauffeur and the reception clerk evaporated and Dex wrapped his wife in a big hug followed by a long, luxurious kiss.

They were interrupted by rapid knocking at the door.

"Damn!" Dex muttered. He called out in English, "Who is it?"

They could both hear the woman's low-pitched, cool voice. "Faith Cortlandt. Is Andrea there?"

"Good Lord!" Andrea exclaimed. "I forgot all about her. But

you do remember her, darling, I said I wanted to put Faith on the payroll. I'll be needing a secretary, and so will you."

"When we return to California." Dex looked annoyed.

"Well, I do have that pile of mail. And it's getting bigger every day. I'm going to show those so-called advisers that we can run Lombard Enterprises just as well as they do. Maybe better."

He was already on his way through the foyer. She didn't know what he was going to do, and she was for the first time frightened by him.

She heard their voices in the hall and then in the foyer. Determined to smooth things over, Andrea put aside the sternness in Dex's voice and started through the big suite to welcome Faith.

NINETEEN

FAITH THOUGHT it was surprising how one could mend a heartbreak, or at least seal up the cracks, by getting a wardrobe together, packing it into two Gucci bags with great care and setting off for—of all places—Capri. . . .

On the flight to New York, Faith ran through her mind all that had brought her this far. When she had first received Andrea's cable she had wanted to refuse her friend straight out. It was bad enough being Brooke Lombard's social secretary. But working for Andrea would allow the world to assume she was a poor relation, taking charity.

On the other hand she certainly didn't want to go back to Wells Fargo as a stenographer, nor did she wish to ask Frank for help.

She thought about the last conversation she had with him.

"She needs you, Faith," he had said. "Someone's got to protect her."

Faith was so tired of hearing Frank tell her about what Andrea needed. She needed someone, too. And then he had made things even worse.

"It isn't right to be taking advantage of the kid's hospitality. I for one can't just stay here and use her house as if it were my own. I'd even hesitate if I were her husband."

That came as a shock.

"You're not likely to be her husband, Frank. Don't flatter yourself." Faith knew she was being harsh but she couldn't help herself.

"I couldn't be a worse choice than the gigolo she's taken up with. I'll bet he's already got her bank accounts in his control. She deserves better."

"You?"

His face became red and he stammered, "Well, she could do worse. At least I care about the kid herself, not her damned money."

It was then that Faith blew.

"If you care so much about Andrea, maybe I'd just better move over. I think you'd better leave here now, Frank."

He was already up and dressing; so her offer came a little late.

It wasn't as if their parting were forever. They saw each other the next afternoon, after his last class. She was waiting outside Sather Gate when he came through. He was flanked by two female students, who tagged after him as he walked toward Telegraph Avenue with his books under one arm.

Whatever her quarrel with him was, Faith knew he still loved her when she saw his face light up as he caught sight of her. He crossed the street with such long strides that he left his hangers-on back at the gate.

"Hi, Faith! Boy, am I glad to see you. I thought—"

She cut him off. "I wanted you to know I'm off to Italy. I've decided to take up Andrea's offer to be her assistant."

He hugged her.

"I knew you'd do it." He grinned self-consciously. "If you look as good as the way you do now, Andrea will have to watch her husband around you."

"I think Dex is a very attractive man. I've got a good notion to—"

"Now, honey..." Was he jealous? "...Just don't hurt Andrea. You're tougher than she is. You don't understand the girl's vulnerability. If you trade on it, you'll destroy her."

Afterward, she thought about that a lot. In one respect it gave her a real sense of power. That and her brains were her only weapons in the face of the enormous power of Lombard Enterprises.

When Frank kissed her good-bye, he had stepped back for a moment and looked as if he were about to say something. Then he seemed to change his mind, turned and walked away in the direction of Telegraph Avenue....

On her arrival Faith saw nothing of Italy beyond the Fiumicino Airport and the evening train to Naples. She spent the night at a small, inexpensive hotel near the dock and was one of the first to arrive on deck the next morning, carrying her Gucci duffle and her small Gucci pullman bag she had received as gifts from Brooke. She saved as much as she could out of the check Andrea had authorized, thinking it would come in handy if she and Andrea quarreled and she had to pay her way home.

She arrived at Capri on the morning boat a few hours earlier than Andrea and Dex. She spent the time mooning about, fantasizing that Frank was here enjoying the island with her. He would adore the pizza parlor in the little gallery that she discovered when she explored the piazza below the hotel. Frank would appreciate the view through the side arches of the gallery. Naples Harbor shimmered in the sun across the waters, and he wouldn't miss the imposing hulk of Vesuvius off to the right, on the far horizon.

She missed him terribly.

When Faith finally arrived at the hotel, it came as something of a shock to learn how much Dexter Cartaret disliked seeing her. She reasoned quickly that she must be a threat to his hope of controlling Andrea's mind and her huge fortune.

"Sorry. I've only just found out we were expecting you, Miss Cortlandt. Come in." His voice was cool.

She held out her hand. He had a firm enough grip and she liked that. She liked what she saw of him, but she knew she wouldn't be attracted to him—not like Frank.

"I really don't intend to intrude on your honeymoon," she promised him.

Before he could reply to that, Andrea met them and threw her arms around Faith with her usual exuberance.

"It's so good to see you. You're our one friend here. Doesn't she look marvelous, Dex?"

Faith was pleased.

"She certainly does."

"Well, don't get carried away," Andrea teased him.

"Where are you staying?" Dex asked.

"Next door. The balcony next to yours. But don't worry— there's a wall between us. Andrea wanted me to be handy."

185

He accepted her presence, though she knew he must resent the invasion of his privacy.

"I've interrupted you," she apologized, taking a step backward. She looked at Andrea. "Talk about looking marvelous! You look like a million dollars."

They all laughed, and the ice was broken.

"Anyway," Faith said, "I'll see you later. You've only to give a buzz when you need me."

Andrea walked with her to the door. "Is your room nice? Would you like a suite? We can probably get you one. It's so late in the season. And all the bigshots are at the Quisisana."

"I'm fine." She wasn't about to say otherwise.

Andrea seemed to understand. "Sure. I'll just go over and see if they're treating you right. Be back soon, Dex."

The two women looked around the big room which, like most hotel rooms, served as a bed-sitting room. Faith's balcony, though smaller than theirs, had the same fabulous view of the piazza rooftops below, the sloping, flower-strewn mountainside, and then, with breathtaking suddenness, the Tyrrhenian Sea far below, glittering in the sunset.

Faith turned away, noticed the mail on the foyer table and gave it to Andrea. It was the usual assortment, all kinds of private letters as well as several manila envelopes.

"I told them at the desk that I was your assistant and the concierge gave me the mail. There's some for Dex, too."

Andrea took the pile and riffled through it. Faith pointed out the letters on the top.

"Those are your husband's. There's one strange one. Some idiot forgot to enclose the letter. Probably wondering now why there's no reply."

Andrea held the thin foreign envelope to the light. She saw that the envelope was empty. Faith was surprised to see Andrea examining the stamp.

"Don't tell me the stamp is valuable. Is it a rare one?"

"Not that I know of. It's a Mexican stamp. Postmarked in the state of Guerrero." She looked up. "Faith, what cities are in Guerrero?" Andrea's voice sounded oddly strained.

Faith had visited Mexico several times but had only a vague idea of the answer.

"Taxco, maybe. Oh, and Acapulco. I'm pretty sure of Acapulco."

Andrea took a big breath. "Yes. Acapulco fits."

"You're acting awfully funny. Are you all right?"

"Of course I am." Andrea slipped the envelope in among the others. "Let's all go out to an early dinner," she said brightly. "I was sick on the train last night and didn't eat breakfast. I'm ravenous now."

"You're on your honeymoon, Andrea. You certainly don't want me tagging along."

"Dex won't mind. And I need you there, Faith. Tonight is one night when I don't think I want there to be just the two of us."

Dex was, as always, the perfect gentleman, and he immediately asked Faith to join them. Before they left, though, he wanted to put away the mail that Faith had brought him.

Dex tossed aside magazines, glanced at several letters and then threw the mail on the table, accidentally dropping the door key with its huge tab. When he picked up the door key again the mail looked a little disheveled. Faith was puzzled by the way Andrea watched him, then went off into the bedroom with her own mail.

Maybe she was jealous already, Faith reasoned, afraid he was getting love letters from other women. She found herself growing to like the man, however grudgingly.

When Andrea came out she had an elegant French fashion magazine in her hands and showed the quarter-page picture to Faith. Something of her more familiar childlike excitement remained in her manner when she pointed out the photo of herself and Dex. She was wearing a Russian sable jacket and looking very chic as she was pictured walking along the Seine in Paris with Dex.

"I think the designer got this into the magazine. Trying to get free advertisement."

"It's not a bad picture, though," Faith said, eyeing it critically.

"At the time I thought it looked super. Now I guess it is a bit dowdy."

Dex glanced at it over her shoulder. "Sweetheart, you look

smashing. But I don't expect a photograph could ever hope to capture *all* of your natural beauty."

Andrea, it seemed, needed his reassurance badly. She looked up at him with what Faith thought was a desperate appeal. "Honest?"

"Honest, my love."

She smiled. "Then let's go. I'm hungry."

Everyone was relieved. The curious tension had been broken.

On the way out they discussed a suitable eating place. Dex asked the girls if they wanted to eat at the obvious place, the terrace of the Quisisana. Andrea hesitated. Faith mentioned the charming little pizza place she had discovered. She went on to describe the view and the general ambiance of the place, and Andrea thought it an excellent idea.

Dex objected, however. "Pizza may bother your ulcer."

"I've never felt better in my life. I'll go get that little silver pillbox of mine and we're off."

He gave in, but Faith was sure he didn't like it. The tiny box was charming and very heavy for its size. It was monogrammed elaborately: ALC.

Because Andrea and Dex hadn't eaten since their dining car brunch that day, the three of them started immediately toward the piazza's heart as dusk settled down over the island and the high, rugged peaks surrounding the piazza on three sides. The fourth side was the terrifying plunge downward to the sea, beyond the Quisisana Hotel and a cliffside road. They decided they would explore that later.

The evening was unseasonably warm and the piazza's outdoor cafes were crowded and inviting. But even though the bottles of Chianti and Orvieto looked tempting and the hum of voices speaking Italian had a certain pleasant music, Andrea was determined to see the place Faith had mentioned.

They turned into what looked like an arcade, a deserted passage which opened on the right into the little pizzeria. On the side facing the Bay of Naples the cafe was open to the evening breezes and the splendid view.

They were the first customers for the evening meal and the waiter made a great fuss over blonde Faith, calling her "la bella signorina" and welcoming her. After the fuss Andrea always got wherever they went, it flattered Faith to be noticed first.

They all gorged on the antipasto tray while waiting for the pizza to be lifted out of the oven on its blackened iron paddle. They drank the locally popular Orvieto instead of the more familiar Chianti so as to better fit into the scene.

They fell silent as the first twinkling lights of Naples and Sorrento came on, a necklace of diamonds around the bay. Then an oil tanker moved in, blocking their view. The tanker reminded Andrea of what she had learned earlier today about Dex's acquisition of the Century-Planet stock.

"What do you think, Faith? My brilliant husband made a killing in the stock market today. Planet Oil is up seven points and we own a thousand shares." She put her arm around Dex amiably.

It took Faith several seconds before she realized Andrea wasn't joking. Good Lord! Could Andrea not know the whole story? Andrea was watching her closely.

"Why? What's wrong with Planet Oil?" she demanded, wanting to hear someone else speak aloud the damning evidence.

"Nothing. Not a thing. I only meant—" For once she had put a fly in the ointment without intending to. "I guess it's a good idea. One way you look at it."

"*Why*, for God's sake?"

"Well, Planet is trying to buy out your dad, to get control of Prysing Productions."

There. It was out. There was a shattering silence. Andrea turned and stared at Dex. She was pale. The flickering candle made her face look odd.

Just then the cook drew the pizza paddle out of the oven and they all saw flames like forked tongues licking at the iron. He brought the pizza over, slipped it out on a platter and offered cutter and fork to Dex.

"*Caldo! Caldo!*" the cook informed them unnecessarily.

Dex gazed at the pizza. He seemed stunned.

Faith found it hard to believe he hadn't known about Planet Oil's Hollywood maneuvers. But he didn't say anything. He just gave Faith that sardonic smile of his. Then he raised his wine glass to his lips, tipped it slightly in her direction. A salute. Then he drank.

For a few seconds she didn't understand. Then she realized that he thought she had staged this deliberately. He was saluting the enemy.

She couldn't stand the silence.

"A thousand shares of an oil company is no big deal," Faith said finally. "I think it's kind of funny, anyway, Andrea infiltrating the enemy camp, so to speak. Think of your shares as a Trojan horse, Andrea. Too bad you didn't invest yourself, Dex."

"I did," Dex said curtly.

Andrea stared at him, stunned. She lowered her gaze and picked at the pizza with her fork.

Faith sighed and began again. "It's such a great night. You two ought to take a walk along the cliffs, down that road they told me about. It's awfully romantic. You can get a great view of the Faraglioni—I think that's what they call those rocks out there."

Andrea laughed shrilly. "What a wonderful idea, isn't it, Dex?"

"Certainly suits me, if you'd like it." He was still reserved, but Faith suspected he was anxious to straighten things out with his wife.

Faith understood. She stifled a yawn and declared that she would be going to bed early. "But they do say that view is terrific. You two have fun."

Andrea startled her. "Don't be silly. You're going with us, Faith. I wouldn't dream of going alone your first night on Capri. Besides—" She patted her husband's arm. "That sounds like a dangerous walk. And you can protect me from my sinister companion here."

Faith choked on her wine.

"Do come along," Dex offered. "As Andrea says, you will be our protectress. One might call you our guardian angel."

With her glass to her lips, Faith returned his toast silently.

CHAPTER
TWENTY

ANDREA REFLECTED that it was surprising how much more cheerful things looked after four—make it five—glasses of that lovely Italian wine. When she walked out of the little pizzeria between Dex and Faith, she had a sneaking suspicion that they hadn't kept up with her in drinking. She walked a bit unsteadily, though her mind was clear. She felt lightheaded, in fact.

They strolled down a curving path, past tightly shuttered little shops. They passed the rambling marble-based Quisisana Hotel which struck Andrea as well suited to the breathtaking locale. Until an hour ago in the pizzeria, she had been happy in the brooding splendor of the Monte Augusteo Hotel, which overlooked the entire village. She had thought Dex chose the Monte Augusteo to save her money. Maybe he had other reasons....

She breathed in the night air. The early evening wind had died down and the air was full of perfume. Perhaps it was mimosa. Or honeysuckle. Something sweet and romantic. Andrea felt Dex's arm around her waist, his cheek against her hair.

Only Faith looked unaffected by the beauty of the night. Her eyes were set on something far out to sea, the thought of Frank Kelly, no doubt. With the euphoria of wine and the Capri scene, Andrea felt sorry for her.

The three came out on a cliffside road to the breathtaking sight of the night-blue sea, its horizon cut by the silhouette of a fishing boat, a distant oil tanker and very close, the black hulk of the Faraglioni Rocks.

Moved by the scene before them, Andrea and Dex kissed

191

each other, all problems laid aside for the moment. Faith hesitated, then walked down ahead of them.

"How would you like to spend the rest of your life here, in one of those houses?" Andrea asked Dex, looking at the villas clinging to the cliff above them. Their red-tiled roofs were like stepping stones planted among the rugged greenery.

He stood back to look up at the villas. "The rest of our lives? No. Now and again, perhaps. But there is a good deal more to the world than Capri."

"Maybe." She pointed to one villa that perched on an outcropping of rock above the others. "There. Say what you will, that one must be the ruler of the world."

He stepped back further to get a better look. Suddenly the pebbles rolled away underfoot and the cliffside crumbled. Just then Faith turned, saw his foot catch and slip. She screamed. Andrea swung around in terror and grabbed for him. But Dex had already regained his footing.

"Careful, sweetheart. Don't you try that. Unless you're an exceptionally good diver," she said lightly.

But she peered intently over the broken edge of the cliff at the white foam and spray far below against the blue-black waters.

She held Dex tightly, though he laughed at her concern, and they went on down the road toward the complex called Piccola Marina, complete with lights and swimming pool that Dex claimed belonged to a famous British entertainer. It was open to the public.

They waited for Faith at the turn in the road. She scrambled toward them.

"My God, I must have screamed like a banshee when I saw you almost slip over the edge there."

She smiled nervously at Andrea.

"I'm so glad I happened to see him step back on those loose stones."

Dex offered his hand. "Many thanks." He added lightly, "I had no idea you cared."

Her smiled faded. Nevertheless, she let her hand remain in his for what seemed to Andrea as longer than necessary. Faith was behaving oddly, she thought. Not like the cool, unruffled woman Andrea had always known.

But Faith recovered, to Andrea's relief. She pulled her hand away. "I'm dead tired. I left San Francisco two nights ago. This jet business gets to me. I'm off for a little shut-eye."

Dex didn't stop her. "Can you find your way back?"

"Certainly. How big can an island be?"

Andrea felt as if she ought to stop Faith but Dex restrained her. "She's a big girl now. She knows how to take care of herself."

"Okay. But she's acting so strange. Do you think she had a fight with Frank?"

He shrugged, took her arm and led her into a nearby bar. They ordered Campari and discussed where to go after Capri. They avoided all talk of business, for fear of the subject of Planet Oil.

With the full moon visible in the island sky, Dex and Andrea started back up from the Piccola Marina. Their walk took them past the dark, shadowed Faraglioni, and they returned to the spot where Dex had slipped backward on the stones near the crumbling edge of the cliff.

Andrea carefully examined the area.

"Right there. You slipped on those pebbles. Here's the mark where your shoe skidded."

Dex didn't seem to think she had the right place. "Around the next bend. Further south of the rocks." He tested the place he spoke of, but the moonlight had illuminated the whole area by this time and the place looked different.

After the highs and lows of the evening—and with a head full of wine—Andrea felt brave enough for anything. She let go of his hand and investigated. Pebbles shifted under her foot and rained over the cliff. She could now barely see the white foam that rimmed the tidal waters below.

She sensed Dex's presence behind her and stiffened. An idea flashed through her mind, so monstrous it was comical. A little push would send her over the cliff. She eluded his touch, stepping back. She laughed to show that this was all in fun. When she saw his amused smile, his eyes shadowed and almost somber as he turned away from the moonlight, she wondered at the trick of her imagination which had momentarily turned her beloved husband into some kind of monster.

She took his hand. "Darling, I'm sleepy. Let's go to bed."

"By all means." He gave the dark sea waters one more glance, then took her arm and they climbed up the cliff highway and walked on through the narrow alleys to their hotel.

Andrea made love to Dex that night with a special passion, to blot out the horrible moment on the Piccola Marina road when she actually allowed her imagination to get the better of her. They slept in each other's arms, hearing faintly in the distance the mandolins playing the romantic "Anima e Core."

In the morning Andrea started to work on her mail while Dex was out walking. She learned in a note from Frank Kelly that he and Faith had broken off their relationship. She was sorry, but not surprised. She had suspected it already.

Frank wrote simply.

Dear Andrea,

> *I know you must be having a great time. I envy you and your husband, seeing all those unforgettable places together.*
>
> *Just a word about Faith. We are no longer together. But please be tolerant of this wonderful girl. She gets a little brusque and defensive sometimes but her feelings run deep. I sometimes think you are her only real friend, and know that she loves you very much, as does*

> *Your friend always,*
> FRANK

She felt a surge of homesickness for her friends and relatives and for the white fogs of morning and the brisk golden afternoons of San Francisco. This feeling was reinforced by the announcement by Sam Liversedge that Gene Rafael, one of the Lombard legal advisers, was currently conducting exploratory talks with the Nevada Gaming Commission about permits for a casino in the soon-to-be-opened Lombard Hotel in Reno. Sam considered that there would be no problem since their application for a gambling license would certainly be approved.

But Andrea wasn't interested. She was infuriated that Sam had completely ignored her suggestion that the hotel be free of gambling. He hadn't even mentioned it. She decided to dictate a letter and also arrange for a phone call to him.

She picked up the phone and called Faith's room. No answer. Faith had probably decided to eat breakfast downstairs rather than on her balcony, as Dex and Andrea enjoyed theirs. Just as well. Andrea took the time to compose what she would say to Sam and to make a few decisions about the rest of her mail. She wanted to be fully prepared before she met with Faith.

She tried Faith's room again twice in the next hour. Still no answer.

She began to compose what she hoped was a cool, professional note to Sam Liversedge. The letter would contain certain demands not to be construed as mere suggestions. But she wanted to sound the way Steve would have sounded. She wished she had asked Dex's advice. She knew she shouldn't shut him out of her business affairs. He would think she didn't trust his advice. But she had to prove her own ability.

She got up and went out to the balcony wondering where he had gone on his walk. Then she saw him strolling up the narrow passage leading to the hotel. He was not alone. Faith was with him.

The thought crossed her mind that Dex's unknown feelings troubled her most. Faith was tall and blonde and beautiful. Maybe a little like his elegant ex-wife. . . .

She left the balcony and went out to meet them in the hall. They seemed in excellent spirits. Faith was laughing, and explained quickly that she had just met Dex out in the street. Andrea accepted Dex's kiss on the cheek.

"Faith, could you get your notebook and join me? I have several letters to get out. That gang back home is just messing up everything."

Faith was all business at once.

"Sam Liversedge again? It figures. I wouldn't trust that old pirate as far as I could throw him."

Dex stopped with his hand on the doorknob.

"Really? I would be interested in your reasoning behind that pronouncement."

"Call it a hunch." Faith said. "He probably fooled Steve Lombard the same way."

"Nobody fooled Steve!" Andrea put in fiercely.

But Faith only shrugged and went to get her shorthand notebook. Andrea turned to Dex.

"Why did you defend Sam? You don't even know him."

"Very true, my love. But he was good enough for your clever grandfather and served him for a lifetime, if I am informed correctly. Don't be so quick to throw out all the old crew. They just might have a few things going for them. Advice from outsiders, including me, isn't always as reliable."

Andrea raised her chin. "He should treat me with more respect."

He looked at her for a long minute before he opened the door for her and they went in. "Then you must earn it," he said evenly.

She was offended, especially because she knew there was some truth in what he said. She had wanted him to advise her on her dealings with Sam and the others, but his implied rebuke hurt her. He probably believed like the others that she would never fit into her grandfather's shoes.

She started to seat herself at the writing desk in the living room. Dex pulled out the desk chair, but she shook her head.

"It's too nice to stay inside. I think I'll just make my headquarters out there on the balcony. Would you believe this Thanksgiving weather, darling? Isn't it glorious?"

"Glorious. I wish you had gone walking with me a while ago. And don't forget. We want to hire a boat for the Blue Grotto."

"I know. But business first."

He nodded and seemed to understand. She sat down at the table where they had eaten their romantic breakfast, but Dex didn't join her. He opened the balcony doors for Faith, stood there and looked at his wife and then went out for another walk. Faith watched him leave, shook her head and came to join Andrea.

"I think his feelings are hurt. He doesn't want to be left out."

Andrea was worried but she busied herself with the task at hand. She began to dictate her first letter to Sam, which Faith took down in shorthand. The letter was short and to the point.

She simply informed Liversedge that she did not want to pursue the question of a gambling permit for the Lombard Hotel in Reno. Second, she wished no action taken on ranchland property in the Modoc, Lassen and Siskiyou counties until she could be present. Third, she planned to overhaul the Lombard stock portfolio.

She tried to remember some of the up-and-coming companies Dex had mentioned to her. The Canadian uranium thing seemed very shaky. Its excitement had almost blown out. She wondered why Grandpa Steve had begun to invest in Japanese automobile manufacture when Detroit seemed to be the place. He had even been in the process of dumping some General Motors shares and investing in two Japanese companies when he visited Tokyo. The Japanese car thing didn't look as promising to her, though, as several radio-television investments.

Dex would help her...

She stopped dictating, heard her voice trail off as she glanced over the balcony, wondering where Dex had gone. Was he really angry? Or hurt?

Was he finding their marriage harder then he had expected?

Faith was studying her.

"Are you all right?"

Andrea recovered, collected her thoughts. "Certainly. Why?" She didn't wait for Faith to give her an answer. "Let's go on. Who's next?"

Ads, investment offers—she set them aside and looked over her personal mail. Letters from her stepmother, Aunt Brooke, a note from Danielle Friedrich and a postcard from her mother. She turned over her postcard.

"Hi, darling. Caracas traffic unbelievable. Glad you aren't here. Best love, Eden."

Andrea smiled. No reply needed there. Correspondence with her mother was simple, if limited. She dreaded opening her stepmother's letter, knowing it would contain money problems and her incessant concern with her husband's studio struggle. Aunt Brooke's perfumed lilac envelope intrigued her. Faith offered her the letter-opener.

Aunt Brooke had apparently forgotten her fury over the loss

of her escort. She wrote warmly about returning to the Nob Hill house, and about how Sam Liversedge missed her.

> Would you believe it, my dear? I had a Thanksgiving note from Genevieve de Sulka, past president of the Bay Shoreline League, full of the most absurd gossip about dear old Sam. She claims he's been seen at the opera opening and a Curran Theater play with Hollis Widekind's widow, that ancient creature who persists in having her hair dyed henna color, if you can picture it.
>
> However, New York seems to have palled on me and I'm homesick for those bracing Golden Gate winds.
>
> Hope to see you soon.
>
> > Love,
> > BROOKE
>
> > P.S. Say hello to Dex. Are you bringing him back home?

Andrea laughed and handed the letter to Faith.

"My God!" she said, sniffing the paper. "This thing is bathed in *Bellodgia*." She read, gave the letter back. "That should be cozy. You and Dex and Brooke, all in the same house."

Andrea had been thinking about that very thing.

"Don't be silly. That will be my first project. We're going to buy our own house. An apartment. Or whatever. I'm sure Dex would be the last one to live under the same roof with Brooke."

"I can imagine."

Andrea gave her a sharp look, cleared her throat and dictated a short, friendly letter to Aunt Brooke, then gave her attention to the more difficult matter of her stepmother.

Jany was deeply depressed.

> My poor Tony, my heart aches to see his struggle. The first scenes of Klondike shown at the stockholders' meeting were not what he hoped. Those dreadful columnists are writing such things! Worse than on the film that opened this month in New York. They said Titian's Lady was unworthy of Eden Ware. They were kind to her. She is a favorite of theirs, I believe. But they said a period story is wrong for her modern image. Well then, there was no business at the theater. Cruel!

198

I cannot believe the next blow, but Eden has told Tony very sweetly that she will not renew her contract, which is up. She is signing for a Stanley Kramer film and then she goes to Alfred Hitchcock's next. She prefers films of terror to films of grandeur. One wonders! But her action has given more ammunition to those dreadful stockholders. Tony says they are selling out to an oil company, one by one.

But Tony calls me. I must go. I have had your prescription filled once more and enclose it here. Tony asks, as I do, how the ulcer is. Much better, we hope.

Now, I send dear Tony's love to you. As for me, let me say, je vous embrasse comme toujours.

JANY

"How can Father lose control of the studio?" Andrea wanted to know. She emptied the box of little white scored pills in among the pills she had brought with her in the silver box. "Father owns over fifty percent of the stock."

Faith considered. "Maybe he's been putting up stock to finance the new slate of films."

"Oh, God! I thought we took care of that." Andrea's hands were shaking. The old guilty conscience ate at her. She laid aside the letter, placing her pillbox on top of it. "You know something, Faith. I was a lot happier before I got all that money."

The telephone buzzed in the living room.

"Shall I answer that?" Faith asked, then got up to do so. Andrea heard Faith's cool voice as Dex came into the foyer from his second walk of the day.

"*Si.* The Signore and Signora Cartaret. He isn't here at the moment. Would your party talk to the signora?"

Andrea waved away the idea.

Faith raised her voice. "Who is your party, operator? Where are you calling from?"

Dex was behind her. "Someone giving you trouble?"

"I don't know. It's confusing. The Naples operator seems to be speaking Spanish. It doesn't make sense." She gave the phone to Dex.

Andrea watched him. He took the phone.

"Who is this? Who is your party calling?... You have the

wrong name. Try the Quisisana...Very well." He hung up. At Faith's questioning glance he explained, "They wanted someone named Carter. Calling from Barcelona. The hotel operator thought it was us." He came out to Andrea on the balcony.

"All finished with your work for the day, sweetheart?"

"Just about."

He took her in his arms. Over his shoulder she caught a glimpse of Faith's expression.

Faith's puzzled gaze went from Dex to the white telephone on its cradle, and then back to Dex. Something was definitely bothering her.

Andrea soon forgot about it when Dex announced that he had made arrangements to visit the celebrated Blue Grotto that afternoon.

She wondered how she could tell him the truth without hurting his feelings. What she really wanted to do was to go home.

CHAPTER
TWENTY-ONE

THEY DID leave Capri several days later at Dex's own suggestion. He wanted Andrea to visit his family home in the English countryside, and thought it was as good a time as any to leave Capri.

Having hired a Daimler in London, Dex drove Andrea and Faith down to Wiltshire, where they traversed long plots of green fields and went up over a hill to find an old Tudor house nestled in the valley below them.

Andrea hadn't been prepared for what she finally saw once they crossed a rickety board bridge over the bed of a dry brook. At close range she saw an enormous gray manor house, softened by a patina of autumn red leaves. As Dex pointed out, the flame-colored surface covering the ancient stones was ivy.

"Any day now," Dex told Andrea and Faith, "all that beautiful color will disappear. If we returned next month you would tell me that house looked dead. Forgotten. But in the spring it comes alive again, and you would love it. There is the gatehouse. Looks deserted."

Here on the edge of winter Andrea did love it all, especially the gatehouse. "The ivy makes it look rustic and warm. So does the westerly wing that's built out from the rest. It welcomes you."

Faith agreed with Andrea's description of Cartaret House. It definitely had style.

Dex stopped the car on the pebbled estate drive near the westerly wing that Andrea had pointed out.

"My favorite part of the house. It hasn't changed much. I was born in the bedchamber, as they called it, behind that corner room which was my father's."

Just then a huge, muscular man in a British army uniform topped by a kind of Montgomery beret came toward them along the drive, tightly holding the lead of a Doberman pinscher.

Dex reached over to be sure the car door was still locked. In the spacious back seat Faith leaned forward, tapping Dex's arm.

"Let's get out of here."

The guard came around to the open window beside Dex.

"You're trespassing, sir. This is the property of General Sir Sidney Croyde-Halesham. No visitors permitted."

Andrea felt Dex's keen disappointment, and was proud of his casual manner, the way he shrugged off the rebuff.

"Sorry. I was born here. I just wanted to show my wife the place. I can see it's been very well kept up."

"Just back up the way you came, sir."

Dex smiled, but his face was tense. He started to back the car up slowly when Andrea leaned across Dex's body and rolled down the window.

"I'll have you know this is Dexter Cartaret. His family *built* this place."

Dex's smile broadened. "Never mind, sweetheart. I'm afraid the name means nothing to this gentleman."

"Sorry, Mr. Cartaret. General Croyde-Halesham is aware that his home was once Cartaret House... Now if you'll turn that way it will just do the trick, sir. Back down to the corner of the west wing and swing around. Easy does it. You'll find yourself headed back toward the village."

He gave Dex a military salute. Dex backed along the drive to the point where he could swing around and head out across the narrow plank bridge over the brook. The Doberman didn't settle down until the Daimler was climbing the estate road up over the hill.

"So much for nostalgia," Dex remarked finally. "Are you all right back there?"

Faith muttered, "I think so. Did you see those fangs?"

Andrea tucked her hand in Dex's. "All the same, it was a lovely idea. I'm sorry it didn't work out. I wish you still owned it."

Dex's expression was wistful, almost bitter, Faith thought.

The return to London was less lively than the trip out. Andrea worried about the breakfast meeting scheduled for the following morning. In the Savoy's grill room she was to meet a sheik of the United Arab Emirates to discuss the subject of Lombard Enterprise's investments in, among other things, tankers and anchorage in the Persian Gulf.

"I suggest you call it the *Arabian* Gulf when you are with the sheik," Dex warned her.

There were so many things for her to learn. She went to bed that night with her brain full of things to remember:

The tankers are not as important as the anchorage. The government view must be kept in mind. The Soviet influence must be counteracted in the gulf by supporting the young shah, but Lombard Enterprises should diversify; since the Saudis—

She wondered what Steve would have done.

To make matters worse, her usual big portfolio of problems had come from Sam Liversedge and Gene Rafael. They had turned down the offer of a big stockholder in a new frozen food processing company. The man needed quick cash and the stock was underpriced.

Andrea's every instinct favored making a counteroffer for the stock and Dex agreed with her. Tomorrow she would have to get on the phone and instruct Sam to buy. It would make more trouble.

But for tonight she had to keep her worries confined to the meeting with Sheik Abdullah.

Andrea woke up about 2 A.M. in their Savoy Hotel suite writhing in pain. Her ulcer had kicked up again.

Dex was up instantly, and upset and angry when she asked for some pills to calm her stomach.

He reached for the phone. "I don't like it. I'm going to bring in a local doctor. Those pills just make you sleepy."

"They help me, honey. They stop that grinding pain. It feels like a screwdriver going through my stomach."

He sighed, put down the phone and reached for her silver box. She took the pills with a gulp of water, and the pain gradually subsided. Dex gave up the idea of calling a doctor. Andrea was fast asleep within minutes.

In the morning, however, she was so groggy she couldn't make it to the breakfast meeting downstairs with Sheik Abdullah Fahmi. All her memorizing and worrying had gone for nothing. Dex took her place after she assured him that Faith would keep her company until he returned.

"Shall I remind you of all the things you're supposed to know?" she asked Dex, only partly in fun.

He smiled, kissed her and promised to remember.

When he had gone Faith wanted to know the particulars of her latest attack.

Andrea, who only wanted to get get some more sleep, dismissed the question and closed her eyes. She was secretly relieved to have surrendered the breakfast meeting to Dex.

"Dex will do the right thing," she murmured sleepily. "You needn't stay, Faith. I'm fine."

Faith settled down in the big chair between two windows. She had turned her back to the faint sunlight over the Thames and her face was in shadow. She nervously fooled with her wristwatch.

"You're having these ulcer flareups more frequently, aren't you?" Faith asked Andrea, who was nearly asleep.

Andrea opened her eyes. "What's that supposed to mean?"

Faith started to say something, hesitated, then went on. "I mean—since you've been in Europe."

"I guess so. It must be all the excitement and the rich food." She yawned. "Why do you ask?"

"Nothing. Where do you get these pills you take?"

Andrea wished she would either go away or just be quiet.

"From a doctor in Beverly Hills."

"Who recommended him?"

"My father." Andrea opened her eyes and propped herself up on her elbows. "What's this all about? What are you getting at?"

Faith turned toward the armchair facing hers and touched the stunning Balmain coat and dress Andrea had expected to wear to her breakfast with the sheik.

"Pretty clever, kid. Wearing green to meet an Arab. Isn't that their sacred color or something?"

Andrea smiled. "That's something I do know."

She lay back down and dozed off, then snapped awake.

"What's the matter?" Faith asked. "Bad dream?"

204

Andrea's face was ashen. She knew it was bound to come up sooner or later. "Faith, did you know that Dex was married before, during the war? Her name was Terri."

"He was married? Then he's a widower." Faith sounded shocked.

"Divorced."

"British, I suppose."

"I wouldn't know. She lives in Mexico, I think," Andrea said, then could have kicked herself... *Why did I say that?*

Faith's mind seemed to be somewhere else. Her green eyes were focused on the far skyline of London. It had begun to rain, though the faded winter sun was still visible.

Faith got up. "I'll just hang around in the next room. If you need me, call."

"I'm fine."

Andrea settled back against her pillow. Now she found she couldn't sleep.

The room slowly darkened and the drizzling rain trailed down the corner windows. The Thames began to look misty. Andrea pulled up the covers around her shoulders.

Think of something else, she told herself sternly, trying to ward off her growing uneasiness.

But her thoughts kept returning to Faith's questions about her pills and about the doctor her father had chosen for her. The implications were preposterous, she knew, but... And then there was the empty envelope addressed to Dex, with the Mexican postmark. The telephone call from a Spanish-speaking operator. What was going on, she wondered, afraid now.

She reached into the drawer of the nightstand and fingered the exquisite gold minaudiere that had belonged to Dex's family and was proof that he loved her. Could she imagine a life without him? She wouldn't think of that. She was sure that nothing could possibly change her feelings.

CHAPTER
TWENTY-TWO

THEY LEFT London in the rain and fog and after nearly two days' traveling, arrived in San Francisco barely in time for Christmas dinner with the Lombard family. Andrea knew how important it was that they be present, that they *all* be present. This was the first Christmas since the war that Steve and Randi wouldn't preside over the long table in the large Victorian dining room. Her grandparents' absence this year would be keenly felt.

They were met at the airport by Tony and Jany in Brooke's limousine. Andrea was touched that her family should take the time to come north to meet her and Dex. She ran across the tarmac to him while Dex got their luggage and Faith was welcomed by Jany.

"Daddy!" Andrea said, breathless. "I'm so glad to see you. It feels so good to be home. You still forgive me?"

Tony's voice was a bit off-key, and he looked tired.

"Honey, I never was angry. Hurt, maybe, but that's all gone. I felt much better after I called you in Paris."

She hugged him. Faith walked over with Jany.

"Jany! You look wonderful." She kissed Jany's cheek.

"So do you, *chèrie.*" Jany was smiling.

"You remember Faith, daddy. She's been helping me out."

Tony shook Faith's hand, then behind her saw Dex coming toward them. He was followed by a skycap with a truckful of baggage, most of it belonging to Andrea. Tony's smile fixed itself stiffly on his handsome face. Andrea looked at her father anxiously.

The skycap wheeled the pile of bags and boxes, which had been badly retied after Customs inspection, over to the limousine. Dex walked over to Tony, who looked at him for a minute without speaking.

Dex offered his hand. "Sir?"

Andrea knew he was only being polite, but Tony's back was up.

"Please. Not that. You make me feel like your elder. We happen to be damn near the same age."

One of the proudest moments of Andrea's life—the meeting of the two men she loved—was a disaster.

They shook hands. Forced smiles abounded. Jany chattered so fast to Dex as he and the chauffeur loaded the car that Andrea wondered if he even understood. At least she was trying; Tony merely stood by in silence.

A camera flash suddenly went off and everyone jumped. The young photographer leaned around the uniformed chauffeur, then scrambled to the other side of the car. Clicks and flashes began again.

The reporter's voice was shrill in her ears.

"Miss Lombard? How did you find Europe?"

"Get in," Tony ordered her.

Andrea looked around at the newswoman.

"I'm glad to be home. And just for the record, my name is Andrea Cartaret." She got in beside Jany.

The reporter stuck her head through the open window.

"Buy any countries, Miss Lombard?"

Andrea waved her away. "*Mrs.* Cartaret."

"Never mind the baggage," Tony ordered the chauffeur. "Cartaret can handle it. Come here and close the window."

Somehow, when they all fitted into the car, Dex wound up sitting beside the chauffeur. Gracefully, he made it seem that he preferred the front seat, but Andrea resented the careful maneuvering that separated her from her husband.

Tony managed to recover something of his normally buoyant disposition. He slapped Andrea's knee playfully.

"Anybody would think you were a movie star, honey. They make almost as much fuss over you as they do over your mother."

She was staring at the back of Dex's head, willing him to

turn around. The glass partition was pushed open, and he could hear their conversation. She wondered what he was thinking, whether he resented his father-in-law's snub. When Jany reached for her hand she was completely taken by surprise.

"Merry Christmas, *chèrie*," she said brightly.

She had almost forgotten it was Christmas Day. She and Dex had celebrated quietly the night before while waiting in the airport, exchanging presents they had purchased in Europe. Dex's gift to Andrea was a little ebony pin in the shape of a black kitten's face with small sapphires as eyes. Andrea's present to Dex was a wristwatch, with a heavy gold band and with a diamond in place of the numeral 12.

He was wearing it now but it seemed to chafe his wrist and he rubbed the flesh under the band.

There was a traffic jam when they crossed Market Street. Though Jany was chattering away nervously, wanting to know how Andrea had found her beloved Paris, Andrea tried to listen to Dex and the chauffeur, who were engaged in conversation.

"I was here a few months ago and got lost somewhere on one of these Lower Market streets," Dex was saying. "I was headed for the St. Francis Hotel."

"Once you get to Union Square there it is."

"So I discovered."

Andrea made up her mind that tonight she was positively going to find out the truth about Dex's San Francisco visit. She had so many unanswered questions. Why had he left town so abruptly? Did he, in fact, ever see Aunt Brooke?

The limousine pulled up in front of the old stone Lombard mansion. This time a new houseman came out to help the chauffeur with Andrea's luggage.

Andrea put her arm around Dex and they passed through the wrought-iron gate and up the walk. Tony and Jany walked behind them while Faith, with her usual efficiency, gave orders about the luggage.

A welcoming party met them in the doorway. Sam Liversedge, Gene Rafael and Frank Kelly were all there keeping Aunt Brooke company.

"Merry Christmas, darlings," she greeted them, hugging Andrea and kissing Dex squarely on the mouth. Andrea stifled a laugh when she saw her husband try to remove the lipstick from his mouth with his handkerchief.

Andrea turned around and spotted Frank standing alone in the dark hallway. He pointed to the mistletoe overhead and kissed Andrea quickly on her left temple. She liked his embarrassed smile and put him at his ease, kissing his cheek and patting him on the back.

"Good to be home with friends, Frank. Merry Christmas."

"Same to you." He asked in a low voice, "Are you well?"

"Well and happy."

"You look—" He hesitated, bit his lip. "I don't mean this in a derogatory way, but you do look tired."

She resented it all the more because she knew it was true.

"No wonder. We've been so very busy. I think I see Faith coming."

He looked beyond her toward the front door.

"Did you get my letter? Then you know Faith and I aren't together anymore. I hope we'll always be friends, though."

Impulsively she kissed him again on the cheek.

"Things will get better. You'll see, Frank."

"Thanks. I hope so."

Sam Liversedge and Gene Rafael came over just then, raving about how well she looked.

"Never better," Gene assured her, his grin cutting across his good-humored face. He was just about Andrea's height when she wore high heels but he made up for his lack of inches by a friendly, country-boy naivete that often fooled his opponents and won him most of his court decisions.

Sam seemed to be on his best behavior and seconded all Rafael's compliments.

"They want you in the den, sweetheart," Dex called out.

Andrea hurried along with him, but watched over her shoulder as Frank Kelly met Faith at the front door and kissed her under the dangling mistletoe.

As she walked through the house she took pleasure in the delicious smells coming from the kitchen. She could smell the turkeys browning, and the lingering piquant scent of the celery, onions and mushrooms that had gone into the dressing. She could tell, from the warm, sweet, spicy aroma, that they were baking pumpkin and mince pies.

In the family den Andrea and Dex discovered that Brooke had brought up the subject of investments, and everyone was engaged in a heated conversation. Andrea didn't think Christmas night was a good time to discuss business. She wished for once the family could just forget about money.

Frank looked as bored as she was. He set down his half-filled glass of scotch and stepped out into the hall where Andrea joined him. He sniffed the air appreciatively.

"Those smells! My favorite part of Christmas."

"Mine, too." She glanced over her shoulder. "I think Dex is probably more used to plum pudding and roast goose and all that English stuff."

Frank looked down at his stomach and grinned.

"I'm absolutely starving, but if I don't start watching myself I'm going to get some paunch here." He patted his belly, and looked up wistfully. "I had a tough father. Worked on the docks, but he was fat, all the same. I guess I come by my love of food honestly."

It was a touching thing for him to confess. She liked him very much for it.

"Look. I was going to say hello to Mrs. Trentini when she wasn't so busy, but let's go now. Maybe she'll let us steal a taste. I know we can sniff to our hearts' content."

"Sounds great to me."

She took his hand and led him along the hall to the kitchen. The huge, old-fashioned room was a beehive as three women and a boy bustled around between the kitchen, pantry and storeroom. The dining room swinging door was propped open. One of the girls had begun to set the long mahogany table, and the complications of a formal table setting with its seemingly endless formation of Waterford crystal required Mrs. Trentini's supervision. She ran back and forth between the dining room and the big kitchen stove where another girl was boiling artichokes.

Everybody was in excellent spirits. Frank and Mrs. Trentini argued in a friendly manner about being in the way as Andrea went around sampling whatever tidbits remained outside the double ovens, offering them to Frank as samples. True to his word, he ate everything offered.

Aware of a sudden and unexpected silence, Andrea turned around while chewing a stalk of celery and saw Dex standing in the hall doorway.

She wasn't doing anything wrong—she knew that. But for some strange reason she felt as if she had been caught at something. Frank, likewise chewing celery, looked as guilty as she felt, and Mrs. Trentini still had her hand over her mouth to stifle a laugh.

What made it all look so bad, Andrea thought, was the fact that she hadn't felt this relaxed, this comfortable, since she had left home.

TWENTY-THREE

FRANK GAVE Dex a humorous, apologetic grimace and swallowed hard. His voice was hoarse when he spoke.

"I'll just be getting back to the party now. The—er—food tastes delicious."

He slid away and vanished into the hall. The door closed behind him.

"We missed you, sweetheart," Dex said calmly. He held out one hand. Andrea recovered her composure.

"Mrs. Trentini, may I present my husband, Dexter Cartaret."

"How do you do?" Dex asked formally.

"Happy to make your acquaintance, sir."

Then she went to the refrigerator to get the cranberry sauce.

"I think we are in the way, Andrea. Shall we join the others?"

Despite his good manners Andrea suspected he was jealous of the camaraderie that had existed in the kitchen without him. When they joined the rest of the family no one had even missed them. Sam and Tony were deep in a discussion about the question of television superceding the movie industry. When the downstairs maid announced dinner Tony was still arguing his point stubbornly that all the industry needed were films with more scope.

At least Dex would be impressed by the long formal dining room, Andrea thought, with its new green and beige wallpaper, its Hepplewhite chairs upholstered with green silk that matched the wall, plus the ormolu mirrors that reflected the long electric tapers in the chandelier and the wall bracket lights. The long windows, as in all Victorian homes, were more narrow than Andrea would have liked, but the house was built in the 1870s by Andrea's great-great grandfather and was the only building on this part of Nob Hill that had survived the 1906 earthquake and fire without major renovation.

There was a jarring moment when the dinner guests wandered into the dining room. Everyone except Frank Kelly had been here on previous Christmases and the absence of Grandmother Randi at the head of the table and Grandpa Steve at the other end was sensed sharply.

Aunt Brooke assigned Tony to his father's chair and she herself reserved her sister-in-law's place, which seemed right to Andrea. Unfortunately, however, she found herself sandwiched between Sam and Gene Rafael, with Faith opposite her and Dex on the left of his hostess. Together, Gene and Sam talked nonstop business at her. When Gene started to mention something about the advantage of signing some land sale near Fresno, Andrea cut him off, reminding him lightly that she was trying to concentrate on her dinner.

"Gene's reasoning is sound, all the same," Sam said eagerly. "It's a huge corner lot and a food chain wants to put up a market there for the heavy Valley traffic."

Why doesn't Lombard Enterprises build and then lease the building?" Dex wanted to know.

It was clear that he hadn't missed a thing. It was also clear that Sam didn't like this interruption.

"Because," he explained patiently, "it's a gamble at present. The property won't show its true potential for years."

"But why is this food chain willing to gamble?" Dex looked at Andrea across the table. "Wouldn't it be a good idea to get some traffic figures on it? And find out the cost of other new structures in the area? Not to mention the tax advantages."

Gene wiped his mouth with the damask napkin.

"These surveys cost money. It might be throwing away good cash."

Even Andrea saw the fallacy there. "What about the tax write-off? Dex is right. Steve Lombard would have said to at least investigate."

It was a very small deal in the scheme of Lombard Enterprises and the two men must have realized their mistake in bringing it up at Christmas dinner. But from a few words Andrea overheard later between them, the Fresno area deal had only been the first of a dozen similarly small deals on which they had expected to get her okay tonight. They probably figured that at a family dinner she wouldn't ask questions.

Andrea became aware that Faith was watching her and when she caught Andrea's eye she nodded approval. She had been the first to encourage Andrea to stand on her own feet, to make her own decisions.

Faith herself seemed to be much more cheerful. She and Frank were busy whispering, both of them full of smiles.

The evening went much better after they got off the subject of Lombard Enterprises. Everyone left the table groaning and complaining that he had eaten too much. There was a tree in the formal Victorian living room, carefully decorated with matching silver glass balls, but it was the more casual sunroom upstairs to which they all adjourned.

In the worn comfort of the sunroom—which had always been Randi's favorite spot—the presents had been gathered around a small tree. Brooke appointed herself Santa Claus, handing out expensively wrapped boxes to everyone present.

Before midnight the party broke up after a round of egg nogs. Having seen everyone off, Andrea and Dex climbed the heavy main staircase together.

All the goodnights having been said, Dex opened the bedroom door and laid the evening's presents on the satin chair. Andrea was still out in the hall. She had caught a glimpse of her father's tense and anxious face, and put her hands on his shoulders.

"Daddy, it will turn out right. You'll see."

"Thank you, honey. I knew I could count on my little girl."

Jany lingered behind him to have a whispered word with Andrea.

"Thank you. My dear Andrea, it is you who will save him. If it costs all your fortune it would be worth the effort. He is a very great man, your father. *Bon soir.*"

Dex called to Andrea. "Are you coming, sweetheart?"

"Right away." She didn't feel safe until she was inside her bedroom with the door securely closed. "Would you mind locking it?"

He was surprised but snapped the lock. Then he came back to her, drawing her to him.

"Our first night at home," she told him, smiling.

"Home? Well, I wouldn't go that far. But never mind that for the time being. What happened between you and your father?"

"Nothing, really."

"You looked funny a minute ago."

"Thanks a lot."

He lifted her off the floor. "What's going on?" she demanded with a laugh.

"Just that I haven't had you this close for more than twenty-four hours." He swung her into his arms and kissed her, hard. Nervous over the encounter with her father and Jany, she tried to respond, but again he read the symptoms and sat down on the big bed with Andrea on his lap.

"Righto. Tell me all about it."

She certainly trusted Dex enough to confide in him, didn't she?

"They expect me to bail out my father."

He knew there must be more. "You couldn't stand by and watch him be sued by his stockholders. You knew that. Once he is free and clear of the big studio operation, he can go into a smaller unit, make those films he did so well immediately after the war."

"Unfortunately, father and Jany don't expect to lose control of Prysing itself. They intend to keep both the Hollywood and Culver City studios, which includes their upkeep. And you can imagine what that amounts to—"

"Are you sure?"

"Jany said they knew I'd come through even if it meant spending the whole Lombard fortune on the studio. But even that won't last forever if it keeps going down the drain."

He agreed. "Especially since he's on the wrong trail."

"Track."

They looked into each other's eyes. She blinked and smiled. "But that will keep."

This time when they kissed she responded fully.

It was almost an hour later when Andrea turned over in bed

215

suddenly, remembering that she had something to discuss with Dex before she slept.

"Dex?"

"Umm?"

"Remember the night I saw you the first time? The Ruby Room?"

"I remember very well."

"Did you know you would meet me there?"

"Do you mean—did I have a premonition that I'd meet my future wife—the woman of my dreams?" He stroked her hair.

"Did you really like me?"

"You know I did. But I didn't know I'd see you there. I didn't even know who you were."

"When you went to the Wharf, did you expect to see me?"

He laughed over the memory. "You want the truth? Well, I came out on the street and saw you practically jumping up and down with excitement before getting on a cable car with your friends. So I jumped on that car behind you. You reminded me of a little girl I once... You reminded me of my sister Deirdre."

The sister he had lost in the Nazi fire raids. She had known that he had been originally attracted to her youth and vulnerability, what he thought of as her innocence. This had aroused in him the tenderness formerly reserved only for his memories of Deirdre Cartaret who died so young. He told her now that his feeling for her changed to something more sensual the hour they were together at Ferrante's. That was why he had walked away, returned to New York.

He sat up and stared at her in the dark.

"I know you have more questions. So here goes. First, I came out to San Francisco at Alec Huntington's suggestion to meet his mother, which I proceeded to do. But not at the house. When I found out who you were, I had my qualms about meeting you in Brooke's presence. I thought you would think... Well, that's neither here nor there."

"I know, honey—"

This time his laugh was hard-edged. Something in his tone, in his touch, suddenly changed, hardened.

"You thought the gigolo came to the Ruby Room to meet

216

you and all your fortune. Is that what you've been thinking?"

The wound was deep and painful.

"I wasn't rich then, so you couldn't have been after my fortune. It simply didn't exist then."

The silence lasted too long in the cool dark of her bedroom.

"That would hardly have been good business, and I'm a sharp trader, as anyone will tell you. Goodnight."

"Goodnight, darling. Merry Christmas."

He said nothing.

CHAPTER
TWENTY-FOUR

ANDREA GAVE Dex all the files submitted to her in copy form by Sam Liversedge's office. It was a peace offering; also she wanted to go over every proposal with him before making her own decision. Before many days had passed he was familiar with most of her holdings, and nothing more had been said about that painful night.

It was disconcerting, though, to find that he had sold out his own Century-Planet Oil holdings bought with the earnings from the profits he had made for her. Perhaps he just wanted to test the waters on something else before he ventured her money. She took Sam's advice, however, and retained her own Planet Oil stock despite the company's attempts to get control of her father's studio. She even bought ten thousand shares in Planet preferred and gave orders to purchase more as the market fluctuated slightly with the Middle East's volatile politics. She had her reasons. Buying their stocks was one way to get a handle on Planet's operation and possibly save something for her father.

Some things didn't go as smoothly. Andrea found everyone against her, including Sam and Dex, when she stuck to her guns about opening the Reno Lombard Hotel without a casino license. There was nothing she could do about the ever-present slot machines that would line the free space on the ground floor of the hotel, but at least without gambling there would be a more spacious, elegant feeling about the lobby and several intriguing cocktail corners, with the best chef they could steal to oversee the lobby cafe as well as the elegant river-view dining room, or so she imagined.

The latter would be called the River Room and would have

comfort as well as beauty. She saw it perfectly in her mind. The north wall was to be entirely of glass, with the Truckee River ambling by at a safe level below the riverbank. The banquette padding against the south wall would be of the best leather imported from Italy.

All this would hopefully mollify those who hankered after the craps and roulette tables. . . .

Andrea could hardly wait for the opening. Inevitably, the whole project made her extremely nervous and she had several bad ulcer flareups. Once when she complained of the headaches caused by the long, knockout sleep her pills gave her, Dex wanted to have the pills analyzed. But Andrea put up a fight.

Then Faith joined Dex in badgering her. They now told her she must go and have a new gastro-intestinal series at the hospital and get herself straightened out before she developed something worse. Andrea was adamant about not having the pills analyzed, but went along with them and admitted herself to the hospital.

During her two-day stay Dex and Faith even visited her in the hospital together. She wondered what made them suddenly warm to each other. Was Dex attracted to her cool, blonde good looks? . . .

Just as Andrea had predicted, a half dozen specialists found nothing wrong except an inflamed, ulcerous area in her duodenum, and she went home with a new diet and another prescription that calmed the ulcer but couldn't prevent the basic cause.

Because Andrea suspected that the real reason behind her steadily worsening ulcer was her insecurity over Dex. There was the nagging worry over how long her husband would continue to love her without enjoying the fortune he might possibly have hoped to control. The medicines could not prevent these fears, but they could calm her pain. So she continued her routine, relying on first one and then another of the tiny white pills.

Faith Cortlandt divided her time now between Andrea's heavy work schedule and Aunt Brooke's social obligations. Andrea offered to hire someone else, but Faith was adamant.

"I was in on your kingdom from the time of your coronation, honey. I want to see it through to the end." She laughed when she saw Andrea's expression. "Make that—just see it through."

It was true that Faith's efficiency made Andrea's life a little simpler than it might have been. But her friend did have a way of uncovering troublesome matters that Andrea would rather have left undisturbed.

One morning early in spring Andrea was fussing over her portfolio of immediate things to do at her grandfather's old desk, anxious to clear things so she could leave for the Reno hotel opening. Faith was in the midst of balancing Andrea's personal checking account.

"Hey! What's this?" She held up a blue Wells Fargo bank check. She waved it to Andrea, who was busy sketching her idea of how the lobby floor furniture should be arranged in the Reno Lombard Hotel.

"Looks like a check." Andrea went back to her sketch.

"Yes, but it's not yours."

Andrea raised her head. Why was Faith making such an issue over one check? Obviously, the bank had made a mistake. It was not unusual. Among them, the family had a half dozen accounts at Wells Fargo.

"So, what are you getting at?"

Faith was a bit taken aback by Andrea's brusqueness.

"Well, it's not important. It's only a check with Dex's signature. Got in this bunch by mistake. Hmm...San Diego."

Andrea would have much preferred to ignore the whole thing but that was not to be. She tapped her pencil against the desk.

"Well, since you're aching to tell me, what has San Diego got to do with it?"

Faith reread the check. "Nothing, only the check is made out to some bank in San Diego. Two thousand dollars for deposit to an account. A numbered account—no name." She laughed and teased, "Maybe he's piling up getaway money. In a border city." She saw the hard look Andrea gave her. "Only a joke, Andrea. Believe me. Only a joke."

"Better send it back to the bank. Otherwise, Dex will have a terrible time balancing."

"Sure. Okay. Sorry I interrupted your train of thought."

Too late. Hours later Andrea was still wondering about the check and why Dex was stashing away his profits from the Planet Oil deal in a city supposedly foreign to him. Or was it foreign?

She brought up the subject of San Diego at dinner that night, relieved that Faith was out for the evening. She had gone to Berkeley to help Frank move into a new apartment. They had resumed a tentative bond, both being careful not to expect too much too soon.

Aunt Brooke was present at the dinner table but much of the business conversation went past her. They were discussing the Reno hotel opening when Andrea began her probe casually.

"After Reno, I wonder what town we'll honor next with a monument to Lombard Enterprises. Mr. Bursten, Gene's law partner, thinks we're ignoring a terrific market in the south."

"The south?"

"Southern California. Los Angeles sort of belongs to father. I don't like to crowd him. But we have some shares in a water-front project in San Diego, don't we, Dex?"

He seemed genuinely surprised. "You may have. I've never run across them."

"Do you know San Diego at all?"

"Never been there. I understand it's a beautiful city. Brooke, you have an eye on that piece of cake. Let me serve you."

Brooke looked at him indulgently. "You are a gentleman. Thanks."

Andrea ran a few crumbs of the homemade three-layer chocolate cake around the plate with her fork.

"Dex, there must be lots of reasons for investing in Southern California, wouldn't you say?"

"I should think so." It was not a subject that seemed to interest him. "I've been told that the future of the state is in the south. I must say, I like what I've seen of Northern California better."

But he said he hadn't seen the south, so how could he have a point of reference? If what he said was true, why the secret bank account in San Diego? She stared down at her plate. San Diego was close to the Mexican border...

Dex's hand closed around hers and he made her a promise with warm, loving amusement.

"Sweetheart, I'll get you another piece. A whole cake. Don't look so sad."

She was shaken out of her mood, smiled and closed her fingers over his hand, responding to his tender touch. She banished her doubts to the back of her mind.

Andrea couldn't bear to confront him with any more questions. One day she would hear the truth. Sooner or later she would find out why he had set up that account in the San Diego bank. . . .

She found herself rushing out to glance at his mail each day before the houseman picked it up and distributed it. One morning Dex caught her at it. He and Frank Kelly had been having breakfast at the Fairmont and discussing Frank's position at the university. Frank would be up for tenure this year and wanted Dex's advice on how best to ensure getting it.

Caught poring over Dex's stack of letters, Andrea gave them to him sheepishly. He opened the letter on top. It was from an insurance company asking him what would happen to him as family provider if he should die suddenly and leave his family penniless.

Dex handed the letter to Andrea and they both laughed at the irony of it.

She was delighted when the date of the Reno hotel opening approached and she became too busy to worry about herself.

Never having seen the fabulous Sierras at close range, Dex drove Andrea over Donner Summit just after spring had opened up the treacherous passes. They were trying out the new white Porsche he had chosen for her. Aunt Brooke and Faith, Sam and the Rafaels flew into Reno and they all met downtown at the brand new Lombard Hotel. Surrounded by reporters from Nevada, San Francisco, Oakland and Sacramento, they were all photographed as Andrea cut the big blue satin ribbon across the main entrance.

A crowd had collected for the occasion but, as Sam pointed out to Andrea, there were a lot more people outside than checked into the hotel.

"What do you mean?" Andrea asked him. "The desk clerk said we were full."

"Freebies, my dear. Guests of yours, ours, everybody. The house has been papered, as they say. I was talking with DeCenzo, the manager, and he says the future bookings look bad. They want something more, Andrea. It's only natural. They came to Reno to gamble."

Since the plan to eliminate gambling from the hotel was Andrea's first real contribution to Lombard Enterprises, she stubbornly refused to listen to all reasoning.

"Well, I must say, you don't help matters with your negative attitude. We'll have to advertise more heavily. In Los Angeles. And back East. Also down in Arizona and Texas."

Dex grinned as camera shutters clicked. "You're more like your father every day," he said out of the corner of his mouth.

"You mean my grandfather."

"No. Your father. Pursuing the impossible dream."

She was relieved when the group, including a television company filming a TV Western series in town, moved inside to inspect Andrea's brainchild.

They loved it. Photographers from the movie company shot film of Andrea and Dex in the handsome black and red lobby, and soon the entire movie cast and crew had fanned out to pose against various slot machines. For a brief hour or so the three cocktail bars were jammed.

After that, however, the crowd disappeared across the nearest bridge to the gambling center of town.

When Andrea and Dex had dinner that night in the River Room, the place was almost empty. The strings of colored lights above the riverbank cast little pockets of brightness across the empty tables, highlighting all the expensive glass and silverware, the fine quality linens. Even the banquettes were deserted except for one elderly couple at the far end of the room.

Dex reached over to the bowl of flowers on the ledge behind Andrea and broke off one of the tiny pink roses and held it under her chin.

"I can't tell whether you like butter or not. Your skin doesn't glow yellow."

She stifled a giggle. "It's buttercups you're supposed to use."

He flicked the rose back and forth, tickling her throat.

"Then this one must tell me you like strawberry ice cream. You glow pink."

"You're an idiot." Her eyes caught the many lights from the riverfront and sparkled. He leaned over and kissed her nose.

"You are enchanting."

"No. I'm a failed entrepreneur."

"That's a big word for someone who's had a bottle of Montrechat," he teased.

"Pour some more and let's get on with our celebration." She leaned forward. "It's not a failure, you know. It's just ahead of its time."

"Of course."

"Don't make fun of me. You'll see I'm right. Sam, the others—they'll all see." She leaned over and squinted her eyes. "Do you want to go across the bridge and gamble with the others?"

"No, indeed. I want to stay here and flirt with an entrepreneur. I've never done that before."

She sipped a little more of the wine. "I love you, Dex."

It was just as well that they could enjoy this last quiet evening alone. The morning brought endless problems, beginning with a dozen local phone calls, plus visits by Sam and Gene with the news that two members of the city council were interested in a conference. The subject was the possible use of the new Lombard Hotel for civic meetings, provided that one of the large third-floor offices could be adapted to the purpose.

An exclusive men's club needed a meeting place as well. This sounded fine to Andrea until she heard the provisions.

"Tell me about it," she said, drinking her morning coffee.

Gene explained. "The Pioneer Club would like to see some sort of casino arrangement installed for the benefit of their members."

So much for that idea. Andrea realized the struggle to keep casino complications out of the hotel hadn't ended with the opening of the hotel. It was all beginning again.

Sam examined the end of his cigar. "Gene, tell her the rest of it. Might as well."

Gene Rafael shrugged. "There's one guy. The city manager.

His wife is mad about the hotel as is. She wants to buy a piece of it. Or at least, lease several rooms. Hold weekly meetings, have daily lunch chitchat. You know. A clubhouse for women. But she insists on talking to you in person. Thinks you're a celebrity."

"And so she is," Sam put in gallantly. "But Andrea, Mrs. Petronelli flies out at noon for Europe. And she's hard to pin down. She'll have a hundred other ideas before she gets back, according to her husband. You've got to impress her. You have snob appeal for her. She saw your picture last month in Town and Country, the one taken of you and Dex at the War Memorial Opera House."

"No problem." Andrea looked at Dex. "See? I told you this place would be a success."

Dex kissed her. "You'll win her over."

"Can't say I see it, myself. The woman's pretty fly-brained and unpredictable," Gene cut in. "You'll have to pin her down in writing."

"I will."

The phone was ringing and Gene and Sam were badgering her but they moved to one corner of the big room when Dex answered the phone.

"For you, sweetheart. From Hollywood."

"It's got to be father." She took the phone from Dex anxiously. "Don't go. I bet he's in trouble with the company. I might need your advice."

Tony was calling from his den in the Hollywood Hills mansion where Andrea had grown up. His voice was tight.

"Honey, I know you're busy. I read about the Reno opening. The *Times* carried a picture this morning. "You—" He cleared his throat. "You photograph like a million dollars."

"Thank you, daddy." *Please let it not be too bad.*

"Believe me, I'd rather do anything than ruin your triumph. But I'm afraid I have to make a decision soon, and I wanted to know the bottom line."

"What do you want me to do exactly? Tell me, daddy."

"I'll get to the point. I don't suppose there's much hope that you can get leverage with Century-Planet Oil, is there? Heavy purchase of stock that might help in the take-over?"

"But they can't take over Prysing without allowing for your position. You're the major stockholder."

"They've now got their hands on the shares I put up to borrow the remaining money for the next season. Don't tell me I was a damn fool. I've been kicking myself for days. Doesn't seem to have done any good."

Before she had time to respond, Tony cut in. "I think I have my answer. I've got to rethink my position at Prysing Productions. Andrea, I'm at least bright enough to know we can't fight Planet Oil. We'd be fighting half the countries in the Middle East, besides their British pipeline interests. We can't take on the whole world."

"Oh, daddy, I'm so sorry. I wanted to help. I really did."

"I know, honey." There was a painful silence. When he spoke again Tony had pulled himself together. The warmth and the old devotion were back.

She remembered Dex's talk about Tony's early films.

"You made some great pictures in the early days. And profitable, too. That kind of film would have an enormous TV market if you had your own unit."

"There's the rub. My own unit. I'll have to do a lot of thinking, fast. Planet Oil is holding stockholders' meetings today and tomorrow. Maybe a white elephant movie studio won't look like such a big deal to them."

She didn't remind him of what he must suspect himself, that Planet would probably tear down the studios and turn the lots into luxury skyscrapers. She covered the mouthpiece of the phone and hurriedly explained to Sam and the others what was happening.

"I'm going down to the Planet stockholders' meeting in Los Angeles this afternoon and tomorrow morning," she whispered to them.

Sam shook his head. "You do that and you've lost the only nibble this hotel has got—that is, if you still want to keep a casino out."

The Petronelli woman, of course.

"Daddy, we've hit a snag. What we want is to get enough clout at Planet Oil to give you control of your own unit. We don't have to try and outbid the whole world. Just a little power would do. So hold on." She put her hand over the mouthpiece. "Can't you and Gene handle it? Lay on the charm with Mrs. Petronelli?"

"No chance. She told Gene she wanted to meet you."

"She wouldn't even discuss it with me," Gene admitted.

Andrea and Dex were the only ones who had dealt with Planet from the first. She glanced at Dex. Sam and Gene stared at him as well.

She was confident. "Darling?"

He looked at the little gold clock on the nightstand and nodded.

She went on. "You could get to L.A. in less than two hours from here. You know about the company. You talked to that sheik in London. I've got to clear up this hotel mess. I know if I leave them now, Sam and Gene will be talked into the casino business. I can join you by the night flight, if I have the nerve to get into the damned plane alone."

"Well, now," Gene began but Sam stepped on his foot.

"I'm all set." Dex leaned over the bed and kissed her. Andrea realized that it would be her first night apart from him since their wedding.

"Daddy, sorry for the long delay, but it looks as if Dex will have to come in my place."

Tony agreed reluctantly.

"And remember, we can't buy them out," she warned Tony.

"I know. I've been thinking about it the last few minutes. I may be through at Prysing, but by God, I'm not through in this business!" She was surprised by the renewed courage she heard in his voice. "You wait, young lady. I'll triumph yet. Oh! Jany wants to talk to you."

Andrea heard whispered arguing in the background.

"Hey, now, it seems Jany can't make it to the phone. You tell Dex I'll be waiting for his call this afternoon . . . And honey?"

"Yes, daddy."

"We love you. Don't you ever doubt it for a minute."

As she hung up, Faith walked into the room. When Dex's trip was explained to her, Faith offered to help out.

"I can get your air tickets. The office is just down the street."

Dex quickly refused. "I'll get them. I'm rather good at spur-of-the-moment trips."

He left within minutes, not allowing Andrea the time to change her mind and go with him.

"All right," Andrea said after he left. "Tell them to send for Mrs. Petronelli. Meanwhile, I'll bathe and dress."

"Sure," Faith said in the doorway. "By the way, Frank and I were talking on the phone and he's coming up tomorrow after his one o'clock class. He called your home to see if there were any messages and Mrs. Trentini said you and Dex had a lot of mail. He wants to know if he should stop by and pick it up on the way."

"Fine. Tell him thanks."

It would be nice to have his company when she and Faith dined the next two nights.

She missed Dex already. She would count the hours until his first phone call from Los Angeles.

TWENTY-FIVE

FAITH CONGRATULATED Andrea heartily after her luncheon meeting with Mrs. Petronelli. The woman had flown off to Rome and Marbella happily under contract to the Lombard Hotel and already planning the bylaws of her club as a rival to the all-male Pioneer Club.

Andrea was pleased within limits. It was only half a triumph, not able to be enjoyed fully without Dex beside her, she explained to Faith. And Faith understood. She had been alone, without male companionship for a long time. But tonight Frank would be arriving, and for once she and not Andrea would be the favored woman.

Walking out on the lanai the evening before in her diaphanous blue nightgown and chiffon robe, Faith had caught a glimpse of distant hills to the northeast, above the low skyline of Reno. Beyond those she could make out the huge, snowy peaks of the High Sierras to the west. She had thought then of the Sierras as a wall separating her from Frank. She missed him terribly.

There were things that Faith knew instinctively about Frank and one of them was that he loved her, not Andrea, no matter how much he flirted. She sensed it every time he touched her, knew it by the way he had kissed her on Christmas Day when she returned from Europe. His shy passion was unmistakable.

Andrea and Faith were in the bar of the hotel when Frank Kelly checked in that Friday evening. In one hand he carried a battered valise. His only other luggage was a Gucci attaché case, which Faith had bought him in Italy for Christmas. In this he carried the Cartaret mail.

He came bounding over to where they sat, kissed Faith gently and shook hands with Andrea. Andrea leaned forward when he gave her the attaché case and kissed him on the cheek.

"Thank you, Frank. For bringing the mail and yourself." Andrea smiled at Faith.

"I picked up everything Mrs. Trentini had collected. A little package came special delivery just before I came by. She thought you might need it. It's here somewhere."

"Never mind," Andrea said. "I'll find it. You let Faith take you on up to see your room. Put your bags away. I'll be fine down here. I need time to go through my mail anyway."

"You're sure you'll be all right?" Faith said.

"Sure I'm sure," she said, winking at her friend.

Frank pointed to the attaché case. "Hope there are no problems."

"How about coming to my rooms when you get settled, and I'll go over things with Faith?"

"Fine," Faith answered. She saw the way Frank watched Andrea, and knew he was as impressed as she was by the change in Andrea. Tonight this sophisticated young businesswoman carried herself like someone used to wielding power. She was growing up fast. And she looked great. Her green Givenchy suit matched the color of her eyes, and looked stunning with her dark hair. But there was more. She didn't seem quite as natural and spontaneous as she used to be. There were little worry lines around her eyes, though in some ways these enhanced her looks, added maturity. They did make her look different.

Faith caught the elevator with Frank. They walked to his room in silence. When he closed the door, however, they fell together in an embrace that hinted of all the unspoken longing they both felt.

"We've got to get back soon," Faith reminded him.

Frank was nuzzling the back of her neck.

"Where is *Mr*. Cartaret? Why isn't he looking after his wife, as he should?"

"He's in L.A. on the Planet Oil deal."

He looked surprised. "Good God! Does she know what he's up to?"

230

"She sent him. I think it's part of an effort to save Tony Lombard. He's in big trouble."

"I think Andrea gets into things way above her head. She really needs a keeper. Why can't she have some of your good sense?"

Faith punched his shoulder playfully. "You're such a gallant soul. What girl could resist your way with words?" She saw him glance at the door and understood. "All right. Let's go before Andrea misses us."

While they waited for the elevator, he turned thoughtfully. "She's got another package from Los Angeles. It came special delivery."

"So?"

"It was from Jany Lombard." He said, and shrugged. Faith took a deep breath. "She's been acting funny. Wouldn't speak to Andrea yesterday on the phone. Frank, sometimes I wonder. It would be easy enough to substitute some other pills. About the same size. Andrea had several bad spells on her honeymoon. Did you know that?"

The elevator door opened but he stood with his hand against the door, staring at her.

"When did they start? I don't remember that she had spells before she went to New York."

"She did. But they got worse on her honeymoon. Frank, remember that account in the San Diego bank that I told you about?" She described their discovery of Dex's check.

He waved that aside as irrelevant. "He's in the marriage for the money—we knew that from the beginning. It doesn't surprise me that he has a hidden bank account. I just hope he's not milking all her accounts. Damn him! And she's so trusting she'd never know the difference."

They rode up to Andrea's suite on the penthouse floor. Before they entered the foyer of the Cartaret suite, Frank made a proposal.

"If we could persuade her to have every pill in the package Jany sent tested, that might straighten things out. Unless—"

Faith interrupted. "You know, we're forgetting someone with a powerful grudge against Andrea. Good old Aunt Brooke."

"Brooke? You've got to be kidding."

"Christmas night, after you left and everyone went upstairs, Brooke and I had a nightcap together. It loosened up her tongue and I got the distinct impression that Dex Cartaret originally belonged to Brooke."

"Well, I'll be damned."

They were ushered into Andrea's suite by Sam Liversedge, who was there with Brooke enjoying cocktails. Sam immediately buzzed around making drinks.

Faith went over to Brooke and whispered in her ear.

"Bet you he wishes mine was arsenic." They both laughed.

"No. It's Dex he dislikes. And that's odd, because the truth of the matter is that Dex agrees with Sam most of the time. They seem to think alike."

Faith felt Frank nudge her. She tried to avoid his eyes.

Andrea decided to meet Dex by the early morning flight. He had called and told her he would fly back to Reno to meet her instead. "I'll call you later," he had promised. She was hungry to hear his voice before she slept tonight.

"May I freshen your drink?" Frank offered.

"I'll do it." She couldn't figure out why Faith and Frank were here and not off with Sam and Brooke at the gambling tables across the river.

"Listen," she said after she had made the drink. "Do you two really want to go through this junk with me? Why aren't you off somewhere having fun?"

Faith and Frank exchanged glances. After an uncomfortable pause, Faith explained. "We're worried about those pills your stepmother sent you, Andrea, especially after what you told me about her not wanting to speak on the phone yesterday."

The long blue evening of the desert country, which had seemed so romantic the first night Andrea and Dex spent together in Reno, depressed her tonight. She resented Faith's remark because that very question had nagged at her ever since she saw the package come to her in such a rush. It *was* odd, as Faith pointed out, considering how antagonistic Jany had been recently. But Andrea had already acted on her secret fears.

"All right. You want the truth? I've already sent it air mail to Doctor Firth in San Francisco."

They all laughed nervously. "No harm in having him check the pills out," Faith said. "Anything else of interest?"

Andrea flipped through her mail. Faith was meanwhile examining the small pile of letters addressed to Dex, fastened with a rubber band. Most of his mail consisted of ads, but there was one personal letter which was stuck under the flap of a real estate ad for a luxury villa in Marbella, Sardinia.

Faith slipped the letter out. A Mexican stamp. The writing was probably female, small, with a lot of flourishes, addressed to Mr. Dexter L. Cartaret.

Andrea saw her look at Frank.

"What is it? Don't tell me it's a threat. I get them every time they mention me in print." Her voice trailed off. She had seen the stamp. "Let me have it."

Faith's hands shook slightly. "A mash note, my grandmother used to call them. Don't forget. He's famous, too."

Andrea snatched it away from her, and with a coolness that would have done credit to Faith, Andrea asked Frank to hand her the mother-of-pearl letter opener.

The letter inside was dated seven days earlier. Before reading it Andrea turned the page over and glanced at the bottom.

It was signed: *For all those glorious times we had, I am always your own, Terri.*

Faith read over her shoulder. "Good God!"

Frank took a step toward the women but Andrea waved him back with the letter. She began to read it to herself but it was obvious her two friends would have to know. She coughed and took a deep breath.

"Darling Dex," she read aloud. "I have the original of the newspaper notice. You must have seen that the one I sent you was a photographed copy. A friend made it for me. Surely, you understand the significance of it. José Gonzalvez, a clerk of the court of the district of Guerrero, died in Taxco of a disease of the stomach. That nasty little man was recommended to me by my lawyer who swore he was a judge, but we were deceived.

"Well, *mi querido*, all our efforts were in vain. As I hinted to you, the divorce must be done over. I am currently leasing an enchanting villa above the bay. *Monte Marques,* it's called. Belongs to that dashing Italian cinema genius, Luigi Bartolo. He always did have a thing for me, remember? He is generous about the rental, but I have exceedingly expensive servants, so I'm afraid we must tap the till of your mistress, the one who calls herself—" Andrea raised her voice. "The one who calls herself Mrs. Dexter Cartaret.

"Come and discuss that ridiculous little Mr. Gonzalvez with me. Monte Marques is just around the corner from Acapulco Bay, darling. The San Diego money arrived safely. However, it was only a drop in the bucket, as we both know so well.

"For all those glorious times we had, I am always your own, Terri."

Andrea dropped the letter on the sofa. Frank made a grab for it, and he and Faith bent over the table and reread the letter.

"Damn them both," Faith spat out.

Andrea began to laugh, softly at first and then slightly hysterically. Faith went over to her.

"I'm okay. Honest. It's just that I really thought it would ...Damn it." Her voice was not as controlled as she wished it to be. "I honestly thought this marriage would last." She tried to stifle weak tears.

"We may be jumping to conclusions," Frank said quickly. "It might be blackmail, mightn't it?"

"Leave it to a man to stick up for this joker," Faith said. "The way I see it, the language is clear enough. They're in it together. He marries rich and sends his money to her care. But something went wrong with the original divorce—or maybe it was planned that way—and she expects you to panic when he tells you you're not really married. You'll pay up and drag this marriage out a little longer."

Andrea suddenly felt as if she were going to be sick. She stumbled to the guest bathroom and leaned over the wash basin. The feeling passed but when she looked up at her face in the three-way mirror, she saw a young woman whose face she barely recognized as her own.

Her skin was bluish white, framed by her heavy black hair. She raised her finger to outline the full, soft lips that looked drained of all color. Two nights ago Dex had followed the curves of those lips with gentle touches of his mouth. Even then he had been sending money to his ex-...No, To his *wife*. Apparently, they were still married, which made Andrea his mistress. The image in the mirror blurred and she blinked back the tears angrily.

She clenched her fist and hit the mirror as hard as she could. Fortunately, the glass didn't break.

"If there's one thing I don't need it's seven years' bad luck."

She felt a surge of nausea again and leaned tiredly over the sink. Nothing happened.

Faith stuck her head in the bathroom. "We're going to give you some privacy now, okay?"

Andrea nodded, not trusting herself to speak.

Andrea was vaguely aware of Frank in the bathroom behind her. He touched the back of her hair with a gentle hand, then kissed her temple. "We'll be here when you need us. Just remember, we love you."

He left Andrea with a reluctant backward step. She would remember his tenderness and understanding.

When she was alone the world seemed unusually silent. Her hands were slippery on the edge of the wash basin and moist with her tears. She hadn't been aware that she was crying again. She closed her eyes but the stinging tears seemed to flow of their own volition. Her thoughts were calm....

Darling, I know you love me a little. I must be very careful to believe that. It's something to hang on to. You really thought you were free when you married me. You couldn't have done this thing to me knowingly....

I'm not his wife. He has a wife.

Oh, please, dear God, don't let that be true....

She never knew how long she stood hunched over the basin in the bathroom. When the room finally stopped spinning she pulled herself together, washed her face and laid a cool, wet washcloth over her face and closed her eyes. She still looked flushed, her eyes flat, lifeless.

She returned to the living room where she perched herself on the end of the love seat and picked up the telephone. She called Dex's Los Angeles hotel, asking for his room. Almost immediately the answer came. Mr. Cartaret had checked out.

"When?"

"This afternoon, early," the hotel operator said.

"Did he leave a forwarding address?"

He hadn't. Andrea cut the connection.

It took her some time to recall her father's telephone number. Her mind was in such turmoil she almost called her own number before she remembered.

He wasn't in.

"Let me speak to my stepmother," she said to the servant who had answered. Jany was now gushing with friendliness.

"Andrea, *chèrie*, I'm sorry I couldn't speak to you the other day. I wasn't feeling well and I—"

"Thanks awfully for the medicine. Yes. I received it. It was thoughtful of you. Jany, is Dex staying with you?"

He wasn't.

"I just thought he might have gone there to explain what happend at the Planet meetings."

"Your Dexter is a fine man. He took Tony to the meeting of Planet stockholders. Afterwards he talked at length with Tony about his plans for future films for TV. You are fortunate, Andrea. He is a good man."

Lucky me. "Thank you, Jany." She could hardly speak. She stopped and tried to compose her voice. "Where is Dex now?"

"I do not know, *chèrie*. He left the meeting this morning. He said he had an errand out of the city."

"And you haven't seen him since?"

"No, but Andrea, you do agree, things are looking up for Tony—"

"Good. Wonderful. Would you give my love to daddy? And of course to yourself." She hung up, feeling nervous and jumpy as a cat, and dialed Faith's room. Faith answered at once.

"We're right here."

"Is there anything we can do? Tell us," Frank called out.

"Come up to my suite right away." She clicked off.

Andrea felt that her brain was running on double time. It was imperative to get the truth from Dex at once. Nothing else mattered. Even her precious Reno hotel deal wasn't so important.

She took Terri's letter and read it again. Terri must have hoped Andrea would see it. She wanted money. Not Dex. And there wasn't a shred of evidence that Dex still loved Terri.

She caught herself. Except for the San Diego money.

But Frank could be right. It could have been blackmail.

Faith and Frank Kelly arrived within minutes.

"I don't want any arguments," Andrea announced. "I'm going to go right to Dex and get the truth."

"But will he know the truth?" Frank asked. "I'd think the woman would be the one to see."

"No. I trust my husband, oddly enough. I want to hear his side. I know he left Los Angeles this afternoon. I've got one or two ideas. Frank, you wanted to help me."

"Yes. Anything."

"Good." Her hands were shaking and she put them behind her. "Can you check the San Diego hotels? I'll see if he's in Acapulco. And Faith?"

"How about if I check Acapulco? I'm a whiz at Spanish."

Andrea smiled grimly. "My project."

"No, it isn't. Andrea, you sit down. You need a square meal. And while you're doing that, I'll call Acapulco."

Andrea's legs were trembling and she sat down abruptly. She tried to keep her mind clear, but everything was moving too fast. She had an awful feeling she might faint.

Perhaps Dex was on his way back to Reno to surprise her, she thought, and huddled further into the comfortable couch, pressing her hands against her abdomen, trying to stop the grinding pain that was her usual ulcer alarm. She roused herself when she heard Faith calling room service and fumbling to order dinner for Andrea.

"Just make sure to order some wine. See if they have a blanc de blancs. I had it in Paris once."

She remembered vividly the good time she and Dex had that day. Danielle and Carl Friedrich were along too and for once, nothing went wrong. Carl drove them all to Barbizon, the artists' town on the verge of the Fontainebleau Forest. It had been one of those perfect fall days with a piercing, windswept blue sky that was so like San Francisco.

The little hotel-restaurant was full, so Carl ordered a bottle of a local blanc de blancs and the four of them sat drinking in the deserted patio garden. Having emptied the bottle, they went back inside and found a vacant table. They ordered a salad of crudités and followed it with seared and buttered steaks which came only a quarter of an inch thick but still managed to be rare. The pommes frites had the exquisite, faintly sweet-salty taste that Dex said he had never found anywhere except in France.

It was all being repeated tonight. Only Dex was missing. . . .

Somehow, the grinding ulcer pain slipped away. Too much to do. Too many secret doors to unlock. Her mind simply refused to accept the pain.

Frank was busy phoning all the prominent hotels in San Diego. So far, no Dexter Cartaret had checked in.

"Try Dexter Leland," Andrea called.

No Dexter Leland either.

Faith, on the other hand, succeeded with the fifth hotel she phoned in Acapulco. The resort was crowded and apparently Dex had been forced to stay in a hotel outside the bay area of the city. Or maybe, thought Andrea, Dex wanted to be close to Terri, whose villa was on the heights beyond Acapulco Bay.

Faith turned to Andrea. "He's not in his room."

"Good," Andrea said. She took the phone away from Faith.

The Acapulco hotel operator spoke to her in fair English.

"Is this Señora Cartaret? He is expecting a call from the Señora Cartaret."

Andrea was shaken. "*Si.* I mean yes. This is Mrs. Cartaret." But he couldn't possibly know she would call him in Mexico. It took a moment before she realized he was expecting Terri Cartaret's call.

"What is the message, Señora Cartaret?"

She thought fast. "I will call him again, late in the morning. Or perhaps in the early afternoon. Tell him to keep his room there."

"But señora, the señor has informed us he will probably leave early in the morning."

"Tell him."

"Yes, señora."

Andrea set the phone back. She felt a little heady, drunk

with her own anger and power and beneath it all, a sense of her terrible loss.

"I'm flying to Acapulco. Tonight. All by myself."

Faith protested. "No, Andrea. It's too much. You're not up to it. You know how you are about planes."

Frank spoke up. "There are no more planes out of here tonight. I already checked. I have to get back to Berkeley tomorrow morning. I've got term papers to grade. But you can get a Los Angeles plane tomorrow surely, and go on from there."

Andrea stood up and stretched graceful, tense arms toward the ceiling. "Oh, no. You both are forgetting something. I'm Andrea Lombard. I can get any damn thing I want. And I want to rent a plane. Now. Reno to Acapulco. Hell, I'll buy it if necessary." Frank and Faith both seemed jolted. Andrea had *never* talked like that before. This was a different woman from the one they both knew. Or perhaps not different—just desperate.

"Might as well buy a pilot too, while you're at it," Faith suggested drily.

"Don't be funny. I want a plane and a pilot and a flight plan that's okayed, and border permits and anything else. And I want it in the next hour."

"My Lord, kid! It'll take half an hour just to get you out to the airport. Suppose they don't have—"

"Faith," Andrea said, "just do it! Frank, if you want to help me so damn much, go ahead and help Faith. I'll pack a suitcase."

Frank opened his mouth. Andrea read the uncertainty in his face. She reached up and kissed him very gently. "I'm sorry. I know you and Faith are worried about me. Don't be. I'm a big girl now. And I'm off to the wars. On a plane."

CHAPTER
TWENTY-SIX

IF FAITH had been with her, she would have been a great help. Faith spoke Spanish with some fluency, and she wasn't intimidated by Customs, police or concierges. But Andrea knew she had to learn many things, not the least of which was the ability to stand on her own two feet, to do things for and by herself.

She felt a definite triumph when she found herself being raced around Acapulco Bay in the limousine that had been waiting for her only a few steps from the airport runway. She had come a long way, alone. And it hadn't been easy.

During the long flight with its hair-raising stops and its forbidding but polite Mexican officials, she distracted herself from her flying phobia by reading over and over the woman's letter. She was now firmly convinced that Terri Cartaret was making an attempt at blackmail. The attempt had already been partially successful.

Dex had to be down here to settle with her, she thought now. If he had intended to bleed Andrea for some large sum he would have done so already.

Maybe that would come later....

In her childhood Andrea had been the only "little person," as everyone called her then, in a family of grownups, tall and powerful, looming over her. A world-famous movie-star mother. The head of a great movie studio for a father. A grandmother who practically ran the finer community interests of San Francisco, and a grandfather who was on a first-name basis with presidents, kings and queens all over the world.

It had taken Steve's bequest to show her that at least one of those glorious beings rated her higher than she rated herself.

Her grandfather had expected her some day to follow in his steps.

But now all that was being shattered by the aching uncertainty of Dex's love for her. . . .

She settled into the comfort of the Cadillac's back seat, hardly noticing the fabulous half-moon of bright waters that must be Acapulco Bay. She had seen Mexico once as she saw Europe, bit by bit, in the company of her mother who was filming a movie in the Yucatan. It had been ungodly hot on the set, and her mother had kept Andrea busy with guides explaining why someone threw someone else into the pits as a sacrifice. Nor had it helped that the rest of her knowledge came from Faith Cortlandt who described frequently and in bloody detail what happened in the Tijuana bullring.

She told herself now that she was learning Mexico all over again, seeing beautiful Acapulco, all green and sparkling blue, with her own eyes. If Dex were beside her, he would explain things to her in his wise way. If . . .

Andrea was determined to prove to herself and the world, if necessary, that Dex was innocent in this mess. And at the same time she would prove to herself that she was capable of handling her own life.

The highway wound around Acapulco Bay past a strip of new beachfront hotels, elaborate Moorish-Spanish complexes catering largely to wealthy foreign tourists.

She watched the tanned hotel guests as the car sped by the beachfront with curious detachment. Her own preference was for crisp, cool, foggy San Francisco. This was the world she knew best, however inseparable it was from the often frenetic considerations of real estate, stocks and high finance.

She couldn't wait to get back to that world. With her husband beside her, there were so many things they could accomplish together.

To begin with, there was the big lot in the valley near Fresno where she was going to hold out for building and leasing, rather than selling. Not to mention the properties at the border of the Lombard ranch in Northern California. Whole communities could be built in those vacant fields bordering the highways.

Some day, she and Dex might even find the time to turn their attention to modernizing procedures for papaya and pineapple crops in the Hawaiian fields near the house where she was born on the windward coast of Oahu.

So much to do, and Dex was in all of it—that is, if he loved her. Each of these separate pieces, like parts in a jigsaw puzzle, was just waiting for her to act upon it. Once she had her husband back....

Leaving behind the traffic jam around the bay, the big black Cadillac climbed the highway and crossed a headland with many Mediterranean-style villas perched on the jungle-green hillside. Coming into sight of the next bay, much smaller but equally dazzling and dotted with bright colored sailboats, Andrea got a better view of the red tile-roofed villas.

"Monte Marques, señora," the chauffeur announced, taking his hands off the wheel to make a sweeping gesture toward the hillside bungalows.

He made a sudden sharp left turn across the highway and just missed a broadside crash from a jeep headed north. Andrea was so badly scared by the near-miss that, once arrived at Dex's hotel, she opened the door herself and got out. They had arrived at their destination, in any case. The chauffeur jumped out, pouring out a spate of incomprehensible Spanish.

"Never mind," she told him impatiently. "Just wait here. I'm not sure of my plans."

She started for the spacious hacienda-type office building with fists clenched and her back very straight, dreading the encounter that was coming. It would have been so much easier just to wait in Reno or at home on Nob Hill for Dex's return. He would probably keep the blackmail secret along with the sudden emergence of Terri Cartaret. Andrea would innocently accept all his explanations and live happily ever after.

But then, according to Terri's letter, sooner or later her demands or her ability to make trouble would invade Andrea's bank account. Andrea couldn't possibly go on like this any longer without a confrontation.

She went into the office, found a man on duty and asked which of the bungalows was taken by Dexter Cartaret.

"Ah! The señora." He turned his dark Spanish eyes on her. "Señor Cartaret is expecting you. Please. I will take you to the señor."

"It isn't necessary."

But it was to the amiable little man. He left his desk, walked her across the tiled floor and out through a cool side hall.

They climbed the hillside road, past guests sunbathing around the heart-shaped pool.

Dex had signed for the fourth bungalow, heavily camouflaged by bougainvillea and two flaming double hibiscus bushes. Above the last two bungalows the thick green tropical growth rose to the peak of the hillside.

The man carefully helped her up the steps onto the brick veranda of the bungalow and opened the barred door.

"Señor Cartaret?" he called out.

The living room of the bungalow was darkened, the shutters half-closed against the afternoon heat. With a quickened heartbeat Andrea made out Dex's figure standing at the far end of the room. He had his back to her. He had been in the process of closing the shutters.

"The señora, Señor Cartaret."

He bowed elegantly and left the stage to Andrea.

Dex spoke, still turned to the deep-set window. His voice was like a whiplash. "You weren't due until evening. Make your case. You'll find I'm not quite so naive as—"

Andrea could not mistake the contempt in his tone that was instantly broken off when he saw her.

"You!" She could imagine his shock. He recovered with an effort. "I thought you were...Oh my God, Andrea, I didn't mean—I wasn't speaking to you, sweetheart."

She laughed, trying not to sound as frightened of the situation as she felt. At least she could tell he was glad to see her. He moved toward her, then stopped. It was plain that he had forgotten—and just now remembered—all the unpleasant reasons for her being here.

"You know what has been going on, then?" he asked without inflection.

She wet her lips and plunged into an explanation, wondering

243

why she could feel so guilty when he was the one who had lied.

"They brought me the mail and I read your w-wife's letter. I thought you might need me."

She could sense his overwhelming relief at her manner and her words. He reached for her, crushed her in his arms. She collapsed in his embrace.

His tender concern for her hadn't changed.

"Sweetheart, I hoped it would all be settled. I didn't want you involved in this. Everything that woman touches she destroys."

"I thought I might help."

With his arms around her waist he led her to a heavy oak chair. He straddled the arm and pulled her to him. His hands rested squarely on her shoulders, and she saw he was wearing the heavy gold wristwatch she had given him.

"I asked you once to believe me. It's about all I do ask of you. And you came through." She smiled, pretending a strength she still didn't feel. "What did Terri's letter say?" he asked.

"I think she's trying to blackmail you about the judge who gave her the divorce. It turned out he wasn't really a judge. She says the divorce was invalid."

He nodded. His eyes gazed deep into hers. "I don't believe that, sweetheart, and you mustn't either. When I finished that business with your father, I hopped on a plane to get the truth from her. So far I haven't even been able to contact her. But I'm ready. God knows, I'm ready!"

She felt his hands clench against her spine. She wanted so desperately to believe him.

"What can I do to help you, Dex?"

"I won't let her get her claws into you. She isn't coming here. I'll see to that." He kissed her eyes and then her lips. As always she couldn't resist his magnetism. She reached out, clasping her hands behind his neck, drawing him to her, his cheek against her throat, her lips on his forehead.

"I'm not afraid of her, darling. Not as long as you're with me." She knew in her heart she was afraid of nothing except losing Dex.

244

He kissed her throat sensuously. "You're using the perfume I like."

"You gave it to me. In London at the theater intermission, when you ordered tea and we got all those little sandwich things and the pastries. You hid the bottle under the pastries. I loved them. And the perfume, too." She lifted her head. "Darling, tell me. Have you seen her yet? What does she say? How far will she go?"

He, too, turned serious, tight with anger, the way he was when she first arrived.

"I'm still waiting to see her. I've visited the Bartoli villa several times but they kept telling me she was due back this morning. The latest story is that she'll be coming in late today. I mean to camp here until she does return."

"About the clerk who died and wasn't a judge or something—do you think it's true?"

"No. I don't." He was emphatic. His hands tightened on her bare arms. "I've already hired an investigator to check out this Gonzalvez matter. I don't believe the man who died was the same José Gonzalvez, judge of the court, who signed her divorce decree."

She began to see the first rays of hope. "It is a common name."

"Exactly. She simply seized on it in the hope of bleeding you, through me." He studied her face, and his eyes became concerned; he must have seen now something of the anguish he had put her through. His voice was gentle. "Sweetheart, I haven't heard from her for years, but she saw our picture in some New York paper at the time of the wedding. God knows how she found our itinerary in Europe, but I received a copy of the Gonzalvez death notice in Paris with a note from her to the effect that the José Gonzalvez who signed her decree had never been qualified as a judge. I tore up the clipping of the death notice and threw it away with the note. Then I kept getting empty envelopes. Reminders."

"I remember."

That startled him. "You knew?"

"No, I didn't know. I saw the envelopes, and I just guessed.

You were—" She fumbled for the right word to describe his moodiness and silence that night when they had gone through their mail at the St. Jean Imperial. "I thought you seemed preoccupied with something." She looked into his eyes. "You received an empty envelope in Capri also, didn't you? I remember."

He nodded. He added with a flash of anger, "I ignored that. But in San Francisco she wrote again. She said next time she hoped you would open my mail. Still, she didn't address you. I suppose she knew that would be the last straw. So I sent her two thousand dollars, via a bank in San Diego, to keep her quiet while I investigated the Gonzalvez thing. I couldn't involve you. I wonder if you know why."

She hoped she did. "Because you didn't marry me for the reason everyone thought, did you?"

"No, sweetheart. I didn't. If I paid this woman, it would be in my own way. Personally, I'd rather strangle her. But I'm afraid commando training would be thought a little out of place on these social occasions. Anyway, I thought about it on the flight to Los Angeles. After your father and I were through at Planet Oil—by the way, I think he has a chance there with his own unit, but we'll talk about that later—I took the first flight down here. I called you in Reno this morning, but the desk said you had left for San Francisco."

She looked away. "You didn't intend to tell me the truth, did you?"

"If I told you, you would have said: Pay. But you see, if you paid, this marriage would have been what they all thought it was."

She was confused but she hoped she understood his reasoning.

"What did you plan to do? Anything short of murder?"

"Anything," he bit off grimly.

"Then tell me how we handle her."

He smiled. "*We* are going to learn the truth from my investigator, Cruz-Madero. He thinks he has a lead."

"Meanwhile?"

"Meanwhile, I'm going to keep you out of the way while I confront Terri. It isn't going to occur here, near you."

"Don't be silly. I've never met a blackmailer before. I'd never forgive myself if I missed it now."

"You will—"

She put her hand over his mouth. His eyebrows raised. She took her hand away, smiling.

"You've grown up lately, Andrea. You're no longer my impressionable twenty-one-year-old."

"The one you fell in love with?"

His eyes searched her face. "Yes. I love what I see now, but it is unfamiliar. I'm a little afraid of it. Will this very mature young woman feel the same toward me?"

"I'm twenty-two, remember. Practically over the hill. You're my last hope."

He sighed. "As old as that. I never intended to marry an old woman."

They both laughed, but afterward there was an awkward silence. Andrea spoke quickly, almost bubbling, to cover the deepest of her fears.

"I guess I was just lucky to meet you when I did, wasn't I darling?"

She never knew how he would have answered. The telephone began its shrill ringing and he turned away from her to answer it. She watched him, wondering if it was Terri.

Dex's features hardened and his voice was harsh.

"*Si*. Who is this?" Dex's face relaxed. His excitement seemed to mount. "Yes. Good... You can't trust me for a few hours... I'll be there. How much?... Not prohibitive. It should be worth it if he's the one. I'd like to see Terri's face if he is. In fact, I will see it. She'll be ready to cut my throat."

Andrea was slightly unnerved to see his twisted smile. She felt that she really didn't know him at all, and wondered if she would ever grow up enough to understand him completely.

He hung up.

"You're going somewhere, aren't you?" she asked.

"I must, sweetheart. That was Cruz-Madero. He needs a few hundred pesos to bribe a waiter who insists he's been delivering meals to some high-echelon gentleman who he claims is in hiding."

"Oh, no."

"Don't worry. The man we're after, we hope, is busy enjoying the weekend with his secretary. He left his wife in the capital."

"But who is he?"

"We hope the elusive gentleman is our original Señor Gonzalvez. A judge. We can't be sure until we meet him. Meanwhile, promise me you won't have anything to do with Terri if she calls."

She didn't answer but he went on cheerfully. "Let's see you bid me *adios*." He kissed her, squeezed her shoulders and started out.

She called after him. "That's my limousine outside. Take it."

"Sorry. Big cars give the wrong idea when you are in the bribing game. I'll take one of the Monte's jeeps... Remember, sweetheart. Don't answer the phone. I'll be back in half an hour... Be my brave girl and we'll come through this."

"I'm Mrs. Dexter Cartaret," she shouted after him as he walked away, causing several heads at the pool to turn. "Nobody better forget it." She lightly kicked her elegant Adolfo shoes on the tile floor. "I really am, you know."

He laughed, waved and was gone.

Andrea walked back into the little stucco house and wandered around, thinking over everything that had just transpired. Despite her anxiety to have Dex return, she realized that there would be serious problems, first when he bribed the waiter, and then when he and the investigator visited the judge in his hiding place. The judge wasn't likely to be receptive. He might deny any knowledge of the divorce decree. It could take a long time.

When the phone rang its noise cut through the quiet air and sliced across her nerves. She walked away from it, remembering Dex's words. The ringing stopped almost immediately. She walked out the back door of the cottage and stood under the desert mesquite and lush jungle growth that crowded the hills above the cottages. The long green tips of an exotic fern tickled the back of her neck. She jumped uneasily.

At the same time she heard a car engine on the hillside drive in front of the cottage. Acapulco was only a few minutes' drive, she thought. Perhaps Dex had returned early.

She rushed into the cottage and threw the door open.

A tall, slender, red-haired woman, elegant in a lime-green linen dress and a large straw hat with a silk band, stood there smiling brightly.

Andrea hadn't the slightest doubt who she was. This was clearly the woman who claimed herself to be the first—and the only—Mrs. Dexter Cartaret.

TWENTY-SEVEN

"MY DEAR, we meet at last," Terri said with the most elegant of British accents.

Andrea was instantly disarmed. The woman was as beautiful as Mariella Cavalcante had described, though she had to be Dex's age at least. She exuded graciousness and charm. Aware of her own sullen bad manners but unable to control them, Andrea stood blocking the way into the cottage.

"He isn't here. He won't be back for hours."

"I know that. I watched him leave. What a dear, husky voice you have, Andrea! I knew you were incredibly young, though. Dex always picks them right out of the cradle."

Andrea's courage began to revive. She managed a cynical smile.

"On the contrary. Before he met me Dex's companions were much older. But you ought to know that."

The woman's eyelids flickered. Her lovely mouth suddenly looked thinner, harder. Andrea added, "So you are Terri, Dex's loving ex-wife."

"His wife, dear. I'm afraid I was cheated out of my divorce. These wretched lawyers. One simply cannot trust any of them. I discovered only a few months ago, when the judge died, that he never was a judge at all. It was just a hoax to get my money." She wrinkled her nose charmingly. "Or Dex's, as I recall. How desperately he wanted that divorce! He must have had several prospects in mind."

"He doesn't seem to have married them in all the years since your divorce."

Terri shrugged. "They weren't such fools as to marry him.

250

I mean—a penniless man. And, of course, they were all dev-astatingly rich. Though not, I think, as rich as you are."

"I understood that you divorced Dex so you could marry your own rich boyfriend here in Mexico. Didn't he come through?" Andrea was shaking inside, but had to show confidence.

"Ah! Dex's little sugar cookie has a dash of salt. My dear, may I come in for a minute or two? It's getting dreadfully hot and I'm dying to take this silly hat off."

Andrea stood her ground.

"What on earth have we got to talk about? We're hardly what you'd call friends. As for your dead clerk who wasn't a judge, I don't believe it. Matter of fact, Dex has proof that your little blackmail scheme is just that. A phony scheme."

"But my dear! May I confess something to you?" With a graceful gesture Terri Cartaret raised her hands and lifted off the wide-brimmed hat. She shook her head and the bright red hair, in long, fine tendrils, caught the light and glinted in the sun. But the sunlight also illuminated the woman's eyes, and she looked her age. The tiny crow's-feet and the drying skin were all signs.

She made a charming plea. "I must get out of this heat. You really don't want me collapsing at your feet. That wouldn't look good at all to those eager creatures staring up at us from the pool."

Andrea was curious to hear what Terri had to say, so she stepped aside with a shrug.

Terri looked over the cool, dark living room before seating herself with proper consideration for her bare knees and shapely legs. She wore cream-colored sandals, expensive and beautifully made.

"Now, then. This is nice." She patted the couch seat beside her. "Come and sit down, darling, and we'll talk like sensible girls."

Andrea didn't make that mistake. She was shorter than Terri and would never be able to hold her own in the conversation. Instead she draped herself casually against an arm of the couch. This gave her the slight benefit of height as well as a jaunty pose of youthful confidence that the older woman couldn't quite match without loss of dignity. Terri had to turn toward the full light of the only window whose shutters weren't tightly closed. It was not the most flattering pose for her.

"You said you had a confession, Mrs. . . . Cartaret."

"Yes. I really *am* Mrs. Cartaret. But my dear, it needn't last."

"Really."

Terri ignored the sarcasm. "I'll place my cards on the table," she said in her clipped accent. "I have acquired a lifestyle that is beyond my means. Various friends have helped me along. I am by nature a friendly girl."

I'll bet, Andrea thought. Aloud, she said, "Go on. When do we get to the interesting part?" She wasn't being very ladylike but though Terri frowned, she decided not to be upset.

"I am quite willing to divorce Dex. At once, if you like. And I may add one more card on my side; I won't reveal your situation to a soul."

So that was her threat, Andrea thought, her trump card. She would work on the shame of it all. She figured that hushing up the so-called scandal would be worth a considerable sum to Andrea. Andrea was amused, but hid it.

"And for how much won't you reveal my . . . situation?"

"Andrea, my dear, your quiet little wedding was fairly well publicized. And now it seems that my divorce is worthless, so your marriage is invalid. In effect, you are Dex's mistress."

"This is nineteen sixty-three, *my dear*. You mustn't judge modern girls by the women of your day. Is that your best card?" Andrea smiled inwardly.

Terri was beginning to get edgy.

"No. Bigamy is a criminal offense." She raised her eyes innocently. "Or am I wrong?"

This finally succeeded in shaking Andrea.

"Then we are to make ourselves responsible for your . . . ah . . . expenses while you get a quiet second divorce, and in return, you forget that nasty word *bigamy*."

Terri examined her long polished fingernails.

"That is my proposition."

"How much do you need for these expenses?"

Encouraged by this businesslike tone, Terri rolled off the figure quickly.

"Two hundred and...two hundred and fifty thousand."

"Pesos?" A little humor there.

"Dollars." Terri watched Andrea's face, saw the tightening of her features.

"And will you blackmail us every time you need *expenses?*"

Terri reminded her quickly, "I could never do that. Furnish your own legal counsel if you like. I'll get the divorce. I swear I will. Then I won't be able to harm you, even if I wanted to. And my dear, I don't." She held her hand out in a friendly fashion but Andrea ignored it.

Andrea got up, walked to the front door and opened it. She became rigid.

"I think you had better leave this house. Now."

Terri Cartaret sat there looking like a beautiful statue.

"Are you serious? You mean to throw Dex to the police? Let him be arrested for bigamy?"

Andrea pursed her mouth, waiting. With an enormous effort at self-control she said nothing.

It was the best thing she could have done. Terri Cartaret could cope with anything but her silence. She got up finally, strolled to the door. Her own effort at nonchalance didn't quite cover the slight rasp in her voice.

"I think you will change your mind, darling, when you see my husband behind bars."

Andrea was ready to explode. All her self-control dissolved.

"Why don't you just drop dead?" She knew she sounded like a child.

Terri gathered herself straight, arranged her hat on her head and sauntered down the hill, past the curious poolside crowd.

Andrea barely resisted kicking the door as she went back inside. She spent the next hour glancing at her watch.

When she heard footsteps on the brick walk again she was sure Terri had returned with more threats. She took a deep breath, straightened her shoulders and marched to the door.

But before she could reach the door it opened and Dex walked in looking as furious as Andrea felt. He held his arms out to her. How good and reassuring it felt to be close to him again! He was certainly tense, however, and she sensed that the business with the judge in his hideaway had gone badly.

253

"Sweetheart—"

"I know. It was bad. Tell me about it."

She had never seen him quite this worked up. The pulsing vein she had noticed occasionally along his temple was throbbing. He rubbed the skin above his temple and Andrea saw for the first time an old scar at the edge of his hairline.

"Look, sweetheart, to coin a cliché—" He smiled with an effort. "This calls for a drink."

She led the way to the modern bar across the room and leaned on the dark, shiny surface. He poured himself two fingers of scotch and began to sip it. She was impatient to hear the news but managed a reasonable calm until they were sitting together on the big, clumsy leather couch, side by side, her hand in his.

"The judge didn't give her the divorce?" she ventured.

"Gonzalvez refuses to see us. Cruz-Madero is still hanging around the villa. He insists he'll wear Gonzalvez out."

"Did Gonzalvez deny he was the man you want?"

"Of course. Claimed to this waiter that he is Jorge Gonzalvez, from Durango. Cruz-Madero swears it's a lie. The waiter claims to know him from Mexico City, but I can't be sure of the waiter. He'd say anything for a hundred pesos." He took another swallow of the scotch. "And that's not it."

"Terri?" She was uncomfortable. She knew Dex would be even angrier if he knew the woman had threatened her in person. "You saw Terri, then?"

He hesitated. "I intended to. When we couldn't get hold of Gonzalvez I phoned her from town. I thought I could get her to confess that Judge Gonzalvez really did exist. But I should have remembered. She was always a practical woman."

"She didn't believe you?"

He loosened her hand, pounded his fist into the leather cushion. "She wouldn't... In the end, it's hard to say. But she thinks he won't help us. Or he would have done so before this. She knows I don't run a bluff."

Andrea was chilled by the possibility of not being able to prove Terri Cartaret was a liar. But this was no time to add to Dex's violent anger. She ran her fingers along his neck.

"Well, honey, there's always tomorrow. We can wait it out."

He finished off the soctch and started to get up for a refill. He glanced at her tall gin-and-tonic and saw that the glass was still full. He looked at her, a long, tender look that made her lean across the space between them and kiss him.

"Dex, I'm not afraid. We're together. Isn't that the way you feel? I mean—that we're together, and what else is important?"

He hugged her, but she knew his thoughts were still elsewhere.

"Tell me about it," she begged as he held her there, her voice muffled against his cheek. "What can we expect for the future?"

That made him smile. "You've never met a demon until you've met Terri. She intends to send out her story to leading newspapers in the States. *Her story.* She's got some contact at *Life* magazine. She threatens a spread."

Andrea struggled to feign surprise.

Dex stood up and began to pace. She reached for his sleeve. His face was red and flushed.

"Sit down, darling, and rest. I've got an idea that can stop all this. You never lied to me. You've told me the truth about that judge and the rest of it. That's all that matters. Trust. So let's just pay her the two hundred fifty thousand in installments, the big payment predicated on the final decree."

"We can't pay blackmail. Everything I've tried to prove since I married you would go down the drain. That was the only thing in my life I've been proud of. I turned over a new leaf with you. But this just proves I'm everything they..." He broke off, stared at her. "How did you know the amount of money she's demanding now?"

It had to come out sooner or later. She wondered why Terri hadn't told him during their phone conversation.

"She came here."

"What? I might have guessed that she'd get to you somehow." He was furious, as she had expected.

"Don't worry. I threw her out. I even told her to drop dead."

His eyes widened. Then he began to laugh. She didn't know why he thought it was so funny but she was relieved, at any rate.

The sudden rasp of the telephone made them exchange glances.

"Terri?" she asked.

"Probably Cruz-Madero. I hope to God it isn't more bad news."

He picked up the phone. She walked over to him, hearing her heels click on the tile floor beyond the woven Mexican rugs.

"Cruz-Madero?" As the investigator talked, Dex closed his eyes briefly. He opened them to smile at Andrea. Covering the mouthpiece, he filled Andrea in. "We may have the judge. It's all your doing, sweetheart. Cruz-Madero sent a message that the one and only Andrea Lombard was involved. Do you mind?"

She waved him on. "Great. Tell him I'll do anything. *Anything,*" she repeated.

He returned to the phone. "How did you get our names to him...My God! That's blackmail, too...No. Far from it. My compliments on your finesse. Yes. We want her to meet him. At once. Great. But it's dusk now. I noticed it was market day in town. You'll have to give us a little time. And many thanks."

He set the phone back and seized Andrea around the waist.

"We're to meet Cruz-Madero outside Judge Gonzalvez's hideaway. The judge sent a note out to ask if this divorce was in any way involved with the famous Lombard heiress. It seems he was impressed by your grandfather's fame."

It was almost too good to be true. "Thank God! But how was the judge persuaded to help us? What did you mean about blackmail?"

"That was Cruz-Madero. He hinted to the judge that Gonzalvez's wife in Mexico City knew nothing about the judge's Acapulco business...at least not yet."

She laughed. "We seem to be surrounded by blackmailers."

"But this one is on our side. Let's wash up, get ready and go see the judge."

Ten minutes later they were on their way down the hill to the Monte Marques office where the chauffeur was waiting for her still. They found him sipping bourbon and chatting with the desk clerk.

"Leave him there. We don't want to drive a Cadillac through those narrow streets after dark," Dex said. "It's the jeep, I'm afraid."

256

"I'm game."

He boosted her into one of the Monte's jeeps and they took off along the highway with the fading sunlight pouring across the road. Out in the bay the water had turned golden with the sky.

The light quickly faded and dusk fell. Dex sped around the high green cliffs. By the time the jeep reached the outskirts of the city itself, Acapulco was shrouded in the blue light of evening.

Andrea saw that Dex was headed inland, away from the resorts, toward the heart of the crowded city. The jeep bumped along between the tired, two-story office buildings and the new skyscrapers, past shadowed figures packing away fruits and vegetables from the age-old market stalls.

The street was littered with discarded green tomatoes, crushed bananas and berries. The faces in the market looked almost sinister to Andrea. As night fell rapidly over the area, these blurred movements disturbed her thoughts and her hopes.

The jeep began to climb into a flower-scented residential area where villas and their lush gardens lined the winding road. By the time the jeep pulled up to a pair of wrought-iron gates it was dark and the stars had begun to appear. A lean, sharp-faced man met them and led them through an overgrown garden to the side door of the two-story Victorian house.

Dex introduced the man as Manuel Cruz-Madero, the private investigator.

The detective turned to her. "The señora will be pleased to know Judge Gonzalvez is seeing us only because of the señora. He has read about you in the press."

"Never mind that," Dex cut him off hurriedly.

A big, portly man ushered them into an overfurnished living room. They caught a glimpse of the judge's reason for hiding here. A blonde girl in a lounging robe peeked in at them from an interior hall. The man gave the girl a brief look under bushy, graying eyebrows and she vanished. He then turned to his guests.

In spite of his ferocious eyebrows, José Gonzalvez had the dignity and appearance of a Spanish nobleman, with manners to fit his appearance. Well along in his sixties, he kissed Andrea's hand gracefully. Then he addressed Andrea in flawless English, ignoring Dex.

"Nothing makes me more delighted than to be permitted to oblige the beautiful Señora Lombard-Cartaret. I believe that is your married title? I had no idea that you were involved in this matter. Only last year I had the pleasure of being entertained by your grandfather in San Francisco. It concerned some properties I own in Baja. He wished to invest in our future, as he called it. He was a generous man, with a vision. May I welcome you to my home in turn, señora?"

Dex watched intently as Andrea, touched by the man's tribute to her beloved grandfather, returned the judge's graciousness. She told him that he, and only he, could save her from dishonor in this divorce mixup.

The judge paused long enough to pour snifters of Napoleon brandy for his guests.

"I am given to understand, señora, that Señor Cartaret's previous wife claims her divorce was invalid because a clerk named J. Gonzalvez died recently. A clerk who did not have the power to sign her decree. But, señora, there are other men of my name. And I assure you, I have the power to sign a divorce decree."

"Yes, sir."

"Then I am pleased to be of help to you. The first Señora Cartaret is not a lady easy to forget. I may say that applies to both ladies," he added diplomatically. "But it is one divorce I do remember, because the first señora planned to marry a friend of mine. The marriage, I believe, did not take place. However, her divorce was unquestionably genuine. Señora, you wish me to face this lady and remind her of these little details?"

"If you would, sir. It means everything to me."

"For you, a great pleasure." He finished his brandy, and finally glanced at the men. "I understand that I may count upon your discretion."

"Believe me, sir," Dex told him firmly, "Even if you feel you cannot accept my word or that of Mr. Cruz-Madero, my wife would never permit any betrayal of your private life."

"Oh yes, sir."

She gave him her hand. He took it, held it for a long time. "Sir, could we go to her right away? I want to get it over with."

The judge sighed, threw a mournful look toward the direction of the blonde who must be waiting for him.

"Very well. It should not take long. You say it is the Bartoli villa? Your car or mine?"

"We borrowed a jeep from the Monte," Dex admitted.

The judge grimaced. Fortunately, Cruz-Madero had his car, which he volunteered to provide for the comfort of the judge.

They started south past the city and around the headlands. The judge sat in the back seat while Cruz-Madero drove and Dex sat silent beside him, looking thoughtful.

Andrea became more and more nervous. When Cruz-Madero maneuvered the big car off the highway onto a narrow estate road along the dark, jungle-covered cliff above the Marques Bay, Andrea felt stiff with apprehension. Nor did it help that two cars with headlights blazing passed them at high speed headed toward the highway.

"Maybe she's making her getaway," Andrea said.

The judge laughed and glanced back at the speeding cars.

"That is most strange. I believe I know the man in the first car," he said.

Andrea raised her eyebrows in question. "Oh?"

"A DFS agent." As she continued to be puzzled, he explained. "The Directorate of Federal Security. Our CIA. Or FBI, if you prefer."

"Maybe Terri Cartaret is a spy." She wouldn't have been the least surprised.

"The DFS has a wide breadth of subjects for its investigations. Whatever it is, Mr. Cartaret's ex-wife seems to have been visited by the police."

They saw ahead of them the pretty white villa with its tile roof jutting out of wild greenery, illuminated by hanging lanterns. Bougainvillea masked the front of the house where several cars of assorted vintage blocked the driveway.

Cruz-Madero was forced to park his car on the edge of the cliff, only a few yards from a sheer drop to the bay waters far below. Andrea glanced over the edge. Far down through the dim starlight she made out the foamy shoreline. Even at night these waters were often alive with swimmers, but there seemed to be no swimmers directly below the cliffs tonight. Perhaps there was a dangerous undertow.

Before moving from the car the judge turned to Andrea. "I am here to be of service, Señora Lombard-Cartaret. That is my sole reason for being in Acapulco."

"Certainly, sir."

"I have signed many decrees, as you may imagine, but I recall Mrs. Cartaret very well. A great beauty, with bright auburn hair. She became something of a social figure here and in Mexico City."

"Yes, sir."

"You must not look so. There is no problem. José Gonzalvez stands by his signature. I will order a copy of the divorce decree forwarded to you tomorrow, señora. It will be certified." His gaze encompassed Dex with less enthusiasm. "And afterward, I prefer to forget our little meeting this afternoon at my house in town. In fact, there is no house. You comprehend, señores?"

"*Si,* señor," Cruz-Madero agreed gruffly.

"Perfectly. Thank you." Dex was also tense, though he must know there couldn't be any problems.

Cruz-Madero walked behind them toward the door, staring at the parked cars and scowling. He shared the general uneasiness.

Andrea looked up at Dex. He nodded and gave her a faint smile meant to relieve her. He, too, felt that something was drastically wrong.

Judge Gonzalvez raised the knocker. The noise reverberated but nothing happened. The judge pushed the heavy door open and walked in. They followed. They didn't get far inside the cool interior with its busy plant life and painted wicker furniture. A stout, elderly woman wearing an apron over her heavy, handwoven skirt, walked blindly into the judge. She was weeping, and stumbled out of the long room. Andrea looked around, saw the starlit sea view at one end of the room. The sight made her long to be out there sailing away from this troublesome business.

"Something must have happened," Dex whispered.

The judge took a step toward the open hallway which led to a brightly lit room at the far end of the cool hall. The buzz of voices came from there.

Judge Gonzalvez raised his voice, calling out in Spanish. "Who is there? This is Judge José Gonzalvez."

His name had its effect. Several men appeared to be standing around talking, and a stocky man in street clothes broke away from the group and came out to meet the judge in the hall.

The judge recognized the stocky man with the penetrating dark eyes.

"I call him *El Capitan*. Emilio Perez is an agent with the DFS. A skillful man, formerly in the army."

Andrea didn't doubt that. The man terrified her.

Meanwhile, Judge Gonzalvez was explaining his presence and that of his companions. "We came to visit the Señora Cartaret. A short visit. I signed her divorce decree some years ago."

Captain Perez shook his head. "I am afraid it is not possible to see her, señores, señora." He looked around the judge at Dex and Andrea. His English, though accented, was perfectly clear to them.

"What is this all about, captain?" the judge asked.

"The Señora Cartaret is dead."

Andrea gasped. Dex put a hand on her shoulder. His fingers dug into her flesh.

"But what a tragedy! How did it happen? And how is the DFS involved?" the judge wanted to know.

Captain Perez consulted his notes.

"The Señora Cartaret seems to have fallen backward, some time this afternoon, struck her head on the corner of the mantelpiece. We believe she slipped on a rug before the mantel. The tiles are very slippery." He closed the little notebook. "As for myself, we are investigating a ring of smugglers, drug dealers, bringing hashish into the cove below the cliff."

Dex asked, "Is there a connection between my—between Mrs. Cartaret's death and the smugglers?"

"Possibly." The agent looked Dex over suspiciously. "The servants report that Mrs. Cartaret quarreled with someone shortly before her death."

"But then—" The judge looked startled. "It was murder, then?"

"Possibly. She was found alone. The yellow rug is piled against the mantel and there is blood on the brick corner of the mantel itself. The sharp brick penetrated the skull. The woman appears to have clutched at a chair to save herself. There are her prints which may have been caused when she overturned the chair."

"I see." The judge reflected on this and turned to Dex. "Perhaps we had better leave. We seem to be in the way of these gentlemen."

Dex agreed. They had all turned away when Captain Perez stopped them.

"It seems that the Señora Cartaret had a man's watch in her hand when she fell. The diamonds in her ring and the impact of the fall apparently scratched the inscription beyond recognition. All we can tell is that it was a gift." He called to one of the Acapulco police and the man delivered a heavy gold wristwatch, wrapped in tissue paper.

Andrea recognized it at once—the watch she had given Dex for Christmas. There was the diamond in place of the numeral 12, and on the back would be the marred inscription: LOVE EVERLASTING—A.

She didn't look at Dex.

"We have not yet discovered why the lady had the watch in her hands," Captain Perez went on. "Would you know anything about it, Judge Gonzalvez?"

The judge gave it a casual glance and shrugged. "I am not an expert on these things."

Captain Perez returned the watch to his assistant. "Now," he said matter-of-factly, "We will all sit down and the señor and señora will tell me why they are here. You are Señor Cartaret, the dead lady's ex-husband, are you not? Let me ask you a question. Were you with the deceased at any time today?"

Andrea fumbled behind her for a chair. She had never known such terror.

TWENTY-EIGHT

JUDGE GONZALVEZ came to the rescue.

"Captain, my friends spent the afternoon with me. That is to say, we gentlemen were together and then Señor Cartaret drove out to pick up the señora." He widened his eyes in mock astonishment. "Unless—can it be possible?—you suspect the señora of something?"

"No, Excellency. Certainly not." But while Captain Perez denied any suspicions, his hard eyes studied Andrea. She tried to look indifferent, even ventured a flickering smile.

"Señora, were you a friend of the Señora Cartaret?" He pretended to find the subject awkward, but she was sure he meant to embarrass her. "I find it difficult. Two Señora Cartarets. Forgive me. I am clumsy."

"Not at all, captain. I am Mr. Cartaret's wife. The woman you call Señora Cartaret was formerly married to my husband."

Dex cut in coldly, "I can't see how my wife is involved in any way. As for me, I haven't seen Terri Cartaret for almost ten years. The judge, however, has seen her since she and I parted. He signed her divorce decree."

"Quite true," the judge agreed.

Captain Perez ignored this.

"It must have been an unhappy time for you, Señor Cartaret."

"Unhappy? How?"

"When the beautiful señora divorced you. What else?"

Andrea sensed Dex's anger at all this needling. She was uncertain, though, of the extent of her desire to defend him before this vicious man. She was still stiff with the shock of discovering that he had been with Terri that day. No wonder he had returned to Andrea shaking with rage. And something else? Fear, because he had watched Terri die and he might be accused?

Dex managed to retain a chilly facade of reproof.

"We had separated years before the divorce. It was something we both wanted. I wanted my freedom and Terri wanted to marry a Mexican industrialist."

"But the Señora Cartaret did not marry the industrialist."

"No. Therefore, I turned over to her various small incomes such as my wartime settlements."

"Leaving yourself without income?"

"I retained a small annuity."

"And survived in other ways. I understand."

Dex colored angrily, started to say something. The judge and Cruz-Madero looked at him furtively.

Finding renewed courage, Andrea diverted the man's attention toward herself.

"I don't understand, captain. If there is some question that Mrs. Cartaret's death was accidental, how are we concerned? I have been at the Monte Marques since noon. Mrs. Cartaret visited me there." The captain studied her intently. "And she left some ten minutes later while my husband was in town with Mr. Cruz-Madero and Judge Gonzalvez." Her voice raised. "I assure you, Mrs. Cartaret was very much alive when she left the Monte Marques."

"Easy, sweetheart," Dex murmured. He put his arm around her, but she shifted her position uncomfortably. Had it been an angry push that sent Terri hurtling backward into the brick corner of the mantelpiece?

Captain Perez wrote only two words in his little notebook. Unnerved, she tried to get a look at the words. The captain looked up.

"No one is accusing you of anything, señora. Except you yourself. You must not let us make you nervous."

"I am not nervous."

"Certainly, señora. It is always well to obtain the facts in a matter of this kind. The cook reports that she heard voices raised in a quarrel this afternoon. It would be helpful if we knew the person with whom she quarreled."

"Was it a male or a female?" the judge asked.

"The cook is not certain. 'A low voice,' she says. Probably a man, but it is not definite. The watch could very well belong to that man."

The judge considered. "How do you know she did not obtain the watch at some earlier time?"

"Nothing is certain," Perez agreed. "Except that the Señora Cartaret is dead. And it would be of great help if we knew the man or woman who may have witnessed her accident."

"Is it certain that the person she quarreled with was present when she died?" the judge asked. "Do you know the time she died? Did she die instantly? These are questions that will be asked and should be answered now."

Captain Perez ignored this. "Señor Cartaret, you expressed no sorrow at your wife's tragic death."

"My ex-wife. I haven't seen her for many years."

"Yet you have been here repeatedly since you arrived in Acapulco, trying to see her."

Dex now had control of himself. "And never made it. Today I expected to have better luck when I brought my wife and my friends. As you see, we came too late."

Captain Perez excused himself, stepped back into the hall and exchanged a few words with one of the local policemen. He then addressed Judge Gonzalvez.

"Excellency, since you can vouch for the Señor Cartaret at approximately the hour when the señora was heard in heated argument—"

"I can. He was outside my—er—hotel. I saw him there for some time before I admitted him. I had been busy. I had work to do and didn't want to be disturbed. But he was there." The judge threw a sidelong glance at Dex.

"Except for the fifteen minutes it took me to drive to the Monte Marques. After that, my wife and I were together for several minutes before we received a telephone call from Mr. Cruz-Madero. We met the judge and Mr. Cruz-Madero about twenty minutes later. We drove here."

"Excellent. All in order. There are usually half a dozen guests at the Monte's swimming pool. They will be happy to corroborate the times of your arrivals and departures."

Andrea suddenly remembered having yelled at Terri in front of the hotel guests: *Why don't you drop dead?*

The captain jotted down times and initials. While he did so, Andrea tried to drown her fears in indignation.

"Judge Gonzalvez, we've told the truth, every detail we can remember. There is nothing else we know. I'm going to call my company's legal counsel. We're innocent, God knows. But we need protection. I can see that."

Dex and the judge protested. They too recognized that the police might find it convenient to involve them, and they didn't want to antagonize the tough captain.

"Sweetheart, don't overreact. The captain has his job to do," Dex said carefully.

Captain Perez gave them an amiable smile.

"These technicalities are regretable, señora. But without them there is no law. You comprehend?"

"I comprehend perfectly. As soon as we are free to go, I will call my legal counsel."

"Very wise, señora."

In another fifteen minutes they were released with a polite warning. "It is unnecessary to ask you not to leave Acapulco, señor. Señora."

Andrea thought it ominous when Judge Gonzalvez remained behind. "I would like to talk over another matter entirely. My nephew is interested in the DFS. I have suggested he start with the police or the judiciary. We will see what Emilio has to say," the judge explained.

"I don't believe it," she told Dex as Cruz-Madero drove them back to pick up the jeep. "He wants to tell that stormtrooper something about us."

She was sitting beside Dex in the back seat. Cruz looked in the rearview mirror and spoke to her.

"He isn't really that bad, señora. The captain is a very good detective, and honest, too. But don't worry. He will find the truth about Señor Dex's wife. Ex-wife," he added as Dex stirred slightly.

Andrea looked straight ahead as she spoke to Dex.

"What do *you* think the truth is?"

Dex had made no further effort to touch her since she had rebuffed him in the Portali Villa. He must sense that there was a change in her since the discovery of Terri's body. She wondered if he really knew what she suspected... If he had been there that day it would explain his agitated manner when he returned to the Monte Marques. Could mere anger at an unpleasant telephone call do that?...

She reserved her questions for the time half an hour later when they were jolting back to the Monte Marques in the jeep.

"Dex?"

He started. He too had been deep in thought. "We would know the whole story if we knew how she got my watch," he said to her.

"When did you wear it last?" Andrea forced herself to believe that he himself hadn't given it to her.

"I left it in the hotel room this afternoon. He was silent, then added, "Sweetheart, I don't want to hurt your feelings." She braced herself. "But frankly, the watch chafes my wrist and I don't wear it too often."

Was that all? She burst into sudden laughter.

"I'm sorry. It doesn't matter."

But he had worn the watch this morning. She remembered seeing it on his wrist when they were in the room together. When had he taken it off—if indeed he had taken it off?

"I was hot when I came back from town. I washed up before we went to meet the judge. I must have left my watch on the basin in the Monte."

They said nothing after that until they reached the office of the Monte Marques. Dex and Andrea walked up past the strings of multicolored lights around the swimming pool. The buzz of conversation stopped abruptly as they passed.

"They've been talking to the police," Andrea decided. "And my suggestion that Terri drop dead is probably the main talk of the Acapulco police by now."

He laughed. "I doubt if anyone seriously thinks you were involved." They reached the cottage. He held the door open and she ducked under his arm and walked into the cool interior.

"I wonder how long they'll keep us here."

267

"You had better call Sam Liversedge."

"Sam! You know what I think of him." But she admitted he was right. "You're right. I should call him."

"Meanwhile—" He went into the bathroom and seemed to be searching around for something.

She looked up from the telephone. "What are you looking for?"

He came out of the bathroom waving his gold wedding band.

"I took this off when I took my watch off. Whoever took the watch apparently wasn't interested in the ring."

She had long distance now. Dex spoke again but she was too involved with the operator to make out what he was talking about.

"Do you suppose Terri... when she was here with you... do you think—" he was asking.

"Is this the Reno Lombard Hotel? Okay. Samuel Liversedge, please."

He had checked out and couldn't be reached.

"Oh, damn! This is Andrea Lombard speaking." She saw Dex's reaction at the use of her maiden name. "Is Faith Cortlandt there?" Meanwhile, it occurred to Andrea that she might as well first speak to a more useful person. "No. Give me Gene Rafael, please."

He was still in Reno, but he was out shooting craps at Harrah's, his wife explained. Andrea asked that he take the first plane to Los Angeles and then Acapulco.

"He should be there tomorrow morning, at the latest," Mrs. Rafael promised. "Incidentally, your Aunt Brooke flew back to San Francisco last night. After you and Dex left, and then Sam, she got bored. But you know Brooke, my dear."

"I know. Thanks awfully. Don't forget to tell Gene we're at the Monte Marques."

She turned away from the telephone, feeling exhausted. She felt for the couch and saw Dex move toward her when he saw her waver. He stopped, however, and went to the window, opening the shutters a few inches.

"Captain Perez didn't waste any time. One of those plain-clothesmen is questioning our happy little group at the pool."

She jumped up.

"Easy does it. We've nothing to worry about."

She sat down abruptly. "I'm glad you're sure."

He pretended to watch the pool but she sensed that he was more concerned with her than with the police. He closed the shutters with a sharp clap. Andrea jumped.

"Frighten you?"

She avoided his eyes. "No. I keep thinking about that FBI man, or whatever he is. Do you think he could have found anybody else's fingerprints on the watch?"

He shrugged. "I've no idea. The question I have is: how did it get into Terri's hands?"

She looked up into his eyes. "What did you feel when they told you she was dead?"

"It was a bad way to go. But I suppose any way is bad. Do you want the truth?"

"Please."

"There was relief, too. And regret. We shared a life together once. A long time ago." He crooked a finger under her chin. "Sweetheart, a very long time ago."

She tried to smile. As always, Dex was the perfect gentleman.

"But that isn't what bothers you, is it? Speak up, Andrea. A husband and wife should have no secrets."

"It's not me. I don't keep secrets."

"Meaning that I do?"

He was aiming to get hurt. But her instincts told her not to spell out her real fear. It would be the end of everything between them.

"I don't know, Dex. How can anybody understand about another person? I don't really know my father. And no one understands my mother! How can I know you?"

He caught her shoulders. "Look at me. Listen!" He had never used force with her before, she wondered if this was how he had looked when he had quarreled with his first wife before she fell back against the mantelpiece and died. *No*—

"I'm listening. Were you there with her today?" Somehow the terrible question popped out involuntarily. But she couldn't back out now.

He set his teeth. His fingers bit painfully into her flesh. She expected him to shake her. He looked into her face.

Then the dark anger seemed to drain from his features. What remained was worse. He looked at her with such sadness that her heart ached for him.

"So this is how it really is, Andrea. There can't be any real love between us because there isn't any trust. You believe me capable of watching another human being die and doing nothing. Maybe it's worse. Maybe you believe I hit Terri or pushed her. In fact, you may even think me capable of murdering her in cold blood."

"No. Never." Her mouth was dry. Whatever she had thought before, she was now so moved by his quiet manner that she was ashamed of her suspicions.

"Sweetheart," he told her, "the one thing I really can't help you with is your fear. Now, calm yourself." He let her go.

She composed herself, wanting desperately to believe him.

She stammered, "M-my lawyer will be here tomorrow. Gene is your lawyer too. You can count on him."

An invisible wall suddenly sprang up between them. A wall dividing them, separating them. She couldn't explain how it happened. Somehow, her assumption that he needed a lawyer had done it.

"Gene is my friend. He can do anything. He'll help..."

"You still think me desperately in need of help, don't you?" he said quietly.

There was a terrible finality in the way he said it.

They looked at each other.

And in that moment she knew it was all over. Her great romance, the passion they had shared, the wonderful moments. He had needed understanding.

And now it was too late.

Gene Rafael was the bearer of good news when Andrea's hired car and driver picked him up at the airport. By the time he arrived at the Monte Marques he had already been questioned by Captain Perez.

"Didn't hurt you a bit to have a judge for an alibi, believe me. He's well thought of in these parts. But anyway, this cap-

270

tain said you two would be free to go—shortly. His word. The testimony of the houseboy corroborates the cook's story, with one exception. Dex, the last time your wife was heard alive she was quarreling with someone over the phone. This occurred *after* her male visitor left. No one seems to have seen him, but they heard his car drive away. So Mrs. Cartaret was definitely alone when she had her accident."

"She was on the phone," Andrea slowly repeated. She caught Dex looking at her. Gene's statement indicated that Dex had told her the truth.

Too late...

Andrea had already endured two miserable nights in one of the twin beds, with Dex virtually miles away in the other bed. They spoke politely. They agreed on their meals. The day before they had watched the famed divers as they risked their necks from the cliffs beyond the El Mirador Hotel terrace. Then they had driven back to the cottage on the hillside and politely went to bed in their separate beds.

The hours dragged. The nights were sleepless and full of regrets.

Andrea tried in a hundred ways to make up to him for her expression of mistrust. She used all her charms but nothing worked. She herself had managed to fulfill all her most dire predictions....

Now here was Gene Rafael adding salt to the wound, pointing out, innocently enough, that her suspicions had indeed been false.

"We will be free to go?" Dex asked. "I promised Andrea's father I'd do what I could about the take-over of his studio. It's a small independent, but it obviously has its uses for Planet."

"For the land?" Gene asked.

"No. At the stockholders' meetings there were comprehensive reports on diversifying. They're thinking of television. There's a good chance that Tony may be able to write his own ticket for an autonomous unit."

"Oh, Dex, how wonderful!"

He kept his cool. "He's good at what he does."

Gene Rafael agreed. "Great. Dex, you're all right. Andrea, you made a smart move when you chose this fellow."

She smiled weakly. She hadn't missed the remote look in Dex's eyes.

Neither she nor Dex mentioned the watch found in the dead woman's hand. It hardly mattered now, of course. Soon they would be back in San Francisco, and life—however they arranged it—would resume.

"Now, then." Gene kicked aside his overnight bag and got out his attaché case. "Sam gave me these papers for your signature. Nothing much. Strictly routine. We'll save the new stuff for when you get back to San Francisco."

"All right. But I'm not signing anything to put a casino into the Reno Lombard," Andrea said stubbornly.

Gene shrugged. "Okay, but believe me, we could shoot off a cannon and not hit a soul in that place. There's just no business."

"I'll leave that to Dex when we get back. I rely on his judgement."

Gene grimaced. But Dex beat him to the punch.

"Sorry. I won't be able to handle it. As I said, I'll be staying on in Los Angeles. To see what I can do there."

Gene Rafael was so busy going through his papers and passing Andrea the folders to sign that he hardly caught the significance of what was being said.

Andrea had refused to accept for two days now the fact that her marriage to Dex was over. The finality of his refusal to go home with her came like a blow, shattering her careful composure.

TWENTY-NINE

ANDREA FELT ten years older and infinitely more sophisticated in her dealings when she returned without Dex to San
Francisco. She wasn't quite sure why she should feel so free
in facing down her critics but it had something to do with the
loss of her husband's love and protection. She found herself
making up her mind and carrying out her own plans, fighting
down all opposition with the secret thought: *If I must survive
without Dex, then nobody else matters.*

During those first few weeks she tried to study both sides
of every plan presented to her, to reason with and cajole those
who differed with her concerning the various enterprises that
came under the Lombard banner. But after three long weeks
that soon became an entire month, she began to develop a hard
shell with her advisers. She still hoped that somehow she and
Dex would get back together. Jany had been giving her glowing
reports about Dex's help in the take-over by Century-Planet
Oil. It looked very much as if Prysing Productions might become a subsidiary of Planet Oil by 1965, but Dex and Tony were
holding out for Tony's own unit—and winning, so far. Tony's
stock control of the private company swayed them, but his TV
plans, sparked by Dex, gave him the control he wanted.

On several occasions, Andrea called Dex personally to ask
his advice about some point on which she and her advisers
differed. His answer was always the same, polite but noncom-
mital. She tried to persuade him that Jany and Tony were sin-
cere when they asked him to stay with them in their mansion
in the Hollywood Hills. But again he treated the suggestion as
if it came from a well-meaning stranger. He was renting a studio

apartment in a run-down building on Wilcox Avenue in the heart of old Hollywood.

All of this was alternately painful and annoying to Andrea. Sometimes she found herself furious with him. Surely he knew the evidence had been particularly damning against him, and that she was not completely farfetched in her suspicions. As far as she could tell, no one in Mexico had discovered yet who owned the watch or why Terri was holding it in her hand when she died. Andrea now tried to convince herself that she should be excused for reasonably suspecting him. . . .

Faith had been told only that Dex's first wife had died in her villa after trying to make Dex think they weren't really divorced. But she, too, voiced a suspicion that Dex had somehow triggered Terri's death.

"It isn't as if it matters, Andrea. Don't get so touchy. Terri had it coming to her."

"Faith, if you keep on like this I'm going to leave the room, okay?"

"Sure. Listen. The Fresno deal is being pushed. I got the lowdown from Sam's secretary. He wants to sell the entire half-block to that food chain. The chain has invested a lot of time and money in sizing the land up and they're not going to back out now, whatever you decide."

Andrea had been glad to get off the subject of Terri's death, which Judge Gonzalvez informed her by mail was now officially "death by misadventure." So she turned her attentions to that piece of land in the town a few miles north of Fresno.

She decided to look it over at first hand and drove down on a particularly hot June day, with the San Joaquin Valley scorching the brown fields bordering the highway. Since Faith had been busy helping Aunt Brooke chair a meeting of the Bay League Committee, and Frank Kelly was still so anxious to be of use, Andrea decided to take him along. He turned out to be a great comfort to her.

Getting into her new car before the valley trip, Andrea said, "You can spell me at the wheel. That is, if my little red monster isn't beneath you."

Frank laughed. She had bought the sleek, daring little Karmann-Ghia to replace her white Porsche. "I do prefer something more solid, but I'm willing to try this. Just give the word," he said.

Andrea started the red car with a terrific jolt, then roared off down Nob Hill toward Mission Street and the distant Bay Bridge ramp. By the time they had made their way through the massive complexities of Oakland and hit the Valley Freeway, Frank had given up holding onto the seat and the door.

"If any of my students drove this way, I'd have them hauled in for driving lessons," he warned her.

"Coward!" she teased. "You belong in the nineteenth century. I bought this car to show off the new me. I'm a free spirit now."

He took this far more seriously than she had intended it.

"I know. I'd have gotten a lot further if I could loosen up and play more."

"That's ridiculous, Frank. Everyone likes you just the way you are."

"Do you?"

She was touched. Now more than ever she needed Frank's devotion. But there was Faith. She said as much.

He nodded.

"I suppose I'll always have a soft spot for her. But everything seems to be changing now. I'm not sure what I want anymore." He gave her an apologetic smile. "My life seems to be one long cliché."

She laughed.

"Won't you always have a soft spot for your first love?"

"I most certainly will. Did you know, Frank, that you were my first love? Faith and I saw you at the same time, the day we walked into your lecture on the English novel. I guess I didn't speak up in time. Faith started raving about you and about how she went to your office about a midterm or something and you got acquainted."

"I remember." He wasn't looking at her. He must be reliving those days while he stared at the high brown hills of Livermore Pass. "I'm going to tell you something. I saw you in class. One seat in from the aisle. About the fifth row. You were wearing a funny little dress. With that cute, innocent look and that ribbon in your hair, you made me think of a dark-haired Alice in Wonderland."

"Good Lord! I'd forgotten all about the idiot I used to be."

"No. Don't. I adored that girl." He added quickly, "I'm sorry. I didn't mean to shock you. But you see, when Faith came to my office that day, I asked her about you. Then, somehow—well, you know Faith. She can be overpowering. And when you seemed so remote, I felt that it would be robbing the cradle if I were to smile at you in class, or speak to you about your work." He looked at her hesitantly. "You gave me very little reason to hope."

"But I thought you cared for Faith."

He said nothing. She understood that he didn't want to blame Faith and she respected that. A year ago she would have been wildly thrilled to think the handsome professor and ex-football hero liked her better than the stunning-looking Faith Cortlandt. Maybe, if she had known, she would have avoided falling for a man who was far too sophisticated and experienced to be satisfied with Frank's dark-haired Alice in Wonderland.

But the idea of never having met Dex, never having known his love, sickened her. It was even worse than the prospect of ending their marriage now. At least there had been the months of exquisite happiness before she had ruined it all. . . .

But her private turmoil had nothing to do with Frank's feelings. She reached over and touched his hand.

"Dear Frank. Maybe it's better now. We're friends. And I need a friend more than I need a lover, believe me."

"Friends. I'll remember that." He settled back after slapping her hand in a comradely way.

As they headed through the first of several medium-sized valley towns, centers of some of the world's largest fruit and vegetable crops, she began to pick his brain on the subject that brought her here.

He got interested in the subject at once and, as she had suspected, he broke down all the possibilities and began to analyze them from every angle.

"And your deductions, professor?"

He ignored, or maybe didn't understand her teasing.

"Well, of course, I'd have to examine all the aspects, the land deeds, the potential for other development, the neighborhood." He laughed at himself. "I do sound professorial. But believe me, I have reason. When I was a kid, a fast-talking con artist talked my mother out of her savings account. Nearly seventy-three dollars. I never forgot it. The fine print means everything."

"Very true," she agreed. "I must remember that. Read the fine print."

He refused to be daunted. "Even rich people have to keep close tabs. Maybe closer tabs. In those days, our landlord, Mr. Allegretti, used to say that people who owned things had a lot more to lose than those who didn't. He was right."

Even when they reached the Lombard lot in the small farm town north of Fresno, he was still talking about deeds. Andrea surveyed the physical locale. The big grass-grown lot was only a block above the valley's railroad tracks, and hardly a first-class neighborhood, but in its function could possibly change all that. Her aides hadn't yet obtained all the reports made by the food chain in coming to their decision, but she could still see various advantages. Although much of their produce was trucked in, even the railroad could serve its purpose. It would provide a bargaining alternative in the event that trucking expenses got out of hand.

As for the location, she could see one thing very clearly. The lot was within a block and a half of one of the Yosemite Valley turnoffs. If the food complex was big enough, it would draw those thousands of campers who stocked up before entering the valley campgrounds of the popular park. And if it offered bargains for large purchases it would certainly attract the shopping public of other San Joaquin cities besides Fresno. Even as far north as Merced there might be interest.

She looked over the scene, standing out in the sun with her hand shielding her eyes, wishing she had brought one of the cowboy hats she had been given in Reno.

"Anyway, I think I see what that market chain has in mind. It's got potential," she admitted to Frank.

He agreed. "But they won't lease. They're sure to insist on an outright purchase."

"Then they won't get it. And they aren't going to buy that bank building, or this dry goods store."

Frank could be stubborn in his conservative views.

"Still, you'd do a lot better to consider what your own time is worth. Leasing a building to them would entail endless time and fuss. Look at all your other business problems. This only adds to them."

"That's why I need friends, Frank dear," she teased him.

He hesitated. "You do have Dexter."

She thought her laughter sounded at least as convincing as Frank's disclaimers of Faith's influence over him. But she didn't trust her voice to answer Frank.

"Well, no use in kidding around," he said after a pause. "I can't say I'm sorry. Though he doesn't seem to be the type we all thought he was."

She found her voice now. "God, no! Just the opposite. Dex and his monumental pride. You want to know something? I'm thirsty. Do you see any likely places around here?"

He ruffled his tawny hair and scratched his head. "Not unless you'll settle for the Red-Hot Doggie Haven up the street, and frankly, I don't advise it."

"Great. They ought to have a cold soda pop."

They walked along the cracked and aging sidewalk to the red-roofed, tent-shaped drive-in and sat on counter stools. It wasn't the sort of thing she would have dreamed of doing with Dex. But then she remembered those moonlight walks in Capri and the times during their courtship when they had haunted the little Third Avenue bistros. Dex *would* eat at the Red-Hot Doggie Haven, she decided. But he would give it class...

Along with her drink she ordered a chili dog. "And make it hot," she said defiantly.

"Should you be eating that, what with your ulcer and all?"

"Frank, do me a favor. Don't be so damned—fussy."

That shut him up, and he became sullen. She ate the chili dog, firmly enjoying every bite.

On the way back to the car, with the dry valley heat beating down on them, Andrea apologized and took his arm.

"Don't be mad, Frank. You've been a guardian angel to me since Dex walked out."

He was at once pleased and embarrassed and went overboard helping her into the car. She got behind the wheel and they speeded back up the valley.

"Are you all right?" Frank was looking at her with concern.

"Certainly. Don't I look it?"

"Well, you've been frowning and swallowing."

"It's the heat."

"I hope it's not what you ate."

It was, but she wouldn't admit it for another half hour. By that time the traffic from the south had merged with the Stockton-Sacramento traffic, all pouring into the Bay Area cities. Andrea had to keep her wits about her and it wasn't until she stopped the car at the Bay Bridge tollbooth that she gave up. The familiar, dull screwdriver was twisting through her abdomen and she doubled up with pain.

With a line fast gathering behind the Karmann-Ghia, Frank paid the toll. She fished through her purse for her pillbox and swallowed two pills before Frank could stop her. As they started up toward the Yerba Buena Tunnel, he put out one hand to stop her.

"Please, Andrea. Use common sense."

"What's the matter?"

"Faith told me you've had trouble with those pills. Remember, we discussed them in Reno?"

"I had those pills checked and analyzed, remember?"

The pills didn't do an awful lot for the pain from her ulcers, but by the time the little red car reached the Nob Hill house she was so sleepy she had to be helped into the house. She wouldn't have minded so much except that Frank refused to let the matter lie.

"They're too strong. Anybody can see that."

She wanted to argue that they were prescribed by her San Francisco physician, but she passed that by.

"It's funny I never had any trouble while I was in Mexico." Her speech was slurred.

279

Frank stopped on the steps and whirled around. "Is that true? Then you think—"

"Andrea, darling!" It was, of all people, Eden. She rushed out the door and hugged Andrea. "It's really you. It's been ages. Since your wedding, in fact. How's my girl?"

Aunt Brooke was behind her with Sam Liversedge.

Frank tried to head off the well-meaning onslaught.

"Please, Andrea isn't feeling well. The ulcer again. Excuse us. Can I help you upstairs?"

"For heaven's sake, no. I can at least climb the stairs."

Eden accompanied her daughter to her bedroom and then sat on Andrea's high four-poster bed as Andrea washed and came back into the bedroom, too tired and sleepy to shower. She gave in to her mother's comforting concern and stretched out on top of the rose and white coverlet Randi had bought for the bed when Andrea first came up to San Francisco to go to college.

"So you drove down to Fresno. And in this heat! But darling, you should have relied on Sam. He can handle those things. You don't have to—"

"Later, mother. Besides, Dex is handling the Planet Oil business for daddy."

Eden scoffed at that. "Not so you can notice. That husband of yours is nowhere to be found."

"What?"

"That's what I said. And if you ask me, Tony is in on it. Jany is acting very cagey as well. Claims Tony is on location. But I've a hunch your Dex is with him. What they're up to, I've no idea."

Andrea raised her head. Eden waved away her protests.

"You shouldn't speak like that, mother. They're not crooks, for heaven's sake! It's just to secure Tony's units. I'll bet that's what it's all about."

The door opened and Faith came in. She certainly wasn't happy. Andrea wondered guiltily if her excursion with Frank was the cause. He claimed he and Faith were, for the moment, not together, but Faith might have different ideas. She paid no attention to Eden's surprise at the sight of her bursting in on Andrea.

"He's positively senile, that Sam Liversedge. Do you know, he's got a Polaroid. He's running around taking pictures of Mrs. Trentini and the help. Also Frank. What kind of an album is that, for God's sake? He caught me with my mouth wide open."

Eden laughed and Andrea tried to hide her own smile. Faith came over to the bed.

"How are you feeling, Andrea?"

"Okay. I must have been out of my mind. A hot dog with chili. Frank warned me, but I got bullheaded."

Faith hung onto one of the bedposts, swinging back and forth gracefully.

"Has Frank told you we split up again? He claims we can't get married on his salary. He doesn't even have tenure yet. It's all very complicated." She raised her head and stared at Andrea. "That's why he's spending so much time with you."

She smiled as if to soften the remark, but her eyes remained steely.

Andrea was still more than a little foggy but she mustered up as honest an answer as she could at the moment.

"I'm not in love with him, Faith. He's not my type. Besides, he loves *you*. He's not interested in me, no matter what he—"

"What he says?"

Andrea licked her lips, which felt dry and cracked.

"I didn't mean that. Anyway, he doesn't love me the way he loves you, Faith. But I need him. I need someone honest to keep things on an even keel. I simply don't trust—" She looked over her shoulder. Eden kicked the door shut. "Sam and his crew. They've tried to run my affairs from the very first."

"Well, honey," Eden reminded her, "that's their job. They worked with Steve for a long, long time. They were good enough for him."

Andrea knew her mother was right. She wondered if she was really just being bullheaded. She and Faith had come to disagree with everything Sam did and said. If he said black, they would say white. And Andrea knew that a lot of it was fueled by Faith's dislike of the man.

"If Frank can help you, it's fine with me. Maybe he can even earn a little on the side." Faith said, ignoring Eden's raised eyebrows. "How about cutting Frank in when he saves you money on something?"

Andrea thought it more likely Frank would talk her *out* of some action. "He's the conservative type. I don't know."

"Well, try, anyway. It sure might hurry my wedding."

"Okay, Faith." She was too groggy to argue.

Eden got up. "I think we'd better give Andrea a little peace and quiet. We're all going out for dinner in a couple of hours and we want you on your feet, honey."

"Sure, mom. I'll be fine."

Eden ushered Faith out with a strong hand against the small of her back.

The room darkened gradually after sunset and Andrea remembered a moment like this in London, a morning when she had felt closed in, depressed, after a similar experience with her ulcer and medicine. She had felt surrounded by sinister forces that day. When her mother left the room now she seemed to take the light with her.

Some time later the door opened with a gentle creaking and she heard Aunt Brooke's voice.

"Hi, honey. How are you feeling? We'll be leaving in an hour."

"Okay."

"Oh, I almost forgot. Sam says he'd like to see you for a few minutes tonight. Time is running out on some deal or other. He has to have your signature. It's vital."

"I might have known," Andrea muttered. "Tell Sam to leave the papers here. I don't want to talk to him."

"Honey, he means well. But you see, he still thinks of you as a child. You know—Steve's granddaughter. My Lord, Andrea! To Sam, even your father is a child."

Andrea settled back against the pillows. In her present mood of depression she mistrusted everyone but her mother. She missed Dex and felt bitterly the loss of his love, his care for her and his trust.

She got up and went into the bathroom to shower. Brooke came in and left a sheaf of papers, mostly contracts and one

282

preliminary escrow report on the little table next to the chaise longue.

When Andrea had dressed and started to leave her room, she glanced back and saw Sam's papers. She didn't want to come home to all that work. She went back and looked it over. As Sam had said, two contracts were of timely importance. She initialed these. She wasn't happy about another, the Siskiyou County lease to a fast-food chain in an isolated area. She wondered if they could expect more activity up there soon.

She heard Frank Kelly's voice out in the hall. He was standing outside Faith's bedroom door. Andrea decided suddenly to make them both happy and test Frank at the same time.

"Frank, would you do me a big favor? Brief me right now on this one about the Siskiyou property."

Pleased, he looked over the lease but then shook his head. "I'm sorry, Andrea. You want the truth? I don't see the sense of renewing when you told us in Reno that you wanted to do something about a community of markets. This calls for yearly renewals. Options. Ten, in their favor."

"Nice work, Frank. How about analyzing the others and giving me a report?"

He was delighted. "I'll do it tonight, right after dinner."

Faith had come out of her room, and nodded to them both.

In better spirits she started down the stairs with Faith and Frank. They saw the rest of the group in the foyer below.

"They all look like waxworks," Faith whispered. She thought it over. "Except your mother, of course."

Andrea grinned, and they all began to giggle. Brooke frowned at them as they walked downstairs.

"Sam just had a call from the Reno Lombard," Brooke said breathlessly. "We could hardly believe it. Too ghastly. Andrea, honey, you must fight him."

Andrea didn't know what she was talking about but was resigned to hearing about some new scandal that delighted Brooke's soul.

"Brooke, for heaven's sake, will you tell me what's going on," Andrea said impatiently.

"Well, if you must know, your disgusting husband is in

Reno. Dex is divorcing you, honey."

Andrea started to laugh. She heard a distinct buzzing in her ears before the dark overwhelmed her.

Frank Kelly caught her as she fell.

THIRTY

"KEEP HER head down, Frank," Faith said, the first to speak. "Bring her to the chair here in the hall. No. She mustn't lie down. Sit her here."

Andrea began to come to when she settled back in the big oak armchair. She tried to wave everyone off.

"I'm all right. I'm okay."

Meanwhile, Eden and Aunt Brooke were exchanging angry words.

"Brooke, what the devil made you say that? You know it isn't true."

Brooke had begun to cry. "I didn't do it purposely. I only thought what everyone else already does. Andrea, honey, I wouldn't hurt you for the world." But she raised her chin defiantly at Eden. "All the same, you know that unspeakable man is in Reno for one reason only."

Sam Liversedge stood over them. He was uncharacteristically stern.

"Brooke, you don't know anything about it. I've got to leave you now. I'm going to get to the bottom of this. Can I count on you, Eden?"

Eden nodded, but to Andrea she looked somehow scared. It was odd. Something was going on here. Faith brought Andrea a glass of water, waited while she drank it, then carried it back to the kitchen. When she came back into the hall she almost walked into Sam Liversedge. He stood in a dark corner, obviously waiting for her.

"Miss Cortlandt."

"Do you need me? Is she worse?"

"No, Miss Cortlandt, but I do need a big favor. My secretary

285

is home because of illness in the family, and I've got to make a quick trip to Reno. Just overnight. Returning by the dawn flight. I need a secretary. May I count on you? I'll make it worth your while."

"Now? With Andrea sick? I don't get it."

"Will you make the trip?"

"Do I have a choice?"

He looked at her hard for a long moment.

"I see I don't have a choice. Well, why not? You said you'd make it worth my while."

"Quite correct."

Sam, she knew, had never liked her. He probably knew she was the one who had persuaded Andrea to make her own decisions.

She tried once more. "Do you think Andrea will be all right?"

"I sincerely hope so. She'll be surrounded by her family at all times." He gave her a sharp look.

Twenty minutes later she had her overnight case packed and was looking her best in a two-year-old gray flannel suit.

Neither she nor Sam said anything while Brooke's limousine drove them out to the airport. The flight itself was uneventful, with one brief stop at Sacramento before they reached Reno.

To Faith's astonishment, Tony Lombard and Dex Cartaret met them in the deserted Lombard Hotel lobby. They greeted her coldly, then all three men stood there looking at her against the red, gold and green lights of a slot machine.

Dex broke the eerie silence. "Shall we take our little walk?"

She kept her cool. "Gentlemen, I get the distinct impression I am not here as a secretary."

Tony Lombard looked uncomfortable, but it was Dex who worried her the most. His expression was hard, ruthless.

"Miss Cortlandt," Tony said, "We want the truth about certain things that have happened in my daughter's life recently. Would you mind walking across the street with Sam?"

"Right now?"

"If you would."

There was nothing across the street except a row of offices, which at this hour, nearly ten o'clock, would all be pitch dark.

"I've no objection to going across the street for a walk, as you put it, but there are three of you and only one of me. How do I know I am safe?"

"God knows you are safe," Dex remarked and turned away. "I'll go on ahead."

Whatever was up, Faith didn't like it, but there was no way to avoid whatever they had in mind. She swung around and started out the side door. Dex walked past her and went ahead. She felt herself escorted like a criminal between the two men. They crossed the dark street. The lights were on above the counter in the airline ticket office and a girl was there, a tall brunette.

Dex knocked on the glass door. The girl went over and unlocked it. Faith found herself ushered into the office.

"Am I supposed to buy my ticket home?" Faith asked, but no one answered her.

The girl looked Faith over, then shook her head.

"I've never seen this woman before. And the woman who called and asked for the ticket had a much deeper voice."

"I don't know quite what I'm accused of, but as you can see, I'm not guilty."

Sam Liversedge brought out an envelope filled with the Polaroid pictures he had taken only a few hours ago at the Nob Hill house. He fanned them out and leaned over them with the tall brunette.

The tension in the air was unmistakable. The girl went through the pictures twice, then set one on top.

"Are you sure?" Sam asked.

"Positive. The voice sounded so different on the phone."

Faith tried to get a look at the top picture but Sam shuffled and then replaced them in the envelope. He nodded to Tony and Dex.

"That ought to cinch it."

It wasn't until they had thanked the young woman that Faith found her voice.

"Please, Mr. Liversedge. Dex. I've got to know. What is this all about?"

Tony Lombard was more polite than the other two, she thought, and seemed sympathetic to her fears.

"We all owe you a debt of thanks, Miss Cortlandt. You've

been an enormous help. Now, if you like, there's a suite waiting for you. Except for the desk clerk at the hotel, we're through for the night."

"The desk clerk?" she echoed faintly.

"A formality. We just want to see if she remembers you and approximately what time you checked out four weeks ago."

"Why in God's name do you want to know that? I was here until the evening flight."

"Feel free to order dinner, Miss Cortlandt. I'm sorry you were cheated out of that back in San Francisco," Sam added.

Faith had a horrible sense of some big explosion building up.

Nor did Dex's anxiety reassure her. He muttered to Tony, "I wish we could get home sooner. Do you suppose she's all right?"

"Eden has been warned." But Tony looked anxious too.

There was a new doctor chosen by Eden. Not that Andrea needed a doctor at eight in the morning. She had been feeling as good as new ten minutes after her collapse the night before, but Eden suddenly began to fuss over her like a mother hen.

Eden's specialist, Dr. Patricia Rovetto, though very stout, carried a lot of assurance.

"I don't make house calls," she announced when she showed up at eight o'clock. "I'm a fan of your mother's, young lady. I happened to be willing to oblige her. Matter of fact, I live in back of you on Jones Street, so I figured no harm in doing her a favor. Where does it hurt?"

Andrea had been sitting up in bed, listening to Frank Kelly read various company reports to her. If anything was calculated to put her back to sleep, that was. When Dr. Rovetto arrived, Eden made Frank leave so suddenly he was forced out protesting that he had left his papers. He asked in vain for someone to hand them to him.

Eden firmly closed the door on him. Andrea noted that Eden refused to leave her alone and had made her uneasy by spending the night on Andrea's chaise longue.

Dr. Rovetto proceeded to take her blood pressure.

"What if the studio calls you?" Andrea asked her mother.

"The hell with the studio, darling." Had Eden gone mad? Andrea wondered.

Dr. Rovetto unwrapped Andrea's arm. "All right. One hundred thirty-two over eighty. You seem to be in fair condition. Not great, but we can't expect miracles the way you young people live today. I'll look over your X-rays, but your problem seems to be confined to a troublesome ulcer. This medication seems to be making you sleepy, so I'm going to change it."

Dr. Rovetto stood up. "Now, Miss Ware, about that autographed photo you promised me."

"Sure thing, doctor. And thank you ever so much. Just send your bill to Bursten & Rafael. They will authorize payment by my daughter's accountant."

"In the old days," Dr. Rovetto grumbled, "we got cash in hand. At the door, as we left."

"You aren't that old, doctor," Eden teased her. "You couldn't possibly remember that."

Dr. Rovetto's face turned pink but she waved aside the compliment.

"Just don't you forget the photo."

Andrea threw the covers off her body and sat up. "I'm okay? Then I'm on my way to Reno."

Eden swung around. Andrea couldn't remember seeing her so worked up before.

"No, you don't, young woman. You stay right there. Don't you move. You're to remain quiet until I come back. No visitors. Just rest."

It was ridiculous. Andrea felt fine.

"I've got to go. Don't you understand? I've got to stop him," she began to cry.

"Nobody is getting a divorce. Besides, Sam flew out last evening. He'll be the messenger bearing all your precious greetings. Now, calm down. Rest. If you still insist on flying up to Reno tomorrow, you may."

Eden closed the door firmly but not before Andrea heard her say to the doctor. "The poor kid is crying. I do think we—"

The doctor's deep voice remarked, "She doesn't seem the type to harm herself in any way. But you can't be too careful.

I heard them say downstairs—"

What on earth...The voices faded.

Andrea waited until there was silence. She put one foot out of bed, then the other, and tried to stand. She felt woozy and sat down abruptly on the bed, but after another try she made it to the chaise longue.

Frank Kelly had left a sheaf of papers here, including contracts, company reports and other memoranda. She hadn't yet initialed or signed them. She cleared her mind and read the top paper, put it aside. Most of the reports had been neatly arranged for her signature, so all she had to do was thumb through the lower right-hand corners to initial the typed changes and copies.

She yawned and set the folders aside. She would have Frank read them to her later. Then she noticed that the back of one of those blue cover sheets had stuck to the top of the sheet behind it. If she had been thumbing through she would have missed it. She turned back the two sheets and their blue cover.

Frank Kelly's name had been typed into the document.

She read it closely now, her hands trembling. A power of attorney. The power of her signature. He had evidently intended to have her sign automatically all the dull legal reports and his power of attorney along with them.

It was absurd. The minute he used it she could stop him.

But what if she was in no condition to do so? What was he hoping for—dear loyal Frank?...

How much of what had happened to Dex and to her could have been contrived by Frank? she asked herself, badly shaken. If Frank was up to something, he certainly would have had to get Dex out of the way first.

She got up, reached for the bedpost for support and sat down on the bed to make a phone call to the registrar at the University of California. She had an idea.

"This is Andrea Lombard. May I speak to someone in the English department?"

She had used her maiden name for faster results—her grandfather had been a regent there once.

Only the summer session personnel of the department were

available but the woman who answered proved to be extremely helpful.

"Oh, yes, Miss Lombard. How can I help you?"

"I was interested in putting Professor Kelly under contract. I wondered what his situation was there."

"Oh, I'm delighted. Professor Kelly is mighty popular. We all adore him."

"I can imagine. But I wanted to ask you about Professor Kelly's attendance record this spring."

The young woman hastened to assure her that Frank Kelly's record was excellent.

"He's always on time. All that sort of thing. Except for that spell of flu last month."

Andrea fingered the satin quilt under her hand.

"Just about four weeks ago?"

"That's the time. Right after classes he drove up to Reno. Then he called in sick the next day. He was sick all weekend. Wasn't able to make the finals on one of his classes. To tell the truth, that may have affected his chances for tenure. I'm delighted that you're thinking of employing him. Such a fine man. And bright, too."

"All of that. Thanks."

It was beginning to add up. Frank hadn't flown back from Reno to his job. He had remained away during the time covered by Terri Cartaret's death. The police said her death was accidental. So be it. But had Frank perhaps intended to implicate Dex in his ex-wife's death? . . .

She heard the door open, and spun around. The windows were heavily shuttered, though, and the room was dark. Who was in the room with her?

She stiffened with fear. Very slowly she walked to the window and tilted the blinds open enough to let in a dim light. Frank was leaning against the door.

She did not want him to read her eyes. If he was indeed guilty, she wanted to be able to prove it.

"Frank? I'm glad it's you. I'm so tired. Maybe you could do a little work on those papers. I'm just too tired to handle it right now."

He came a step further into the room.

291

"I really shouldn't be in here. Your mother won't let anybody come in here to see you, and I guess that includes me." He glanced at the papers on the table beside the chaise. "I really meant to take those with me when the doctor came. You probably aren't up to reading and signing them now."

"You could read them to me, Frank."

"I don't know. Your mother has given strict orders that we all let you rest. There's one of those reporters downstairs right now, trying to interview her or she would be up here marching me out by the ear."

"You think mom is behaving oddly?"

"Well, you know how bright and breezy she always is. But ever since last night she's been jumpy. She loses her temper, talks sharply to us all. Not at all like Eden Ware. Everything is odd. Sam Liversedge took Faith with him to Reno. Hasn't he a secretary of his own?"

Why were Sam and Faith in Reno? she wondered.

She groaned, grabbed her stomach and pretended she had a severe ulcer attack. He picked up the papers.

"Shall I call someone? I suppose you want your pills."

"Yes. I have them in the pocket of my robe, right here." He reached into her robe and got out the pills, poured her water from the silver carafe on the table. "Meanwhile, I'll sign that stuff you have in your hand. Just give me a brief rundown as I go along."

She stuck pill after pill into her mouth, storing them under her tongue while Frank watched her, frowning.

"You really shouldn't, you know. They aren't good for you." But he did nothing to stop her.

"Read," she ordered him. The instant he turned away she spat the pills out in her hand and then sank against the back of the chaise.

He looked uneasily at the hall door. "I don't want to be caught in here. Your mother will have a fit."

"All right. Just let me thumb through them and I'll sign. God! I'm sleepy."

He set the papers before her, holding onto the pile and presenting them so she would merely flip up each lower right-hand corner. She began to initial and occasionally sign. She knew the sheet he was waiting for and saw that his fingers tightened their grip on the pile of papers as she neared the one giving him power of attorney.

She let her own fingers slip. "So...tired." She looked up at him foggily. "I heard doctor say...something about suicide. It's ridiculous how they're worried about me."

"They think you are suicidal," he told her very quietly.

She dropped the pen.

"You see? I don't need Sam and the others. Just my old friend Frank. You know what?"

He began to get nervous. "Andrea, please lower your voice. Do you want your mother to interrupt us? We aren't finished yet. Just a few more."

She sighed. He handed her the fallen pen. But she was hoping to get him to betray himself in his anxiety to get the power of attorney signed.

Before her grandfather died leaving her his fortune, Frank hadn't shown the slightest interest in her. What he had said on the drive to Fresno about having originally preferred her to Faith was all a lie.

She signed the power of attorney and passed on to the next page. She was pushing him now. Having the power of attorney would do him no good if she lived. She supposed he would hide it until she died of "natural causes." That must have been his plan all along. And he'd be able to make it look like suicide.

She pretended to stumble to her feet. Andrea realized she had to move fast. But even with the evidence of the paper she had no proof that Frank was responsible for all that had happened in Mexico, or even that he knew Terri Cartaret.

"Think I'll lie down now."

She looked at the hall door situated near the nightstand beside her bed. If she was in danger, it would be the nearest way out. Her other bedroom door led through the bathroom between her room and her father's generally unused bedroom. Frank probably hoped to sneak out that way if her mother came back.

She looked up at him. "Did I take my pills? My stomach hurts."

"No. Do you think you need them?" He didn't blink.

She saw him take out his handkerchief and pick up the pill-box, careful not to get his fingerprints on it. He poured out two, hesitated, then poured out half a dozen.

She had given him the opening. He actually intended to kill her. Or at least leave her permanently foggy. She pretended to stumble toward the bed without taking the pills from his handkerchief.

"Got to get water."

"Right here." It was at her hand.

She was near enough to the door to touch the knob but something had happened. He was looking down into her eyes and he read the truth. He knew she was not drugged and he knew she was frightened. The realization triggered his own desperate fear. He forgot caution. His hand, filled with the pills, clapped over her mouth. She fumbled for the door, struggling to keep those damned pills from being forced between her lips. She kicked hard but her slippered feet had little effect.

"Damn you! Damn you! Swallow!" His tough hands were forcing her. She maneuvered frantically, twisting in his hands, but she only succeeded in wedging his body against the door. She heard herself make choking noises as she tried to spit out the pills.

Suddenly his body slammed against hers and he fell on the floor on top of her. The door was opened, and Dex appeared in the doorway. He kicked Frank, who groaned and rolled away. The door from the bathroom opened at the same time, and the room was suddenly, inexplicably filled.

Dex's arms closed around her. He raised her shivering body against his and held her to him. He was murmuring things she only half heard.

"My love...it's all right. It's all over, sweetheart."

At her feet Frank stirred, tried to get up. Andrea was shocked when Tony pushed him forcefully back down.

Andrea saw faces in the doorway, her mother and Faith. Faith was pale, her eyes wide. Andrea had never seen her cry before and she knew those tears were for Frank.

"I'm all right. Just take him away. Don't hurt him," Andrea said, staring at Faith.

Then Eden was there holding her hand.

"I should have stayed. I meant to be gone only a minute. I shouldn't have left you alone, honey."

But in Andrea's confused mind that mistake of leaving her alone had been made long ago. She smiled mistily at her mother and then at Tony, but she felt only the comfort of Dex's love.

CHAPTER THIRTY-ONE

"YOU OWE me, damn you!"

Faith ran downstairs after Sam Liversedge. Angry and desperate, she followed him only minutes after Frank had been taken away.

For the first time in her life Faith found herself in a daze. There was so much she didn't understand. She chose to believe Frank had done it all for her.

She caught Sam's arm as he went into the den. He turned to face her.

"The man is guilty. He has confessed. Gene Rafael advised him to say nothing. So it was Kelly's own choice, and it will help him in the long run. But how do we owe you something, Miss Cortlandt?"

She moved in front of him, her eyes blazing.

"You dragged me up to Reno last night and somehow I helped you get evidence against Frank."

Sam nodded, walked over to the bar. He poured bourbon into a glass and handed it to her. She made a face but drank.

"Well, Miss Cortlandt, that trip was for your protection. Dexter Cartaret believed you were Frank's accomplice in this. Cartaret watched you in Capri but couldn't find evidence that you were the one responsible for informing his ex-wife of his and Andrea's every stop."

"Certainly. Because I was innocent."

"But someone was providing Terri Cartaret with information and probably advice. Someone who wanted to get a piece of her blackmail. Motive number two. Now, as for motive number one..."

"It was for me. He did it all so we could get married. He wouldn't marry me when he didn't have a cent."

She hated Sam for the chilly smile with which he responded.

"That may be. But his first motive was to destroy young Andrea's faith in her husband. He tried that first by sprinkling Demerol tablets among her Donnatal pills. Later, he flew down to Mexico, stole that watch from your hotel room and gave it to Terri Cartaret. He expected her to flaunt it in front of Andrea, apparently to make her think Dex was resuming a relationship with her."

"But he didn't kill the woman," she pleaded. "It must have been an accident."

He swept aside the Cartaret woman's death as if it had been a mere detail. "So the DFS believes. Luckily for your friend Frank the houseboy saw his rental car driving away some time before Miss Cartaret died. The man who rented it gave his name as Bob Kelly. It was some time later that the cook overheard Mrs. Cartaret's argument *on the phone* with Dexter Cartaret."

"Then Frank didn't commit a crime in Mexico."

"No. According to the Mexican police, there is nothing of a criminal nature they can hold him for." He took a long swallow of whiskey and studied her. "It wasn't his first trip to see Mrs. Cartaret. He made a trip to Acapulco last October while you were in Europe with Andrea and Dex. I guess it was to point out his value to Mrs. Cartaret. Or did you know that?"

She hadn't known.

"Do you know how Frank had access to Andrea's medicine?"

"You saw him when he stayed here several weeks. He knew where her medicine was kept. I myself sent her pills to New York at the time of her marriage. I suppose he must have put in those others. But as you see, there were not enough to kill her. Not then."

"Not then, indeed. But today there were."

"He panicked. That's all. He just panicked."

He rolled his eyes at this. "So you still want to defend him."

"He did it for me," she insisted.

"Have you guessed why we took you to Reno?"

She didn't want to know. "I suppose Frank went down to Mexico that last day from Reno."

"That's right. He told you he had to return to his classes in Berkeley. He covered up rather stupidly. He was afraid someone might gossip while all of us were there, so he called the airline office, changed his voice and told them he was Faith Cortlandt ordering tickets for her employer. In the airline office he gave his name. Bob Kelly. The name on his passport."

"But that's not his real name."

"Frank Robert Kelly, I believe."

She didn't answer. The lump in her throat threatened to choke her.

"So you see, Miss Cortlandt, Frank had involved you. Dexter Cartaret was suspicious of you all along. Frank must have known that. Tony Lombard, on the other hand, thought you had nothing to do with Kelly's scheme."

She leaned against the bar, devastated. Her desire to protect Frank had not disappeared. He was like a child, she thought. A child with a little kink in his brain. A boyhood of poverty and struggle had left its mark.

She set the drink down and clenched both fists.

"I'll help him get the best legal defense available. I don't want that man in jail, damn it. Just watch me!"

She swung around and started upstairs to see Andrea. Her friend was the only one who could help them now.

Andrea sympathized with Faith, but quietly said that she couldn't help her. It was now all up to the courts.

Faith was crushed, but managed to walk out with her head held high. She would help him, somehow. . . .

A great deal besides lovemaking was accomplished in that first night of Andrea's reunion with Dex. He was more loving and more caring than he had ever been. For the first time she could look into his eyes and be sure he loved Andrea—the woman and not the heiress.

The next morning she told him just that.

"It hardly comes as news that I love you. . ." He shook her a little. "This idiotic, exasperating, tantalizing girl who finally grew up. Did you think I'd stopped loving you when we said good-bye in Mexico? I wanted you to grow up, to feel as strongly as I did about this relationship. A day after you had gone I wanted to call you back. Tony will tell you that. I almost ruined his studio deal, mooning over my lost love. But we had to settle this whole business that threatened you and our marriage. Besides," his manner softened, "I wanted you to miss me, to realize what our marriage meant."

"Oh, I did, believe me."

"I've been waiting over a year for the girl I fell in love with to return what I felt."

"But I did. I adored you."

That made him smile.

"What makes you think I wanted a girl who adored me? I wanted a wife. I knew you were too young. But I loved you. I wanted to share my life with you. I knew the money thing would stand between us."

"It didn't."

"Don't lie. I had to prove myself every single day."

He pulled her to him, folded her in his arms.

"The truth is, sweetheart, I loved you when I married you, and I'm not at all sure you loved me."

"Oh, but—" He silenced her with a kiss.

"You were interested, intrigued. Infatuated, perhaps. But you didn't *know* what love is. I think your friend Faith Cortlandt does. She's a fool, but she does love that man. I tell you, Andrea, you and I have a lot of learning to do before we can thumb our noses at all those who predicted the worst."

She wanted to deny his words, but in her heart she knew he was right. There was still so much growing up to do...

They went downstairs arm in arm to say good-bye to her parents, both of whom had pressing engagements in Hollywood.

"I suppose you two will be the next to desert me," Aunt Brooke said mournfully.

"I'm afraid so," Andrea answered. "I'm taking Dex right now to a house I once saw. We're finally going to have a home of our own."

Brooke's eyebrows raised. "Is she making all the decisions now? Doesn't sound like the Andrea I know, at all."

"No," Dex corrected her. "Only those we agree on. For instance, that Reno hotel will have to put in a casino or go broke." He knew that would get a rise out of Andrea.

"Okay. You win on the casino. If you agree to a new home."

Brooke scoffed at the deal. "This marriage of yours is going to take some work. I can see that."

It was Andrea who answered quietly, her eyes on Dex shining with pride and with love.

"We've got a whole lifetime together to work on it, don't we, Dex?"